SCISSORS

By the Same Author

Novels
Sails of Sunset
The Love Rack
Little Mrs. Manington
Sagusto
David and Diana
Indiana Jane
Pamela's Spring Song
Havana Bound
Bargain Basement
Spears Against Us
Pilgrim Cottage
The Guests Arrive
Volcano
Victoria Four-Thirty
They Wanted to Live
One Small Candle
So Immortal a Flower
Eight for Eternity
A Terrace in the Sun
The Remarkable Young Man
Love Is Like That
Wide is the Horizon
A Flight of Birds
The Pilgrim Cottage Omnibus

Miscellaneous
Gone Rustic
Gone Rambling
Gone Afield
Gone Sunwards
And So To Bath
And So To America
And So To Rome
Half Way
Portal to Paradise
One Year of Life
The Grand Cruise
Selected Poems (1910-1960)
A Tale of Young Lovers (Poetic Drama)
The Diary of Russell Beresford
Alfred Fripp; a biography
A Man Arose
The Growing Boy; an autobiography/Part 1
Years of Promise;   Part 2

SCISSORS

A NOVEL OF YOUTH

BY

CECIL ROBERTS

HODDER & STOUGHTON

All Rights Reserved
First Published by
William Heinemann Ltd. April, 1923
June, 1923, October, 1923,
1924, 1925, 1926, 1927, 1928, 1929, 1930,
1931, 1932, 1933, 1934, 1935, March, 1936,
October, 1936, 1938, 1940, 1941, 1949,
This Edition, 1968
SBN   340   04421   7

REPRODUCED FROM THE ORIGINAL SETTING
BY ARRANGEMENT WITH
WILLIAM HEINEMANN LTD.

PRINTED IN GREAT BRITAIN FOR
HODDER AND STOUGHTON LIMITED,
ST. PAUL'S HOUSE, WARWICK LANE, LONDON E.C.4.
BY
COMPTON PRINTING LTD.
LONDON AND AYLESBURY.

HOLT-JACKSON
11/4/72
£1-75p

CONTENTS

BOOK I

TO
HARRY CUNNINGHAM BRODIE

FOREWORD

The twenty-second reprint of this my first novel, published forty-five years ago, perhaps justifies a foreword. When it appeared I was a young author, anxious and hopeful. It had not been easy to get it published. Perhaps its history will give heart to other young authors. An agent sent it to ten publishers who all declined it. I was sorry for my agent and indignant with the publishers. After all, I had some qualifications, I thought, some reason for believing I could write. Between eighteen and twenty-seven I had published six books of poems — without paying for publication! I had been a literary editor and critic on a daily newspaper, a war correspondent with the Army, the Navy and the Royal Air Force, and, aged thirty, I was the editor of one of the oldest newspapers in the Kingdom, on which James Barrie had begun his career.

A man can write many things, of course, and not be able to write a novel. A novelist may in turn not be able to write poetry. A great novelist, Joseph Conrad, told me that he looked in awe at anyone who could write poetry. It was a mystery beyond him. The gifts of dialogue, characterisation and psychological analysis are the essential stock in trade of the novelist, apart from experience of life and a lively imagination. I thought I had these. I felt more challenged than daunted by the rejection of my novel. It was not a literary man but a cricketer who helped me to open the door to my future career. He was Aubrey Faulkner, a world-famous bowler, who gave me a letter to a friend of his, an enthusiastic cricketer. The essential point about this friend was that he was a director of a famous publishing firm. Armed with my letter to him, and with my rejected manuscript in hand, I went to London. In those wonderful days, in the year 1922, you could buy a return ticket from Nottingham, where I then lived, to London, a half-day excursion, of a distance there and back of two hundred and fifty miles, for five shillings! It proved for me a good investment. I was courteously received by the publisher, an urbane gentleman who loved cricket. He had had a career as a singer, and now possessed a small *palazzo* in Venice — altogether a somewhat romantic figure in my eyes. He listened patiently to my 'sales' talk. I told him what I had already done. Finally, I asked him — "Do you think I look like a young man who can write a novel?" He blinked at that question and said — "Well, I should think it's quite likely you can. Leave it for us to read." "Oh, no!" I replied, "that won't do. I want you to say now that you will publish it." He laughed at my audacity. "My dear young man, we've never done anything like that!" "You've never met a Cecil Roberts before," I retorted, full of the egotism of youth. "Show a little courage for once and take a chance."

By this time there was an element of comedy in our conversation. "Have a glass of sherry," he said, taking a bottle out of a cabinet. He began to talk about Aubrey Faulkner, then, as we rose in termination, he said, putting a hand on my shoulder, "I should hate to disappoint him and I've a feeling that we shall publish your novel — but do let us see what we're taking!"

I agreed and left the manuscript with him. I walked over to my literary agent. "I believe I've placed *Scissors*." I told him of the interview. "With the English a little touch of cricket does wonders," he observed . . .

The next Spring they published my novel. There was a strange sequel to this event five years later. I was in the Austrian Tyrol, staying in a schloss that had been turned into a pension by a war-impoverished countess. One of the guests was an elderly Russian lady, the widow of an Excellency. She was a *grande dame*. By this time I was an established novelist with six novels to my credit. "Are you writing anything here?" she asked. I confessed that I was. "It would be delightful if you would read some of it to me," she said. Flattered, I agreed to; few authors can resist such a proposal. In front of a log fire, with a samovar on the table, with a companion, the mouse-like little Belgian countess who did embroidery all the time, I read to them. It was rather like a scene from Chekov, I felt — the country house, the Russian 'Excellency', the samovar, the lady-in-waiting, and the young author.

One evening Her Excellency surprised me by saying, "You

know, I feel very proud that I'm the cause of your being a
novelist." Startled, I exclaimed "But how?" She told me.
After the Russian revolution, impoverished, a widow, she
sought to earn some money. She had met in her prosperous
days, taking the cure at Bad Homberg, my publisher.
Fluent in five languages, she applied to him for some
translation work. Later, impressed by her judgment, he
sent her manuscripts to read. "That was how I came to
read *Scissors*. I liked it and strongly recommended
publication," she said.

When my novel appeared I was tense with mingled
excitement, confidence and apprehension. Hoping that I
was a born novelist, I wanted to succeed in order to escape
from the ties of editorship and be free to travel. Years later
Somerset Maugham said to me, about the publication of
his first novel—"I was so scared I daren't open the packet
of press clippings." I felt like that. I trembled when they
came but the critics were very kind; they usually are to first
novels. They wrote — "He shows considerable promise and
one day, perhaps . . ." Years later when the novelist has
established himself firmly in public favour they tell him
that he has never fulfilled his early promise, or they ignore
his work. A curious race, critics. I have been one.

At the time of my advent there was an influential critic,
elderly, by name Clement Shorter, who edited *The Sphere*,
foremost among those vanished illustrated weeklies. He
wrote a famous book page each week. He was a pundit
like Edmund Gosse and Arnold Bennett. He was, naturally,
assiduously courted. Testy and somewhat disappointed
with life, he often showed his claws. He reviewed *Scissors*
at length mingling praise with acid denigration. It looked
as if I was going to be too successful, too easily, too early.
He wrote —

"Surely recognition never came to young men of an
earlier generation in the way that it comes to-day.
Charles Dickens awoke to find himself famous at
twenty-five with *Pickwick*, but Thackeray made no real
reputation until he was thirty-seven. George Meredith
was thirty-one when he attained some small measure of
fame with *The Ordeal of Richard Feverel*. Mr. Thomas
Hardy was thirty-four when *Far From the Madding*

Crowd proclaimed him a great novelist. *The War of the Worlds* made Mr. H. G. Wells at thirty-two. I do not know of any prose writer who made much noise in the world before he was thirty. But nowadays young writers can get a public at almost any age. The younger generation has all the luck . . . I am thinking for the moment of Mr. Cecil Roberts. He is only twenty-eight."

Now actually I was just entering my thirty-first year, so in those magic thirties enumerated by him. He continued:-

"I always like to hear of the success of the young. I did not drag in Dickens's early success on account of there being any analogy but only because the exceptional character of his success and that of Mr. Roberts. I do not think the latter will prove another Dickens. If Mr. Roberts had awaited two or three years more he would doubtless have given us a more vital book, more mature."

So only two or three years cut me off from the chance of ranking with Meredith, Thomas Hardy and H. G. Wells. How rash of me not to wait. Even so, despite maturing years, it might not 'come off'.

"We have all one novel in us, and perhaps this is to be Mr. Roberts's one effort in this department. The style is good, which it is not always in these modern novels now appearing so plentifully, but style is not everything and in *Scissors* the account of school life could not be better done, frequently as we have seen it done of late. The description of the outbreak of war, however, should not be done at all."

Clement Shorter, forgetting me, then proceeded to pay off an old score:-

"Nor am I thrilled that the personality of Sir Philip Gibbs has been presented in this book, as we have been carefully informed by the inspired paragraph. Sir Philip once put me into a book and very offensively. I did not much mind. I have been used all my life to anonymous letters of the foulest description, and I assume it is the fate of most people who try to be honest in their work on newspapers to make more enemies than friends. Moreover, I think Mr. Roberts is all wrong in his psychology. He makes his heroine at one moment very much in love, the next moment throw over her lover to marry a blind soldier she has nursed. Even if it happened under Mr. Roberts's very eyes I should say this was too abnormal to be worth putting in a novel . . . But there is poetry in the book, and many good qualities. Above all there is promise of better work to follow."

I had every reason to know that he was wrong about the girl who threw over her lover to marry a blind man, but on the whole I was grateful for a very kind review. It had another merit. It took up, with a photograph, almost the whole of his book page. I had not reached the cynical stage of the writer who said "I never read reviews, I measure them," but I felt proud of the space alloted to me. Clement Shorter, I am sure, despite those 'letters of the foulest description' addressed to him, had some very good qualities. After his death, by a quirk of fate, I succeeded to his book page in *The Sphere*. I hope his shade approved.

Regarding that 'one novel in us', with which Shorter threatened me, I, too, had my fears. Could I stay the course? Well, *Scissors* has stayed it through forty-five years, and for companions I have added twenty-three more novels down the years.

And now I must make a confession, *Scissors* opens in Asia Minor. It has been much commended as a portrait of an English Public School. I was never in Asia Minor and never at a Public School. This does not disqualify me from writing about either. Gibbon wrote *The Decline and Fall of the Roman Empire* in five volumes, without ever having seen it. All he saw of it for a few days in 1764 were the ruins of the Capitol that inspired his masterpiece. To write about a place you have never seen is more difficult than to write about one you have seen but it is likely to be a more accurate account, and much more laborious. The eye and the mind are fallible things, as any barrister knows who has his victim in the witness-box.

How did I come to place the opening scenes of my story in a country I had not visited? In 1917 I had reviewed a book about a journey made by its author from Samsun, a port on the Black Sea, to Amasia, a township of Asia Minor. The journey was made on foot, with a mule and an old Turkish *kavass*. The description so impressed me that it lingered in my mind. About 1917 I sketched the first draft of my synopsis; and boldly from this ancient town I sent my young Scissors into other terrain unknown to me, to an English Public School, from Amasia, in Anatolia, set in a valley between mountains through which courses the Yeshil Irmak, or Green River.

And now a little history concerning Amasia in Anatolia. A town of about 20,000 inhabitants, it is situated some seventy miles south of Samsun, a port on the Black Sea, the ancient Pontus Euxinus that figures in the Argonautic legend. The Black Sea, with Russia for its northern shore-line is, in winter, a cruel sea, notorious for its black fogs. The Argonauts found the people living on its southern shore savage, and the sea so treacherous that they called it the *Ageinos* (Inhospitable). Then, not wishing to seem unkind, following the euphemism of the Greeks, who abstained from words of ill omen, they reversed the name, calling it the *Eugeinos* (The Hospitable). Samsun, one of the few good ports on the southern shore, was the terminus of a road going inland, a caravan route that brought trade from Baghdad, 800 miles, S.E., along the Tigris, via Mosul (Nineveh), Bitlis, Sivas, and then to Amasia and Samsun. Long before Jason went to Colchis with his Argonauts to obtain the Golden Fleece, this long peninsula south of the Black Sea had been inhabited. Since 3000 B.C. it had known people of the Bronze Age, and of Hittite and Phrygian origin. The ancient town of Amasia was founded on the mountain side where the citadel stands today. What history this natural fortress above the green valley of the Yeshil Irmak has known! It was captured respectively by Phrygians, Cimmerians (Gk. *kimmerios;* people in perpetual night, thus regarded after the bright Attic lands), Medes, Persians, Greeks and Romans. The Greek profile can still be seen in Samsun and Amasia, and Xenophon's Ten Thousand, marching to the Black Sea, may have left Hellenic mementos of their passage. Lucullus, the Roman governor, soldier-gourmet, once ruled the province of Pontus in which Amasia was situated. Since the Black Sea offered the easiest route, the Emperor Nerva bridged the Yeshil Irmak and carried the road through Amasia to the

Roman line on the Euphrates established by Domitian.

Famed for its romantic grandeur, Amasia lies in a defile between two massive cliffs which tower above the course of the river. The city-fortress was impregnable on every side. The garrison based on the fortress controlled the route to which the town owed its importance and prosperity. In the face of this high rock, approachable only by terraces and an internal stairway, were the burial places of the Kings of Pontus and Persian princes. Strabo the geographer, born in Amasia about 54 B.C., left a description of these rock-tombs which are in existence to-day. In the last part of the second century A.D., Amasia was a royal capital. It rose to its greatest splendour as the seat of power of the kingdom of Pontus after the time of Alexander, who conquered it. The last king to rule there was the father of Mithridates the Great, who, after a long struggle against the Romans, was defeated by Pompey. He made it a free city. In turn, Amasia became one of the chief towns of the kingdom of Trebizond. It was a bishopric in the Byzantine period (A.D. 323-327), and was restored by the tyrant Phocas, the East Roman Emperor. A monster of humble origin, he murdered the Emperor Maurizio and his five sons in order to gain the throne. He was assassinated in A.D. 610. By a trick of history this benefactor of Amasia has a monument that survived the downfall of the Roman Empire. This is a fluted column of beautiful proportions. It is the only monumental column that has survived intact and erect in the Roman Forum through thirteen centuries.

In 1075 the Turks captured Amasia. In 1193 it was annexed to the Seljuk State and restored to glory. It withstood a seven-months' siege in 1402 by Timur the Terrible (Tamerlane) who had defeated the Turks in a great battle at Ankara, making the Sultan Bayezid I a prisoner and dragging him in his train. But the son, Bayezid II, returned and became one of the governors of Amasia. He built there a fine mosque.

The little town in the ravine is still beautiful with its mosques, mausoleums, minarets, a caravanserai and a covered bazaar. The caravans from the East come no more but the place is prosperous being at the centre of a rich terrain producing grain, fruit, olives and tobacco leaf.

A popular brand of cigarettes sold today in the kiosks of Istanbul is called 'Amasia' after its leaf.

Scissors, like all first novels, is in part autobiographical. Renstone Rectory is the old Rempstone Rectory, near Loughboro', on the edge of Leicestershire. As a boy I was invited there to help in the rector's garden. It had an enchantment that has not vanished, with its timbered gable, long lawn and a blue vista of the Charnwood Forest. The Marsh family, inhabiting the Rectory, is wholly imaginary.

In re-reading *Scissors* I find that after almost half-a-century it has become a period piece. It presents an Edwardian England that has vanished, with its large house-parties, numerous servants and the graceful affluence that marked the era of the upper middle-classes. The 'upper' and the 'lower' classes have been engulfed in a tidal wave of the general prosperity marking the Welfare State. The world has become as classless as a Royal Garden Party. I think it is a happier world despite the crushing taxation and predatory rapacity of successive profligate Governments.

Each age breeds its own words, discarded in turn. The nineteenth-century 'Egad, sir!' has disappeared, as also the feminine 'vapours' of the eighteenth century. At the beginning of the twentieth century objectionable men were termed 'cads'. Schoolboys used 'ripping' in moments of ecstasy. 'It's simply ripping!' replied Scissors, describing his delight. In turn this has given place to 'scrumptious' and 'wizard'; doubtless other adjectives are coming up over the schoolboy's horizon. I have resisted a temptation to revise these words. One would not tamper with Jane Austen's dialogue. *Scissors* is a portrait of an age and can now claim the immunity of a period piece. My young hero was 'highly sensitive'. Today schoolboys are sophisticated and thick-skinned, or pretend to be. The excitement of doing forty miles an hour in a motorcar has been supplanted by the six hundred in an aeroplane, done by Smith minor once or twice a year on his way to the Riviera. In turn this speed will be outdated for the supersonic schoolboy.

Down the years since this novel's appearance I have been written to and visited by people who had been to Amasia, to my embarrassment. Before prefacing this twenty-second reprint I thought it time to visit Asia Minor. I found little had changed since I imaginatively set my scene there. Turks still smoke hookahs at cafés in the shade of giant plane trees, picturesquely situated amid blue-tiled mosques and finger-slim minarets. The latter, alas, have been modernized. The imam no longer climbs his high minaret to make the call to prayer. From the ground floor he summons the faithful through tinny loud-speakers affixed to the parapet. But on the old caravan routes, now main highways for local buses and cars, one encounters a string of melancholy camels led by an old Turk sitting on a donkey. An animated bundle of rags, he greets you, and at the hour of prayer he dismounts, to touch the earth with his brow in the worship of Allah and his Prophet. Peering in a silk factory with its hand-operated loom, I saw a large sign above the rackety machine. *Allahin Dedigi Olur* it proclaimed. 'What God Says Happens'. It is akin to Ali's 'Kismet' with which he decorated Scissors at their parting. Amasia has in no way changed, somnolent in its river-bright ravine.

There is much in this novel that I would now write differently, having practised my craft through a lifetime. There would be no clichés, there would be a suppression of sentiment. But inevitably there would be something else, a sophistication that comes with long experience. Nor would there be that youthful note of 'the first fine careless rapture'. Above all, one thing that the years take with them would be missing; the bloom of adolescence in the morning of life.

January 1968.   CECIL ROBERTS.

SCISSORS

CHAPTER I

A COLD spray blew over the deck of the steamer as it left the calm waters of the Bosphorus, making for the open and wind-swept expanse of the Black Sea. Although it was springtime, and the promise of summer had made Constantinople a city of warmth and cheerfulness, the wind cut through the shivering crowd on the deck of the Austrian-Lloyd boat. A north-easterly gale was blowing from the Russian Steppes, and at intervals, through mists and clouds closing and parting, the passengers caught glimpses of the Anatolian coast with its long mountainous barricade rising from the surf-beaten strip of shore. In lee of the deck-houses there was also a nurse, a fresh-complexioned English girl, in charge of a boy of seven, evidently the son of the Englishman and his wife. The Captain of the steamer, an Austrian, regarded the strange party from time to time, for it was rarely that Englishmen came to this part of the world, and seldom were they accompanied by their women folk. Impelled by his curiosity, he approached the tall stranger who had now risen and was surveying his fellow passengers with amused interest.

"You make to Trebizond, sir?" he asked, in broken English.

"No, for Samsoon."

"Ah—then you are of those who make the harbour

there. It is a good scheme. The English have much wisdom, but it is a terrible land," he continued, and swept his hand expressively toward the grey coastland. "Barbarians there—Turks, Armenians, Greeks, Syrians, Circassians, Kurds, and some Americans, they go everywhere, like the English. Ah, a terrible land." He shuddered and drew his fingers across his throat, and then rolled his eyes as if the country transcended all words at his command.

"Do you know Asia Minor?" asked the stranger. "I am going to Amasia."

"That is inland—a place of the wolves, the bandits— no, I would never tread that soil. It is enough to sail the sea. The Black Sea—ough!" And once more he shuddered. "The lady—is it that she goes there, and the child?"

"Yes, I have business in Amasia."

"That is the illness of the English,—business, for this they come to these lands. They are great fools, and brave fools, sir! The sea is more safe. I hope soon never more to see this coast. I will live in Vienna. Ah! one can live in Vienna, but there!—" He gave a short laugh and then went about his work.

But as Charles Dean leaned over the taffrail and watched the flowing coastline dimly streaming into distance, it was not without a stirring of deep interest. This was the classic land of great adventure; they were near the coast of Phoenicia; behind that range was Sidon, looking towards Palestine. This sea had seen Jason and his Argonauts searching the coast of Colchis for the Golden Fleece. All the ancient world of the Greeks was here, and the tides of barbaric splendour had swept over that land; Greek, Roman, Byzantine and Ottoman rulers had shaped its destiny. It was the great battlefield of the world; the

Greeks sailing for Troy, the Ten Thousand, had all known that shore and the mountains still slept by the thundering seas as in the days of Alexander and of Cæsar. Peak after peak of those mountains with their historic names arose and looked inland, the mountains of Ionia, Ida and Casia, of Bithynia, Pontus and Paphlogonia; violet and blue and amethyst, they stretched like sleeping animals in the March sunlight, clothed with a forest growth and fringed with pine trees.

So all day long the little steamer went along its pathway of foam; during those hours, Charles Dean and his wife were sustained by the excitement of their entry into a new world. The last four years of their lives had been spent in journeying from city to city, from country to country. Amsterdam, Berlin and Bordeaux had held them for a short time. Eastwards then Charles Dean received a call from the trading company employing him, this time to Constantinople. That had been the pleasantest of all their sojournings in foreign lands. The city of mosques and minarets, with its beautiful gardens and golden sea, had seemed like a dream from one of the Arabian Nights' Entertainments. And now the gradual extension eastwards of business, was carrying them to Amasia, the city unknown, dwelling inland behind that great mountain barrier. It was a strange life, yet not without its fascinations. Mary Dean insisted upon accompanying her husband. She had the choice of remaining in England, but she swept it aside unhesitatingly. Devoid of fear and devoted to her husband, she went with him from land to land. With them also went their young son, John Narcissus Dean. Narcissus! exclaimed everybody, hearing the name. "Yes, Narcissus," answered handsome Charles Dean solemnly, while the light of humour danced in his grey eyes; and then followed the story of that honeymoon

in Naples, when Mary, after seeing the famous statue of
"Narcissus listening to Echo," had pleaded with her young
husband, assisted by a Jew curio shopkeeper, for a copy
she coveted. "But I want a real Narcissus," whispered the
young man, pressing her hand quietly, while the Jew dusted
the expensive bronzes on his counter.

"You shall have one—if I can have this," she answered
roguishly. He nearly kissed her in boyish ecstasy.
"Done!" he cried—"and we'll call him 'Narcissus.'"

Charles Dean was not only a man who kept to his word,
but also to his joke. The announcement of the birth of
John Narcissus at the historic manor of "Fourways"
filled old Sir Neville, the grandfather, with delight and
protest; a boy—excellent, Narcissus—preposterous! But
Charles was obstinate, Mary amused, and Sir Neville protested anew. It was like Charles—independent, obstinate
Charles, who had always been so irrational. It might have
been expected of a man who had thrown up a diplomatic
career to breed horses, which he could not afford to breed,
who had married penniless Mary Loughton, his land-
agent's pretty daughter. Charles had always been the
fool in contrast with Henry, his level-headed elder brother.
Sir Neville did not protest long,—he died one month after
the coming of the grandchild with the freak name; and although all babies seem to look alike, many ladies, calling
on the young mother, vowed the child was a veritable Narcissus—so handsome, so bonnie, so—

The new baronet made one formal protest, but Henry
knew well he could do nothing with his odd-minded
brother; still, as uncle, head of the family, and sixth baronet, he felt he had some right to protest against "Narcissus," if not for himself, then for his own girls, who were
cousins to this piece of Greek mythology. The young parents only laughed, and John Narcissus, as if seeing the

joke, gurgled whenever he was shown the statue and told to grow up like it—not altogether of course, for the statue proved to be cracked over the left breast, where the dealer had carefully kept his thumb.

Sir Henry, annoyed, kept aloof. When he heard that Charles had ruined himself and lost "Fourways" in a mad scheme to sink a shaft, over-persuaded by a gang of company promoters, he declared he was in no way surprised, shrugged his shoulders, and waited to see what would happen now. The sale of "Fourways," its contents and its horses, must have been a hard blow for Charles, but he certainly gave no sign when he called to say "Goodbye," before taking a position as continental agent offered him by an old friend.

"And—the boy?" asked Sir Henry, unable to make himself pronounce the ridiculous name.

"He is going with us."

"What—all over the Continent!" cried the astounded baronet. "You can't take a boy there—why not send him to school?"

"He's too young—we want him—and I don't believe in preparatory schools."

"Crank!" exclaimed Sir Henry to her ladyship when his brother had gone.

Thus came John Narcissus Dean to be swinging his sturdy legs on a box aboard an Austrian-Lloyd steamer bound for Samsoon. He was a fine boy, well matured for his seven years, and already he had a manner of command which made a slave of his devoted nurse Anna, a big fresh-coloured country girl, one of the small group that had gathered, seven years before, at the foot of the staircase at "Fourways." Anna had never intended going to Asia Minor, which she looked upon with the same horror as she did the South Sea Islands. Her first excursion, to Amsterdam, had been taken with great daring. Only love of the child she nursed and the mistress she served, could have prevailed upon her to leave England, for as all the peasant class, she had a loathing of foreigners. But from Amsterdam to Berlin had not seemed so far, and then the change to Bordeaux was like coming half-way home, so she remained with the family, and, as the years went by, became more tightly bound by affection to her young charge. For, however much she admired her mistress, she never doubted for one moment that, without her, young John Narcissus could not live. She had nursed him from a baby, was familiar with all his complaints, and also his moods, which were peculiar and trying.

It was Anna alone who could curb those terrible fits of passion which so alarmed the fond parents. The child had a way of working himself into a fanatical frenzy when pleased by anything. At first these moods had been attributed to infant naughtiness and had been punished, but without result. An eminent Berlin specialist, whom they had consulted in distress, had said that the child's brain was abnormally developed. He was to be humoured and closely watched. With time and careful guarding he would outgrow those storms of passion and ecstasy. So Anna immediately took the specialist's words to heart. Without her the child would not live. When the change to Constantinople was announced, her first intention was to give notice. She did not object to France or Holland, but Turkey was a barbarian country where Christians were crowded together and shot at with bows and arrows, or cut to a thousand pieces with terrible knives like those which grocers used for carving hams. But she could not think of leaving the child; and, after all, she had been to Berlin, which was almost half-way across Europe. She decided to go to Constantinople, for the more she considered the matter the firmer grew her conviction that her master and mistress were mad.

When therefore, one morning, seated on the deck of the steamer as it entered Samsoon roads, she was told by Mr. Dean that the white path, climbing past the squalid little houses up the mountain side, winding in and out like a ribbon, was the way to old Baghdad, the ancient city of Haroun-al-Raschid and Sinbad the Sailor, she wondered whatever her people, far away at home, would think when they heard she was travelling in these fairy-tale lands. The only real things in her amazing life were John and his father and mother. She looked at John as he sat swinging his brown legs on the side of a box, and wondered that such a morsel of life should drag her across the world into strange and terrible lands.

The passage ashore was made in a small boat, and the adventure was a somewhat perilous one, for the frail craft was swept by the waters. They were finally landed on the beach some distance away from the town. Here a small crowd of customs officials and Turkish luggage porters met them; then they were driven along the front of the town in an *arabya*, a native conveyance with curtains for warding off the sun, drawn by one horse in the control of a Turkish driver.

And now the irresistible glamour which the East throws over the hearts of all who venture into her domain, entranced the small party as it was driven for some two miles along the edge of a sandy yellow beach into the town of Samsoon.

The buildings were low and inelegant; the streets narrow and filled with that accumulation of smells and filth that are to be found in all cities under Ottoman rule. But there was, despite these disadvantages, a definite charm in the little town of forty thousand souls. Samsoon is the one accessible port lying on the fringe of a tableland containing the richest cornfields and tobacco country of the world. The city itself was built at the great gate of the mountains over which the roads wind through the few low passes along that impregnable coast. It was the gate of that great historic highway running through Turkey in Asia, along which all the traffic had rolled for centuries. It was traffic that had scarcely altered in any detail since the day of the Caliph Haroun-al-Raschid; the sight which met the eyes of Charles Dean and his family was one that had greeted the traveller for the last ten hundred years.

As the *arabya* climbed up the steep road leading to the centre of the town, it breasted a stream of traffic coming down from the high pass. Young John shouted with glee as the solemn camels trudged by, their bells tinkling, their backs loaded with great bales of merchandise. Wagons, bullock-carts, donkeys, packhorses, *arabyas* and men carrying great bundles, all seemed destined for one place, the block of warehouses above the harbour. Here and there a tired camel knelt for rest in the shade of a wayside tree. The drivers were vivid figures in their white cloaks, dusty and travel stained, while beside them moved, talked, and gesticulated such a mixture of races and colours that the eye was dazzled with the indistinguishable medley of blue, scarlet, gold, yellow and green gowns and cloaks, nearly all richly embroidered; and above all, rose the noise of innumerable bells in all keys, some ringing deep and slow, others tinkling incessantly as the donkeys wound by, urged on by cries and blows.

Sounds, colours, smells, all mingled in this small town, along this crowded highway, and Charles Dean was not slow to notice the prosperity of the place. Every man and animal was burdened with merchandise of some kind.

Carts rolled by with shrieking axles, loaded with wheat and barley. The camels were weighed down under great bales of wool, tobacco, mohair and boxes of fruit and nuts. Brown-legged boys from the hills drove their flocks down the main street. They had started for the town at early dawn, and by eleven were in Samsoon, a distance of twenty miles. They were chiefly Turks, but occasionally one noticed the sharp features and clear skin of a Syrian youth, or the dark lean profile of a Circassian, always mounted and belted with daggers and pistols. The Greeks too were in evidence, walking about with a superior air of possession, for they and the Armenians were the chief citizens. They kept the shops and ran the small hotels and cafés.

That night, Dean and his family slept in Samsoon, but they were early astir, and after a short call at the local office of his company, Dean, with his wife, child and nurse, were seated in the curtained *arabya* with a Moslem driver urging his two cream ponies along the high street. They were now travelling on the Baghdad road, and they had for companions on the way an unending line of betasselled camels, with great bells clanging as they lurched forwards, caravans winding slowly up the mountain side, and many *arabyas* loaded with human beings or boxes, which once, to Dean's amazement, included American sewing machines destined for Baghdad. There were also many picturesque pedestrians or travellers on the humble donkey. For miles the broad road climbed up the side of the great ravine. Early in the afternoon they passed through Chakallu, the Place of Jackals, a village in the deep valley, and twilight found them at their first halting place. The town of Marsovan lay amid vineyards, orchards, and walnut groves. Above the flat-topped houses towered the slender minaret, rose tinted with the flush of waning light. Around the town, beyond the open plains, stretched the dark mountain ranges running north and south. As they descended into the town the driver pointed with his whip to an enormous blue precipice which towered up on the distant horizon some thirty miles away.

"Amasia," he said briefly, and Charles Dean and his wife looked at the distant horizon where lay the city in which they were destined to abide. In Marsovan they were fortunate in finding an American Medical Settlement where they were hospitably entertained for the night. It was with regret that they set out next morning for Amasia. It had been a great delight to live for a space among English speaking persons, to exchange opinions with the cheerful nurses and listen to the tales of the resident doctors. There was even an English garden, a fresh, green, home-like space within the walled compound, bordered with cherry trees and Easter lilies. Here at least was a place of refuge when the solitude of Amasia became unbearable, and as Mary Dean drove out of the courtyard and waved farewell to the little group of women gathered to speed their guests, she looked back with a feeling of comfort. She would be but a day's journey from them, and those who know what the sound of one's native speech means in an alien land will realise the comfort Mary Dean derived from the workers of the Mission.

The road to Amasia was a gradual crescendo of delight. The soft blue mountain ranges towered up above the travellers as they approached the entrance of the gorge. Here and there a column of smoke wound up the mountainside from the fires of the charcoal burners, whose little tents were pitched on the slopes. It was afternoon when they entered the ravine along which the white road wound into the town. Above them they saw the Baghdad road, on the opposite side of the ravine, half obscured by the clouds of dust thrown up by the miscellaneous traffic of carts, herds, camels and donkeys driving into the town. Now the plain appeared, and the vision stretched before them was like a new garden of Eden, a land flowing with colour, and scents from luxurious gardens. The smooth, quickly flowing river tumbled over its weirs; they could hear the singing of the water and the creaking of water mills built along the banks. The great crags stretched sheer to the sky, blazing with crimson shrubs in the bright, hot sunlight, and the further they progressed, the richer, the more varied grew the colours of this wonderful land.

Presently with a sharp turn in the road, they emerged from the rocky ravine into a tremendous gorge, with Amasia nestling between the folds of the towering mountains. The town itself was a maze of little white houses, dotted here and there in the small fertile valley, and stretching along the two banks of the Yeshil Irmak. A dozen bridges, all of quaint design, some going back to Roman times, spanned the bright river, and above the banks rose the minarets of the mosques, khans, colleges and public buildings. The best houses built along the river each possessed wonderful hanging gardens blazing with luxuriant growths of semi-tropical plants and fruits, but the wonder of Amasia lay, not in the gardens or buildings, but in the immense cliffs that walled in the town from the outer world. These precipices, scarcely a mile apart, rose up on each side of the town to heights of three thousand feet on the western and more than a thousand on the eastern side. They did not rise as mountains, but seemed to be walls of rocks guarding the town. A castle stood boldly silhouetted against the bronze sky, perched on a frowning crag dominating the town. This was indeed an ancient dwelling place, an old world town of wonder, where history seemed to sleep, for Amasia was once the capital of Pontus, the home of the great Seljuks, the birthplace of Mithridates the Great. On the face of the western precipice there were still the five rock-hewn Tombs of the Kings. When Strabo wrote of them in B. C. 65, he was telling an ancient story, yet they remained untouched as when he had seen them.

As Charles Dean and his family drove into the town it was early afternoon, but already one half of the place was in shadow, the other half blazed with sunlight streaming over the western precipice. They were driven through the main street, a well observed party, giving as much interest as they found. The company employing Dean had a house for its agent on the outskirts of the town and to that they made their way. Presently they turned off from the road and went down a slope which led them through a beautiful garden into a small courtyard. Here, their home came into view, and as the large, low, white-faced building rose up among the trees, they all gave a cry of delight. On one side ran a large pergola built of yellow stone and black wood, leading to a garden which, even at this early time, rioted in colour. Beyond the pergola, approached by broad stone steps, lay the river, bordered with trees beneath which several boats were moored. One end of the house, raised upon piles, overlooked the river, with a wonderful view down the gorge towards the dazzling minarets and towers of the town.

They had scarcely noticed this enchanting vista when the *arabya* pulled up in front of a large porch, screened with a swinging rush curtain. Before it, with a smile of welcome on their faces, stood the bronzed Englishman and his wife, whom Dean had come to relieve.

Greetings exchanged, they were led into a large, yellow room with French windows opening on to a verandah. Passing through the windows they were confronted once more with the view down the gorge. Tea was laid, and the travellers were soon exchanging the news. The agent, Mr.

Price, and his wife had been in Amasia for twelve years. It was six years since they had had their last holiday in England. Now they were going there, never to leave it again.

"And to think—in six weeks we shall walk down Piccadilly!" cried Mrs. Price, the delight of anticipation in her voice. "It is just the same I suppose—the same crowds, the same lights and hurry?"

They laughed like children. It was so good to think they would be in England again. It was a little cruel to show their joy in view of the new exiles. But six years away from England had filled them with irresistible longing. Their questions too were all of home. The political crisis—was it over? The new Premier, how long did they think he would be in power? They had a boy at Winchester—was the tone there still considered good? He was sixteen—his mother fetched a photograph from the drawer to show them. He was going into the consular service.

And then Mrs. Price turned to the little boy standing beside Mrs. Dean. Until now, his whole attention had been divided between the novelty of his surroundings and the piece of cake he held in his hand. They hoped the summer heat would not be too intense for the child.

"The poor little chap will find it lonely here," said Price, "unless he makes friends with the Turkish children." Privately he wondered what insane motive had caused that couple to bring a child to this extraordinary land.

"John has always been with us," remarked Mrs. Dean, as if reading his thoughts. "The child seems to be quite happy without playmates, though of course, I devote most of my time to him."

And then they passed to business matters; the two women discussed domestic arrangements, the men their own trading affairs. Dinner was served in the long yellow room that evening. It was only six o'clock and yet it was quite dark. The light departed rapidly from the gorge, for the moment the sun had dipped below the precipice, the valley below was plunged into darkness. But as they sat at dinner, and looked out westwards over the mountain barrier, they could still see the daylight lingering in the glowing sky. A few stars glimmered in the twilight, their brightness and the light blue sky contrasting vividly with the black gorge and the dark running river.

They were waited upon at dinner by two Armenian boys clad in white jackets with brass buttons.

"We have practically brought them up in our service," said Price. "Their parents were killed in the last massacre."

"Massacre!" Mrs. Dean dropped her hand on to the table and looked across at the speaker—"When did the last occur?"

"Four years ago—it was a bad one too. Some squabble in a bazaar began it, I believe. The Armenians here are skilful in trade. They make hard bargains, and the Turks never forget the fact. There was a dispute in the bazaar; it set a light to smouldering passion, and the town was ablaze in half an hour. These Moslems are curious people. They kill deliberately, and though the massacre begins with a frenzied outbreak, it goes on with a dispassionateness which is terrible. The Armenians immediately flocked to the bazaar. It's in a walled compound with strongly barred gates. I had been out in the country that morning and knew that something was astir. The Turks looked askance at me and were sulky whenever I spoke to them. On returning my wife begged me to go down to the bazaar and see what I could do, for it is wonderful the weight we English have here. The Turks will listen to an Englishman, for they have never forgotten our Consuls and their firm, honest treatment of them.

"So I went. In front of the bazaar door, I found a horde of Moslems, rifles and pistols in hand, waiting for their victims to emerge. The outbreak had occurred at ten o'clock that morning. It was now four in the afternoon and they showed no signs of dispersing. I knew they would wait there five or six days if necessary. It was useless to argue with them. Moslem blood had been shed. The Armenians would have to bleed for it. Finally I succeeded in obtaining a concession. They would allow the women and children to go to their homes. But not the men, they said. So the door was opened and the terrified women and children passed out between a sullen crowd of Moslems. When the last appeared in the gateway there was a rush, and I saw a helpless woman surrounded by a mob of angry faces. Pushing my way towards her, I attempted to give her my protection but before I could reach her, she fell forwards, stabbed in the back, and as she fell, I saw that the Turks had not broken their word. Under the folds of the garment covering her was the Armenian pastor who had tried to escape in disguise. There was a murmur of intense satisfaction at this slaying of the leader of the hated community. In all these affairs, the pastor is the first to go; they seek him out as the figurehead, and these poor leaders of a timid flock know that; you can see perpetual melancholy in their faces, hear it in their voices. But they are brave men, and there is never any lack of pastors. These two boys who wait on us are the sons of that unfortunate man."

There was a long silence; then, fearing he had alarmed his guests, Price added in a cheerful voice—

"Still, they never touch us you know. European blood

is sacred to them, and I have always found the Turks very docile, but if you are wise, you will keep in when the drums begin to drone."

"The drums?" asked Dean, eager for information, although he could see his wife was being unnerved.

"Harry," interposed Mrs. Price, "don't you think this is very trying for Mrs. Dean—she has only—"

"Oh! please go on!" cried Mrs. Dean, "—there's no safety in ignorance."

"Well—you can generally surmise that trouble is brewing when you hear the drums begin to drone. They start at sunset and grow louder towards midnight. It is an awful sound, weird, oriental. You will probably hear a few of them to-night, there's always a strolling drummer entertaining at one of the khans. When trouble is brewing however, there's not one drum, but hundreds. They sound everywhere. You hear them in the streets, down the gorge, up the mountain-side. They sound as if Timur the Terrible was gathering his army again." He broke off with a laugh, "Really, Dean, I shall give you all the creeps— you are quite safe being English and life is very pleasant here, but lonely at times. You will find even Constantinople a change—have you lived there?"

"We have been there two months," answered Dean.

"Two months!—then you will know Therapia—lovely Therapia! We took a bungalow there for two months each year. I have a cousin at the Embassy. We had a delightful time—nights on the Bosphorus, gay little parties embarking in *caiques,* sunset beyond Therapia, the house parties at Buyukdereh. Oh, it was enjoyable, but to think now—Piccadilly, Oxford Circus, Henley week—days in Surrey!—there's no place like England."

With a boyish gesture of delight, he pinched his wife's arm who laughed gaily in response.

"We are now going to leave you to talk business," she said, rising. "I am sure Mrs. Dean is tired and wants to go to bed, and we two will have a busy day tomorrow." And with that the two women said good-night. When they were gone, Dean and Price sat smoking for a time.

"Come on to the verandah," said Price, leading the way. "The moon will be up soon, and moonrise here is one of the wonders of Asia."

They seated themselves in low wicker chairs. It was so dark that it was impossible to distinguish anything clearly. There was a sound of running water, and a muffled roar came back on the wind from the place where the river leapt its weirs down in the gorge. Price's cigarette glowed red in the darkness with each draw he took. The air was perfumed and warm. There was something in the atmosphere which made the senses very acute. It seemed as if one was waiting for something to happen—the singing of the stream, the wandering breeze, the perfume and the impenetrable darkness were all a prelude to the first act of an unknown drama. The silence grew so oppressive that Dean felt he would have to speak or cry out. He was about to force a remark to his lips when his host suddenly sat erect, intently listening, his face turned towards the valley.

"Listen!" he said after a pause. "Can you hear anything?"

Even as he spoke, the other man heard a subdued sound. It was borne on a wind which died down, but gradually its note was more insistent, deepening in tone until it seemed to make the darkness tremble. As Dean listened, he experienced a strange thrill creeping over him. There was something so weird, so redolent of the strange land in that music as it was borne along the gorge and gave expression to the mystery of the night. Such a sound it was as had been heard many centuries ago when the invading

Turkish hordes had swept over the land. Those drums had heralded the approach of Timur the Terrible on his devastating march across Asia, leaving a track of blood behind, his name sending terror in advance of his ruthless army. The drum now throbbing down the gorge had the same barbaric note, the same sinister significance, and as Charles Dean listened he knew that this city of old Asia had never changed from the days when the Seljuk sultans ruled or Haroun-al-Raschid kept his court in Baghdad.

And then, as if to add to the wonder of the night, the two men became aware of a slow change in the scene before them. The objects in the garden grew into vision slowly. Along the gorge they could see the houses and under them a chill light on the black swirling river. The dim minarets changed from blue sentinels of the darkness to long white fingers pointing skywards. And above the black edge of the precipice it seemed no longer dark, for even as they looked and wondered, the moon came up over the edge, round and full, with its white face peering over the great wall shutting in the gorge. The scene before them was now one of indescribable beauty. The little white flat houses, the mosques and minarets and gardens, all glimmered brightly in the serene light flooding the gorge. As the river ran between the banks, leaping the weirs and rocky obstructions, it flashed silvery under the rays of the moon, and as if to keep measure with this revelation, the drum-beats grew louder and louder, throbbing in the perfumed air until the sound seemed to be closing in from all sides.

How long they sat spellbound before this magic of the East they knew not, but their inactivity was broken at last by the noise of a footfall on the gravel below the verandah. Instantly Price was on his feet, peering over towards the garden. His companion too had heard the noise, and jumped up just in time to see a white figure turn in the path and pass from sight under the darkness of the cherry trees.

Both men looked at one another for the space of a second.

"I'm sure there's some one moving in the garden," said Dean.

"No one has any right in here."

They listened. The drum droned louder than before and as the sound died with the veering of the wind, they heard a footfall again, less distinct. The trespasser was going in the direction of the drum.

Without hesitation, Price vaulted lightly from the verandah to the path below, his companion following. Quickly they traversed the downward slope until they reached a grove of cherry trees into which Price plunged. Behind him, Dean, following silently, heard his guide give a short cry; peering into the shadow, he saw a small figure some ten yards ahead, garbed from head to foot in a loose white gown, which fluttered ghostlike in the moonlight. Price, running now, had caught the white form; when Dean came up, he turned to him with a nervous laugh. As the latter stopped, he gave a short cry of surprise, wondering what trick the enchantment of the night was playing upon his senses, for there, firmly held by Price, was his own boy, barefooted, in his white nightgown, looking up with startled eyes.

"John! what are you doing here?" The father stooped and lifted up his boy. The child's face wore a half puzzled expression as if he had suddenly been awakened from sleep and was dazzled by the light. For a moment or so he gave no answer, but clutched the lapels of his father's coat, his small frame shaking with fright.

"Daddy, I had to come! Something called me, something—" and as if unable or afraid to give words to the fear in his heart, he sobbed violently in his father's arms. It was in vain that Dean tried to sooth the child; he shook from head to foot and clutched at his father's hand in wild terror. They carried the sobbing child indoors, and when they had gained the lamplit drawing-room, calmness had once more come over the child. He looked about him and blinked in the brilliant light like one waking from a dream.

Price pinched the boy's ear playfully—

"A nightmare, old son, eh?—you've been having too much cake!"

"How did you get out of bed?" asked the father, looking anxiously at the boy.

"I don't know, Daddy—I can't remember until you found me." It was obvious that the child was speaking the truth.

"Well, we can't have you sleep-walking like this, John. You'll frighten your mother to death."

"Take the boy up to his room, Dean," said Price. "What a good thing it hasn't roused Mrs. Dean! Come along, I'll show you the way, he's sleeping next to your room."

They took the boy upstairs and placed him in his bed. The child was quite calm now and his head sank on the pillow as if heavy with sleep. For a minute Dean waited in the room and then stooped over the bed.

"Will you be all right now, John?" But there was no answer for John was already fast asleep again, his head buried in the pillow. The two men tip-toed silently out of the room. When they had gained the verandah Price mixed himself a whiskey and soda.

"Drink?" he asked, with an ill-concealed attempt to be at his ease.

"No thanks."

There was a long silence; the two men were thinking.

Price knocked the ash off his cigarette and watched its end until the glow died down.

"Is John subject to those—er—to sleep-walking?" he asked at length, making his enquiry as casual as possible.

"No, he's not. I have never known him to do this before."

"H'm, perhaps the journey's upset him—the excitement; children are easy victims of nightmare."

"Yes—do you think it was nightmare?" asked Dean. His tone plainly conveyed the belief that he thought otherwise.

"Of course!—why not?—the child has no reason for going down the garden."

"Where does the path lead?"

"To the river—there's a footway into the town—it cuts off the bend in the road."

"To the town?—towards the drum?"

Price started. Dean had noticed then! He gave a short laugh, and got up and stretched his arms.

"Perhaps you'd like to turn in now?" he asked, and then as if changing his mind, he sat down suddenly.

"Look here, Dean," he said earnestly, "I'll be quite frank —it is perhaps better. You've guessed what drew the boy out of his bed?"

"The drum?"

"Precisely—and you're right, I think, though we may be making a silly mistake. I would never have believed it myself, but it is certainly curious."

"What?—the sleep-walking?" asked Dean. "Because I'll say plainly that I'm sure the boy wasn't sleep-walking, he was wide awake."

"You noticed it?"

"Yes, I did—but I can't account for his expression."

"His half-dazed look?"

"Yes—it was uncanny. I've never seen John look like that before. He seemed almost—" Dean paused as if reluctant to use the word upon his tongue.

"Hypnotised?" suggested Price. The other nodded, and they both relapsed into silence.

"I don't want to alarm you," said Price quietly, after a long pause, "but this thing makes me half inclined to believe what I would never credit. Now, remember what I am going to tell you is only an old legend. There's hundreds of silly tales you will be told by the natives here, if you encourage them to talk. They spend nights embellishing these yarns in the khans until they believe in their own imaginations. But it is as well you should know, in case to-night's event may be repeated. You noticed the boy went in the direction of the drum? Well, it's said that there are certain souls which can be allured by the *saz*—that's the name of the drum. They cannot always be allured, only when the moon is full can the sound attract the souls of its victims, but when that condition is fulfilled, there is no power, save intervention by a person not under the influence, which can break the spell—it's a silly tale of course, these old khan entertainers always make the flesh creep."

"But the victims—you say they are allured—where?"

"I don't know, these old legend-spinners never say."

"But surely there is some point in this hypnotic influence —why are they drawn by the sound?"

"It's a mystery—as I've said, there's no sense in the whole story. What an ass I am to tell you all this. It's late, hadn't we better turn in?"

The change in the conversation was clumsy, and it did not deceive Dean.

"You're keeping something back, Price—what is it?"

Price looked steadily at his interrogator. It was evident that Dean would go to the bottom of the subject.

"Oh,—er, there's not much else to be told, only a silly sort of nightmare ending, that's all."

"What kind of ending—death?"

"Yes."

"Violent—dreadful?"

"Oh no, in fact, I should think rather sudden, or peaceful, that's how it seemed to me."

"Then you've seen it? Tell me all about it, Price."

"Really, Dean, you know this sort of thing is very stupid—a coincidence, that's all, and I may have been mistaken."

"Perhaps so, but I want to hear."

"It happened three years ago, just such a night as this —full moon, those damned drums droning away—when my *kavass*—the fellow who takes me about the villages here, came running in. He was in a fearful state, so excited he could hardly speak. Had I seen Hafiz? he asked, —that was his son. I told him I hadn't. He said he had seen him crossing the bottom garden, going towards the river path."

"Towards the drums?"

"Yes, we had heard them at dinner. They were very loud that night. I told the *kavass* he was mistaken. Hafiz couldn't have gone that way, it was full moon and we should have seen him, but the old fellow wouldn't be denied. It was the drum of Timur, he said—no one could resist it who heard. I didn't know the story then, but the old father was so distressed that I offered to go with him along the path. So taking my revolver, we set out. We had gone about a mile along the river's edge when we came to an old khan. The drum was being beaten inside, so

we thought, but my *kavass* said it was impossible because
the khan was roofless and no one lived in it. Anyhow,
we could hear the *saz* droning away. So we pushed open
the creaking old gateway.

"Inside the courtyard there was a pool, and a fountain
that never flowed. The moon shone down on the pool
which was so still that it reflected the stars. Round the
old khan buildings ran the galleries, in rectangular form.
The moon threw a deep blue shadow half across the courtyard, and as we stood there, peering into the deserted place,
it seemed as if we had entered into a strange world where
only the shadows moved. We stood there, I should think,
for quite a minute, transfixed by the silent beauty of the
place, when the old man suddenly gave a cry. I followed
his gaze and saw what he had seen. There, on the other
side of the fountain, lay the naked body of a youth. At
first I thought it was a marble statue, it was so white and
perfect in form, but the old man ran forward and as I
came up to him, I saw the head of the youth was covered
with a mass of loose, black curls. The poor old father
flung himself on his knees and gathered up the body in his
arms, sobbing as he did so.

"I never saw such a youth as Hafiz. He was quite naked
and the whiteness of his flesh was intensified by the moonlight bathing his body, and the head of black hair. He
had fallen sideways, with one hand resting on his thigh,
the other clenched and stretched out towards the basin.
There was no sign of any struggle. The face was composed, just as if he had fallen asleep, and there was nothing on the ground or anywhere about to suggest violence,
but his clothes were all missing and to me this was conclu-
sive proof that robbery had been the motive of the crime;
no doubt he'd been strangled. The poor old father who
had been speechless with grief for some time, shook his

head when I spoke of strangulation. 'No, effendi,' he said quietly, with a touch of fatalism in his voice, 'It is the drum of Timur—look!' His finger pointed to the left breast of the youth, and I saw what had escaped me in the first hurried examination. Just over the heart there was a short, red line, not the incision left by a dagger, but such as a penknife might make.

"There was hardly any blood, a little stream had trickled down the breast and dried. I told the old fellow that his son had been shot, but he only repeated, 'The drum of Timur,' and that was all he could be got to say. The *zaptiehs* searched the khan the next day. They were stupid fellows, and shared the old man's conviction. The fact that the unfortunate youth's clothes were never found proved conclusively, in my mind, that robbery had been the motive. You mustn't believe a tenth of all you hear out here. Anyhow, Dean, when the moon's full, watch your boy if you really think there's anything in the tale. I don't. Why should John be attracted by the drum of Timur, even if there were such a thing?—he's English, born in England! This is a native spell and only works upon those of Moslem blood."

The two men talked on for a short time and Price watched his companion closely; he was greatly relieved when he saw, on retiring, that Dean had dismissed his strange apprehension.

CHAPTER II

I

O N the verandah, under the shade thrown by the blossoming almond tree, sat a boy who at first sight would seem to be some fourteen years of age. It was a hot day without the suspicion of a breeze, and he stretched himself out in a wicker chair while he fanned himself with a broad, soft-brimmed white hat. He was dressed, although it was only early spring, as boys in England dress in the hottest days of summer, that is when they are holidaying and have escaped the vigilance of their mothers. A white cricket shirt, open at the neck, showed a chest and throat tanned to a rich brown by the suns of Asia Minor. His face had the deep healthy tone of one who had exposed himself to the fiercest heat of the sun, but the tan could not hide the pink and red which mantled the clear skin of the boy's face. His head was covered with a disordered mass of brown hair that had a tendency to curl. The impression of all who saw young John Dean, was that of a remarkably handsome English boy. The mouth was finely shaped, the nose straight, with a curious little curve in the nostrils which gave at times an expression of disdain to the face. But the eyes were the arresting feature, they looked out from beneath long lashes, with a light in them so luminous that they appeared to be always on the verge of laughter. John was now twelve years of age, and not thirteen or fourteen as his robust frame suggested. Dressed in a pair of short white knickers, with a long length of brown leg showing, his sleeves rolled up at the elbows, he gave promise of a wonderful manhood. For Charles Dean's whim was daily growing true. This straight tall boy had a classic mould that followed the grace of the "Narcissus" which had given him his name. And to this distinction was added a manner that attracted all. The boy's voice was clear, his laughter infectious; he had an air of command which probably was half innate and partly due to being a European among foreigners. For he ruled his playmates imperiously. The *arabya* drivers who gave him many a lift along the roads, the *zaptiehs* whose rifles he handled, and whose stories he listened to breathlessly, down to the Turkish and Armenian boys of his own age, recognised without question his imperious will. He was "John effendi" in the eyes of all the inhabitants of Amasia, not only because he was the son of the Englishman, but also by reason of that will to rule.

But there was one follower of John effendi who not only respected and obeyed, but worshipped silently. It was Ali, the son of the watermill owner. Ali was a Turk and proud of his blood. He was a year older than John, tall, and in a different way quite as notable as his friend. He had fair wavy hair, always kept close-cropped. His whole life had been spent playing on the banks of the Yeshil Irmak, or the Iris as it was popularly called, and his young body was lithe and brown as a panther's. When he moved it was with the sleek grace of that animal. The muscles slid under their satiny sheaths with a suggestion of cryptic strength. He could run like a hare and swim like an otter, accomplishments which quickly endeared him to John who was his rival in all these things. Ali, by his father's position,—for he was a well-to-do, judged by oriental standards—though more because of his own spirit and strength,

was a boy who reigned among his companions. Only to
one was he known to give way, to John, whom he followed
with an intense, doglike devotion.

It was of Ali that John was thinking this morning as
he sat on the verandah. Where was Ali now? Probably
he had gone to the mosque with his father, for it was nearing noon. He wondered whether Ali would come round
to the house. They had planned a great adventure for
that day. They were to meet by the market drinking-
fountain at eleven o'clock and then to climb the great rock
on whose summit stood the castle. Ali's uncle, the war-
den, was going to show them all the dungeons and court
rooms. It would have been a wonderful treat, and now
he had been forbidden to leave the gardens because of a
silly suspicion of his father's. Last night they had heard
the drums droning even louder than usual. The sound
grew to such a volume that the whole gorge had reverber-
ated with it, and it had awakened him although he always slept soundly. At breakfast his father had looked
worried, and it was plain to see from Anna's nervousness
that something was upsetting them. His father had been
in the garden soon after rising, and he heard him tell
Anna that Achmed was like a bear with a sore head. Then
Anna did a mean thing. She said, "Do you think that
John should go up to the Castle, sir," and his father immediately said "No." It was in vain that he pleaded that Ali
expected him. Ali would have to go alone, he was forbidden to leave the garden.

So John sat on the chair idly swinging one leg over
the arm while he fanned himself. Anna was becoming
a nuisance. She had increased her authority ever since
his dear mother had died two years ago now. The
thought of his mother led his mind back to the almond
tree he and his father had planted on the grave in the little

cemetery of the American Mission at Marsovan. He re-membered that day clearly, because he could never forget seeing his father as he bent down, stamping the soil about the roots of the sapling. His father's shoulders seemed to be twitching curiously and when John looked at his face, he saw he was crying. It was strange to see his father cry, he did not know men could do that, and it hurt him so much, that he had grasped his strong hand and cried "Don't Daddy!" which did not improve matters, for his father had gathered him up in his arms and pressed him to him until he could scarcely breathe. And then John too cried. He would never forget that day.

If only his mother were living now, thought John; she would not let Anna be so strict with him, although he knew that his nurse was like a second mother.

As he sat there with nothing to do on this lovely morn-ing, the spirit of rebellion was strong within him. Rest-less, he got up and ran down the verandah steps towards the courtyard. In front of the stable door he paused, as if thinking, then swung back the door and entered. It was but the work of a minute to saddle his pony. There was just time in which to reach the fountain and tell Ali that he could not go and then be back for lunch with his father.

A few minutes later John was cantering down the high-way into Amasia. He passed the heavily laden camels trudging along with their deep-sounding camel bells slowly tolling, a cloud of dust rising about their pounding feet. Now and then a Turk would greet the boy with a profound salaam, but he could not help observing that the greetings were not so cordial or numerous this morning. A few of the Turks he passed, who knew him well by sight, turned their faces away as he went by, and John recalled his father's words when he had come in from the garden before breakfast. Had they all got sore heads, he wondered.

In the market place he passed little groups that stood talking around their merchandise spread out on the ground, but he had no time this morning for sauntering in and out of the motley gathering. When he reached the fountain, it was exactly eleven o'clock but there was no sign of Ali. So dismounting, John slung the rein over his arm and waited. A number of dusty *arabyas* rattled by, evidently coming in from Marsovan. Two Circassians, their coloured waist-bands gleaming with dagger handles, and long breeched revolvers, rode up to the fountain to water their horses, two superb animals which these wild men rode as if born in the saddle. With characteristic insolence they pushed away a Turk who was watering his mule, and the angry old fellow went off waving his arms and leaving a stream of abuse behind him.

It was very hot and the increasing heat made John realise that it must be getting near noon. There was still no sign of Ali, but John dared not wait any longer, for he knew the penalty he would have to pay if his escapade were discovered. So mounting his pony, he gave it a flick with his whip and started off at a sharp canter on the way home. But he had not gone far before he became aware of a great commotion in front of him where the street narrowed just at the entrance to the bazaar. A crowd of loose-cloaked Turks were seething towards the door, and a frantic yelling broke on the boy's ears as he approached. Impelled by curiosity he urged his pony forward and soon reached the fringe of the mob. As he did so a Turk caught hold of his rein and forced the pony back on its haunches. The frightened animal immediately wheeled and kicked out, scattering the dense crowd left and right, and when the boy had managed to rein in his frightened mount, he saw that he was hemmed in by the crowd, with his back to the wall.

Even then he was not aware of the danger in which he stood, but at his side in a heap, huddled against the wall, was a figure. Hastily looking down John saw it was a man. One glance told him that the Armenian was dead, and as he stared at the corpse, with its bloodstained tunic, the yelling broke loose again, and the crowd surged up towards him. From the bazaar door another Armenian came out. Before the man saw his peril, his retreat was cut off, and he flung himself behind the pony and the boy. Mounted on his saddle, John's head was just above those of the crowd, and as he looked down upon the scowling angry mob, his heart thumped in his chest.

With set face, the boy backed his pony so as to cover the terrified Armenian. But the crowd would not be baulked of its prey, it was determined to set blood flowing. A bullet sang through the air and hit the wall with a sharp thud, and a fat dirty Turk, drawing a wicked-looking knife from his belt, tried to get between the Armenian and his protector. Instantly John raised his hand, the lash of his whip whistled as it cut through the air, and the man backed with a howl of rage and pain. John raised his whip again, his eyes blazing in his tense face.

"If any of you want a thrashing, come and get it!" he cried, his young voice sounding shrilly above the low muttering of the crowd. They stared at this young English boy, with his firm set face and defiant head. Perhaps his courage stirred them, or it may have been the fury of this child bare-throated and slim, who looked at them unflinchingly. The crowd backed a little and as it did so John saw in its midst, Mehmet, the brother of their gardener Achmed.

"Mehmet!" he cried, "if anything happens to this man I shall give information to the *Zaptiehs* about you."

The threat had its effect, the English never invoked the authorities in vain. Seeing his opportunity, the boy turned his pony sideways.

"Keep between me and the wall!" he shouted to the terrified Armenian, as he urged the animal forwards. Out-manœuvred, the mob made no attempt to follow, and the Armenian and his protector went their way down the street. When they were at a safe distance and the clamour had died away, the boy pulled up his pony to give the man time to get breath.

"Oh, master!" cried the man, "my poor brother!" John looked down at the Armenian. He was a man of about fifty, thin, with black straggling hair and pinched cheeks.

"Was that your brother?" asked John.

The man nodded his head, choked with tears.

"How did it begin?"

"A boy stole a ring from our stall. He fled into the street and my poor brother ran after him and was beating him when the father came up—Usef the butcher."

The Armenian shook from head to foot, and John waited while he gathered his breath, then they moved on again. After going for about half a mile, the Armenian stopped and clasped the boy's hand.

"Young master, God bless you for this!" he cried, kissing the boy's hand. "I am safe here, my home is near by. I shall never forget you, young master," and kissing this time the boy's knee, he turned and disappeared down a narrow courtway.

On the outskirts of Amasia, John realised how near he had been to disaster. His courage was sinking rapidly, no longer sustained by the excitement. Whipping up his pony he cantered up the home drive and rode with a clatter into the courtyard, and as he did so, he saw that his thoughtlessness had betrayed him, for his father, hearing the sound, came out on to the verandah.

John stabled the pony, and then entered through the dining room on to the verandah where his father sat waiting.

"Well?" was his greeting.

John hung his head a little; he was still quivering with the excitement of the last half hour, but he tensed his muscles and threw his head up with a determined look. Dean watching his son closely, saw the lithe young body stiffen, and he mistook the effort of self-control for one of defiance.

"You know I forbade you to go out: Have you anything to say?"

"No, father."

"Very well,—fetch the switch."

II

Three days later, John sat with his father having dinner on the verandah, for it was a warm evening and the stars glimmered in a cloudless sky. Over the western precipice the daylight had not quite disappeared, there was a strip of red which higher up changed to a light green and gradually merged into the dark blue of the night. They could hear the Iris singing along its bed, a deep full-toned note now, for the melting of the mountain snows was increasing its volume. John did not usually sit up to dinner, but to-night he was enjoying a special privilege which his father gave him occasionally. After dinner he would sit on his father's knee while he was read to from an exciting story book—a custom of his mother's which had been faithfully retained. So when the dinner had been served and the servants had cleared the table and shut the windows behind them, John fetched the book for his father to read. As he handed it to him, Dean took the child's hand in his own, holding it while the boy stood between his knees.

"John, why didn't you tell me what happened when you disobeyed me the other morning?"

John looked into his father's face; some one had told him then.

"I didn't think that was any excuse, Daddy," he said simply.

As he spoke, Dean looked at the boy. What an astounding sense of logic the child had! Of course it was no excuse, he had disobeyed and had accepted his punishment; but it was amazing that no advantage had been taken of the incident at the bazaar. For a minute there was silence, in which neither spoke, and Dean's hand closed tightly over his son's. This boy was made of good stuff. A great pride in him leapt up in Dean's heart.

"John," he said gravely, "I am very proud of you. You were a young Englishman that morning. You made no excuses—which I loathe, and you didn't flinch in a tight corner, which makes me proud of you," and with that said, he lifted the boy up on to his knees and began reading.

John's taste for fiction had undergone a change. Once he had loved tiger stories, and hunting yarns in India; now he wanted school stories. It fascinated him to know how English boys lived in that far country where he had been born. Their escapades at school, their tricks on masters, their friendships, sports, quarrels, the fagging and the lordly prefects, all filled him with wonder and delight. As he listened to these tales, a great desire grew up within him. He longed to be with them, to go to an English school. It would be St. Martin's or St. David's—for all big schools began with St. something he discovered. He

would be among English boys there and perhaps share a
study with one of them. They would be great friends and
then they would quarrel and "cut" one another. He didn't
like the idea of the quarrel, but it was necessary, otherwise
he couldn't get hurt on the football field, scoring the goal
that won the match for the school.

Yes, he would have to quarrel, because how otherwise
could his friend help him to limp back to his study, and
then shake hands, and sit down to make toast, as in the
days before they had quarrelled? John also wondered
what the school chapel would be like. He had never been
in a chapel. He imagined there would be hundreds of
boys bowing their heads, and the stern-faced headmaster
would speak in a deep voice (that was really kind although it would seem terrible), and at his side there would
be a big boy crying, a prefect—for was not this his last
Sunday? There would also be the pealing organ—he wondered how an organ would sound—and the light would
stream down through the high-coloured windows and rest
on the heads of the boys while the lines of the last hymn
died away. For the light always streamed through highly
coloured windows in school chapels—that was what helped
the prefect to cry. It would be—

"John, you are not listening—are you sleepy?" said
his father.

"No, Daddy—I was only wondering—"

"What?"

"If only I could go to a big school like that, and have
friends and—"

"Well, you will one day."

"Oh! In England?" asked John, his eyes dancing with
excitement.

"Yes—when you are a little older."

"O-o-oh!" cried John, flinging his brown arms round

Dean's neck, and wriggling his body until his face touched his father's. "And shall I have a study, and a big box with my name on it—'J. N. Dean' in great black letters?"

"Yes, Anna will pack it full with your clothes."

"Oh, how glorious—and you will come too?" Dean laughed, and pinched his son's leg.

"No, old son—they won't have daddies at school." Then seeing the young face cloud over, "But I shall take you there. When you are fourteen we will all go to England for a holiday, and I shall leave you at school."

"And come back here?"

"Yes, you see your father has to make money to pay for your schooling."

The young arm tightened around his neck, and in the dim light Dean saw the boy's mouth quiver.

"I don't want to leave you, Daddy."

"It won't be for long, not very long," he said, "and when you have grown up you will be able to keep your old Daddy always by your side—if you want him."

"I shall always want you. There's—there's only us."

There was a silence then between the man and the boy. Dean stared out across the valley. The stars glittered frostily and the moon was coming up behind the precipice. But he hardly noticed that, for his thoughts were far away in England. In two years or so he would be alone— out here, an exile, with his boy far away.

The moon slowly climbed, peered over the precipice and then flooded the gorge. A breeze came wandering along the night and stirred the boy's hair as he lay sleeping in his father's arms. It was growing late, but Dean sat on, moving not, just looking down on the sleeping face of the tired boy.

CHAPTER III

IN the shadow of one of the walls of the castle of Amasia two boys were resting during the hot noon-tide, for it was near the end of May and the summer sun was already scorching the plains and reducing the size of the Iris as it flowed along the gorge.

Another two years had wrought a change in John and his friend, Ali the Turk. They were fourteen and fifteen respectively, but John had outgrown Ali, both in height and breadth. This slight period had further developed the English boy who now looked sturdy and thickset in comparison with the slim Turk. They had climbed all the morning, starting out before the sun had dried the dew on the ground. Ali's uncle had shown them over the castle, a treat that had been postponed through one cause and another until this day. The excursion had been made at last because the two boys would soon be parted.

In three days' time, John was setting out with his father for England. Of that journey and the wonder that awaited him at the end of it, John had talked for months, and Ali eagerly listened to every detail of the new life his friend would soon be living. England, to Ali, was a country of fabulous wealth, where great lords lived in wonderful houses; most of them were soldiers, and the country in which they lived was so small that open spaces were almost unknown. It was from John that he gained his first conception of a public school, which seemed something very unlike the great schools in Constantinople where his father would send him one day. As the two

37

boys rested in the shade they were busy with their
own thoughts. Below them, almost under the high rock
where they lay, crouched the town of Amasia. They had
a bird's-eye view down the gorge, and across to the opposite precipice walling in the valley. They could see the
course of the winding river until it abruptly turned from
sight in the bend of the valley; they counted the bridges
intersecting its silver stream, and saw behind the trees
fringing its banks, the flat-topped houses, the slender minarets, dwarfed by the height from which they looked, and
the patternless maze of baths, domes, khan courtyards, and
mosques covering the narrow valley. Far up the eastern
precipice they could follow the winding highway, climbing
like a white ribbon, until it reached even higher than the
rock where they lay, and disappeared over the pass leading to Marsovan.

As they watched and half dreamed, they heard the muez-
zin calling to prayer. Ali straightway arose, and as if
John had not been present, performed his elaborate genu-
flections, bowing his head to the ground. John did not
watch Ali closely. On such occasions he always felt a
little awkward and hardly knew what he should do. He
did not wish to give Ali an impression of irreverence; on
the other hand, he was English and a Christian, and felt
he had something which he should uphold. He pretended
therefore, whenever Ali performed his religious exercises,
not to be aware of them. The subject was one they never
discussed, each avoiding it with caution.

When Ali had finished, he stood up and looked at John
in silence for a minute. His friend lay on his back, one
leg crossed over the other, with a brown arm propping up
the sunburnt face and head. As if aware that Ali was
watching him, John sat upright.

"Ali," he said, "let's have a bathe, I'm baked! Is there
any water near?"

"There's a stream half a mile down, it runs into the
Iris, I've often bathed there—shall we go?"

"Yes!" cried John, springing up. They set off at a
brisk pace over the rocky ground. They found the stream,
and as if constructed for bathing there was a deep pool
where it turned into a rocky crevice. Eager to cool their
sun-weary limbs, the two boys were soon stripped, and
splashed and shouted in the clear water. As they swam
they seemed like silver fishes in the crystalline stream, and
long practice had made them adept swimmers. John who
had been looking for a place from which to dive, soon
found a jutting rock lower down the stream. Calling to
Ali, he mounted it and stood poised for the dive. As he
did so, he stood up straight, cutting the brilliant sky
with his slim brown body. Ali, looking up stared at his
friend, for although only fifteen he had the Asian's keen
appreciation of beauty. Behind John's head the sunlight
danced in his wind-fluttered hair, it gilded his shoulders
and rimmed with silver the outline of his young body, and
as the muscles quivered, the wet flesh gleamed like a burn-
ished shield.

As he watched, John raised his arms straight above his
head, the slim body was taut for a moment, the muscles
contracted, then suddenly relaxed themselves and rippled
as the shining figure leapt through the air and fell like a
silver arrow into the blue pool below. For a moment the
diver disappeared under a broken bubbled surface, and
then, spluttering and laughing, John had reappeared. Ali
stood on the bank, shivering despite the heat. He was
unhappy and could not shake off a heavy sense of doom.
What oppressed him he did not quite know, he could only

attribute it in some way to John going away from him to a distant land.

Swimming to the side, John climbed the bank and was amazed to find Ali not there. Their clothes lay together all in a heap, so it was impossible for him to have gone far. There was nothing to be heard save the hum of insects and the soft whisper of the grasses as they bent under the breeze. Ali would come back soon, he thought, as he lay down in the grass. It was delicious to feel the wind pass over his body. It touched him as though it delighted in rippling over the flesh and he felt its cool hand play on his shoulders then run swiftly down to his stomach, along his legs and finally make a queer sensation on the soles of his feet. He let his head fall and half-turned on his side. The wind blew down his back and between his legs deliciously. Why didn't Ali come, where had he gone?—it must be nearly two o'clock, they would have a . . . .

When John awoke he had a feeling it was late afternoon. The sky above him was not such a brilliant blue, some of the lustre had gone out of it. The stream sang louder than before, otherwise there was perfect quiet, for the insects had ceased humming. All at once he realised he was naked. Of course, he had been bathing and had slept in the grass, waiting for Ali! Where was Ali? John got up and then gave a low cry. His friend too, was fast asleep at his side. John stretched out his hand to wake him, when he felt something upon his head. It was a wreath, twined out of asphodel, pressed over his brow like a crown. He drew it off with a laugh. Ali had been playing tricks. His laughter woke Ali, who sat up.

"Hadn't we better get dressed?" asked John, standing up. "What's the wreath for?"

"To crown you."

John laughed gaily, and then checked himself, for there was an expression of pain on Ali's face. His friend was now on his knees, his sunburnt body erect, and he was looking at him from under a brow half hidden with hair tousled by the wind. John had never seen Ali look like that before. The eyes were no longer those of a merry lad, but belonged rather to a suffering dumb brute. As John looked down at him, their eyes met, and a low cry escaped Ali's lips.

"What is it, Ali?" John asked, stooping, and his question seemed to loose a floodgate of the emotions, for Ali flung his arms round the boy's ankles, and sobbed as if his heart would break.

Like all males, John hated the sight of tears; it made him feel awkward; he knew not what to say or do. So he just stood still and looked down at the bowed back of his friend. Then, unable to watch Ali's distress any longer, he bent down, and with sheer strength, lifted him on to his feet and held him just as a mother would a troubled child. Somehow, John felt years older, and Ali seemed like a baby—it was strange, because Ali had always been so silent, so reserved, with a kind of hidden strength which had often made John admire him secretly.

"I say, Ali—you mustn't go on like this,—what is the matter?"

"You are going away, John effendi."

"Yes, but I shall come back,—besides why do *you* worry so?"

"You are my friend, John effendi—I would never leave you—you are more to me than a brother."

"Thanks, Ali—we—we've been great friends, and when I come back—"

"You will come back?"

"Of course I shall! I shall spend my summer holidays at Constantinople with my father. He wants to take you there with him, unless you are there at school. I didn't know you—thought so much—of me, Ali."

"Have I not always followed you, effendi? You are English, I am a Turk—but we are brothers—and now you are leaving me."

He stood there holding John as if he would hold him thus through time. The English boy, embarrassed, with the British instinctive dislike of emotional display, knew not what to say. He wanted to say something that would express all he felt, his love for his friend, and all the happy times they had had, but no adequate words would come. So he just gave a short, forced laugh, tightened his grip on the other boy, and then turned and picked up his shirt.

"I say, we must get dressed!—it's getting late."

Ali was now calm. The storm had passed. They made their way down the mountain side almost without words. The sun had not set, but the town below was already in deep shadow and they could see the lights glimmering. Now that the inevitable moment of parting was drawing near, John began to feel something of the emotion which Ali had shown by the pool. It was a break in his life, this parting; the first he had ever made. They had been jolly days, and although the future had its glamour, things would never be quite the same again. Ali would grow up, and he would grow up, each in different worlds, with different customs. They would meet in two years, but two years was a long time. Dear old Ali, if only he could take him with him!

They had now reached the fountain at the foot of the steep street where the ways parted. The inevitable moment had come. John took Ali's hand and gripped it, English fashion.

"Good-bye, Ali—I'll write to you often. We'll meet in two years."

"Insh' Allah—God willing," said Ali gravely. "I will make you a gift, John effendi, will you give me a promise?"

"Yes, Ali—what is it?"

Ali opened his shirt at the neck, and lifted over his head a thin chain. At the end of the chain hung an oval moonstone; on one side it had Turkish characters, on the other the etching of an eye. John had often seen this charm against the evil eye hanging on his friend's neck, but as it no doubt had something to do with his faith, John had refrained from asking any questions.

"See, effendi—I give you this talisman. My father brought it from Mecca. It will keep you from harm, and also you will remember me by it. Will you wear it always?"

The tone was so earnest, and Ali spoke with such gravity that John nodded his head, which he lowered while Ali passed the chain over him until the talisman hung on his breast. For a moment there was an awkward pause. Ali seemed about to say something, but his lips did not move. John feared another outburst; so gripping his friend's hand, he looked into his eyes for the last time.

"Good-bye, Ali!" he said, and was quickly gone into the darkening twilight. Down the street he felt an overmastering impulse to turn and wave to Ali, who, he knew, would stand watching his going, but such an act would only prolong the agony. With a firm resolve he strode on along the way home.

It was dinner time when John reached the house, and he just had time to wash before the gong sounded. Seated at table he was very quiet during the meal, and when coffee had been served and they had passed out onto the verandah where so many happy evenings had been spent, Dean drew John down into his big wicker chair.

"You are very quiet, John—anything the matter?"

"No, father—I was only thinking."

"What of?"

"Oh—of England, and leaving here, and—Ali."

The moon had come up over the precipice and flooded the garden in soft light. They could see the river, like a silver shield where it turned in its course. Not a leaf stirred in the garden, but there were sounds floating about the night. From the orchard came the first notes of a bulbul; more distant, they could hear the musical rippling of the water as it sang in and out among the rocks, and further off, subdued, pulsating with mystery, sounded the low droning of a native drum. It rose and died in the night air with its barbaric note insistently calling. Calling what?—they did not know; perhaps it drew towards it the Moslem spirits, as it had drawn them on that night long ago when Timur came near, red with conquest.

Dean looked down at the boy sitting quietly by him. The moonlight glinted upon something on John's breast. He slowly drew out the chain with its talisman.

"What's this?" he asked, reading the Turkish characters —"Kismet!"

"Ali gave it to me for a keepsake—what does Kismet mean, father?"

"Destiny—all Moslems believe in it."

"Do we?" asked John. Dean paused before replying.

"Some of us do, some of us don't," he said quietly. Then there was silence again, save for the drum calling through the night.

BOOK II

WEST

CHAPTER I

THE guard's whistle sounded shrilly, and in John's ears it seemed to be cutting through his life as he stood on the platform at Sedley and felt his hand held in his father's farewell grasp. The last carriage door had been slammed, the perspiring porters mopped their brows under the hot September sun, the train drew back a little with a hissing of steam and a rasping of brakes, then slowly crawled forward. John ever afterwards carried a distinct impression of his father as he saw him that afternoon leaning out of the carriage window. The tanned face, the clear grey eyes and clean-cut features all stamped themselves upon his memory. The ring in his father's voice as he said—

"Good-bye, John—you'll soon settle down,"—then the long pause, the last look into his eyes, and the tightened hand. These impressions burnt themselves upon the boy's brain, and, somewhat overwhelmed with the pain of it all, he stood watching the train dwindle down the line. It drew out of sight, first the long length of carriage windows, then the shortened perspective, until the back of the guard's van covered the train, finally the lamps, the two buffers, and a coiled up brake connection—and a long stretch of shining steel rails that converged to a point. He wanted to run along that iron way, to catch that train, to get away from this terrible desolation creeping over him. He stood, lonely and miserable, in a crowd of shouting boys and porters struggling with luggage. Just outside the station, beyond the white palings where the ticket collector stood, was a waggonette packed with boys of all ages. John looked at them curiously. They were to be his companions, to form his life in the coming years.

In Amasia he had looked forward to mingling with boys of his own age and race, but now their noisy behaviour and boisterous good humour repelled him. He thought how much preferable was Ali with his quiet oriental manner. There was also another disconcerting experience which depressed him—his new clothes irritated him. He had worn trousers for a week now and hated them. His waistcoat was like a chain round his chest and he wanted to tear the vile Eton collar from his throat in·rage. He longed for his loose open shirt, his easy shorts and socks. There were other clothes packed away in that white wooden box, with black iron flanges. John stared at his initials, black-lettered on the front—"J. N. D."—did they belong to him? Somehow they seemed to shout at him, to possess him, and the "N" in the middle grew and swelled until it dwarfed its companions. John was terribly afraid of that "N". Why hadn't the porter stuck the luggage label over it? He recalled what that awful boy, at the house where his father went to dine one day, had said, when he told him his name.

"Narcissus! Good Lord, you will get ragged!"

"Ragged—what's that?" he had asked.

"Oh—knocked about—chivied." And then, in a friendly tone, "You'd better keep that name quiet."

John must have stood thinking on the platform for a considerable time. It was almost empty. He would walk back to the school. His housemaster's wife had asked him to have tea with her. He instinctively liked Mrs. Fletcher. She was motherly and there was such a pleasant ring in her voice, also she was beautiful and probably young Her cheeks were very fresh, as if she had walked in the wind all day, and John liked the style in which she did her hair. Fletcher too had attracted him, though he had not been able to notice him much, for his father had talked to him about Eastern affairs.

When John reached the school, he tapped on his house-master's study door and entered. He was in no genial mood, but full of warlike thoughts. Mrs. Fletcher smiled at him as he entered and motioned for him to sit by her side. There were other boys in the room, seven or eight, all laughing and talking with Mr. Fletcher, and John won-dered whether he would ever be on such familiar terms with the master as these boys were. There was something about the book-lined study which pleased John—it had such a homely look and Mr. Fletcher seemed all the more attractive because of his study. The books, portraits and pictures were interesting, the chairs were very comfortable, and Mrs. Fletcher gave attention to John. Soon he was laughing at something she had said which amused him immensely, and he laughed as only a boy can laugh. Mr. Fletcher turned from the group about him and looked across at John.

"Now I wonder what I am missing, Dean?" he said. "Come here. This is Mason—Rogers, Russell, Thomson, and Vernley." He indicated the boys with a sweep of his hand, and John surveyed his new schoolfellows. One boy attracted him, a heavily-built fellow with carefully brushed hair that was thick and shiny. John saw that he was strong, so strong that he looked ungainly in his suit, which tightened with every movement, but what at-tracted John was Vernley's smile, it was so good natured, and warm, like sunshine. He was pleased when Mr. Fletcher added—

"Vernley is in your dormitory, Dean." Then turning to the boy, "You must take charge of Dean until he finds his way about. Now you'd better get along, all you. Don't forget to see the Matron about your things, and chapel's at seven-thirty."

John followed the boys out into the corridor. He shivered as he closed the study door. On this side of it he was in the school and it looked so depressingly barren after the cosy study. He watched the other boys with envy as they walked down the corridor to the Matron's room. Vernley was among them, and seemed to have forgotten the master's injunction, but at the Matron's door he waited for John.

"Come along, our boxes are up in the dorm,—yours has been put next to mine—I'll show you the way up."

Putting his arm in John's he led the way, talking as they went. To John it was a novel experience. He had never talked to another English boy in this free manner, and the friendliness with which Vernley had taken his arm gave him a slight thrill. It was pleasant to be noticed like this, and already he liked his companion. There was something so placid and solid about him which appealed to John. There was nothing Eastern about this boy, he talked without reserve and his clear brown eyes seemed like those of a young animal rather than a human being.

Vernley sat down on John's bed and explained the various contrivances in the room. It was a long well-lit chamber with eight beds on either side, bordered by two long strips of carpet. The middle of the floor was bare.

"It's jolly cold too," said Vernley, "when you stand on it with the wind blowing over you."

"Stand on it, why?"

"Oh, it's Lindon's fad—he's a physical culture crank, he's prefect here. He makes us all strip night and morning and has us squirming on our backs with our legs in

the air,—but he's quite a decent chap. You'll get on with
him well."

"Why?"

"Oh, you look so splendidly fit—he's simply mad on fit-
ness. He spends half his time torturing me to get my fat
down."

"But you're strong," said John admiringly.

"Oh, yes, but it is not strength he believes in—it's what
he calls form, the Greek ideal—he's always talking about
some Greek johnny, and he's rather like one himself.
What's the J. N. for?" Vernley broke off abruptly and
stared at the box.

"John Narcissus—"

"Narcissus!"

"Yes—it's Greek too," John smiled, and Vernley
laughed. John noticed that he had teeth like an animal's
—white and strong.

"Well—they'll call you 'Cissy' for short."

"Oh, please don't tell them—I hate it," he said, looking
at Vernley imploringly.

"Very well—then it'll be Scissors—that's more cutting!"

"I don't mind that—what's your name?"

"What do you think—there's only one name for all persons like myself—Tubby—isn't it a libel?"

"Yes—you're not too fat. I think you're—" John hesitated,

"Well, what—let's hear."

"You're quite—splendid."

Vernley laughed again in his fascinating way.

"Thanks—I can return that compliment."

John flushed. He was glad Vernley had laughed like
that.

"That's strange, you know—saying that," added Vernley.

"Why?"

"Because most fellows never think about appearances—
I always do, and you do. I loathe ugliness. Lindon's always preaching on that text. You'll hear him later, 'the
good and the beautiful' that's his pet phrase. He's beautiful enough, but he isn't good."

"Why?—does he swear?"

"Good lord, yes—we all do, there's worse things than
that." He stooped down and took a book out of the box
at the foot of his bed. Then he glanced at a watch on his
wrist.

"Glory!" he exclaimed, "it's a quarter past seven.
Come along or we'll be late." He hurried out, John following. He wished Vernley had gone on talking, he interested him in Lindon. What was it Lindon did? Perhaps he drank secretly, or cribbed, or—John hurried on,
his head filled with speculations. He was looking forward
to seeing the terrible Lindon.

CHAPTER II

I

JOHN'S first week at Sedley passed with amazing rapidity. It was all new to him, and enjoyable also. The masters were such a decent set of fellows, and already John had formed a strong alliance with Vernley. He had had tremendous good luck in this. Vernley was in his second year and entitled to a study. A small room at the end of the corridor was vacant, but it was only large enough for two boys. All the other studies had four occupants, save fellows in the fifth and sixth forms who had attained to the dignity of separate rooms. When Vernley discovered that he was the odd man out with a study of his own, he went straightaway to Mr. Fletcher and asked permission for John to share it, which was readily granted. He and John entered into partnership. So far the alliance had been a great success.

It was the Wednesday half-holiday and John had just had his first game of football. Exhilarated by the exercise and the novelty of it all, he had changed from his muddy shorts and red and white shirt, wallowed in the bath, and now sat stiff and tired in a wicker chair, holding toast to the fire, while Vernley got out the tea cups. Tea was the one meal they had in private, and both boys gloried in it.

John, burning the toast furiously, sniffed with delight.

"I say Verny—toast is the incense of the appetite—isn't it good?" and he sniffed long and loud. Vernley looked at him. John's curiously turned nostrils always

53

fascinated him, they were just like the faun's in the draw-ing class.

"You ought to be called Bunny, not Scissors," he said, pouring hot water into the teapot.

"Why?" asked John turning round in the chair.

"Damn!—watch that toast, it'll be black! Why, be-cause you twitch your nose like a rabbit. That's enough, don't toast any more."

There was a long break in the conversation, filled with the noise of crunching.

"I shall have to go in a minute—I forgot to fill Lin-don's kettle," said John.

"Hang Lindon—he's always running you about. I knew he would. He doesn't like your being here."

"Don't talk rot—he's been jolly decent to me, he was coaching me all this afternoon. He's going to give me an hour at racquets to-morrow," said John, defending Lindon stoutly; then seeing that he had hurt Vernley—

"I say, Verny—don't be jealous—only it is decent of him. Why don't you like him?"

He looked at Vernley, who shifted uneasily and kicked the fender.

"I never said I didn't like him," he answered.

"But I know you don't—what's the reason?"

"Well—it's because you're such a kid, Scissors."

"Thanks, you're a year older—but that's no reason."

"P'raps not—but I knew Lindon would go for you—I said so the first night."

"To-day's the first time he's taken any notice of me."

"Is it?—he's watched you like a cat for a week. You don't know Lindon—I do."

"Then why are you so mysterious about him?"

Vernley got up and cut himself a piece of cake.

"Have a piece, Scissors?"

"Thanks."

"Look here, Scissors, you've said I'm jealous—well I am, but not for the reason you think. You're only a kid and a green one at that. I'm a year older, which isn't much, but I've been at school five years, in a prep. and here, and I know who's who. Lindon's a clever chap, captain of the first eleven, our best bat and all that—but keep clear of him."

Vernley would say no more after that. John went out and filled Lindon's kettle and returned. His forced manner made Vernley watch him curiously; John was evidently upset.

"What is the matter," he asked John, abruptly.

"Nothing."

"That's a lie, Scissors—try again."

John flushed deeply—"Well, nothing much," he confessed.

"Has Lindon said anything?"

"Yes."

"About me?"

John was silent.

"I guessed so," said Vernley bitterly, "and you believe him?"

"No—I don't—and I don't understand,—and I don't want to understand."

"But, Scissors, if—in the past," added Vernley. He looked anxiously at John, who had picked up *Punch* and was looking through it.

"Well—the past is the past, that's all. I say, Verny, listen to this," he said, reading from the paper. He had dismissed the subject, and Vernley sat and listened, looking at his friend with a doglike affection.

II

John enjoyed the Saturday evenings when they all gathered in Mr. Fletcher's study. They sat wherever they liked, on the floor, the lounge, or in the windows, while Fletcher talked and his wife poured out the coffee. Fletcher was a man of ideas and of sufficient strength of mind to carry them out. He was never so happy as when, pipe in mouth, he debated with six or eight boys at a time. It was a time-honoured custom for the boys of his house to come in each Saturday evening to talk over the school matches or any other topic that presented itself. There was no attempt to make the conversation "improving." Sometimes, led by a question, Fletcher would tell them about his travels in Greece and Italy, illustrating them with snapshots in his albums, or perhaps Mrs. Fletcher or one of the boys would sing. The repertoire was in no way restricted. Occasionally Vernley had to be forcibly deposed from the piano stool after an orgy of music-hall ditties or waltz tunes, and any outburst of ragging was quickly suppressed. The boys were not compelled to enter into any conversation. They could take down the books and read if they wished and sometimes complete silence reigned until Fletcher stood up, knocked the ashes out of his pipe and said "Time, boys."

There was one particular pleasure to which John always looked forward—that was Lindon's playing. There was a magic quality in it which held them spellbound; even Vernley admitted that Lindon knew his way about on the piano The pianist would sit down in front of the keyboard, wait for the preparatory hush which he commanded as a brilliant performer, run his fingers up and down the keys once or twice as if making their acquaintance, and then begin. Sometimes it was Beethoven he played. John never forgot the thrill that ran down his spine when he heard the *Pathetique* for the first time. Its great soulful chords crashed through him, echoing along his brain like thunder in a valley.

But on this particular evening, Lindon was in a more festive mood. He had won glory on the field that afternoon; his swiftness, his quick decision had brought victory to his house, and some of the seriousness which usually invested his manner was forgotten. It was the last Saturday night of term. The examinations were nearly over. The holiday spirit already made the school restive. So Lindon was in good spirits. He chose Chopin, and sent the melodies rippling from beneath his wonderful fingers.

John, completely fascinated, stood leaning on the flat top of the grand, it being his duty to turn over the music when the demi-god nodded. Lindon started off with the *Valse Brilliante* in four flats. It was hackneyed, but not so to John who listened while the magic movement seemed to lift him up with ecstasy. Then the pianist played *Op.* 64—he seemed scarcely to touch the keys, for they whirred just like the wind blowing through a leafy tree. It was the speed, the superb vivacity of it all that entranced John. Now they were butterflies dancing rapturously, now a spinning wheel. Here was something that reached an eloquence beyond words, a joy greater than anything he had ever known. When Lindon ceased, John's eyes were sparkling with intense delight. The pianist, seeing his pleasure, laughed lightly. The applause he did not appear to notice; it was John's boyish approval which he looked for and found at the conclusion of each piece.

How long Lindon sat at the keyboard John had no idea. His ecstasy was suddenly shattered by the performer who said,

"Only one more, Scissors, then you can sit down."

And this time it was something that stirred John until he felt he must cry out. It was the exquisite pain of it. As he watched Lindon he was strangely attracted; the latter was no longer smiling. He sat with compressed lips and stern eyes. The slender hands flew over the thundering bass and swept like a whirlwind into the treble. The player's hair, shaken with the energy of his execution had fallen over his brow. There was something fierce about Lindon as he sat there, something that made John draw in his breath with half fear and wonder. He had never seen this Lindon before. The gracious, laughing young hero whom he worshipped had changed into a being capable of great passion, and perhaps cruelty.

It was the *Drum Polonaise* which Lindon played. It began like the slow murmur of thunder, and then it broke into a wild ecstatic music like the mad flight of a thousand horses across a prairie. John wondered how so much sound and furious activity could be torn out of that piano, and the player's frenzy almost terrified him as he turned the music, but his fear suddenly changed to a feeling of dread and helplessness. The second movement had begun with its monotonous bass. John listened, breathless; it was the sound of that drum which enthralled him. It grew in intensity and passion, it called, called, called with a horrible fascination, John looked at Lindon, but the latter seemed oblivious of all but the page before him. The sound swelled up and smote on John's ears like a flood of waters; a curious numbness stole over him—the drum seemed nearer now, it was soothing, he would know nothing soon, already feeling had left him, he—

Lindon was the first to jump up as John swayed and fell in a heap on the floor. He sprang from the stool and lifted up the insensible lad. Fletcher and his wife were bending over John when he opened his eyes again. Where was he? He did not quite know, yet he was very tired. Then he heard some one call "Scissors!" and looking up again saw Lindon bending over him, with anxious face. He was safe; he could feel the rigid muscles of his arms as he held him. He let his head sink with a sigh.

"I think it's the air, sir, we're rather warm in here," said Lindon to Fletcher.

"Carry him into the hall, Lindon—you boys stop here."

"Let me take him," said Mrs. Fletcher, all the mother nature of her sounding in her voice.

"It's all right, Mrs. Fletcher, I can carry him. I think the porch would be the best place. The cold air will bring him round."

Lindon lifted John like a baby and went out into the porch followed by Fletcher and his wife. He deposited his burden in a wicker chair.

"Don't wait, sir, I'll bring him in in a bit—look, he's all right now." John sat up and looked at the anxious trio.

"Better?" asked Fletcher, cheerfully.

"Yes, sir—I'm awfully sorry," replied John.

"Don't worry, my boy—you've played too hard to-day. Now sit here a bit with Lindon. Ah, here we are!"

Mrs. Fletcher had returned with rugs and wrapped the boy round with them.

When Fletcher and his wife had gone, John and Lindon sat in silence.

Lindon could see Dean's face in the dim light and his eyes were still very bright as he looked up at the sky.

"Scissors," said Lindon quietly, "why did you faint?"

"I don't know, Lindon—you frightened me, I think."

"Am I so terrible?" the question was asked jokingly but not without an undercurrent of feeling.

"No—but you fascinate me—you have done since the

first. It's only when you are playing that I really seem to see you properly."

Lindon gave a short laugh. "What a queer little beggar you are—I suppose the East is in your blood. I hope Vernley hasn't been playing on your imagination too much—he talks about me?"

"No, he doesn't," said John shortly, "and you shouldn't ask me—I'm his friend."

"I'm sorry, Scissors—it is caddish, only—" he broke off and looked out into the night. John sat in silence and waited. He knew Lindon wanted to say something. Presently he spoke.

"You see, Scissors, I don't want anything to upset our —well, we get on fairly well, don't we? Somehow you've made me feel—oh, I'm talking rot."

"I suppose you've seen how I watched you," said John, "—I simply couldn't hide it—I'm a little fool I know."

"That's what made it all so difficult. It's not easy being a god," responded Lindon. "You've put me on a pedestal—and I want to keep on it." They talked more easily after that.

CHAPTER III

I

IT had been arranged that John should spend the Christmas and Easter holidays with his housemaster. Fletcher had a cottage in Wales where he went at the end of each term to repair his shattered constitution. There, he dressed in a most amazing assortment of tweeds, smoked endlessly, loved to sit in village bars and listen to village gossip, and tramped over the mountains with inexhaustible energy.

John spent the first fortnight with the Fletchers, after which he went on to Vernley's people, who sent him a cordial invitation to their home in Essex. It was there that John first became acquainted with the amazing possibilities of life.

The Vernleys lived in a rambling old house with long corridors in which John could lose himself. Indeed, everything was on the spacious side, with that heavy, solid prosperity stamped on it which somehow fitted the Vernleys and all of John's preconceptions of them. Mr. Vernley was a broad-shouldered man with a shock of black hair and a tremendous voice. Mrs. Vernley was stout and tall, talked rather loudly and made a draught whenever she moved, but she radiated kindliness. The family, too, was on the large scale, for John found himself being introduced to a crowd of brothers and sisters who varied from being wonderfully beautiful to uncompromisingly ugly.

There was Kitty, aged twenty-two, a big-boned woman,

61

who talked horses all day long; then Alice two years her junior, the musical genius of the family. Vernley had great faith in his sister's future as a singer because she was so fat. Tod, twenty, and in the first flush of glory at Balliol, was the Vernley Adonis. He had the good looks that wonderful health and spirits bestow. His cheeks were tanned, his laugh cheery, and when he didn't sing or talk, he whistled. Vernley said that sitting near Tod was like being near a radiator, he warmed you like an animal. With great cheerfulness, Tod offered to teach the two boys how to box. He took them up into a dim roomy attic, stripped them, tied the gloves on to their hands, and made them pound away at each other while he bellowed his encouragement. At the end of half an hour, the two boys being utterly exhausted, he just tucked them under his arms, walked down to the bathroom and turned the cold water tap on them as if they had been two mice he had wished to drown. They emerged from their first boxing lesson with a black eye each. In addition John had a swollen nose and Vernley a cut lip. When they both appeared at tea-time, the family yelled with delight, save Mrs. Vernley, whose motherly instinct forbade further boxing lessons.

And here it was that the amazing complexity of life first dawned upon John's consciousness. Mr. Vernley was a member of Parliament and he brought his friends on week-end visits to "The Croft." John looked at these persons with considerable awe. They were all doing, or going to do something big. Among them was Chadburn, quiet, unassuming, strictly conscientious, with a fine face and a courteous manner.

John walked with him through the woods one Sunday morning, and at the end of half an hour, fell in love with him; all that night he had visions of himself as a private secretary It would be glorious to be near him each day, to go in on a thick-carpeted floor with a sheaf of papers and say, "Will you sign these, sir?" or, "A deputation wishes to see you, sir," or "Your speech is in your bag, sir," and his hero would say, "Thank you, Dean; I shall be back to-morrow—take cuttings from the *Times* and *Telegraph*." Perhaps he could accompany his chief to a big meeting and see him sway the crowd, hear him cheered in the packed hall and he would want to get up, and say, "That is my chief—I am his secretary." John went to bed that Sunday with life revealing a wonderful vista before him, for as he had passed through the lounge where the men sat smoking, he had heard Chadburn say, "That boy's as intelligent as he's handsome." As the two boys undressed, Vernley noticed his friend's elation.

"Are you enjoying yourself?" he asked.

"Oh, ripping! It's glorious here, Vernley—I don't know how to thank you," which sent the devoted Vernley to bed equally happy.

There were two other incidents of that holiday that stood out in his memory for many years. The first dawn of adolescence stirred in him, disquieting, but wonderful. Muriel awakened him, Muriel the vivacious, sixteen, home from school in Belgium, the prettiest of the Vernley girls and just ready to fall in love for the simple adventure of it. They liked each other at sight; she admired his slim grace, the brown healthiness of his skin, the fine ring in his laughter; he, her elusive charm and tomboyish air. Her quick, witty chatter in English or French was music to the enchanted John; and she rode her horse like a princess.

Each morning, after breakfast, three or four mounts were brought round from the stables, the groom waiting until the riding party was ready. Sometimes Vernley and

Kitty made up the quartette, with John and Muriel. John sat his horse superbly, the legacy of Amasian days, with the result that he and Muriel were often far in advance of the other couple, for Vernley rolled on his seat like a sack, and Kitty acted as whipper-in.

One morning, after a breathless gallop, John and Muriel found themselves alone together on the white road running through a little copse of birch trees. The girth of Muriel's saddle had slackened, and John helped her to dismount and tightened it. Then slipping their reins over their arms, they walked the horses on to the soft turf bordering the road. On a barren bough a robin began to sing cheerfully. Muriel gave a little cry of delight, and as John looked at her, his flesh thrilled with her laughter. She was flushed, with her fair hair falling over two pink ears, and as she turned to him with her beautiful eyes, she caught him in the act of open admiration. Muriel looked away, pretending she had not noticed.

"Shall we mount and get on?" she said awkwardly. She placed one foot in the stirrup, and John placed his hand under the other to help her into the saddle. It was the first time he had ever touched her and a queer self-consciousness caused him to bungle, for she failed to gain the saddle. The horse moved, and Muriel fell back into his arms. It was an accident which John took as a gift from the gods. He gave an awkward little laugh as he looked down into her timid eyes and she tried to hide her face on his shoulder. The soft brushing of her hair on his cheek gave him courage; holding her in his strong young arms, he raised her face with one hand and saw the laughter in her eyes. Then deliberately he kissed her lips, her soft wavy hair falling over his brow, her arms pressed tight and warm around his neck. It was a moment's delight, with no passion in it—only youth discovering youth and thrilled with the wonder of it.

Almost gravely John helped her into the saddle, and they started off at a canter. The wind whipped their faces, the superb vitality of the horses seemed to flow through their bodies. Ahead lay the wooded country and the chimneys of "The Croft." John remembered that white strip of road, the birch-tree copse and the laughter in Muriel's eyes evermore. In the years that followed he was to love, but it was never quite the same, there was more intelligence in it, more consciousness, more passion, but not the quick edge of sharp surprise.

II

John's Christmas at "The Croft" was his first experience of life at an English country house, and he saw there how money and leisure could make existence almost ideally tranquil. He learned too, the patrician order of things. Hitherto, humanity for him had only been classed in nationalities. He had recognised, of course, that mankind itself was divided into the rich and poor, those who did what they wished, and those who laboured as they must. But he now saw that Society was more subtly divided; it had its rigorous caste systems, and he was living in the strictest caste of all. The county type that he met at "The Croft" was something distinct. It spoke very definitely of humanity as "the masses." Clearly they were a slightly inferior people, to whom a duty must be performed. They had to be kept in their places, taught to recognise superiority and to render homage without servility; in return for this recognition they were rewarded with the influence and interest of those who controlled their lives.

Down in the village John found that, as the guest of the

Vernleys, he was somebody. The villagers touched their caps to him, the postmistress was effusively polite. All this seemed strange at first to John, for accustomed to the deference of the Moslem before all Englishmen, he had conceived a socialistic idea of the position and powers of all who spoke his native tongue. After a time he grew accustomed to the patrician attitude. It was so easy to assume the air of command, to know that servants, even English ones, were there to serve, and that one could be perfectly polite to them and forfeit no respect or authority.

He admired the young squire manner of his friend Vernley—the way in which he obtained all he wanted. The whole country-side was his, the farmhouses all gladly opened their doors at his approach. The name of Vernley was powerful. The next thing John realised was that the name was loved. The Vernleys had lived on the land for generations, and their knowledge of every family on the estate was unique. They knew the hereditary tendencies of Farmer Jenkins' children, the constitutional inclination of the Wichsteeds to bronchitis, the wanderlust that was in the blood of all the Wilkinsons' younger sons. John's friend too was intimate with all the village boys. He played cricket with them, called them by their Christian names, and assumed leadership in their midst without any rivalry or jealousy.

This was new and strange to John; but it all seemed part of the landscape. The village people were the natural possessions of the Vernleys, just as much as the fine old copper beeches in their drive, or the splendidly level lawn and flower-bordered terraces. It had always been so, and there was no reason why it should ever change. The village church, with its tombs of dead Vernleys also showed that their religion was a family affair, looked after by the vicar who held his living by appointment of a Vernley.

Comfort too was so visible in that home. There were solidarity and security in those massive oak doors under the stone portico. The heavy carpets sank richly under the feet; one felt majestic ascending the broad staircase with its crest-panelled pillars. The bedrooms with the blues, reds, and greens of carpets and eiderdowns and couches had a solemn splendour, particularly after the coldness of a school dormitory. It gave John a peculiar sense of pleasure to watch the maid in the morning enter his room with the hot water. The copper water can gleamed as the felt cover with its monogram came off. The curtains as they were drawn, fell back in heavy beautiful folds, and his bed was a massive thing built to endure for generations.

John revelled in all these things so new in his life and he looked at Vernley closely when that young gentleman expressed no particular delight, no pride of proprietorship. John, of course, was careful not to show his ecstasy. He accepted everything without comment, but secretly he exulted. Life was going to be pleasant enough with such splendid traditions and beautiful houses. He would spend his days visiting friends; he would find such a house himself, and entertain large parties. The wine should stand richly in beautiful glasses, as it did on the Vernleys' table at night time, discreetly lit with shaded candles in the silver candelabra. He would find servants as well trained, a butler as majestic, and the stables at the back of his house should be filled with superb horses, flawlessly groomed.

Dreaming in this manner one night as he lay in bed, he suddenly started with a recollection that his home had once been like the Vernleys. He had seen photographs of "Fourways," and heard his father speak of Tom the groom —a splendid beater or loader. With a thrill of discovery

John recalled his inheritance; it explained so much, his joy in these surroundings, the feeling that somehow he was at home again among the Vernleys. This was no new life; it was the old life, the one his father had known.

And then John realised how much he had lost. The mention of family misfortune had formerly conveyed nothing to him. He had been quite happy in his home at Amasia. There was nothing wanting, and he had often wondered at his father's ceaseless recollections of "Fourways. Now he realised all that the change to that hard, bright, lonely life in Amasia had meant, and the fuller knowledge clouded the boy's happiness. He would build up the family fortune again and take his father back to "Fourways." So thinking, he fell asleep to dream of his father greeting Tom who came to welcome him back, and somehow in that dream he mingled—but he was not alone. There was Muriel with him, flushed with riding, her cheeks whipped with the wind, her eyes bright with happiness, and her hand, soft and warm, holding his as he helped her down from the saddle.

John awoke in the morning to the sound of bells. It was Christmas Day, and springing out of bed he ran to the window that overlooked the drive opposite the church gate. The bells were clamouring merrily and he could see the villagers making their way to the early morning service. Picking up his towel he rushed off to the bathroom, shouted loudly at the shock of the cold shower, dressed quickly and ran downstairs just as the breakfast gong sounded In the dining room the family was busy opening presents. There were three for him, one from Vernley and two from his host and hostess. With boyish impulse he went up and kissed Mrs. Vernley delightedly. Life *was* good!

CHAPTER IV

I

ON Christmas eve John had noticed another guest at dinner, but he had no opportunity of studying the person, who was addressed as Mr. Steer. The next morning after breakfast, there was a walking party to Holdfast Covert, about three miles, whence a fine view of the surrounding country was obtainable. John asked Vernley all about the stranger, for he was attracted to him by his manner.

"The Governor's frightfully keen on Steer," said Vernley. "He's a poet and quite well-known—at least I think so. There's always a mild sensation in the district when Steer's down here."

"Have you read his books?"

"No, I've seen them of course—they're always prominent in the drawing-room when he comes here. He's not like most of those writing people who everlastingly talk about themselves, and he's a sportsman. He'll start love-thirty with any one on the tennis court and beat 'em."

It was on the way back from the covert that John had his first conversation with Steer. The boy had fallen behind to tie up a shoe lace, and the poet was hacking away at a wand he had cut out of the thicket.

"What are you making, sir?" asked John, overtaking him.

"A whistle—can you make one?"

"No—I'm not very handy with a pocket knife."

69

"Well, there you are—that's a sycamore pipe which you can play—like the Idle Shepherd Boys," said Steer, giving the stick to John.

> *"On pipes of sycamore they play*
> *The fragments of a Christmas hymn,—*

I suppose you know that?"

John confessed his ignorance, but he liked the sound of it and wanted to hear more.

"God bless me," said Steer, "you mean to say that you've not heard of Wordsworth? I thought every boy out of a nursery had been brought up on 'We are Seven' and 'The Idle Shepherd Boys.' "

"I've never heard of Mr. Wordsworth," said John naïvely,—"do tell me about him."

"Oh, he's quite dead now—he was what is called a Lake poet—he lived at the English Lakes, Grasmere and Rydal to be precise, where there was a group of these poets and essayists—Coleridge, Southey, De Quincey, Christopher North—names you've probably heard. 'The Idle Shepherd Boys' was a favourite poem when I was a lad. I remember reciting it to my mother for a penny. She used to give me a penny for every new poem I learned. I remember how she laughed when I pronounced 'vapours'— 'vappers.' The first stanza runs—

> *The valley rings with mirth and joy;*
> *Among the hills the echoes play*
> *A never, never ending song,*
> *To welcome in the May.*
> *The magpie chatters with delight;*
> *The mountain raven's youngling brood*

Have left the mother and the nest;
And they go rambling east and west
In search of their own food;
Or through the glittering vapours dart
In very wantonness of heart."

"Oh, how jolly! Do go on please!" shouted John eagerly, and his new friend recited the whole poem. The joy on the boy's face greatly amused him.

"You've evidently got a taste for verse, John—but there's much better stuff than that. Wordsworth was a philosopher, he wrote splendid things like—

Love had he known in huts where poor men lie;
His daily teachers had been woods and rills,
The silence that is in the starry sky,
The sleep that is among the lonely hills."

These words fell upon John's ears as music. It was a spell upon him, something that took him into a realm of wonderful sounds and visions. On that walk home, he plied the poet with questions, and Keats, Shelley, Browning and Byron became more than mere names. He learned how they had lived, of Byron's picturesque, turbulent career; of Shelley's passion for reform; of Keats' struggle against disease and the burning ardour for the glory that was Greece. And then Steer told him of living men who were writing. "But don't meet them if you can help," he advised. "You should never meet authors of the books you admire—they have conserved their best moments in a few pages, and they cannot live up to your expectations —and authors, too, are not the pleasantest of mankind. There is sufficient egotism in a room full of them to lift St. Paul's to the top of Everest."

"But you're a poet yourself, Mr. Steer—and you're not at all objectionable!" said John laughingly.

"Perhaps that's why I'm such a bad one," answered Steer. They had now overtaken the others and Vernley, looking round, noticed John's excited manner.

"Whatever's stirred you up, Scissors?" he asked. "You look as if you'd found a gold mine!"

"Mr. Steer's been telling me about the poets. Oh, Verney, I'd no idea they were such a ripping set. Have you got a Wordsworth at home?"

"Yes—but you haven't come here to read that stuff— you'll have to read it when you get at your 'remove'—a horrible old man, always grousing about some 'divine, far-off event'—no, that's Tennyson. How does it run? I've got it—

a sense sublime
Of something far more deeply interfused,
Whose dwelling is the light of setting suns
And the round ocean and the living air—"

"That's beautiful, it's—" exclaimed John.

"I call it utter tosh. Parse and analyse. Subject: there isn't one, predicate; find it if you can; object— Good Lord, why don't these fellows write sense? Whoever saw a round ocean?"

"But that isn't what he meant—you mustn't take it pictorially."

"Bravo, John, you've got the sense of it," interjected Steer. "Bobbie's attempted to analyse it,—that's fatal."

Vernley stared at John curiously for a moment, amazed at his friend's enthusiasm, then—

"You are a rum beggar, Scissors; I believe you'd like to write stuff like that yourself."

"Perhaps he will—alas," sighed Steer.

"Why do you say 'alas'?" asked John. "You're not at all sad, you're quite jolly and—"

"You can play tennis, sir," added Vernley in a consolatory voice.

II

For the remainder of the day, John's head was full of poetry. He had found a copy of Wordsworth in the library, and after lunch, when every one disappeared for a nap, he stole up to his bedroom, successfully evading Vernley, who, he knew, would cover him with derision if detected. Fortunately Vernley had gone across to the vicarage with a message, and he was detained there with lemonade and mince pies for a whole hour. In that time John read through "The Idle Shepherd Boys" and "Lucy Gray." He then attempted "The Excursion" and found it altogether too much for him, save one jolly bit—

> *"He loved; from a swarm of rosy boys*
> *Singled me out, as he in sport would say,*
> *For my grave looks, too thoughtful for my years,"*

which ministered to his egotism, and helped him to build up visions of long walks with Mr. Steer, in which he saw down into the soul of a poet. He had given up "The Excursion" in despair, but later, turning over the pages, he recognised the lines Vernley had quoted. Like an old friend they seemed. He had just finished the "Lines composed above Tintern Abbey," when Vernley, or Bobbie as the household called him, burst in, searching for him.

"Scissors, I've been all over the house—what are you doing?"

"Reading." John closed the book and half hid it behind him, but Vernley was too sharp and made a grab. One look, and the secret was out.

"Scissors! I've a good mind to scrag you."

"If you can—but isn't it ripping—

> *Whose dwelling is the light of setting suns,*
> *And the round ocean and the living air—*

—it's like eating caramels."

"If you say it again, I will scrag you!"

"*Whose dwelling is the light—*" began John provocatively.

Vernley leapt upon him and they went down together, John underneath.

"Say it again, Scissors!" cried Vernley, holding John's head firmly to the floor. John wriggled and tried to shift the hand over his mouth.

"*Whose dwelling is the—*" he managed to get out before he was choked. There was a wild scrimmage which ended with a great crash. They had cannoned into the washstand, and the jug and basin lay in a thousand fragments.

"Golly!—what a mess!" commented Vernley from where he lay, surveying the ruins.

"Will your mater be angry?" asked John nervously.

"No—she's used to having things smashed—it's a family failing. I've made a mess of your collar, you'll have to put a clean one on. Old Crimp's coming to tea, I've just been to the vicarage. He's a dreadful old bore—but he's got a ripping kid. I can't think how he did it."

"Did what?" asked John naïvely.

Vernley looked at him for a moment, and then went scarlet. "Scissors," he said, taking his arm, "you are a bit of an angel—"

"Whose dwelling—" began John derisively.

"Shut up!—do you want to smash the looking glass next? Get your collar on—there's the gong for tea."

Those days at "The Croft" went all too swiftly, and the morning came when the two boys lifted their trunks into the car and were whirled down the drive to the station. John left feeling that the end of life had come. He had been among friends and had felt almost as if he had been to his own home—the kind of home of which he had dreamed. Mrs. Vernley had mothered him, and John's secret pleasure at being petted had been expressed in many little acts of devotion.

"What a lovable boy he is!" she said to her husband as she watched the car recede down the drive.

"Yes, and sharp too. They may well call him 'Scissors'—that boy will cut his way through," replied Mr. Vernley. "Where's Muriel? I thought she was going to the station with them?"

Mrs. Vernley looked intently at her husband, but his face told her nothing. Ten minutes before she had hurried a sobbing Muriel off to her bedroom, where she was now going to lecture her on the absurdity of falling in love at sixteen, but as she secretly sympathised with her daughter she did not say anything to her husband. Upstairs in the bedroom she found Muriel with watery eyes, standing by the window, and screwing up a miniature handkerchief. Mrs. Vernley looked at her and decided that further words would bring a deluge. So she talked about everything but the thing in both their minds, and the only allusion to John's departure was when she said,

"Now, Muriel, wash your face. Miss Lane will be here for the music lesson in a few minutes."

It was then that Muriel found courage to make her confession.

"I gave him a photograph, Mother—I hope you don't mind?"

"Well, it's a little immodest for you to be presenting your photograph so freely."

"He asked me for it, Mother."

"Oh,—but really, you children are very absurd! I shall dread Bobbie bringing friends home with him if it means you are going to have red eyes every time. But there—you'll get over it," she said kindly, as she stooped and kissed her. "Now come along, dear, I'm afraid you haven't done much practising for Miss Lane."

The subject was never alluded to again, but Mr. Vernley the following morning almost provoked another flood of tears.

"You'll miss John, Muriel," he said genially at breakfast. "No more morning gallops together—you looked quite a loving pair on horseback." There was silence, then looking from Muriel to her mother, a glance told him everything.

"Why, bless me!—you don't mean to tell me—"

Muriel had dropped her eggspoon in a desperate search for a handkerchief. "My dear child!" cried Mr. Vernley, pinching her ear, "I'd no idea young Master Scissors had made such a conquest. The young beggar, I'll teach him to upset my daughter." He laughed good-heartedly, saw Muriel force a smile through her tears, and then diplomatically prevented further observation by spreading out the *Times*.

III

The two boys in the train were very silent. Vernley was immersed in a copy of "The Hill," John sat staring out of the window. But it was not the swiftly passing fields that engaged his attention, for at that moment he was exercising what Mr. Steer, in the explanation of Wordsworth's poem, had called "the inward eye, which is the bliss of solitude." John's thoughts were not at all blissful. He was feeling quite blue. The end of a glorious holiday had come, and having what another poet had called "the passion of the past," he was reluctantly taking stock of his memories. He had found delightful friends. There were Mr. and Mrs. Vernley; he could never feel quite lonely in England now. They represented home for John, being people who could understand and sympathise. There was Mr. Chadburn who had talked to him quite seriously. John had found a great friend in Mr. Steer. They had had wonderful walks together, when John had been taken into a new world that awaited his discovery. Steer had invited him to call at his house when he was in London. He wondered whether Mrs. Steer would be just as delightful.

Then his thoughts turned to Muriel. She would be having her music lesson from Miss Lane now. He had made her tell him all she was going to do that day. After the music lesson she was going to visit the stables. He saw her walking round the wing of the house, he saw her small hand press the catch on the wicket gate, and her short graceful steps as she crossed the cobbled stable-yard to the corner where the horses were stabled. He knew exactly how she would lift the iron bar out of its socket, swing back the half-door, call "Bess!" and then stroke the white patch running from between the eyes down to the nose. He could even smell the stable, with that delightful manure and horsey aroma.

He could see the deftness with which she slipped the bridle over Bess's head, and the firm way in which she led

her out of the stable, for she insisted on attending to
Bess herself, and with a sharp movement she would be
in the saddle at his side, level with and laughing into his
face, and their horses would walk clattering across the cob-
bles, before breaking into a canter in the lane. He knew
every inch of that lane, just where the horses would gallop, and where they would walk. He remembered the crest
of the hill, with its pattern below of fields and farmhouses and stacks; with the dim blue clumps of leafless
trees, and the barren telegraph poles, carrying the singing
wires across the valley towards the railway siding. Half
a mile over that crest was the copse where the robin sang
as he kissed her that wonderful morning when they had
ridden ahead of the others.

And now he was being carried away from all that happiness! He was going back to bare noisy rooms, to a crowd
of boys and worried masters. Would such times as he
had had ever come again? His hand at that moment rested
on something hard in his pocket. It was Muriel's photograph which she had given him before breakfast. He had
looked at it hurriedly then, in its tissue cover. Now he
wanted to take it out and feast his eyes upon it. He
looked up; Vernley was chewing butterscotch and still
immersed in his book. He did not want the old lady sitting near to see him gazing at the photograph, so he got up
and went into the adjoining lavatory. There he bolted the
door and pulled out the precious packet.

Slipping the photograph from its paper cover, he saw
it was a small cabinet in sepia by Neame, New Bond
Street, of Muriel in her riding coat and cap. As he pulled
it out something dropped to the floor. It was a small piece
of tissue paper. He was disappointed, for he thought it
was a note. Then seeing its shape, he knew it contained
something, which, after unwrapping, proved to be a strand

of hair. John immediately kissed it with all the sentiment of fifteen. He was about to wrap it up again, when he had an inspiration. It was another pledge of love and should be placed with Ali's gift. John pulled out the chain with its moonstone pendant, which he faithfully wore, and tied the strand of hair around the link. Then, putting the photograph back into his pocket, he returned to the carriage.

The platform was crowded when they arrived at Sedley and there was a fierce fight for seats in the brake. John found himself separated from Vernley, but half an hour later, as he was going towards Mrs. Fletcher's room, he was caught by the arm.

"I say, Scissors, what do you think?" asked Vernley excitedly. "We've got a new study! Maitland told me, and I didn't believe him, but it's on the list. There's another fellow in with us—what a nuisance! I don't know who he is."

"What's his name?"

"Marsh—Maitland says he's a new kid, tons of money and a motor bike. He was at Eton and has come here for some reason. It looks queer—we don't want Eton's castoffs."

"I beg your pardon," said a quiet voice. The boys turned to find themselves surveyed by a calm young gentleman. He smiled at them in a superior way.

"My name is Marsh—of whom you speak. If my presence is offensive to your secluded domain, I'll remove myself."

"Pompous ass," thought John. Vernley stared at him.

"Well, we are friends y' see," said Vernley at last.

"So I perceive," murmured the tall youth, looking at Vernley, who had his arm in John's. There might have been something offensive in the fact, and the stranger impressed this upon them. Vernley drew his arm away.

"Do you always *perceive* things?" asked John sarcastically.

"When they are worth it," retorted Marsh. "When I've finished unpacking, I'll speak to you again. So long," and he turned and walked down the corridor, with deliberate dignity.

"Well I'm snubbed," said Vernley. "Does Fletcher think we'll put up with that piece of skin and grief!"

"He'll speak to us again!—when he has finished unpacking! Bobbie, we are dismissed!" cried John.

Their next encounter with Marsh was more genial. They found him sitting in the new study. When John and Vernley opened the door they stood on the threshold and gasped. It was an amazing spectacle they beheld. Two lounge chairs covered with chintz were placed on each side of the fireplace. A blue cloth covered the table on which lay a shallow black bowl. In the bowl was water on which floated, in careless design, a dozen narcissi dropped in by the hand of Marsh. The window was draped in chintz and in the far recess was a magnificent bookcase. It towered up to the ceiling and was crammed with sumptuous books in highly-coloured leather bindings. There were four pictures on the walls, of a mysterious nature; those sallow-faced maidens and thin-legged youths in red hose, John learned later, were from the hand of Botticelli. A lady with a curious smirk occupied the place of honour over the fireplace. When John asked Marsh if it was his mother, the boy exclaimed sadly, "Alas, no!" and going to the bookshelf read from a volume a long analysis of the lady's smile written by a person called Pater in prose which, to John, seemed a long time getting to the point.

After the reading was finished and Marsh had pronounced it to be "luscious," he invited them to sit down, which was singular, since it was their study,—but he was a person who evidently took command. Appreciating comfort, and a little proud of the envy their study would arouse in others, they settled down amicably.

At the end of the month, they were inseparable. The trio became famous. Vernley was the athlete, Marsh the scholar, and John—that amazing discovery was made by John almost by accident. It filled his dreams for a whole term.

It was in the school debating society that John made his great discovery. Mr. Fletcher was in the chair. The meeting was in the lecture theatre with its tiers of seats climbing up to the back windows, in one of which John sat listening. There was a mock government in office, trying to introduce a bill for compulsory military training. The debate was opened by the captain of the Officers' Training Corps, a man John disliked intensely, mainly because he had prominent teeth that were not prolonged on parallel lines. John had attended three meetings of the society, but had not spoken. The small boys sat silent in the presence of the sixth form gods. John would not have spoken on this occasion except for an accident. He was sitting on the window seat, jammed in between two other boys, who, in the course of an attack upon each other's head, ejected John from his position. He fell with an amazing noise on the hollow boarding, and the Speaker, looking up, caught John's eye The boy had no intention of speaking but Mr. Fletcher evidently misconstrued his action, and very kindly paused to give John his opportunity. So there was nothing else for him to do but to open his mouth. He stammered for half a minute, uttered a witticism and provoked a laugh, which encouraged him to proceed to a

superb piece of youthful cynicism. The house gasped, but
liked the sensation; the leader of the debate sat amazed
at the junior's audacity.

But John had tasted blood. He felt the flattery of the
attention he was commanding. He grew bolder. A few
of Marsh's grandiloquent phrases came into his head, odd
readings from those leather-bound books pointed his arguments gracefully, his ear for a choice phrase kept his listeners intent. At the end of ten minutes John sat down
abruptly. There was a great silence. He had made a fool
of himself, he thought, and was blushing with shame when
the tide of applause caught him. It seemed to rock the
theatre. He was being applauded, the whole theatre was
applauding him! He was no longer a nonentity, but somebody! It dazed him a little. For the next half hour he
heard his name mentioned in the debate. When they all
trooped out of the theatre, he was smiled at, and patted on
the back. The crowning moment came when Mr. Fletcher
looked at him closely through his spectacles and said—

"I hardly like to approve of your audacity, Dean, but I
am pleased that my house has such an eloquent represent-
ative. I'm afraid the bitterness of your spirit suggests
a misspent youth and the convictions of a Labour leader."
And with a good-natured smile, in which John detected
whole-hearted approval, Fletcher passed on.

A fortnight later, John was the leader of the Opposition.
It was an unheard-of thing for a junior boy to sit on the
front bench, but John had broken all traditions. He was
aided by Marsh who loved to be diplomatic. Marsh carried on an insidious campaign against all who opposed
John's nomination. He held tea-parties at which he collected his forces. He despatched his lieutenants to the
fields, the five courts, the common room, the quadrangles,
the armoury and the tuck shop. Vernley brought round

the athletic vote—"the blockhead squirearchy," Marsh
called it, and the fifth and sixth form 'bloods' were bribed
by the thoughtful loan of French novels.

"Scissors," announced Marsh on the momentous day of
the election, "you should be eternally grateful to the
French scribes. Anatole France, Flaubert, Maupassant and
Daudet—these have won the day. Thanks to the lasciv-
iousness of Madame Bovary and the voluptuousness of
Sappho, the full-blooded gods of Upper School will nod in
your favour. I have seduced them with questionable literature. I have undermined their morals and pandered to
their secret viciousness. In grateful recollection of the
delicious nights I have given them, they are your hench-
men to-day. I have suffered in the cause. This morning,
the Censor, in the heavy shape of Fletcher, produced his
warrant and searched my shelves. His disgusting taste
has been satiated. Look—'A Rebours,' 'Thaïs' and 'Sappho' have been abducted. Those bleeding gaps are the
memorials of my enthusiasm in the cause. In your hours
of triumph, O Scissors, forget not the hand that raised you
to your dizzy eminence. Let me whisper in your ear, and
remind you, as the Cæsars of old, of the fickleness of Fate."

"Shut up, you ass," exclaimed Vernley. "Scissors'll
romp in. I've exhausted the bank in buns and lemonade,
and have given away enough cigarettes to smoke the enemy
out."

"We shall probably be unseated for corruption," said
John. "Your support, Marsh, is a questionable advantage."

"That's the kind of rotten remark one expects from a
politician. You've a great political career in front of you,
Scissors—you have the necessary lack of gratitude and
want of principle. Et tu, Brute! O shades of the departed! Bovary, Thaïs and Sappho, behold the ingratitude

of this friend who wades to glory over your dead bodies! Scissors, the first day you're in power you've got to abolish the censorship. There shall be no peace in your Parliament until I can read Wilde and Baudelaire in bed, without interruption or confiscation."

IV

As anticipated, Scissors headed the poll, and henceforth he was leader of the Opposition. The result was a high political fever. Immediately after breakfast each morning, he rushed round to the library and read through the newspapers. At first he modelled himself upon Winston Churchill, to whom he was supposed to have some facial likeness, but he found he had not the cool self-assumption of his prototype. He found himself more akin to Lloyd George, that Welsh lawyer whose name was as blasphemy to some and holy song to others. The rôle suited John. He was a born iconoclast. He had the Welshman's gift of stinging epithet, and he surprised himself with the veneer of venom that added lustre to his sentences. He learnt from his prototype the art of swift descent from Parnassus to Limehouse; he punctuated his periods with cheers provoked from the blubber-headed section of his audience; he knew the pathetic touch, the 'lump-in-the-throat' moment, as he called it, and he used them until his opponents were powerless to stem the avalanche of his invective.

All this alarmed Mr. Fletcher. He saw his house becoming socialistic. The authority of the prefects was becoming undermined, the junior boys no longer feared the Upper Remove. They frankly stated their dislikes. In one debate they declared their hatred of compulsory cricket with such vehemence that he had to move the closure, whereupon John attacked him as a champion of tyranny, the feeble upholder of bloated tradition. This so alarmed

Fletcher that he had a private interview with John, who suggested very skilfully that his overture was a form of corruption. The fact was that John was getting a swollen head. Marsh, whose hornet-like nature delighted in the stinging of authority, encouraged John in his most daring attacks. Vernley, lost in admiration at John's brilliance, worshipped silently and approved without question. The other boys followed in John's path, hardly realising the power of his leadership.

The awakening came rapidly from an unseen quarter. It fell like a thundercloud over the sunshine of John's triumph, and he resented his defeat all the more because it was the hand of a friend who brought him low, and his fall had no dignity. It was not intellectual. He would have borne that. It was physical, and he felt sick with shame. Inwardly he was conscious that he had provoked disaster, and most of his anger fell upon himself for being such a fool and not realising the need of tact.

It happened one Wednesday half, towards the end of term. Lindon was the instrument of Fate. John was fagging that day and had been told to lay tea at four in Lindon's study. He had always been allowed great liberty by his fagmaster and he took his own time to perform his duties. John did not worry, therefore, when four o'clock struck as he finished a game in the fives' courts. He leisurely walked across to the bathroom, stripped and sat on the side of the bath, whistling while the water ran in. As he waited for the bath to fill, Marsh appeared through the steam.

"Lindon's been calling like blazes for you. He said he told you to lay tea at four."

"Let him call," said John, turning on the cold tap and hiding himself in steam.

"You'd better hurry up, Scissors—he's quite scrubby."

John merely yelled as he plunged his leg into the hot water. He had just nicely soaped himself from head to foot, and was working up a white lather on his head, when he heard his name called, and looking up saw Lindon.

"I asked you for tea at four," he said.

John's face was covered with white soap, but he smiled sweetly.

"I know, I'm coming when I've finished here."

"Indeed!—get out!"

"I say, Lindon, do be reasonable!"

"I have been—too much so. Are you going to get out?"

"No!" answered John, sullenly, rubbing his head.

"Very well!" A moment later the door slammed. John lay back in the bath. He had won. The warm water made him feel very comfortable. He wondered if Lindon felt sick. While he was contemplating, Lindon reappeared. He had a switch in his hand. The business took on a serious aspect.

"Are you coming out?" he asked severely.

John pouted. "No!" he said obstinately.

Lindon immediately pulled out the plug and turned on the cold water tap. John sat still, getting colder every second. Soon he was shivering. At last he had to stand up, and the moment he did so, Lindon's switch whistled through the air and left a red weal across John's thigh. Involuntarily he yelled, then blazing with shame and anger, he picked up the wet sponge and flung it full in Lindon's face. The squelch ruined the prefect's neat collar and tie, but Lindon only looked cooler, which frightened John. The next moment he was lifted bodily out of the bath, and before he recovered from his amazement at Lindon's strength, he was pinned head downwards over the drying rack and being thrashed like a puppy. He screamed at the top of his voice, not in pain but in anger. When he was released, he saw three boys waiting in the doorway with towels. They had seen all, and overcome with wounded vanity and misery, John fell in a heap on the floor and cried. He lay there, moaning, and Lindon as he watched him, relented.

"Scissors," he said kindly, bending down.

John looked at the face, and hated its strength. Madly, he struck Lindon full in the face with all his might. The boys in the door stood breathless at this act, watching. The elder boy was the most amazed of all. For a moment he stared at John, with an angry red mark under his right eye. Suddenly turning, he strode out of the room.

Utterly miserable and smarting, John dressed himself. He had acted like a little cad and Lindon would be quite just in refusing to accept his apology. He was miserable, not because he feared the consequences of this act, serious as they were, but he had lowered himself in the eyes of one whom he admired. Nothing could hurt him so much as that Lindon should hold him in contempt. He hurried along to the study, tapped and entered. Lindon sat in a wicker chair with his back to John, talking to three other fellows. They had finished tea. John hesitated, he had expected to find him alone, and his courage failed.

"I came to lay tea," he said feebly.

"We've had it," replied Lindon without turning his head. John paused awkwardly; there seemed no more to say so he went out of the room quietly. All the evening he hung about miserably. Marsh tried to cheer him up with witticisms about his being honoured with the disorder of the bath. Vernley quite bluntly told him that he had acted like a cad, which John knew very well. So he quarrelled with them both, and was glad when it was bed time. But in bed he could not sleep. He longed for the morning and the opportunity of apologising. Finally he buried his head under the sheets, and in sheer wretchedness cried himself to sleep.

The next morning, immediately after prayers, he went round to Lindon's study. There was no one there, so he sat down and waited. After ten minutes, as the bell rang for morning school, Staveley looked in for a book he had lent.

"Hullo!" he said.

"Do you know where Lindon is?" asked John.

"Yes—in the 'San.' He won't be here again I expect this term. He's suspect—chicken pox. Seven of Field House are down. You'd better cut, that's second bell."

When the end of term came, a fortnight later, Lindon had not reappeared. John went across to the Sanitorium and learned that he was convalescent, but could not be seen. Yet he knew Staveley had visited him. It was obvious he did not wish to see John. So ended a wretched term.

CHAPTER V

JOHN had been invited to spend the first half of his Easter holidays at Marsh's. The second half was to be taken with the Vernleys. John wondered whether his acceptance of Marsh's invitation would hurt Vernley, but Marsh included Bobbie in the invitation. Vernley, however, was unable to accept; he was spending part of his time with an aunt in the north of Scotland. So they parted at Sedley Station, and two hours later John was being driven in from Loughboro towards Marsh's home. The gardener with a trap had met the boys at the station and they had about an hour's drive before they turned off the main road which intersected the village of Renstone. On the right was the Vicarage, standing back from the little street; on the left, across the road, stood the church, with its square tower, and near by, the Hall. Marsh's father was the Vicar of Renstone and Marsh had been born in the Vicarage. As the trap turned off the street, they entered through two wide gates which completely shut off the Vicarage from the village. Inside the gates there was a small courtyard, in the centre of which stood a great holly bush. The yard was closed in by the back of the house and in the middle was the main entrance porch with a wing of the domestic building. When John entered the porch and the door opened, he gave a cry of delight. He looked right through a small hall on the opposite side where wide low windows with small leaded panes overlooked two long lawns. A gravel path led down the centre to a line of magnificent elms that

89

bordered the far edge of the garden, and through the elms John caught a vista of the country with the white main road, along which they had come, stretching away to the horizon.

John's admiration of the Vicarage was cut short by the entrance of a lady. She wore a large straw hat, and a pair of washleather gloves. In her hand was a basket full of clippings. She placed the basket on the settee and coming forward kissed Marsh, then turning to the boy standing shyly in the shadow of the door, said,

"This is John—of whom I have heard so much? How d'you do? We are so glad to see you."

After his momentary shyness, John found himself looking into the face of a fair little woman with kind eyes. She also examined John closely, noticed the shy flush on his face, the darkness of his eyes and the slim grace of his regular features and carriage. They immediately liked one another. John was at home again. She was one of those women who are mothers to whatever humanity seeks their love. So John looked long at her and knew that he had found a friend. He contrasted her with Mrs. Vernley, whom he also liked. But Mrs. Vernley was a woman of the world, determined, a lover of fashion. Mrs. Marsh was quite of a different order. John felt she was one who would understand sympathetically when others would judge harshly. She was the kind of woman to whom he would rather come if he had a confession to make.

He noticed how very frail she was, almost like a saint who had fasted. Her white hair, loosely fastened, seemed as a halo while she stood there in the dim hall with the sunlight behind rimming her head with light. Her hand was so thin that John could feel all the bones in it and her flesh was almost transparent.

Meanwhile Marsh had superintended their boxes.

"Come up to our room, Scissors!" he cried, and John followed him up an old oak staircase, along a narrow corridor that ran the whole length of the house, overlooking the courtyard on one side. Their room was at the end, and the beauty of it made John's heart leap up. It had two low casement windows, bordered with creeper drooping to the lawns below. Their two beds faced the windows; the dressing table, mantelpiece and writing desk were decorated with fresh bunches of violets. The perfume pervaded the room and mingled with the delightful smell of clean linen, which John had come to distinguish as a 'country house smell.'

"What a jolly room!" cried John.

Marsh seemed pleased at his approbation. "Not a bit like a parson's hole, is it?" he commented. "This room is modern—that's a copy of a Cézanne; that's a real Pissarro —you won't find on these walls any woolly legend 'God is Love,' or a dead aunt's knitting in five colours—'Blessed are the meek.' I ejected all those long ago."

"But what does your governor say?"

"Nothing—he merely smiles. I am the cuckoo's egg in the family nest."

John was a little shocked. He felt uneasy when Marsh talked in this strain. It was not that Marsh wanted to shock, but John was in an alien country, which his friend evidently knew well. Every day John was discovering some thing new about himself until his mind was in a condition of fear. Marsh was so splendidly cool about everything. When John asked him questions, he showed no surprise, or superiority, but explained and amplified from familiarity with his theme. Marsh dismissed certain things as "rotten," others he characterised as "smuggy." John always had a feeling that Marsh knew much more than he said. His knowledge of books, for instance, was extraordinary.

John was discovering new books every day of his life, but he no sooner announced a fresh treasure than Marsh knew all about it, had read it long ago and could supplement the knowledge with personal information concerning the author and other books he had written. He was at home in French literature or English, which John accounted for later when he found that Mrs. Marsh had spent her youth in a French convent school. This discovery was made at tea-time in the study, a delightfully cosy room full of books and loose papers, and magazines, with big chairs in which you sank low and all the cushions gradually deflated as though the breath had been crushed out of them. Marsh talked to his mother in French, greatly to John's admiration.

"You mustn't mind Teddie talking French to me," said Mrs. Marsh, as she handed him a tea cup. "He thinks it is such a treat for me, as indeed it is, and Teddie is greatly afraid that I might forget how to speak French."

"I wish I could follow it all, Mrs. Marsh—you speak French so frenchily," said John, munching toast. He loved her already; there was something so comfortable about her.

"Well, you see I was sent to a French school when quite a little girl.

"Jolly good thing for me, Mater, wasn't it?" cried Marsh, linking his arm through his mother's.

"Why, dear?"

" 'Cause I shouldn't have been here if you hadn't fallen in love with a red-haired young curate on a walking tour through Provence!"

Mrs. Marsh laughed.

"You naughty boy—what would your father say if he knew you called him a red-haired curate—his hair was golden then."

"That's the usual story—if a man has red hair they say it's golden; if a girl, they call it auburn."

"My mother had au-red hair," said John flushing. Mrs. Marsh looked quickly at the boy at her side, mingling her love with admiration of his courage.

"Sorry, Scissors—but it can't have been red, for you haven't a freckle. He's jolly good-looking, isn't he, Mother?"

John coloured; further confusion was checked by the abrupt opening of the door. A clerical collar told him that it was Mr. Marsh. After the formal introduction John was able to study the Reverend George Marsh while the latter questioned his son.

He was a tall man of striking appearance. His hair, although almost white, was thick, and a great wave of it lay over his brow. He had a tanned healthy face and laughing eyes. A smile was never long absent from his face, which was handsome in a broad-featured way. John noticed how large and strong were his hands. He had been a great cricketer in his day, and the athlete still lingered in his frame. He would have been recognised as an English country gentleman in any community, and his geniality was blended with an exquisite courtesy. Of the parson there was not a trace, and when afterwards he appeared without a clerical collar, there was no indication whatever that he was anything but a full-blooded English gentleman fond of his horse and his pipe.

He was at least ten years older than his wife, whom he called the "Skipper," greatly surprising and afterwards amusing John. He evidently troubled himself about nothing. If Marsh wanted anything, he was always told by the Vicar, "Ask the Skipper," or "Does the Skipper know?" On Saturday afternoon there was what Marsh assured

John was the weekly tragi-comedy. He confessed he had
not composed his sermon for the following day, and, like a
penitent boy, was locked in his study with the threat that
he should have no dinner until the sermon was completed.
He must have been either a man of quick inspiration or
short patience, for half an hour later as John walked by
the study window he saw the vicar, pipe in mouth, stretched
in his wicker chair, reading the *Nation* which he waved
joyously at John as though to say, "See! I defy the Skipper!"

Later, John discovered that the Vicar was a rebel at
heart. He read the *Nation* religiously, and had an intense
enthusiasm for the Chancellor of the Exchequer, who was
saying rude things about persons who kept pheasants,
greatly to the vicar's delight, who knew how angry it
would make the new tenant of Renstone Hall, who
stood for King, the Conservative party, a covert full
of pheasants and a house full of servants. Teddie, partly
from perversity, and partly because he felt the lordship of
youth, was a conservative, like his mother, and they had
fierce arguments, in which the Vicar bravely kept his flag
flying, despite assaults on either flank.

John's sympathies were with the Vicar. The Chancellor had the gift of phrase and epithet which he admired,
and had also excelled in. He supported him therefore
because that politician's brilliance delighted him. The
Vicar was delighted. He ragged Teddie unmercifully,
and commented gaily on the pleasure he derived from
seeing that the new race at Sedley was enlightened, a
playful thrust at his son's assumption of seniority in his
attitude towards John in political discussions. John loved
those tea-times when argument grew merry. It was all so
good-humoured, the Vicar bantering his son and wife with
great joy, they in their turn exposing his "democracy" by

stories of a "brother" of the soil who had imposed upon him again and again.

John loved these debates. He felt he was one of the family, and after the bleakness of schooldays this comfort and intimacy were something to be treasured. His admiration of Mrs. Marsh grew daily. She was so clever that John no longer wondered at Teddie's amazing ability in all things. She could paint well, and had read deeply and widely; was an authority on Bartolozzi engravings and made beautiful jewellery as a hobby. In the evenings after dinner, they always had an hour's music in the drawing-room—an unique apartment decorated in black and white, with silver fittings and massive candelabra, holding twenty candles—"with enough dripping to make saute potatoes," commented Teddie. The corner of the drawing room was filled by a superbly-toned Bechstein grand, which Mrs. Marsh played with consummate skill.

She had studied at Vienna under Leschetiscky and her interpretation of Liszt and Brahms held John spellbound. Her rendering was quite unlike Lindon's. He played *con fuoco*. She caressed the piano so that it sang as though its heart was filled with grief. When she played Debussy and Ravel, it was as though the wind were making the aspens shake and glimmer in the sunlight. There was a series of delicate currents of sound which followed one another like the reflections of rippling water on the sides of a boat, and one floated down the stream with all the senses quiescent yet acute.

When the music ended and it was time for bed, for they retired early, there was the ceremony of blowing out the candles. Mrs. Marsh, Teddie and John joined hands round the candelabra and a fierce competition ensued. In the small hall they parted. The Vicar went off to his study, where he sat reading until one or two in the morning. His lamp threw a long strip of light across the lawn long after the boys had fallen asleep. On the first night, after Mrs. Marsh had kissed her son on the brow and said "Good night," she turned and half held out her hand to John, then with one of those sudden impulses, which endeared her to him, she asked,

"I wonder if my new boy is too big?" and smiling, she pressed John's head towards her and kissed him on the brow, then turned and went upstairs. John stood still for half a minute. He hoped the light was too dim for his friend to see, for his eyes were blurred. It was silly to be so frightfully sensitive, but kindness like this always upset him. It increased his sense of loneliness and loss and yet it made him happier.

Upstairs in their bedroom, John threw open a window and leaned out into the night. The air was warm, and a full moon hung low over the elm trees at the bottom of the garden, throwing their long shadows across the lawns. The distant woods, black and distinct, were silhouetted on the hills; there was a great silence over everything. The moon would look just like that peering over the gorge at Amasia. He wondered what his father was doing at that moment, and whether he knew how happy he was. Probably he was smoking his last cigarette on the verandah, watching the stream as it ran and flashed along its stony bed; perhaps the night was not silent like this, but full of the droning of the *saz*. And Ali?—he would be fast asleep, tired after a long day in the sun. Dear old Ali, how he longed to have him with him, to show him this wonderful English house, and have him hear Teddie talk—how he would stare at Teddie!

"I say, Scissors, how long are you going to hang out of that window?" It was Marsh, tooth-brush in hand, already in his pyjamas. "I'll bet I know your thoughts."

"You don't."

"I do—you're thinking about another place the moon hangs over and what everybody's doing there."

"How did you know?"

Marsh laughed delightedly at the confirmation of his guess. "Easy—when you turned just now you'd got the East in your eyes."

"The East—what do you mean?"

"Well, you look a bit Eastern at times. I thought so the first time I saw you, but you looked very much so just now, just as I imagine Lindon saw you."

"Lindon—" John gulped at the name— "saw me? What did he tell you?"

"Oh, he was telling us one day how you fainted when he played the *Drum Polonaise*—and how queer you looked at him just before you went. By the way, I don't think I ever told you Lindon lives near here."

The days slipped by at the Vicarage. Indeed, there was so little to do and yet they were so industriously idle that the day was over before all that was planned had been accomplished. John had been at the Vicarage just a week, when, one sunshiny Saturday morning, the trap came round to the door, with its well-groomed pony and shining harness, at which Marsh had laboured for an hour the previous evening with a bottle of polish—and the promise of half a crown. Mrs. Marsh and John and Teddie got in, the latter taking the reins, and they clattered merrily out of the courtyard, down the village street, where the little boys gaped, and the women in the doors curtseyed, out on to the highway stretching away beneath an avenue of over-reaching elms. They were bound for the market town of Loughboro, on a shopping expedition.

"There's nothing worth buying there," said Marsh,

"which is the reason for the Mater's regular visit. She drags me round in the trap while she looks in every window. There's nothing to see and less to do."

"There's the Theatre, dear."

"What a show! 'East Lynne' by the celebrated London company or 'The Girl at the Cross Roads' preceded by the one act comedy, 'Sarah in the Soup.'"

"You should not run the place down—you will spoil John's anticipations."

They passed a couple of ragged men, bronzed and unshaven, who stood still while the trap passed.

"That's the ideal life," exclaimed Marsh, flicking the pony. "Nothing to do and no desire to do it. They remind me of Davies' lines—he was a tramp too—

> *What is this life if full of care*
> *We have no time to stand and stare?*

This road's punctuated with these leisured gentlemen— that's another attraction of Loughboro—there's a fine workhouse. The Governor goes to preach there once a month, and always comes away regretting he's not an inmate—it fits in with his idea of the democratic communal life. But he always drinks sherry when he gets home—to kill the taste I suppose."

There were now signs of the approaching town. Cottages became more frequent, and then villas, pathetically attempting to keep on good relations with the country by burdening their windows with flower boxes and their square little front gardens with shrubs. Two gasometers loomed up in the distance, long monotonous buildings with tall chimneys suggesting some kind of industry. Then with a turn, they were trotting down the streets of the town itself. They pulled up under the Town Hall clock which projected itself over a market place greatly animated with booths and wandering groups of buyers, gossipers and gapers. Mrs. Marsh disappeared in a chemist's shop, where she exchanged her library books, and presently she emerged laden with three novels, the *English Review,* the *Nineteenth Century* and *The Tatler.* These were deposited in the trap, whereupon she walked on again and disappeared in a dairy shop. Marsh flicked the pony and the trap jogged on, halting again outside the shop.

"This is how we progress on a shopping expedition. I follow the mater all round the market place while everybody comes to the shop doors, stares at me, asks, 'Do you know who that is?' until a wiseacre says, 'That's the parson's son—him what preaches at the workhouse.' Last summer I came down here in shorts and socks and the sight paralysed the market place; they had never seen so much male leg before. I shall bring my 'topper' home next term. It'll have a raging success."

For three quarters of an hour they slowly worked round the sides of the market place, while the trap got fuller and fuller and Mrs. Marsh redder and redder. John was busy carrying parcels from the shop to the trap.

"Thank heaven a market square has only four sides!" cried Marsh, as John deposited a two gallon jar of cider in the well of the trap.

"There's more to follow!" cried Scissors, darting back to the shop. He emerged a few minutes later, his arms full of small parcels with Mrs. Marsh following behind. He was so intent upon balancing his precariously held pile that he did not notice a youth and a girl who stood aside to let them pass, but as he turned to hand the things to Marsh he caught a glimpse and his heart gave a great thump as he coloured in confusion. Marsh noticed John's sudden uneasiness and turned in his seat.

"Lindon!" he cried. "What luck—how are you?"

It was Lindon—cool, immaculate. He raised his cap
to Mrs. Marsh, with the alert manner that distinguished
him. The girl at his side was obviously his sister. She
had the same straight nose and keen eyes. Her fresh
beauty made John stare at her. All that fascinated
him in Lindon was there with the added grace of girlhood.

"Good morning, Mr. Lindon—good morning, Miss Lindon. You are shopping too, I suppose," said Mrs. Marsh
genially; then noticing John nervously drawing back—
"You know John, I think?"

"Rather," interrupted Marsh. "John's his fag."

Lindon laughed. "I'm afraid he knows me only too
well." He turned to his sister. "This is Scissors—John
Dean, Mabel." John raised his cap and took the proffered hand.

"How d'you do," she asked, "I've heard so much of you
from Henry."

Then Lindon had spoken of him!—he had called him
Scissors! A hundred thoughts raced through John's head.
Had he forgiven—or was this mere politeness? He had
talked about him to his sister, but perhaps that was before
this miserable affair happened. He must speak to Lindon
somehow before they parted, and say how sorry he was.
The eye, he was relieved to see, showed no signs of his attack. In his imagination he had come to think of it as
quite closed up.

Mabel Lindon looked at the boy who stood so silent before her. Possibly he was tongued-tied, certainly he was
flushed, or was it his colour? He was very attractive,
she thought, and his embarrassment flattered her.

"Will you not come over to see us?" she asked him.
John was in a dilemma. Lindon was busily talking to
Marsh and his mother, he had not heard the invitation.
John waited, hoping he would hear and re-inforce it.

"I'm leaving here on Tuesday—so I'm sorry I shall be unable, thank you."

"Oh, that is a pity, for we are leaving next month, we are going to live in Worcestershire, and it is a shame, for we have such a wonderful garden and pond—you would love it."

"I'm sure I should."

They were saying good-bye now. He shook hands with Miss Lindon. Mrs. Marsh had got into the trap. John was about to follow, when Lindon spoke.

"Having a good time, Scissors?" he asked, in a friendly voice. John stammered with joy and relief. It was *Pax*.

"Awfully, thanks Lindon," he muttered. The reins had been jerked, the trap began to move. Miss Lindon walked on. Lindon raised his cap. "Good-bye!" he called to them. It was now or never.

"Please Lindon—I—I'm awfully sorry I was such a cad to you—and will you forgive me? I—I—"

"That's all right, Scissors," said Lindon, shaking John's hand. "I like fire in a kid. Are you coming over to see us?" he asked.

"I'm sorry I can't—I go on Tuesday—"

"Well—you must come to stay next hols. Good-bye!" and with a smile he was gone. All John's hero worship swelled up within him. How splendidly Lindon had dismissed the beastly affair! John hurried after the trap and clambered in. Marsh smiled at him with perfect understanding, and John felt how good was life. All the way back to the Vicarage his heart was singing within him. At the Vicarage door, as he carried in the parcels, he could not help whistling. Marsh took his arm.

"That storm over?" he asked, sympathetically.

John could not answer, but he nodded. They walked into the house.

CHAPTER VI

I

THE following Tuesday John said good-bye to the Marshs and left for "The Croft" to spend the remainder of his Easter holidays with the Vernleys. Mrs. Marsh and Teddie drove him to the station, and, as the train left and he leaned out of the window to wave farewell, he knew that once more he had found true friends and a house where his return would be welcome. At dusk he had arrived in the village station nearest to "The Croft," where he found Bobbie and his brother Tod waiting for him on the platform.

"Hello, Scissors!" shouted Tod, as the train drew in, "We've a surprise for you. Where's the luggage—give me that, I'll carry it."

"How's the great Marsh?" asked Vernley. "As super cilious as ever?"

"Yes—in great form, he sends his love and recommends Mother Wingate's syrup for fatuous persons," answered John.

"Cheek!" retorted Vernley, "and by Jove—don't you think I'm getting thin—Tod's had me out on the cinder track every morning at six. I'm going to pull off the 'half' and mile race next term."

John looked at him critically, and although Vernley was as delightfully substantial as ever, he had not the heart to disappoint him.

"He's wasting away like our Narcissus," said Tod, bang-

102

ing his way through the narrow booking hall. "Look, my
son, isn't she a beauty!"

He pointed to a racing car drawn up outside the station.
John noticed its long rectangular bonnet, the beautiful
gleam and hidden strength of the thing, admiration showing in his eyes.

"It's mine!—the Governor's twenty-first birthday present! She was first in the trials at Brooklands last
week," said Tod, dropping the bag in.

"We're going on a tour next hols—all round this giddy
old island," cried Vernley. "There'll be a fringe of dead
dogs and defunct old ladies around these shores, that never
did and never will stand under the foot of the—how's the
thing go?"

"—proud conqueror," added John. "She is a lovely
thing—what's her name?"

"Haven't decided yet. I've voted for the 'Silver
Slayer,' Tod suggests 'The Gleam.'"

"The Governor says 'Œdipus Rex' would be more appro-
priate," added Tod, his brown hands on the steering
wheel.

"Why?"

"Because of the murders at the cross roads that'll be
committed. Ready?"

There was a preparatory purr of the engine, then a delightful roaring hum, and they glided forwards, imperceptibly gathering speed. The chill wind whipped John's
face. He looked joyously at Vernley seated beside him
and noted the disdainful pose of lordship. Vernley's utter contempt for a display of feeling always amused John.
The villages tore by, fowls screeched, and flew with fluttered feathers into the hedge bottoms; they roared up the
hills and ran silently down into the valleys. Half an
hour later they had turned in at the familar drive and

pulled up at the stone porch. Inside the hall Mrs. Vernley came to meet John.

"Here you are at last—we are so glad to see you, John."

"Thank you—it's good to be here, Mrs. Vernley." The dogs, as if welcoming an old friend, bounded forwards.

"Down, Tiger—down, Ruff—down, sir!" yelled Vernley, and they cowered and wagged their tails, beating a tattoo on the parquet floor.

In the library, gleaming with a rosy fire, its light shining on the silver tea service, John found Mr. Vernley.

"Hullo, my boy! well, how are you? I hear we've found a great orator at last!"

John smiled, then halted as he saw some one standing at Mr. Vernley's side.

"Ribble," said Vernley turning to him, "this is our rising hope." Then to John, "This is Mr. Ribble—you'll be great friends I'm sure, though I don't know which side of him you'll like the better. Mr. Ribble has written some very clever books, and he's in the Cabinet, so that politicians say he's a good author and a bad politician, and authors say he's a good politician and a bad author."

"And my wife says I should have been a nonconformist divine. How d'you do, John; we must hear some of these famous flights of oratory."

"He's the real stuff, sir," said Vernley enthusiastically.— "Doesn't half work 'em, makes the 'gods' boil over!"

"This empire, this realm upon which the sun has never looked—no, that's not it, sir—I'm no orator," said Tod. "Let's have tea, Mother. By Jove, Governor, you should have heard her sing up Carshott Hill—did it on top, lots in hand. When she's tuned up she'll take a houseside."

"Lord! You've done nothing but tune up since you had her," cried Bobbie.

"Now boys, sit down, tea's ready," said Mrs. Vernley,

pouring out. John hoped every moment that Muriel
would come in. He was disappointed when she was not
in the hall to meet him, and his heart sank when he did
not find her in the library. Perhaps she had gone out for
a walk. He did not want to ask, for Vernley might think
he had come simply to see her. It was not so, of course.
He was glad to be with Vernley again, but he could not
help looking forward to seeing Muriel, of whom he had
been thinking through all those weeks at school. The talk
at the tea-table was chiefly political. Mr. Vernley was
discussing a coming election with Ribble, whom John
thought was the most picturesque old man he had ever
seen. He had long curly white hair, his eyes were surrounded by good-humoured wrinkles, and he beamed
through his spectacles. The mouth was thin and compressed and had a ghost of a smile always hovering about
it. John wondered where he had seen such a face before,
and then suddenly remembered a portrait of Thackeray
in Mr. Fletcher's study. There was a slight resemblance, and Mr. Ribble's character seemed to John to
be somewhat Thackerayish, for John was now half through
"The Newcomes," after a delighted discovery of "Pen-
dennis" and "Henry Esmond."

"Steer has just published a fine book," Mr. Ribble was
saying. "I think that little poem on Muriel is masterly."

John was alert immediately, and Vernley, eating cake
and drinking tea at the same moment, contrary to all laws,
noticed John's interest.

"When's Muriel coming home, Mother?" he asked.

"I read you her letter this morning—to-morrow. You'll
have to drive the trap to the station to meet her in the
afternoon."

"Why can't we motor?"

"I'm going to Brooklands in the morning," said Tod,

"and I'm taking Brown—so you'll have to drive the buggy."

"Oh, bother—I hate the old thing!"

But John would have ridden to Paradise in it if such a passenger as Muriel had awaited him. To-morrow! He looked at Vernley, and it occurred to him that his question had been what Mr. Fletcher, in debates, had called a leading one. Vernley had never shown much interest in John's affair, but he was not so unobservant as the latter thought.

When the boys were changing for dinner that evening, and while John was struggling with a bow, his glance fell upon a silver frame standing on the dressing table. It contained a beautiful portrait of Muriel who laughed at him out of the frame. John looked long at it, and finally he realised that the photograph had been placed there for his delight. It was on *his* dressing table and not on Vernley's. Only one person could have placed it there.

"I say, Bobbie," said John, through the open door leading to his friend's room.

"What?" asked Vernley, standing with one leg in his black trousers, the other kicking its way through.

"You're a jolly decent sort—being here, you know—and in this room again—and the—photograph—thanks awfully, old man."

"Thought you were a bit keen, you know—she's not at all bad for a sister, is she?"

"Rather not!" said John ecstatically, giving his bow a confirmatory pull.

That evening John knew Mr. Ribble much more intimately, for while one of Vernley's sisters was accompanying the aspiring prima donna, John was led off by the politi-

cian into the conservatory. The boy began asking questions about the House of Commons and Mr. Ribble had a
great fund of stories. John learned of Mr. Balfour's
aloof manner, Mr. Churchill's imperturbable genius, Mr.
Lloyd George's subtlety, Mr. Asquith's classic weight and
Sir Henry Campbell Bannerman's personal charm; then he
wished to know all about Mr. Austen Chamberlain and the
hereditary monocle, whether Mr. **John Burns'** mother
really had been a washerwoman, and what tactics were le-
gitimate in catching the Speaker's eye. Leaving these
personalities, the conversation changed to political economy and John found himself on new ground and in a
world of unknown names.

John felt flattered by the fact that Mr. Ribble took it
for granted that he knew these persons and subjects, but
the politician was deliberately whetting the boy's appetite
and trying to lead him into a channel of serious study.
John Stuart Mill, Walter Bagehot, Edmund Burke, Karl
Marx, together with such queer names as Spinoza, Kant,
Schlegel, Schopenhauer and Nietzsche, all rolled off Mr.
Ribble's tongue. He was now in the realm of Philosophy,
and John, for the first time in his life, heard of Comte
and Positivism, of Darwin and the Origin of Species, of
Huxley and Russel Wallace. Mr. Ribble talked and John
listened, experiencing the wonderful thrill as when Mr.
Steer had shown him the world of poetry.

"I think you had better start with Ruskin's 'Unto This
Last,' " said Mr. Ribble when John asked where he should
begin. "He's easy to read and somewhat superficial.
You'll find that philosophy and political economy are
closely related—half brothers in fact, and Ruskin believes
their parents were Social Morality and Private Duty."

Before going to bed that night, John had found a copy
of "Unto This Last" which he took up to bed. The two

boys often read before going to sleep, and Vernley was engrossed in "Kim" so that he did not see what absorbed
John, until growing sleepy, he closed his book and came
into John's room with its light still burning.

"What are you reading?" he asked.

"Ruskin," replied John, deep in the book.

"Golly—what on earth are you reading that piffle for—
what's the book?"

"Unto This Last."

"Holy Moses—you're the queerest mixture I've ever
known. Last hols it was "Whose dwelling is—"

—*"The light of setting suns,'—began John—*
And the round ocean and the living air,
And the blue sky and in the mind of man:
A motion and a spirit, that impels
All thinking things, all objects of all thought,
And rolls through all things. Therefore am I still
A lover of the meadows and the woods,
And mountains; and of all that—"

A pillow landed on John's head. It was returned with
redoubled energy. Vernley made a grand attack, John
defending with a bolster. There was a frantic scuffle, the
bed groaned, the electric light swung furiously, Vernley's
pyjama coat was torn down the back and John was
soon without a blanket or a sheet on his bed. Suddenly
they were buried in a snowstorm of feathers that
floated all over the room; the pillow case had split; it
called for an armistice. John and Vernley subsided
on the bed, silently watching the feather-laden atmosphere.

"Lord! what a mess!"

"We always seem to be smashing something in this

room," said John ruefully—"last time it was the wash basin."

"It's that infernal Wordsworth—there'll be nothing left now Ruskin's on the scene too."

"Well—you shouldn't interrupt."

"Do you think I'm going to lie still while you pour out that bosh?"

"It isn't bosh—Mr. Ribble says—"

"Ribble's an old fool—'a nonconformist crank swaddled in the longclothes of infantile ignorance'—that's what the Governor's opponent called him last election."

The feathers had now settled.

"What a mess!" said Vernley surveying the room. "I've got an idea! Open the door, Scissors!" Vernley threw open the two big windows and the draught thus created swept the feathers out on to the landing. The two boys followed and peered over the banisters as the white cloud slowly settled down into the hall below. At that moment the drawing-room door opened.

"Father!—Just look at this—wherever—" came Mrs. Vernley's voice in amazement.

"Shut the door, Scissors!" They rushed into the room, switched off the light and waited breathlessly. All was quiet again.

"If you go on reading every author you're told about, there'll be nothing left in this house," said Vernley, "and I don't agree, of course, about that libel on old Ribble— he's a decent old boy. Good night, Scissors."

II

The next afternoon Vernley and John harnessed the pony and were on their way to the station to meet Muriel. Spring was in the air. The hedgerows were beginning to burst into leaf, and the birds singing in the lanes filled

the country-side with hope.   John's heart too was singing.
It was so good to be driving through the sunlit lanes with
a crisp air blowing in their faces, the friendly jog-trot of
the pony beating upon their ears.   He looked at Vernley,
the imperturbable Vernley, who was flicking the pony's
haunches with his whip.   There was something comfort-
ably solid about him.   He represented tradition and the
continuance of a settled conception of life.   John had no
difficulty in planning Vernley's future; unlike his own,
it depended upon no caprice of Fate.   He would go up to
Oxford, travel, and then settle down to the life of a country
gentleman.   He would grow stout and red-cheeked, marry
a healthy, unimaginative wife and be the father of a
crowd of noisy, well-developed children.   The hunt, a seat
on the bench, June in London and August on the moors—
that would be Vernley's life.   And he would not bother
his head about political or religious faiths.   He would
probably be a Conservative, despite his father, who was a
family renegade, and a Churchman.   Conservative, because caution and security were better than haste and revolution, and the world on the whole was a jolly old place
despite Socialists and other disgruntled reformers.   A
Churchman, because he knew so little about religion, and
a respectable ready-made creed, tried and found suitable
as an accommodating policy of living was the safest and
easiest to adopt.   Had he been born in Constantinople he
would have been a Mohammedan, in Bombay a Buddhist,
in Hongkong a Confucian, and in Paris a Catholic.   And
whichever creed environment had caused him to accept,
he would have been a credit to it, faithfully observing its
tenets, a respectable, unthinking, clean-living fellow.

Vernley looked at John as the station came into sight;
the far-away expression was in his face, a curious detach-

ment that often puzzled Vernley. Sometimes John seemed
to have left his body in another world. It was uncanny
and he remembered that Marsh, referring to this habit,
had called it "the Eastern touch," though what that quite
meant Vernley did not know.

"The train's signalled," said Vernley. "We shall just
get there in time. I wonder whether Muriel is bringing
her friend back, she said she might—a topping girl."

"I hope not—I don't want any one monopolising
Muriel," said John boldly.

"That's all right—I shall look after her friend—so don't
you worry."

They pulled up just as the train ran into the station.
Vernley sat still in the trap.

"I must mind the pony,—you go in, Scissors!"

Dear old Vernley, thought John, what a tactician he
was! So leaping out, he went on to the platform just as
Muriel descended from the carriage. There was one glad
look of recognition and then a momentary shyness fell
over them. Muriel had brought her friend whom she introduced with embarrassment. John, scarlet in the face,
pretended to be frantically busy with the luggage, which
filled the trap. Homewards turned, the pony trotted
smartly. John sat opposite Muriel and kept looking at
her furtively. She was beautiful. He wanted to touch
her soft flesh, and press back the little strand of hair that
fluttered over her ear and across the cheek. He noticed
the full redness of her lips, and the wonderful beauty of
her long eyelashes. The sight of her filled John with a
kind of ecstasy bordering on intoxication. He was in-
finitely more in love with her than on the previous occasion. The absence of three months had glorified her in
his imagination, but now he saw that reality transcended
his most extravagant dreams of her physical perfection.

He was fifteen and this first flush of love left him breathless with wonder. He did not want to talk; it was enough to sit near her, to hear her voice, to watch the elfin grace of her movements, to see her eyes shine, and the whiteness of her small teeth when she laughed. Had some one told him he was in love, he would have denied it. He was more a worshipper than a lover. This revelation of the woman, as he saw it in Muriel, was like sunrise on a new world; he was so lost in wonder that familiarity became impossible. He was filled with awe, in which ran fear, the fear that she could not always be there, that one morning he would get up and find her changed, an ordinary being, moving on the old earth as he had always known it. But this afternoon was his time of ecstasy—the friendly trot. ting of the pony, Bobbie talking away to Polly, and himself sitting there with Muriel near him while the birds sang in the hedgerows, and the sunset clouds in the west reddened behind a black fringe of trees.

"Polly," said Vernley, "you may think so, but my friend is not really dumb—in fact John is a fearful talker at times."

He laughed at John.

"You've got the field, so I've retired," retorted John. "And I'm waiting for Muriel to tell me what she's been doing all the holidays."

Muriel responded to this invitation, and, the ice broken, they were soon engrossed in each other. At the top of Carshott Hill, Vernley pulled up. He was enjoying himself with Polly, who was sensible, and to his great relief didn't giggle.

"I say, Scissors, shall we go round by Carshott? It is two miles out of the way, but we shall be in time for dinner."

"Oh yes," cried Muriel. "It's such a glorious afternoon."

"I'm not a bit hungry," said John tactfully; any excuse for the prolongation of the drive. So they turned off to Carshott. It was dark when they arrived at "The Croft" gates and turned up the drive, so dark that John had been able to hold Muriel's hand in his and interlace his strong fingers with her slender ones, and he was so overjoyed that he failed to notice that Vernley had done similarly.

Greetings over in the hall, they hurried off to dress for dinner. The boys had a hot bath, and John sat on the side while Vernley lathered himself.

"Polly's a very pretty girl," said John, rubbing hard with the towel.

"Of course!" cried Vernley, banging the sponge on his head, then spluttering, "and Muriel?—well I suppose you've hardly noticed her yet," he added satirically—"it was so jolly dark—but I know she has soft hands."

John coloured, rubbing his head so that Vernley should not see.

"I say, Scissors! I'll bet you I know what Muriel's going to wear to-night."

"What?"

"That white dress with the blue insertion."

John remembered it. It was all fluffy, and she looked like a fairy in a cloud. He had admired her in it and told her so.

"How do you know?"

"Why, in honour of the occasion, of course. I called it the froth and frolic dress, but probably Muriel calls it mode-a-la-Scissors."

"You are an ass!" said John.

"I am your friend," retorted Vernley. "By their companions ye shall know them."

"Are you coming out of that bath—the dressing bell went half an hour ago!"

"I'm getting boiled all over—I want to look my freshest to-night. You are not the only knight on the war-path; and I've got a deadly rival."

"Who's that?"

"Tod," said Vernley. "Personally I fear nothing from him—he's harmless, but he's got a car, and that is usually a winner."

"You are a cynic," said John.

"I've had experience—I've been thrown over for a tennis racquet. You don't know women, my boy."

"Being elderly, I suppose you know all about them."

"Almost, but there's one thing always puzzles me, Scissors, I always wonder how much these girls confide in one another and giggle at us for being such asses."

"I don't think Muriel would," said John seriously.

"Angel!" murmured Vernley, kissing the sponge ecstatically.

III

Mr. Ribble did not come down to breakfast the next morning. He was reviewing a book for the *Nation* and kept in his room. John saw breakfast go in to him and wondered if ever the day would come that he would be so important as to have breakfast sent up to his room. He went to the window and sat there for a time enjoying the early morning scene, the light on the distant hills, the sharp sound of a passing cart down in the lane, and stray noises from the stable yard. Then he watched the country postman cycle up the drive, his fresh healthy face perspiring, a heavy mailbag on his shoulders. John got up and

went out into the hall and received the letters, which he
spread out on the table in neat order. There were fifteen
for Mr. Vernley, six for Mr. Ribble—John paused lovingly
over these. How splendid they looked!

"The Rt. Hon. Ellerton Ribble, M. P."
and as he looked the magic letters changed into—

"The Rt. Hon. John N. Dean. M. P."
Day-dreaming he did not see that Mrs. Vernley had entered the hall and was looking at him.

"Disappointed, John?" she asked. "I am always disappointed when I get no letters. I like receiving them,
but detest answering them."

"Good morning, Mrs. Vernley! No—I was just thinking how splendid Mr. Ribble's address looks."

"Wondering when your own will be like it?" asked Mrs.
Vernley, placing her hand on the boy's shoulder. She detected the pleasure her little guess gave him.

"Well, if Muriel has anything to do with it," she
added, "you'll be the youngest Cabinet minister in
history."

"Muriel?" asked John.

"Yes, last night she gave Mr. Ribble the worst cross-
questioning he has had for many a long hour. I believe
she has planned your whole career, but I hope, John," said
Mrs. Vernley, opening her letters, "that you are not going
to waste yourself in politics. It is the most futile life
a man can lead. I never knew a member of Parliament
who wasn't a harassed mass of vanity. Their lives are
made wretched by pulling wires for a thousand societies
that threaten to extract a dozen votes at their next election.
They are the prey of the parsons, charity organisations
and vested interests—"

"But surely Mr. Vernley—" began John.

"One's husband is always excepted from general criticism, John. My husband is such a bad member of Parliament because he is such a good husband."

"The world has to be ruled, Mrs. Vernley."

"I do not deny it, but why presume that Parliament rules Britain? I'm quite sure it doesn't, any more than Congress rules the United States or the Chamber rules France. There's the gong. I wonder how many of us will appear at breakfast!"

In the breakfast room they found Tod and Muriel, and a minute later Vernley came in and took his seat.

"Let's see—this morning? Ah! it's plaice and sausage," he cried. "Lift the covers, Mother."

Sausage and plaice duly appeared.

"We have a Scotch cook with the mind of a mathematician," said Tod. "Wednesday, bacon and eggs."

"Friday—kedgeree!" added Vernley.

"Saturday—grilled ham!" supplemented Muriel.

"Sunday—two eggs," contributed Alice.

"Monday—" began Tod.

He was interrupted by the entrance of Mr. Vernley.

"I suppose you children are reciting the food calendar as usual?"

"Yes, Dad,—it's your turn," cried Vernley. "Monday—?"

"Monday—liver and bacon!"

"Really," commented Mrs. Vernley, "if cook heard the way you make fun of her infinite variety—"

"She might give us sausage twice a week which would please me!" said Tod. "By the way, Mother, is Mrs. Graham coming to-day?"

"Yes, I want you to meet the 11.15, she will arrive by that."

"Let's all go!" cried Vernley. "Jove, she's a stunner, Scissors!"

"Bobbie dear!" remonstrated Mrs. Vernley, "you mustn't talk of Mrs. Graham like that!"

"Why not, Mother? I told her she was a stunner once and she pinked with delight."

"I don't know where you boys pick up all your slang," said Mr. Vernley.

"We get so many M. P.s in the house, pater," suggested Tod. "Will you play me a round of golf? I did four and seven in bogie yesterday."

"When?"

"This afternoon—three o'clock," said Tod.

"Remember, dear, we have Mr. Crimp coming to tea," urged Mrs. Vernley.

"Then I'll play you, Tod," Mr. Vernley said decisively. "My dear, why do you ask that man?"

"Because, being a tactful wife, I know he is worth two hundred votes to you."

"He turns my tea sour," complained Tod. "The pater and I will stay out to tea."

"That's not fair," cried Muriel. "It means I shall have to talk to Mr. Crimp."

"On foreign stamps," murmured Bobbie. "He'll love Scissors—don't look so glum, Scissors—you look quite crimpled up!"

Tod's aim was unerring; the tea cosy ruffled Vernley's well-plastered hair.

"Stop! I won't have my breakfast service smashed!" cried Mrs. Vernley in alarm, but protest was useless. The cosy flew back with redoubled vigour. Its flight was unimpeded by its destined objective, for Tod ducked. It went over his head. Polly who had sat very quiet all through breakfast, received it on her empty plate where it ousted an egg cup with a clatter, and the familiar sound of a crash followed as it broke into a dozen pieces.

"You awful children!" cried Mrs. Vernley.

"Never mind, Mum," said Tod, bending and kissing her. "You know you're proud of your bouncing offspring."

IV

It was no exaggeration to say that the arrival of Mrs. Graham was an event in John's life. Ever afterwards he could recall vividly the first sharp impression of that bright Easter morning when he stood on the country station platform. His impression was always clear, even in its detail. Recalling her advent and attempting analysis, he was never sure whether his first surprise was caused by beauty, by dress or by aroma. There was something distinctive in the perfume Mrs. Graham used. Only once afterwards did he encounter it, in the foyer of a Paris theatre, when it brought back in swift vision the English Easter morning, and the graceful lady extending her hand to him as he stood, cap in hand, admiring every line of her figure.

True, on the way to the station, above the purr of the car, he had heard the ecstatic praise of Tod, and the no less fervent admiration of Bobbie. But their tribute, faithful and generous, omitted the something that caught John in the mesh. Was it her voice, so rich with its quality, a speaking voice that gave such distinction to all she said, that made a trivial comment noteworthy? Was it her beauty?—that Romney-like picture of colour and contour, the shapely nose, the lovely arched lips, the delicate rose-bloom of her cheeks and the dark, quick vivacity of her eyes? Or was it her ornaments, the grace and style of their choice and use? No earrings ever hung like hers; they seemed to gather beauty from the lobes they decorated. The string of pearls that nestled about her throat, shapely as a swan's neck, in its sheen seemed to derive lustre from the sweetness of her flesh. Was it those all-expressive hands, that tapered so fascinatingly with nails that exhibited the charm of nature and art? Something perhaps of all these, yet something which, without all these, would make her a woman of memorable beauty.

Her dress was elegant, noteworthy, but women had dressed so a hundred times and achieved nothing distinctive. John had seen features as perfect, hands as lovely—but nere was something not wholly extraneous. He knew now why she was always called, "the beautiful Mrs. Graham"; why, to this woman of thirty-five, clung the air of a tragedy queen; why, since that dread period of newspaper notoriety, she had never been allowed to relapse into obscurity, but was photographed and paragraphed. Would her sin ever find full expiation?

Sin! How absurd that word seemed. Was there such a thing in the presence of such perfection? John gazed at her as she sat at his side in the car, talking to Bobbie, while Tod drove. She was alluded to as a "notorious" woman, and as John thought of it, he almost laughed aloud; what chance had all the dull, dingy, respectable women at the side of this empress of life? John, of course, did not know the details of the divorce case which had made her, for six weeks, the most discussed woman in the world. The young peer who had ruined his life and hers, and who, strangely enough, had found all the sympathy while she took all the blame, who had declared himself powerless in her presence. Perhaps so, but if so, why so contemptible in that power, why the ready surrender of her character, the confession of impotence? She was unfaithful, a married experienced woman of thirty-five, and he a young boy of twenty-one. But whose was the sacrifice? She should have known better, said the world, she corrupted a boy. But if his was the ardour, if the passion of first love and the lyrical song of youth were laid at her feet, how could she resist, she a grown woman, who saw youth lapsing like a spent wave on the shore of Life, one whose elderly husband could not guess the tumult of nature beating at the doors of her heart, about to close on summer for ever?

Seven hundred years ago, such love was romance; not even the dagger of Giovanni had been needed to draw, with its blood, the tears and sympathy of lovers of all ages for Paolo and Francesca. But Francesca in the twentieth century must stand in the witness box for legal luminaries to torture, must hear every nameless act given the label of lust, and finally, hear Paolo fling the insult of age and cunning into her face, and plead the ignorance of youth.

And then, when the whole dreadful nightmare was over, another reappearance in a hopeless battle for her child; then peace again, while the world whispers of the disappearance from society of the beautiful Mrs. Graham. But Life would not leave her alone; five years might have brought some healing to a heart that asked forgetfulness. The suicide of the young Earl, with a last love declaration, set the world by the ears again. So he loved her to the last! She laughed almost. He had died for his love of her, said the world. Women envied her the compliment of his suicide. He might have loved her sufficiently to live, she reflected, and once more passed through a night-mare of picture papers; herself as a bride, bathing at Ostend; herself in the box; extracts from the trial; her tears in the last scene, then—God in heaven!—her boy at school, not in the first school he had had to leave, but another, which he would now have to leave. And through it all, as if to excite envy and scandal by obstinacy, her beauty grew, and she remained "the beautiful Mrs. Graham."

But it was not an aura of tragedy that fascinated John.

He had not exchanged a dozen words when he recognised what he had heard, with mirth, the school porter call "quality." In the first place her voice—that was a revelation. What a wonderful instrument the human voice was! When she spoke her words were invested with alluring music; then also there was a hint of—no, not worldliness —of—

"Bond Street, Rumpelmeyer's—cum Papier Poudre," supplied Tod a few days later, alluding to the same hint. She was one of those women of whom one asked inwardly —was that rouge, was that carmine, did she pencil? and you were never sure. If so, it was wonderfully done and fascinating. If not, she was amazingly perfect and unbelievable. But you never knew for sure. Of her powder, she made no secret. No beautiful woman ever does, for it is an embroidery which beauty only can justify.

And as John sat there he experienced a cheap sensation. That it was cheap he knew, and despised himself for it. She was a divorced woman—notorious even. Were not the Vernleys bold? Then a hot flush of shame leapt to his face at the meanness of the thought—he was like the rest.

His sudden colouring was noticed by Mrs. Graham, who, unaware of its cause, thought the handsome lad at her side was shy. She began to talk to him and by the time they reached "The Croft," she had made a fervent disciple. At lunch he sat between her and Muriel, and felt an uncomfortable twinge of his conscience. Had Muriel felt neglected? But she would understand how fascinating it was to talk to Mrs. Graham, or rather, to hear her talk, for she seemed to have been everywhere. Big-game shooting in Africa, the wonder of Lake Louise, the views from Mons Pilatus, the charm of Copenhagen and other diversions of the Tivoli; the house-fringed shores of the Little Belt, the crowded Hohestrasse of a Sunday evening in Cologne, the

colour and *gelati* of the Piazza San Marco, the brightness
of Unter den Linden on a June morning, the approach
to the Brandenburg Gate, Le Touquet and its golf, the
winter sports at Murren—the little glimpses of all these
lighted her conversation.

She had dined at most of the Embassies in Europe;
delightful little anecdotes, pointed with the witty
brevity of a French phrase, scintillated in her talk. Yes,
she had met "Anatole France," and told a story of his
courtly grumpiness; she had crossed the Atlantic with
Paderewski, who had played for her his "Romance,"
on the evening of its composition, played it in the
lonely drawing-room while passengers were at dinner, with
such elegance, delicacy of touch and strength of tone.
Had she read "Mr. Polly?" asked John. That reminded
her immediately; they saw Mr. Wells in an Essex house writing all the morning, playing hockey all the afternoon, and
always the busy little man in a blue serge suit, pouring out
a medley of history, theology, romance and hard-headed
business talk. There was a flashlight of Rodin in his pala-
tial studio. "Madame has beautiful hands—they must be
immortalised," and one saw the robust personality of
Roosevelt at a small dinner party at the Plaza, New York,
with a later snapshot of him speechmaking from the platform of a Pullman at a wayside station in Indiana. "A
lovable man—he made that speech just to enable fifty
country school children to say in after life that they had
heard the President."

What a luncheon hour, with Tod cross-questioning, Muriel laughing, Vernley dumb, Mr. Vernley corroborating
and Mrs. Vernley beseeching her guest to get something to
eat; and whenever a break in the conversation came, Mr.
Ribble restarted the flow of anecdote with a query or a

scholarly footnote. John would have wished that luncheon
hour to last for ever, but before they had risen from the
table Tod had slipped away and a few minutes later the
car was purring in the drive.

"Come along, sir," he called as they rose.

"Not yet, not yet, Tod," protested Mr. Vernley.

"Yes, now—if you go upstairs for a nap, there'll be no
golf this afternoon. Mrs. Graham is coming too."

"But Tod, I have no clubs," protested Mrs. Graham.

"I have—the car's waiting now. Are you coming, Mr.
Ribble?"

"No thank you, my boy—I am still ink-bound. Muriel
has promised me a nice cup of tea in the study at four
o'clock, and we have Mr. Crimp coming, I believe."

"That's why we're going."

"Tod, dear!" protested his mother. "How rude you
are!"

"I loathe the fellow!"

"And you have no reason, dear."

"Loathing," said Mrs. Graham, "is perhaps the safest
of all feelings, it relies more on instinct than intellect."

"And what are you children going to do?" asked Mr.
Vernley.

"*Children,* pater!" protested Bobbie.

"We are having a double on the lawn. Thomson says
it will be quite good playing to-day. He cut it this morning," said Muriel.

"Well, when we return, if you've any steam left in you,
Mrs. Graham and I will take on the winners."

"Good!" cried Bobbie. "Come on, Scissors, let's
change." In his room, Vernley found John a pair of
flannel trousers. There was nine inches to spare round the
waist, and a serious gap above the ankles.

"If I had known I was going to look ridiculous," said John "I shouldn't have played—" He pulled out the top of the trousers. " 'The expanse of spirit in a waist of shame,' that's what I look like."

"Don't be rude, Scissors—you know my figure fills you with envy. Jove, I do hate playing this game with women. Those kids have no idea how to use a racquet. They'll just stand and squeak every time they miss a ball by a yard, and you're expected to say 'Hard luck.' "

"Can Mrs. Graham play?"

"Yes, she can make Tod work. If Alice and Kitty were at home we'd get a good set. I say, Scissors, do you mind playing with Polly?"

"No—but why?"

"Because if I play with her and lose, as I shall, she'll be quite huffy, whereas if she plays against me and wins, she'll be quite nice to me," explained Vernley.

"But what about Muriel?"

"Oh—that doesn't matter. Nothing will dim you in Muriel's eyes." John bent over and tied his shoes.

"How do you mean?" he asked without looking up.

"Well, you're on a pedestal that six-love can't damage. You know you did talk brilliantly at lunch. I don't know how you do it."

"But I was listening to Mrs. Graham."

"And she to you—why, together you held the table, and old Ribble kept persuading you both to go on."

"I hope I didn't talk too—" began John.

"You old fraud, you were both soaring and you knew it. You like it, Scissors. I've seen you take the platform before."

"Rot!" commented John, a little angry at being discovered.

V

When the tea bell rang, four red-faced youngsters trooped in to find the Reverend Crimp mid-way in a monologue on the woes of the Dodenesian Islanders. On the appearance of the tennis party, he put down his cup very deliberately, rose from the comfortable depths of the divan, folded his puffy hands and beamed upon the young people.

"I think you know John," said Mrs. Vernley.

"Ah, yes," began Mr. Crimp in a minor key. "Of course I know John. I have a delightful memory of our last meeting. How d'ye do? I perceive you have grown. Fresh air, eh, and good food, I am sure. It is a true maxim, early to bed, early to rise—"

"Not much good food at Sedley, Mr. Crimp," said Bobbie. "We always go to bed hungry."

"I'm sure," commented Mr. Ribble from a corner seat, "your remarks are libellous; they are certainly belied by your figure."

"That's what I tell Bobbie," cried Muriel, "but he says the cause of stoutness is atmospheric, not gastronomic."

A few minutes later the drawing room door abruptly opened and Tod entered, followed by Mrs. Graham and Mr. Vernley.

"Any tea left, Mother?" he cried. "Mrs. Graham has led us all the way. Jove, she took the last hole in four!" Then, seeing the clergyman, "Good afternoon, Mr. Crimp." Mr. Vernley crossed the room and shook hands with him, while Tod was just about to draw up a chair for Mrs. Graham when Mr. Vernley said, "I do not think you have met Mrs. Graham, Mr. Crimp?"—and turning—"this is Mr. Crimp, our clergyman, Mrs. Graham."

Tod, still grasping the proffered chair, saw her hold out her hand to the clergyman, who moved his in response and then suddenly faltered, paused, and withdrew his hand. Mrs. Vernley, teapot in action, held it suspended. Mr. Ribble seemed intent on selecting a cake. John, Bobbie, Tod and Mr. Vernley were transfixed, waiting the blow. Surely the fellow would not be so insane, so incredibly rude, thought Mrs. Vernley. He would not dare!

Mr. Crimp was speaking in a hollow, affected voice.

"The lady's face is familiar to me—in circumstances I do not care to recall," he said stiffly.

The blow had fallen. It was followed with a painful silence. How would she take it? With suspended breath, John, his heart aching, watched her. Yes, she was superb, and dignity did not desert her. Her face was calm; there was no sign of surprise, not even embarrassment—perhaps this scene was not new to her. She looked at Mr. Crimp, the ugly little man puffed out in his asserted dignity.

"I'm sorry," she said, "to awaken your unpleasant memories. I will retire." She turned to go.

"Julie, dear," cried Mrs. Vernley, putting down the teapot and rising suddenly to intercept her, "you mustn't listen to—"

"You cad!" blazed Tod, turning on the clergyman, who had gone pale.

"Really, sir, after insulting my guest I must ask you to retire." Mr. Vernley's voice hardly restrained its anger.

"If there is any insult, it is I who have suffered," replied Mr. Crimp. "The dignity of my calling—"

"Damn your calling!" cried Tod.

"Sir!" flared Mr. Crimp.

"Tod, be quiet," pleaded Mrs. Vernley.

Mrs. Graham had now reached the door, Mrs. Vernley following, but John was there first and opened it.

"Leave me dear, please," said Mrs. Graham, turning,

and the other woman saw how it was with her and stopped.
Mrs. Graham passed out; John following, closed the door.
He had not meant to follow her but in his confusion he
had closed the door and shut himself out with her. Mrs.
Graham looked at him half blindly, he thought. He
dropped his hand from the handle, and followed her into
the hall.

"Mrs. Graham," he called, "I—I'm—" but his lip
trembled and the words choked him.

She paused at the foot of the stairs, then impulsively
caught his outstretched hand, and pressed it.

"You dear boy—I know, I know!" she cried, holding
his hand for a moment, and then swiftly she mounted the
stairs. John watched her go, the blood singing in his
ears. He heard her bedroom door close, and then silence.
He turned and looked at the drawing-room door. What
was happening in there? As if in answer, it opened and
the Rev. Crimp emerged, alone, closing it after him with
a bang. For a moment he paused in the hall, flushed, uncertain which way to turn, then, seizing his hat from the
hall stand, he hurried out. When the door banged and he
was gone, John started. His brow was damp with per-
spiration and he was trembling. Tod came out.

"Come in, Scissors, and finish your tea."

"No—no, thanks Tod, I don't want any."

"None of us do—the swine!" said Tod fiercely.

John followed him into the drawing-room.

"Has Mrs. Graham gone to her room, John?" asked
Mrs. Vernley. He nodded.

"I must go up to her—poor thing," she said. Muriel,
in distraction, had lifted the piano lid and struck a
chord.

"For God's sake! Don't play that now! Oh hell!"
cried Tod. Then seeing the reproach in his mother's eyes,

"I beg your pardon, Mother—but I could murder some one! Come on, boys—I'm going to the garage."

Bobbie and John followed with alacrity.

Mrs. Graham did not appear at dinner. She kept to her room, and there was a cloud over the party throughout the evening, despite Mr. Ribble's delicious sallies of humour, and a fascinating discussion in the library afterwards between him and Mr. Vernley on Proportional Representation, a discussion very tedious to Tod and Bobbie, who slipped away into the billiard room after vehement signals to John to follow, which he ignored. He absorbed every detail, eager for a political education, and very occasionally he ventured to ask a question, which Mr. Ribble answered fully and seriously as though John had been a grown-up person. Here was a new theme for the debating society! So he sat, listening until the clock struck eleven, and Mr. Vernley and Mr. Ribble lapsed into a silence filled with tobacco smoke, whereon John rose and said good night.

He found Bobbie perched on the edge of his bed, pulling off a sock.

"Good Lord!" was the greeting. "Have you been in the library all the time?"

"Yes—isn't Mr. Ribble a wonderful man?"

"They say so," assented Vernley, "but I always want to yawn when he and the pater get going. It is an awful business having to live in a house where M. P.s are always about. They talk for ever about things nobody would give a brass button for."

"But surely the method of government—" began John.

"My dear old Scissors—what does it matter how we are governed so long as we are left alone? Judging from those fellows who come down here, you'd think the universe

would cease to revolve if they went out of office, and when
they do go nobody would know, if it weren't for their own
newspapers which lament so over 'em. And it's all a
game. I've heard these fellows abuse one another, and
use the vilest terms, and, Lord bless us, they're playing
bridge or golf together the next day."

"But that reveals our sporting instinct."

"That's not yours, Scissors. It's the pater's, I recognise it—he always quotes that when he throws over what he
said the night before about a man." Then ploughing his
hands through his thick ruffled hair, "Lord, what a mess!"
he exclaimed.

"What, politics?"

"No—that filthy Crimp and Mrs. Graham."

John started; in his selfish interest he had forgotten the
incident.

"There's one blessing," said Vernley, slowly squeezing
out some tooth-paste onto his brush, "we shan't be worried
by that swine here any more. He always made me sick.
I wish I could generate a good hate like Tod's."

"Tod always did dislike him, didn't he?"

"Yes. Good night, Scissors."

"Good night."

John did not sleep for a long time. He lived over that
dreadful episode in the drawing-room. Was Mrs. Graham
sleeping now? Perhaps she was crying, and women hated
crying, for it made their eyes red, and betrayed them in
the morning. It would be awkward at breakfast to meet
her as though nothing had happened. Still he looked forward to doing so. They were friends, she trusted him—
that pressure on his hand told him so. Then he wondered
if Crimp was asleep down at the Vicarage. Probably the
beast was snoring now—he looked like a man who could
snore, with those horrible protruding teeth. Then he fell

asleep, and when he woke again Vernley was sitting on his chest.

"You've been snoring," said Vernley.

"I haven't," denied John indignantly. "I couldn't, I don't know how to."

"But I've heard you in my room—you woke me."

"That proves I haven't, I should have woked myself first," said John with a fine disregard of grammar. "I'm a lighter sleeper than you."

"You've been dreaming, I'm sure."

"Well, I have—of old Crimp," confessed John.

"That accounts for the snoring. Hurry up, the first gong's gone."

Downstairs, Muriel was the first to meet John.

"Mrs. Graham's going," she told him. "Isn't it a shame?"

"Going?—what, now?"

"No, soon after breakfast. She told Mother she couldn't stay. Of course she knows we're all sympathetic and all that, but she says she finds sympathy as hard to endure as the other things. There are always scenes like this wherever she goes, and she doesn't intend ever going out again. I'm dreadfully sorry for her."

"So am I, but Muriel, we mustn't show it; we must pretend nothing's happened. Let's joke with her at breakfast."

They went in together. Mrs. Graham was there, and she was not red-eyed. Indeed, to John, she seemed more beautiful than ever. She talked wittily to them all, and Muriel and John found their desperate resolution quite unnecessary. After breakfast they all walked round the grounds. Mrs. Graham was leaving in half an hour. To his delight John found himself walking with her down the rhododendron drive.

"I'm so sorry you're going, Mrs. Graham," he said.

"That's kind of you, Scissors—may I call you Scissors?" she asked, smiling at him.

"Oh, please!" he answered.

"And I hope," she added, "this will not be our last meeting. If ever you come up to town, and would care, you must call at my little flat. I will give you my address." She opened her chatelaine and extracted a card. John took it.

"I should love to, Mrs. Graham—when the next holidays come—will you be in town then?"

"Yes," and he noticed she hesitated before adding quickly, "but you must ask your guardian first."

John's heart stopped. The cruelty of it!

"I shall do nothing of the kind," he said hotly. "I— I think you're wonderful, Mrs. Graham," he added in boyish admiration, and he noticed she turned her head away. A moment later they had come out of the drive and joined the others.

BOOK III

GROWTH

CHAPTER I

I

THE chronicles of youth, filled with trivial incidents, but acute at the moment of experience, swiftly pass. John found himself, on his seventeenth birthday, hardly aware that he was leaving boyhood behind him. He was very different from the shy sensitive youngster who on that momentous day of his arrival at Sedley had stood miserably on the platform watching with an aching heart the receding train. He had altered, almost incredibly, and yet he had not altered. In the handsome, self-possessed lad, a leader of his house, something of a god to the younger boys, with already a distinguished 'career' behind him, as athlete and scholar, a President of the Literary Society, a leading light in debate, the Editor of the school magazine, Sedley indeed had a creditable specimen of its training.

Had Mr. Fletcher, who had watched over him with a father's care, been asked for his most reliable boy, it would have been John that he named, or for his most promising, again, John, despite the dazzling brilliance of the fitful Marsh; and yet Mr. Fletcher knew his weaknesses—the tendency to dream, the sudden sensitiveness that made John seem afraid of life, and occasionally, but rarely now, that strange oriental preoccupation, that came over him, and shut him out from his fellows. There was always something a little mysterious, thought Mr. Fletcher. He loved and knew well all his boys. Even Marsh's fanciful versatility held no secrets from him. But he never quite plumbed the bottom of John's nature. Affectionate, deeply so, revealed in a hundred small acts of tribute, Mrs. Fletcher had drawn out the fires of devotion in the boy's heart, even sometimes, to little whimsical confessions that she knew were signs of his absolute trust. He had talked of his mother often. It was in Mrs. Fletcher's drawing-room, where she had first seen father and son together, that they talked of the reunion, after a parting of three years' duration. She laughed away all John's fears of that meeting, soothed his feverish anticipation.

"Oh, Mrs. Fletcher, will father think I've grown?" he would ask.

"Why of course,—you're almost a man now."

"But do you think I have grown as he would wish?"— half fearfully this, at which Mrs. Fletcher would laugh, "Why you silly boy, are you afraid your father won't be glad to see you?"

"Oh,—it's not that—only you know Mrs. Fletcher—he thought so much of me when I was a kid—I'm almost afraid he might be disappointed."

"Fathers and mothers never change, John, it's the children who do that," she answered him. "And look at all you've done and—" she was going to add, what a handsome fellow you've grown into, but she checked herself. She didn't believe in turning a boy's head.

So the momentous day came. John, up very early, very scrupulously dressed, excited by a confirmatory telegram, was filled with anxiety as to whether the taxicab would be in time to meet the train. He slacked shamelessly in form that morning, but the master was indulgent. Something of his anxiety and excitement permeated his friends. Even Vernley became aware of the meaning of nerves, good old Vernley, fatter and more faithful than ever, sharer of all joys, woes, triumphs, disasters, and food.

But the great moment came; the train drew up, the doors flew open, a sudden flooding of the platform, a boy's flushed face under a straw hat, an eager survey, with heart tremendously thumping, and a strong resolution not to run or cry, a terrible fear that he had not come after all, and then—

There! His father! He had not changed!

"Dad!" he shouted rapturously, waving a hand. The father stared a while.

"John, my boy—what a great lad you are!" There was a swift, astonished survey. This tall, clean-limbed, laughing boy his son! This lad, with the glimmering grace of an athlete, the boy he had nursed at Amasia? His eyes lingered on every feature, noted the broadening shoulders, the straightness of his carriage, the direct level glance of the eyes. Presently they were seated side by side in the taxi, and then, absurdly enough, John found he had nothing to say, not one of those thousand premeditated questions to ask. The father, too, felt restrained, and waited.

"Ali sends his love," he said, at last.

"Dear old Ali! How is he, Dad?"

"Grown, but not like you, and quite a grave married man now."

"Married! What a joke—Ali married!"

"He does not think it a joke, he is very serious about it. He was married the week before I left. I met his father in Constantinople. Ali seemed a little sad because you did not write oftener. I showed him your last photograph. He looked at it for a long time and then said you were a great lord. I told him you were more probably a great anxiety."

Then followed lunch at Mr. Fletcher's— just his father

and Mr. and Mrs. Fletcher, and, by the way of a great favour to John in celebration of the event—Vernley and Marsh as special guests. John was frightfully anxious about his friends He wanted them to admire his father as he did, and in turn he hoped desperately that his father would take to Vernley and Marsh. He was not long in doubt, for the elderly man had soon won his way into the boys' hearts, and had broken down their stiff reserve.

"Isn't he ripping, Scissors!" whispered Vernley, during the second course, "and you're alike as two peas." Under encouragement, Marsh was radiant. John felt his father was such a success that he would ask Lindon to the great tea in his study. A little in awe of the hypercritical god, he had held Lindon in reserve, but Marsh had been conquered and that young gentleman was critical and seldom approved of parents. "An outworn institution," he always declared as he observed them on Prize Day.

Marsh, however, rose to great heights of enthusiasm and made the tea party an unqualified success. It was true there were not enough buns, owing to the repetition of some guests before the plate reached others, and the kettle fell off the fire and soaked the muffins. These were incidents. The great event was Mr. Dean's stories of Asia Minor. And it was Marsh who kept him going, Marsh with an incredible knowledge of strange Eastern ways, and an insight and intelligent curiosity that amazed John's father. When the bell went and they all trooped away, John knew it had been a triumphant day.

Mr. Dean left the next morning. He had business to attend to before his holidays, but he crowned his success with his last act. He asked Vernley, Marsh and Lindon to join him and John for the first fortnight of the summer holidays. He had taken a house at Grasmere for a month, after which he and John were making visits to his friends. With this promise of a happy reunion, Mr. Dean left them.

That holiday became a great memory to John. They had a small house that nestled on the side of Fairfield, with wonderful views from all its windows of Grasmere and the lovely little lake, the road to sylvan Rydal, the fern covered side of Red Bank. These were days when they all set out, knapsack on backs, with stout boots, shorts and sweaters, to climb the mountains. And what talk was theirs! There was Marsh with his inimitable irony; where did he gather all that he knew? Mr. Dean said that he must be a reincarnation.

"No, please!" retorted Marsh. "Have you noticed how all the cranks who profess to be reincarnations always claim something regal or aristocratic or famous, for their previous existence? Mr. Smith will tell you he was Marc Antony, while little Miss Titmouse, who lives on nuts and uncooked food, and believes bad thoughts make bad weather, will assure you she was mother to Marcus Aurelius, which in some way explains that fellow's incessant moralising. Now if I have to be a reincarnation, let me be original. I don't want to be an echo of Demosthenes, or a second edition of Hannibal, or Henry the Eighth— I'm much more likely to have been dustman to Ptolemy the First, providing there were dustmen in that era."

In the evening, after dinner, when tired in every limb with a long jaunt across the mountains, with that pleasant ache that follows exercise, they would sit in the lamplight listening to a reading from the poets; or a passage descriptive of the ground they would explore on the morrow. Perhaps, after many requests, Lindon would sit at the piano and play a ballade or a sonata, while they looked out across the gathering gloom at a solitary light on the opposite side of the valley; and they would notice how bright and lonely were the stars hanging over the mountain heights. As John sat there in the dimly lit room with his friends and his father, listening intently, a deep melancholy stole into his heart. This might never happen again, this strange jolly time, and there was his future in the world and all life so strange before him. But the sadness of these reflections brought him a glow of pleasure. He felt so acutely conscious of everything, he seemed so capable in this fresh experience of Life to accomplish anything he wanted. So he let himself dream pleasantly, which Vernley would notice and suddenly exclaim, "Scissors has gone East again!" for it was that old far-away expression which had so often come into John's face, but was rarer now.

So with crowded hours the end of the holiday came. Invitations to spend a week at Vernley's and at Marsh's were accepted, the rest of the holiday was to be spent by John and his father together. They travelled down with Vernley from Windermere to his home, and here Mr. Dean once more entered that large world of men and affairs with which he had lost touch. His holiday in England was not unconnected with a proposal that might result in his permanent return a few years hence, for which he was striving. It was essential that John should be kept in England and have a large field of opportunity at his disposal. He had made arrangements with Mr. Fletcher for John to enter at King's College when his time ended at Sedley, as it would, next year. It would be time enough then to decide upon John's career, if the boy had not revealed any preference.

He liked the Vernleys and was glad to find John had chosen his friends so well. He had hoped to take his son on a visit to some of his own friends, but it was obvious that John had chosen his friends with a regard for their quality of character. There was something very open and faithful about young Vernley and this was reflected by the whole household. However much Mr. Vernley might try to deceive himself, and believe and attempt to impress the belief that he was a man of affairs, Dean soon detected that he was naturally lazy and extremely good-hearted, with a passion for horses, a glass of port after dinner and a good cigar.

As for Muriel, that little fairy danced her way into the father's heart as she had into the son's. John had been very guarded in his remarks about Muriel, so guarded, that his father guessed all immediately. Muriel herself soon decided that Mr. Dean should have been Mr. Ribble's brother. There was the same genial, somewhat "curly-crinkly" appearance, as she called it, and as she confessed to him one evening when he had begged a kiss in return for a box of chocolates, she was glad he was not as serious as John, "who looks at me like a collie dog and wags his tail when I smile." Mr. Dean laughed heartily at this, it was so truly descriptive of John, who followed her in silence and devotion. When Mr. Dean left, he took Muriel on one side.

"I wonder if I can ask you a favour?—it's for John's sake," he added, as she looked up at him. "You see he has no brothers, and no sisters, which is even more important for a boy, and living somewhat lonely, I'm afraid he may become self-centred, which means being selfish, so I want you to be his official sister. He'll talk to you. I think he'll even tell you his dreams and ambitions, things he would never tell to other boys because he feels he is just a little different from them. I think he is, for instance, too highly sensitive. I want him to grow out of that; and only sharing confidences will help him. So I'm asking you, Muriel, to make a brother of him, if you will?"

Muriel had never quite looked at it in this light; then she had a swift intuition that Mr. Dean was not in the dark. A sister—that meant service in return. It meant something more than having John as a courtier—it meant, yes, running after him a little bit if necessary, and—oh clever Mr. Dean!—sharing him with other friends. She promised readily. She was going to be a sister to John.

Another week and they had left the Vernleys and were at the Marsh's. John's father had been doubtful regarding young Marsh for a day or two. There was no question of the boy's brilliance, but he distrusted precocious persons, and Marsh's omniscient cynicism was not healthy in a boy of seventeen. He attached too much importance to the smartness of a thing. All his opinions were original and brilliant, but they were dominated by those ends rather than by a love of truth. It was not good that John should see the ridiculous, bizarre or cynical aspect of life before he had tasted its wholesomeness; and there was that in Marsh's character, so restless, so desirous of things because they were new rather than good or genuine, which made his judgments unbalanced for all their refreshing enthusiasm.

But fuller knowledge of the boy modified these reservations. His was a razor-edge intellect, and highly combative. John, inclined to be sensitive, introspective, was shaken up and drawn out of himself by Marsh, who challenged all his ideas and made him defend them with passion. Moreover, Marsh had, for a mere youth, an amazing range, not of experience, but of thought. The literature of Greece, Rome, Germany, France and England were not strange to him. He read rapidly and talked volubly;

true, his ideas were ill-digested, but he *had* ideas, and they flowed in his conversation. His curiosity was tireless as his enthusiasm. On their Lakeland holiday Mr. Dean had been amazed by his turbulent spirits, his readiness to rhapsodise, argue, and run, swim, box, climb, read and eat at any time of the day and night. He had no temper in the meaning of the word. His equanimity was never shaken.

"You know, sir," he said one day, "old Scissors thinks I'm the Voltaire of the party, but when he likes to wake up he can make us all take a back seat. Sometimes his quiet efficiency annoys me. He is always so infernally correct. Something-like always does for me, whether it's a quotation or a figure, but Scissors always has the exact thing and knocks you down with it, and the queer thing is, that he's got imagination—and they don't often go together; you don't get the Scottish lawyer working with the Welsh preacher."

Mr. Dean was amazed at this bit of schoolboy psychology, but it raised Marsh in his estimation, and from that time he saw there was something more than scintillating wit in Marsh's observation. With this view of the boy, all his preconceptions of his parents were shattered on meeting them. How came this bird of such bright plumage in so sombre a nest?

Teddy Marsh met them at Loughboro Station, in exuberant spirits as usual. "Good morning, sir," he cried, waving his straw hat as soon as he sighted the guests on the platform. "Hello, Scissors, you rusty old blade! Come along, sir, our wigwam on wheels awaits you. The pony's in a vile temper this morning, and will probably insist on going in the opposite direction. Yes, they're all well, thanks. Mother's got a new creed—let's see, what was it when you were here last, Scissors, a Nutfooder or a

Christadelphian, or was it Rawsonism?—well now she's a Sunrayer. You'll hear all about it; they're a sect she's linked up with in middle America; they lie in the sunshine all day, think violet thoughts, and achieve salvation by sunburn. The governor's horrified and threatens excommunication. All aboard?—won't that bag topple over? Hold on, I'm going to tickle Flossie's flanks."

He whirled the whip and with a running fire of questions, answers and comments, they rolled along the leafy lanes towards the vicarage.

II

As before, that visit was composed of long sunny days in the garden, endless tennis sets, or cricket parties at the Hall, and always in the evening, after dinner, there was Mrs. Marsh's wonderful playing in the drawing-room. Tea-time was the favourite hour with John. He always felt glad when he saw the maid, changed from her pink and white dress for the morning into official black and white, with lace cap, bearing the folding table which she set under the walnut tree. Then hammock chairs appeared; after that a white tea cloth, and the rattle of china and the glint of the silver sugar basin—how he knew the design!—two folding lids, with soft white sugar like flour inside—jampot and teaspoons and cake knives. Then—after what seemed a long time—the glad tinkle of the tea-bell, with Mrs. Marsh crossing to the table, her first appearance for the afternoon. Mr. Marsh would follow a few minutes late, and sometimes Teddie would rouse him in the study, where he dozed after lunch when the weather was hot. Generally there were a couple of guests to make a tennis four, either the solicitor's daughter, or the governess from the Hall, who played the best tennis of any lady in the county and was always in danger of losing her situation because visitors at the Hall would always mistake her for the mistress.

It was a merry tea-time. Mr. Marsh was not always quite awake, and he had, at this function, quite a gift for Spoonerisms.

"Pass me the plake, kease," he would say.

"Dertainly, sad," would respond Teddie.

After tea, John's father and Mr. Marsh usually disappeared. On two occasions they were challenged to a tennis double and to the amazement of exuberant youth, won. But generally they disappeared at the end of the garden.

"They've gone to talk roses again," commented Mrs. Marsh.

"The governor's mouth's watering with the names Mr. Dean's given him—he'll go about talking Turkish to the gardener for the next two months," said Teddie.

Dressing for dinner, too, was like a prelude to the delight of the meal and the music to follow. John's dress shirt and jacket and trousers lay neatly spread out on the bed.

There was, at six-thirty prompt, the copper jug, filled with hot water, with its initialled felt cover; and the country bathroom! John always wanted to sing in his. There was the low music of the running water, the lucid green shimmer, reflected on the porcelain sides, sending waves of rippling light over the ceiling.

Then, with gleaming shirt front and glossy hair, an immaculate boy would descend to the drawing room and wait with the others for the dinner gong. John soon grew to love those country sounds just before dinner; through the windows glowed long stretches of wooded country; often a thrush marked even song, and there was

the retiring twitter of the birds. A cow driven byre-
wards lowed in the valley, and the cawing of rooks in the
Hall drive came on eddyings of the evening breeze.

At lamplight in the drawing-room, after coffee, Teddie
would raise the dark reflective lid of the grand.

"Now, Mother, come and break the Bechstein," he said;
almost a formula, that sentence, to John. And Mrs.
Marsh would rise and seat herself at the keyboard, carefully adjusting the height of the seat, moving back the
music-rack slide, playing a preparatory major scale, that
descended in the minor, before proceeding to the real business.

Then, a momentary silence, the death of talk, and the
first notes trembling into harmony. Never would John
forget that first night on which, squatting on the floor at
his father's feet, he heard Mrs. Marsh play Schumann's
Papillons. It opened a new world to him; he seemed to
be looking down a long grove of trees into a glade filled
with moonlight, where an intruding wind, lost and hesitating, ran from bough to bough awakening whispers. That
hesitating prelude, the slow, then quickening announcement of the theme, and the glad, butterfly-flutter of the
melody, dying away again into melancholy and silence.

Somehow, as John sat there, with his father so near, it
brought back others nights, nights on that verandah overlooking the silver Yeshil Irmak, as it flowed singing along
the dark gorge, with the high moon peering over the cliffs
of Amasia; and a great longing filled him to be back there
again just once, to sit in that hot, spiced dusk, to hear the
tinkle of the camel bells from the highway, and perhaps
the soft voice of Ali, dear old Ali, dignified and melancholy, sitting cross-legged, and reading every mysterious
sound of that Eastern night.

"There, that's enough for me," cried Mrs. Marsh, break-

ing across John's reverie. "Come along, John, you've got
to sing."

"John, sing?" cried Mr. Dean. "I never knew he could
sing."

"I can't, Dad, it's Mrs. Marsh's idea!"

"But he can! Come along, John," and she struck the
opening chords of "Drink to me only." "Why, Mr. Dean,
your lazy son used to sit here, watching me work night
after night, and it was only by accident I found he had
a voice—I heard him singing in the bathroom one morning."

"Mother's heard me in the bathroom," said Teddie, "but
that's why she doesn't ask me."

"No shirking, John," called Mrs. Marsh, replaying the
opening bars, and obediently John stood up and sang in a
light baritone voice. When he had finished there was applause. There was feeling in John's voice; the spirit
breaking through the flesh.

"You should hear him sing, 'Who is Sylvia?' Mr. Fletcher makes him sing it," said Teddie.

"But Mrs. Marsh has no music," answered John finding
a loophole for escape.

"You fraud—you know you can play it."

Mrs. Marsh jumped up. "I believe he can do lots of
things—and he sits selfishly here listening to us all blundering."

John sat down, placed his hands on the keyboard, and
began softly, being very nervous, chiefly because his father
was listening.

> *"Who is Sylvia, what is she?*
> *That all her swains commend her.*
> *Holy, fair and wise is she;*

> *The heavens grace did lend her,*
> *That adored she might be."*

"And now that's finished," said Teddie, "let's have
Sedley Field Song."

"You asked me to sing 'Who is Sylvia,'" retorted John.

"I know, but ours is better."

"All right then, here you are,"—and once more John's
hands pressed down the black and white keys while his
voice went soaring into "Field Song."

> *"Summer days, winter days, when a fellow's young*
> *And friends are many and pains are few,*
> *When the ball going over filled every fellow's lung*
> *With cheers for—"*

Yes, those were beautiful nights in the lamp-lit vicarage
drawing-room. Their memories sank deep into the heart
of a happy impressionable boy. But one more impression.
Enter, on Thursday night, two days before the termination of their visit, Veronica, aged seventeen and all the
Spring sweetness thereof. It was thoughtful of Mrs.
Marsh to ask a lonely girl from a neighbouring manor
house, but she could not have seen the effect on John.
He first saw her in the hall. He had just come down
the stairs, immaculate and well-groomed, with shining hair
and the rose-red of health in his face. He heard a mingling of voices—Mrs. Marsh's and another—that other!
His heart stopped. It was like the trill of a bird. Then
he saw a flimsy cloak fall away, revealing a thin, elfin
girl, with gleaming shoulders and a dress swan-like in the
dim hall light. She turned and he could see her face—
an oval, petite face with a little whimsical mouth which
might be just going to laugh or cry, and the small head

tumbling with curls, short and bobbed, and shaking as she turned. It was a vision and the youth on the stairs paused—would she vanish into the darkness of the doorway again, or—

"Here's John," said Mrs. Marsh coming forward. "Veronica, this is John Dean, Teddie's friend."

"How d' you do," she said to John, and half held out her hand, but John, embarrassed, withheld his, and then bowed stiffly. Mrs. Marsh noticed his gaucherie, and guessed the cause.

"You're to take Veronica into dinner," she said, leading the way to the drawing-room. He should have said something polite in response, but he walked like a stick at the side of the girl, tongue-tied, and furious at his own stupidity. He had never known his self-possession to desert him in this manner. Even Muriel had not left him speechless. Here, he began a comparison with Muriel, and felt a twinge of disloyalty. Of course he was not disloyal—and disloyal to what? But the thought perturbed, with the result that Miss Veronica Chase, used to adoration, found the good-looking youth at her side very dull, despite his romantic appearance. The entrance of Teddie with "Hello, Veronica old thing!" relieved the tension, and by the time they were seated at dinner, John had found his tongue. He had asked her if she lived thereabouts, when followed a minute description of their old manor house, with one of the thousands of beds which that poor restless queen, Elizabeth, was reported to have slept on.

"Why don't you and Teddie came over to-morrow for tea? It's only two miles from here."

"I should like to very much," said John. What an enchanting little hand she had; he watched the thin fingers as they played with a fork. When she turned to speak to

Teddie, he took the opportunity to study her profile, fascinated by the beautiful curve of her neck, the little pink ear, half clouded in a curl, the mouth—with its pensive corners. This is perfection, thought John.

> *"Ah, Boy, it is a dream for life too high,*
> *It is a bird that hath no feet for earth:*
> *Strange wings, strange eyes, go seek another sky,*
> *And find thy fellows of an equal birth."*

—He recalled Richard le Gallienne's lines. And the real John disappeared that night—he was a creature of monosyllables, and Marsh had no flint on which to strike the sparks of his wit. He realised that John had been swamped in the flood of Beauty, and gallantly came to the rescue. True, John emerged somewhat in the drawing-room, and to-night, he sang readily and well, his effort being repaid by Veronica's "you sing beautifully—I could listen all night," although she jarred somewhat slightly by adding, "Do you know any comic songs?" Though he abhorred them, John would gayly have responded, and made a note to add a comic song to his repertoire.

The end of the evening came all too soon; the car waited outside to bear her away. The two boys lingered round it while the chauffeur tucked the rugs about his young mistress. Then she went with a farewell wave of the hand and a musical "Good night," which John, standing there in the porch, heard drift up to the star-light.

"Are you going to stand there forever, O stricken heart?" asked Marsh. "I want to fasten this door—and bar Love out."

John went in. Upstairs, in their room, he was silent.

"Scissors, you poor impressionable young calf, I hope you're not going to pine away in the night."

"Oh shut up!"

"That is not a gift of mine, as you know. Scissors, old thing, you're racing your phagocytes, as Metchnikoff would say, since all love is stimulation. She isn't worth it. I know old Veronica. She's a heart-cracker. She counts her conquests by the hundred."

"I don't think it's very decent of you to—" began John, a little peevish. Marsh's flippancy irritated him.

"To abuse our guest? No, it's not, Scissors, but I don't want to see you going about with sticking plaster on your heart. Old Veronica and I understand each other perfectly. She cracked me once, and then laughed. That kid hasn't the brains of a beetle; she's merely an agitator of pink youth. Flirt with her, yes, and she'll give you a good time, for she's got a sporting instinct—but don't take her seriously—she doesn't know what it means. Did you hear her ask you for a comic song?—and you did sing well to-night, Scissors—the nightingale to his mate."

Marsh touched the tender spot. That comic song request rankled.

"You didn't talk much with her?" asked Marsh.

"No."

"Well—do so to-morrow. Ask her what she reads, what she likes, the pictures she prefers. She's got a mind like an illustrated Sunday paper—you've had the comic supplement to-night."

John groaned. Marsh's. arrows always hit.

"I think you're beastly about her," he said desperately.

"No, I'm not. Veronica and I are great pals, but she doesn't come deer-stalking on this estate. You're a sweet kid, Scissors, and I'm not going to let you cry yourself to sleep for a butterfly with the brains of a bat!"

"Oh rot—you do rag, Teddie."

"Well, well, dear infant, just investigate to-morrow."

Why did Marsh delight in pricking balloons? He was right: horribly right, thought John, as they drove away from the manor house next evening. That afternoon had been one long disillusionment. She was just as beautiful, just as attractive, and John feasted his eyes and heart on her. But she made a mistake when she took him down to pick gooseberries, in the far end of the garden, away from the others.

"Give me your hand," she cried, and he helped her up the bank. He tried to master an impulse to squeeze it, and just failing, was going to, when she anticipated him. That sent the first cool little wind around his heart. She laughed frankly into his eyes. She was irresistibly beautiful, "and she knows it," thought John.

"Shut your eyes, Scissors, and open your mouth."

He obeyed. A cool thin hand held his chin, the fingers of another pushed a berry in his mouth.

"Swallow!"

He swallowed obediently.

"Open!" she commanded.

He opened his eyes, her face was very near to his, her bewitching red mouth smiled at him, and he saw two little devils of mischief dancing in blue eyes that looked straight into his.

John looked back into them. There was a pause.

"You're shy," she said reproachfully.

"I know," he answered. Her hand slid off his shoulder.

"I wonder who's winning the game," she said, moving towards a bush. "Perhaps we ought to go back."

"But I want to talk to you," said John.

"Do you?—you are a strange boy," Veronica said.

"I'm not a boy—at least, no more than you are a girl," he retorted somewhat resentfully.

Another silence. They came to a summer house with

a table in it, on which a book was turned down. John picked it up. It was by a popular woman novelist whose sex sentimentality swamped the bookstalls.

"Do you read Amelia Serkle?" she asked. "I love them."

"No—I've never read her books—are you fond of reading?"

"Awfully."

"What do you like? Have you read Conrad?"

"No."

"Wells—or Bennett?" he added.

"Yes—one of Bennett's—I didn't like it. I like Amelia Serkle and Helena Thinne best."

"Oh," said John. She was fast losing marks.

"And poetry, I adore poetry!" she said ecstatically.

"So do I," said John, warming. "Isn't Masefield splendid, and Thompson and Swinburne—"

"I haven't read any of those, I think. I like Laurence Hope, and oh, I love Ella Wheeler Wilcox! Do you know her 'Poems of Passion?'"

"I looked at them—once," said John. There was no hope left in his voice. He did not disguise the fact very successfully.

"We'd better go back," she said.

They joined the others, who had finished their set. It was late and Marsh suggested going.

"Good-bye," he said, at the end of the drive, down which Veronica accompanied them. Even then John marvelled at her beauty, enhanced by the setting of those elms and the old manor house.

"Good-bye," she said, offering John her hand.

"Good-bye," he responded. And as he said the word it was obvious that they had lost all interest in each other. It really was "Good-bye," and neither minded.

Half a mile from the house, walked in comparative silence, Marsh burst into laughter.

"What's the joke?" asked John.

"I can't help laughing at that poor kid—she's so crude."

"Who—Veronica—why?"

"I'm wondering how many romances she's killed in the gooseberry bushes."

John glanced angrily at Marsh, and then the humour of it caught him and he laughed also.

"How did you guess?" he asked.

"Because I've shut my eyes and opened my mouth," said Marsh. "Poor old Veronica. She is a flirt! If only she had brains—just a few. And there are a lot like her. Now, I'll tell you of a girl that's my type, jolly sensible too. I want to see more of her next Prize Day."

"Who?" asked John interested.

"Vernley's sister," replied Marsh.

"Oh—yes," said John, knocking down a nettle with a swish of his tennis racquet.

Then came the end. The train drew away from Loughboro Station. John's father leaned back in his seat while John hung out of the window, waving to Teddie and Mr. and Mrs. Marsh on the platform, until the arch of the bridge shut them from sight. John sank back into his seat.

"Aren't they jolly, Dad!" he cried.

"Splendid, old son,—you make good friends."

III

There was one unsuccessful event in their holidays, that was the visit to John's uncle. Mr. Dean went, John thought, from a spirit of duty rather than pleasure. John had only seen his uncle once, when he had

come to the school on Prize Day and had treated John as
a child of five and adopted an air of patronage towards his
father, which the boy deeply resented. They had not responded to each other in a single detail. "Just like his
father," said Sir Henry to his wife, the next day, "as im-
practical as Charles and as wayward. The boy wants
strong handling. I told his house-master so." He had
departed without asking John home for the holidays, greatly
to John's relief, for he would have gone in a spirit of
martyrdom. John felt he was resented because he was his
father's son. It must be galling to the uncle with no sons
and two daughters, to know, unless he was more fortunate,
that his nephew would inherit the title. It was the one
unsuccessful fact in Sir Henry's life. He could and did
ignore his brother, but hang it, he could not ignore his
brother's son. He never read without anger in the Bar-
onetage, "Heir-presumptive, Charles Dean q. v." and q. v.
led him to John Narcissus Dean. Narcissus! What a
preposterous name to give a boy—to an heir!

Their visit did not improve the mutual opinion.
Charles Dean resented his brother's air of patronage, his
smug self-satisfaction, his ill-disguised vanity over his es-
tates which somehow he seemed to attribute to his own
ability. Four tedious days, in which every minute held the
possibility of friction, brought the visit to an end. John's
father did not say much afterwards, but John realised all
he thought. Once only did he reveal in words what John
surmised.

"I hope you will never have cause to ask help from any
relations—stand on your own feet, John," he said.

John accompanied his father down to Southampton. It
seemed almost impossible that this was the end, that he
would not see him again for two years. How far away
was Amasia—and now that they were together, so closely

together, it seemed as if they had never been apart.

"Two more years, John—and I shall have a directorship here—it won't be long, old son—you're seventeen and time flies at that age."

They stood at the top of the gangway. A gong was sounding, and an officer came down the deck. "Visitors ashore, please!" he shouted.

Father and son grasped hands. It was a long tight grip, with John trying to look squarely into his father's eyes, summoning a stiff lip to his aid, the father simply saying,

"Good-bye, dear lad."

"Good-bye, Father."

A loosening of the grip, a turn, and his feet were blundering down the steep, trellised gangway. He halted on the quay, while the ship was being warped out. They were too far apart for words, his father high up above him, leaning over the deck rail. Now the boat was away, the last rope drawn aboard; the stern propellers thrashed the waters into a white foam, the gulls cried, wheeled and followed. John pulled out his handkerchief and waved it, though he felt soon he might have to put it to another use. There was a responding flutter, and then distance grew between them, distance across which John's heart was stretching until it well nigh broke; a grey spot on the horizon, and it was all over.

He walked along the quay, the rain began to drizzle down. It turned cold and he shivered as he walked back to the station.

England seemed a lonely place to live in.

CHAPTER II

I

A BUSY year, a year filled with little successes, trials and triumphs, and John, taller and a little quieter, perhaps too quiet for a healthy lad of eighteen. He had achieved his object by winning the Mansell Exhibition, not of great value, it was true, but £50 would help and the real value of success lay in the fact that his father would know he had worked since they had parted. In June, Vernley and he had gone to Cambridge for the King's College entrance examination. It had not troubled either of them greatly, although Vernley, with an unshaken belief in his own stupidity, swore he had been ploughed. Their glimpse of Cambridge filled them with dreams of a golden age. They stayed on for a couple of days after the examination and made visits and excursions. Vernley's cousin was at Trinity and had a large bare room, reached by a winding staircase that looked on to the Backs, with a vista of bridges and elm-tree walks.

The day after their return to Sedley, Mr. Fletcher sent for John. It was late in the evening when young Jones came to his study with the summons, and John was just finishing a game of chess with Marsh. Vernley sat in the window trying to read "Henry Esmond" in the sunset light. The Triumvirate, as they were called, had recently moved into this large room in the corner of the quadrangle. It was regarded as the lap of luxury by the small boys who saw

157

with envious eyes its easy chairs, the cretonne curtains and the piano which Marsh had imported.

"Shan't be long," said John going out. What could Fletcher want him for? Perhaps a house matter—he was a prefect now. He tapped at the green baize door, pushed it open, then crossed the small hall of the Fletcher household, and knocked again at the study door. Mr. Fletcher bade him enter.

"Oh—Dean, I want to see you—come in—sit down. It's about a matter—a—" he hesitated. Why did the man fumble so, and fidget with the blotter on his desk? The room was almost dark, he could hardly see the master's face. Suddenly Mr. Fletcher got up and walked across the room to the fireplace where he stood for a moment with his back to John. Then abruptly he turned.

"Dean—I hardly know what to say—how to tell you— I'm—I'm—you must be brave, my dear lad, but I know you will be—you will be," he repeated. John just stared at him. What had happened—and was he to blame in any way?

"What's the matter, sir?" he asked.

Fletcher drew near and put his hand on John's shoulder.

"I have sad news, John. Your father—"

John started to his feet; why had Mr. Fletcher's hand trembled so?

"There's nothing wrong, sir?" he asked, his heart sinking within him, for he knew now something was wrong.

"No, not wrong, Dean—but everything that could be brave, and like him. My poor boy, your father is dead— there—there, it is terrible for you, I know." Mr. Fletcher pressed him down on to his seat again.

"Dead!" said John,—"not—not dead, sir?" he pleaded, raising his hand as if to ward off a blow.

"This letter has just come, Dean, by express post."

John took it, and the master crossed the room to the electric switch.

"I'd rather it was dark, sir,—I think I can see it," said John.

"Certainly," replied Mr. Fletcher, and with an aching heart he watched the boy go to the window and peer over the letter. It seemed an eternity before John turned and spoke.

"There—there seems no hope, sir—the company has none," he said in an expressionless voice.

"No, Dean, I fear not—it is terrible."

"Yes," echoed John.

Why did the boy stand there so silent, so emotionless, with the letter in his hand? Anything was better than this unnatural calm. Did he realise yet?

"Dad—died fighting," said John, jerkily.

"Yes—to the last, they say. He defended them magnificently—you have that to remember. These massacres are terrible, terrible—I—" he paused. Still John stood there. Mr. Fletcher had expected an outburst, had prepared himself for it; and here they stood in the dark facing each other, silent; nothing but the ticking of the clock sounding in the abyss of these tense moments. The entrance of Mrs. Fletcher was welcome. She moved to John's side, saying nothing, but he felt her sympathy.

Then, folding up the letter, "Thank you, sir. I will go now," he said.

"Yes, Dean—if you would like to stay here—we can—"

"Thank you, sir, but I'll go—I'm—I'm all right, sir," he replied, moving towards the door. Mrs. Fletcher saw his drawn face. He was so pitifully brave. He had reached the door now, was turning the handle. He hesitated a moment, they saw him pause and turn, then swiftly he moved towards them, flung himself face down on the couch, buried his face in the cushions, and sobbed like a child.

Mrs. Fletcher sat down beside him, and motioned to her husband to go. He went out silently, leaving them in the dark room.

"Oh, Mrs. Fletcher—my dear Dad! My dear Dad!"

Mrs. Fletcher put her hand on the bowed head and stroked his hair. There was nothing to say; she sat there, simply, her sympathy tending him, until the storm passed.

II

John never forgot the details of those three days that followed. First there was the anxiety of his father's fate. That he was dead he knew beyond hope, but there was a lack of details, of the manner and the circumstances. The letter from Messrs. Agnew & Cust merely quoted the cable they had received stating the death of his father at Amasia defending some Armenians who had taken refuge in his house during a massacre. That was all, and three days elapsed before they wrote again, enclosing another cable which said that his father had been shot through the head, had died instantaneously, while fighting his way out, with his servants, to effect a juncture with a relief detachment from the American hospital at Marsovan, where his body had been conveyed and buried. John wondered whether his father lay in that cemetery where, on a memorable day he had seen him crying over the grave of his mother.

During those days of waiting, John realised, more deeply then before, the meaning of friendship. Vernley and Marsh were always with him. They said little, for what could they say? They knew that John had rather they did not touch upon the knowledge so heavy on their hearts, and sometimes their watchfulness, their eagerness to serve him brought him to a point of open breakdown. For his own sake John went on with his form work. It was a slight distraction from the anxiety of the days that must pass before a letter could come from Asia Minor. One night, about a week after the receipt of the news, Vernley and Marsh sat in their study doing their preparation. John had been sent for by Mr. Fletcher, and had been absent some time. Vernley looked at his watch.

"Shall I get supper?" he asked—"Are you finishing?"

"Yes," replied Marsh, closing his Euripides. "I say, what a miserable devil old Euripides was; he's always talking about death. A good job some of his plays were burnt at Alexandria—there were ninety of 'em. I hate thinking about death."

"And just now—with poor old Scissors," added Vernley.

"By the way, Bobbie," said Marsh, flinging one leg over the arm of his chair, "what's Scissors going to do? I don't like asking him."

"Do—how do you mean?"

"His future—you see there's the money question. I don't know much about his affairs—but Cambridge means money—and I don't know whether his governor had any —he seemed too jolly for money-making."

"Oh, he'll have left some—and there's the Exhibition," said Vernley. Money matters were always easily dismissed in his presence. "He'll be all right, I expect."

"Well—we've got to see."

"But it's no business of ours."

"It is," retorted Marsh.

"It is?" asked Vernley.

"Yes—supposing there is no money?"

Vernley had never supposed such a thing. He was silent a moment, thinking.

"You mean—he must go to Cambridge with us?"

"Of course—and that's three hundred a year."

"Three hundred?" said Vernley. He had never realised that so much was being spent on him. Then quietly,
"Well—if old Scissors is stuck, we'll find it somehow."

"That's what I'm driving at. Three years at three
hundred a year is nine hundred pounds—and that's college expenses only. It'll mean a thousand all told."

"That's nothing—my guvnor'll never miss it. He'd do
anything for Scissors," said Vernley, cutting the cheese.
"He'd adopt him and depose me to-morrow."

"And there's my governor—he'd want to come in," said
Marsh.

"Well, there you are, that's settled!" Vernley took a
large slice of cucumber. He disposed of money problems
just as easily.

"But it's not settled, my child. You've forgotten the
chief person in the settlement—there's Scissors."

"Well?"

"You can take a mule to the water, but you can't make
him drink—suppose he wouldn't be helped?"

"Oh—he would!—he'd be quite decent about it—he'd
know it would please us. But I don't think we need worry.
He's sure to have some money and there's his relations."

"From all I've heard of his relations—we've a better
chance," commented Marsh. "I suppose you guessed why
Scissors refused the captaincy of the beagles last winter?"

"He wanted to work for his Exhibition."

"It wasn't that—really—he couldn't afford it."

"How do you know?"

"I heard him making discreet enquiries as to how much
it would cost—and old Scissors wanted it awfully."

"I never knew that—I wouldn't have been captain had
I known,"

"That's why I didn't tell you," Marsh explained, "but it shows you that Scissors gets pressed. If he only—"

"Ssh," whispered Vernley as the door handle rattled. John entered. He looked worried and carried a letter.

"News?" asked Marsh eagerly.

"No—only a letter from the firm—about a job," said John.

"A job?" queried Vernley.

"Yes—they've offered me a junior clerkship at £80 a year in case I need it." He did not add that the wording had cut him to the quick with its "in excess of the customary figure at which our junior clerks begin, but in view of probable necessitous circumstances," etc.

"But you're going up to Cambridge with us!" cried Marsh.

"Of course, or we don't go," added Vernley.

"I don't know," said John, sitting down wearily. "It depends,—I may not be able. I don't know yet how I'm—"

"If it's a matter of—" began Marsh, when a warning look from Vernley cut him short.

"You're sure to hear soon, Scissors—I shouldn't worry yet," said Vernley. "We're all going up together, we've always said so. You know if you only think hard enough it always is so."

"Sounds like the mater and the Higher Thought circle," commented Marsh, wondering what plan Vernley had suddenly conceived when he sent that warning signal.

"Well—anyhow, I could eat something," said John, putting the letter in his pocket.

"Righto!—draw up!" said Vernley, passing the bread and cheese. "Oh—I've written home to say that you'll spend the holidays with us."

"He won't—at least he'll spend part with me," corrected Marsh.

"Thanks—but I can't make any plans, you see I don't know what's going to happen yet."

"But you must go somewhere, Scissors," cried Vernley lightly. The moment he had said it, and saw the dumb pain in John's eyes he would have torn his tongue out to retrieve the careless remark. "Scissors, I don't mean it that way—you know I don't!" he added desperately.

"No, I know you don't," agreed John, swallowing hard, and trying to look steadily back. They ate their supper in silence. Even Marsh's forced gaiety failed.

The weeks leading to the end of the term went swiftly. Bit by bit the news dribbled through, news of how his father had been killed—this in a letter from the doctor at the American Mission. His father had been buried next to his mother at Marsovan, under the same almond tree whose blossom John could still picture in his mind, so deeply was the first impression etched. Then later came Mr. Glass from his father's company, somewhat surprised and hurt at John's refusal of the clerkship. His father had been insured for £500. There was that, and a small balance at the bank, not more than £600 in all. Was he wise in refusing the opening, which would lead, in years to come, to a very good position? John looked at Mr. Glass, with his bald head, large stomach and expressionless face, and the result of success did not appeal to him. Mr. Glass prepared to depart.

"Well, you may think better of it, my boy. Your father would have wished it, I know. I don't see what more we can do for you—but there, if you do change your mind and need us, we are there, remember."

Clumsily done, but well meant, and John realising this, thanked him and shook the hand extended towards him. After Mr. Glass had gone Fletcher looked at John.

"I suppose you intend going up to King's?" he said. "I think you will pull through all right with care."

"No, sir, I feel I ought to begin doing what must be done —earn my living. Six hundred pounds is not much, and I shouldn't feel happy knowing that I was using it up."

"But Cambridge may lead to opportunities—a Fellowship—at least a degree, which is useful. At the worst you can become a—a schoolmaster." He smiled apologetically for the joke against himself.

"And meanwhile, sir, make expensive friends and acquire expensive tastes? Why shouldn't I do the last thing first, and learn whether I have the inclination."

"The last?" queried Mr. Fletcher.

"Yes, sir, I thought of getting a junior mastership— if I could. A year would not matter greatly. If I failed at that—then I would go up to Cambridge—it would not be too late."

"No, but you are wasting a year."

"Yes, sir, but I want—oh, I feel I must work it all out. I'm afraid you don't understand, sir," added John lamely.

"I think I do—this has altered your whole life, or at least you feel so—nothing really does affect our lives to anything like the extent we imagine it does. Experience proves that we are always ourselves. As for a mastership—it is not easy without a degree. I have a friend at a scholastic agency. If you wish I will write to him—that is, if you want to take this step. Personally, I advise you to—no, I won't advise you, John—you must decide for yourself."

Two weeks after that conversation, John was glad of the step he had taken. The insurance company had refused to pay the claim; the policy did not provide for the contingency in which Mr. Dean lost his life. John's capital now was £132. Mr. Fletcher's friend had obtained for him a junior mastership at a preparatory school in Hampshire.

"Sixty pounds a year, Dean, not much, but still you're a beginner—it will give you time to think," said Mr. Fletcher, handing him the letter. John wrote accepting the offer. There were vigorous protests from Vernley and Marsh. At the end of the term, after a terrible wrenching from the school, his friends, the Fletchers, and all the beloved corners and places and daily events of four happy years, he went down with Vernley to his home. The latter still believed that John would accompany him to King's. Marsh had gone home with the same belief. Vernley's faith was based on the ability of his father to bring John round to common sense. There was a talk one afternoon in the library that brought a lump into John's throat, and a mist into his eyes, as he listened to the self-effacing generosity and kindly plans of the big, bluff man sitting in front of him. But he remained true to his decision. Mr. Vernley mopped his brow, hot with the attempt to suggest, as delicately as possible, a way out, and afraid all the time of hurting the boy's feelings. John thanked him in a voice that trembled.

"Well, well, John, you're an obstinate boy, but I won't worry you. You can do me a great favour by keeping an eye on Bobbie, and you won't—and I'll owe you a grudge all my life. But if you do want to give me real pleasure— then come to me whenever you will—I won't say more than that. You understand, my boy, don't you?" and with that he placed a kindly hand on the lad's shoulder. "And—'pon my word, I admire your grit—you're the right stuff!"

Dismay, blank dismay, was written on Vernley's face when he heard of the result. It was no use appealing to

John—the latter had heard him to the limit of his patience. Vernley went to Muriel. She could act when others failed. To his amazement she did not agree.

"Scissors is quite right. You can say what you like, or put it how you like, but it's charity, and John would know it, and you would know—and it *might* make a difference. I think you're blind."

"But why?" cried Vernley, plaintively.

"John refuses to be helped simply because he thinks so much of us—he's not going to jeopardise his friendship by indebtedness or reasonable gratitude. But you men never can see these things. Only a woman understands."

"Rot!" said Vernley, but he began to understand. That night he wrote to Marsh. "I shouldn't mention it any more, Scissors can't be shaken—the Governor's failed, and if your Governor tried he might suspect a plot and throw us all over. Perhaps we'll have a chance later. School teaching's a hell of a life." True to his advice, Marsh dropped his own scheme, in which his father had concurred. When John arrived to spend September at the Vicarage the choice John had made was not opposed. They had a jolly holiday, jolly in so far as John, with the momentous events of the last two months in his mind, could be lighthearted. Often he looked into the future and sometimes was seized by despair at its hopelessness. It was not the task confronting him. Earning a living was the common lot of men, and the one in which they found most happiness. It was his loneliness, the apparent futility of his life. He was alone. That was the awful thought. This great, passionate world, and of all its millions, not one inseparably bound to him, to rise or fall with his success or failure! Ungenerous, perhaps, this thought. He had friends, such friends too! But the possession of friendship meant independence; he was not going to be behind and be pulled along in the race of life. They should have no cause to be sorry for him; rather would he have them eager to know him, to cherish his friendship the more for the success that he brought with it. He was of a class that found it easier to do a favour than receive one. He spent his life seeking, not a way out, but a way through. He was now braced for the contest, and the sternness of it exhilarated him with the freshness of a morning sea. He was diving from a great height of sunlit friendship into the cold sea of life.

CHAPTER III

I

IN the art prospectus, printed on a glazed paper with many choice illustrations, Chawley School was a perfect place. The school, once a manor, celebrated for its architectural beauty, was situated in a magnificent park of five acres, with an ornamental lake and a drive one mile long. The gardens in front of the house were extensive and well kept. One of the illustrations showed fifty small boys, all dressed alike, in grey shorts and blue flannel jackets, with grey socks with red tops, and straw hats with red bands, squatted on the splendid lawn, all showing bended bare knees and round happy faces. In their midst were three masters, one middle-aged and two quite young, and a lady. The letterpress under this charming picture of sunlit foliage and smiling humanity, said "Afternoon Tea." The prospectus also mentioned the covered swimming pool in the grounds, the boys' own garden, the large airy dormitories and class rooms. It then drew rapturous attention to the staff. The school was run by the Rev. Shayle Tobin, M. A., Scholar of Balliol College, Oxford, with a double first, a blue for cricket, and for some years famous as a half-back.

One Sunday morning, six head boys, conscious of leadership and the great world of a public school approaching, shuffled their feet in the Manor pew in the village church. Behind them in other pews sat other little boys, more an-

gelic in appearance and devilish in action. They were all
dressed alike, in black Eton jackets, white collars, grey
trousers and shoes. Even at the tender age of ten to thirteen their faces gave promise or otherwise. The new young
assistant master who sat guarding them in the third pew
found himself studying, during the dreary sermon, the
shapes of the heads ranged in front of him like turnips on
a table. There were long heads, round heads, oval, pointed,
blunt, flat and dinted. Handsome, well-made, ugly, emaciated, intelligent, stupid, good-natured, deceitful, mischievous and lovable. John Dean ranged up and down the
row. This was his first Sunday morning in church. It
was his Sunday on duty; the other assistant master had
gone into Southampton.

The young assistant master was not the only critical person letting his thoughts wander from the Harvest Festival
Sermon. John gazed abstractedly at the figure of the Rev.
Samuel Piggin, ringed round with bunches of carrots, a
few grapes and six tomatoes balanced on the top of a sheaf
of wheat, which demonstrated God's bounty, despite a ruin-
ously wet summer and a harvest, half of which lay rotting
in the fields.

Miss Piggin, twenty-nine years of age, with spectacles,
and ardent in romance, was quite thrilled by the first
glimpse, as she turned to the East in the recital of the
Creed, of the handsome young master. His profile would
have enhanced the wrapper of those shilling reprints to
which, for want of romance, she was addicted. Nor was
she alone in her sudden interest. Several young ladies
sitting behind John found great fascination in the clean
curve from the nape of the neck up to the wavy brown
head. Other younger ladies, favourably placed in the side
pews, could not have been more fascinated had Apollo himself renounced his pagan origin and come to church. The

proud mouth, the dark eyes, the fine brow surmounted by a wavy mass of chestnut hair, the whole poised on an athlete's shoulders, were attractions against which the sermon competed in vain. The doctor's daughter, for three years determined to be a missionary's wife, found her gaze wandering from the altar to the school pew.

One little boy with a freckled face and a genius for mischief, ceased making chewed pellets from a hymn sheet when he noticed the rapt attention directed towards the pew in which he sat. He nudged the boy at his side, and both, suddenly conscious of the suppressed excitement that flowed over them, sniggered and brought a reproof from their new master. Something in the freckled boy's mute mirth as he looked at him, caused John to turn round, when he met the troubled gaze of a dozen pairs of amorous eyes. He quickly turned again and felt the blood mounting to his neck and face. The little boys sniggered again. John made a mental note not to the little boys' advantage. Miss Piggin also made one—to call when her father paid his formal visit; and not to be outwitted, the doctor's daughter decided she would motor in with her father on Monday morning, when he paid his usual visit to examine all the boys at the beginning of term.

Hitherto missionaries had absorbed her hero-worship, but then, assistant masters, as a class, had not seemed attractive. The former master drank, to the scandal of the village, which met him in the bar of the "Red Cow" where he grossly libelled all those, and their wives, who kept preparatory schools. His predecessor had a squint, the one before was lame, and the one before him was an old man of sixty, who had suddenly and most inconveniently died of bronchitis in term time. Sixty pounds a year and free board somewhat limited the available supply of assistant masters. Messrs. Sloggart and Slingsby, the scholastic

agents, had told the Rev. Mr. Tobin that they were afraid
he would have to add another ten pounds.

John liked Mr. Tobin on first contact. He was a man
of about fifty years of age, with a tanned face and kindly
blue eyes. The famous athlete was fast disappearing in a
bulky schoolmaster, who added weight each term with considerable anxiety, coupled with a feeling that his appearance
at least was a good advertisement of the school. He had
a genuine love of boys and worked hard with them, being
strict and kind, with a determination to do his best for
them. The boys, in fact, were watched day and night; con-
victs would not have had closer attention, and the same
supervision extended to the two assistant masters.

Mr. Tobin had little imagination, and the whole of it had
been expended in the prospectus.

The grounds of Chawley School were certainly extensive. The former tenant, like the present, had found them
too much so, and let them go wild. The lawns on the front
part of the house were kept tidy; elsewhere the walks were
weed-grown. The ornamental lake stank, and might have
been the death place of Shelley's "Sensitive Plant." The
prospectus mentioned boating on the lake as one of the diversions of the fortunate boys. The only boat was an old
punt, one end of which had been long submerged among
the water lilies. It was the floating end that appeared in
the prospectus photograph. Afternoon tea on the lawn was
also slightly different from the photograph. Three quarters of the boys had never been on the lawn. Every Sunday, as a reward, six top form boys, with the assistant master, were invited to tea with Mrs. Tobin on the lawn. A
fear of her presence was mingled with the love of her cake,
and had the boys had a free will in the matter they had
rather not have been rewarded.

Mrs. Tobin was a tall woman of about forty-eight years. She was cold and looked at people with eagle eyes. Her voice was deep, her features gaunt, framed in straight brown hair brushed severely back. She had the full equipment of a bishopric's conventions and never forgot her very reverend origin. She was the business woman, and constantly reminded her husband of the fact. She knew that to make a school pay, it required at least fifty boys. All over that number represented profit. Chawley School had forty-nine boys. She lived her days as though on the edge of a precipice. Mr. Tobin, as became a sportsman, delighted in feeding his boys, and invited them to a second helping of favourite puddings. Fortunate youngsters who sat at his end of the table! At Mrs. Tobin's end a second request did not bring a refusal, but, "Are you sure you have not had sufficient?" John, who struggled desperately with his pies, found a problem in the differential calculus easier than the elementary mathematics required for cutting a pie into fourteen portions to the satisfaction of twelve hungry boys.

Often, when his fourteenth turn came he received a small piece of pie crust as his share. Sawley, a sharp little fellow who sat at John's right, soon noticed this and generously offered his share. "We get more than usual now, sir," he explained. "Why don't you serve yourself first? The other masters always did."

"Masters?" queried John. "Why how many masters have you had?"

The boy smiled, then looked cautiously round to Mrs. Tobin's table.

"Six, sir," he whispered.

"And how long have you been here?"

"Six terms, sir."

John's heart sank.

"I don't expect you'll stay—will you, sir?" asked the boy in a burst of confidence.

John snubbed him, in duty bound. So he was one of a procession! He began to understand the bubbling curiosity which his arrival had aroused. His arrival! That had marked the end of a long mood of despondency which began as soon as he had left the cheerful faces of the Marshs. The misery he had endured in the three-mile ride from the station to the school! Peering out of the window he watched the long road with its straggling cottages, brown and gold in their autumnal creepers. Then the village stores with a fat man looking curiously at the school cab, next a rise and on the other side a glimpse, through the trees, of Chawley School, fronted by a broad stream and bordered by rook-haunted elm trees. As the cab drew up at the main door, the Rev. Shayle Tobin came to greet him. His box was taken up and he followed the head master into the wide hall. There was no furniture in it except a round mahogany table with an electro plate card tray, and a hat stand. The head-master's living apartments opened off on the right, and a wide corridor traversed the whole length of the building. John was led to the left, which contained the class rooms. If anything more had been needed to depress him the room, somewhat grandly called the Masters' Common Room, would have done it.

"We have not had time to get straight yet. The Matron will make this more comfortable soon," Tobin said. There was certainly room for improvement. A worn carpet covered the floor. On the left side stood a small table covered with a crimson cloth stained with ink. The wall paper was a faded, patternless drab colour. There were two chairs, one a basket chair with a short leg, the other a stiff sham-

Sheraton. There were no pictures on the walls, the fire grate had two broken bars and no fender.

The head-master next led the way to John's bedroom. This appeared to be a great improvement. The size of the room, in contrast to the Common Room, made John feel more lonely than ever, and he shuddered when he thought of winter mornings. But it was well furnished in a heavy mid-Victorian manner. There was a white, marble-topped wash stand with a red-flowered jug and basin, a large swinging mirror and wardrobe. The carpet was faded but good. This at least was an endurable room and he could live in it.

It was shortly before tea on the first day of term that John met his colleague. Gerald Woodman, a scholar of St. John's College, Oxford, was tall and heavily built for his twenty-five years. He appeared much older because of his great reserve and a perpetual melancholy. He had dark hair and dark eyes, an enormous appetite and no sentiment. In his short life he had arrived at a creed of absolute cynicism. He talked with reluctance, but John found later that at heart he was a good fellow whose foibles were the inheritance of a period of religious mania. He was now a robust atheist. The Church no longer seemed a desirable refuge; he had become a schoolmaster. Although fourteen stone in weight, he was possessed by a fear of starvation and deplored his thinness; when in cricket flannels, his thighs wobbled so much that all the boys grinned, but even this did not reassure him.

John had recently passed through the brief pimply period inseparable from youth, and in desperation one day bought a bottle containing five hundred blood pills. As if alarmed at the prospect, the pimples immediately disappeared. Mr. Woodman saw the pills on John's dressing table and asked if he might have a few to set his blood in

order. John gave him them. Those pills probably saved
the first assistant master from a second nervous breakdown.
He swallowed five after each meal and declared with deep
satisfaction that he was putting on weight; he was opti-
mistic until the bottle was finished, when his habitual
melancholy returned.

Their first evening at Chawley School was spent in
a conference with the Head-master who drew up the cur-
riculum. The hours were arranged between them. John
received one afternoon per week off duty and the alternate
Sundays. The class hours were 8:30 a. m. to 11, a break
of half an hour during which they supervised games, then
11:30 to 1 p. m. An hour for lunch, then work until 3
p. m. Games followed until five, a period during which
John changed into football shorts and raced about the field
in a scrimmage of shouting boys. He enjoyed this and
quite forgot all his woes. Tea was at five, a blessed interval of one hour's peace, then school again until 7:30, when
the boys went up to bed. Dinner, in the household apartments, with Mrs. Tobin in an evening gown and facetiously
cheerful, was at eight. After dinner the two masters left
the rosy warmth of the dining room for their own bare
quarters, where the interval between dinner and bedtime
was spent in the correction of the day's exercise books; a
monotonous routine, dulling the senses, and demoralizing
human beings with its hopelessness. There was no sense
of advancement. The end of the term came slowly, then
the holidays, then term again, with the same subjects to
drill into the same reluctant little boys.

Mr. Woodman, in a voice of deepest melancholy, foretold all this on the first night. When he learned that John
was new to his profession he smiled at him like a butcher
on a good sheep delivered for slaughter.

"Whatever made you do it?" he asked. "Do anything,

be a scavenger, a policeman—you will at least retain your
self respect. You will not have to endure the chilliness of
schoolmasters' wives, the scorn of parents, the buffoonery
of boys. We are fools out of motley, something masquer-
ading as gentlemen on the stipend of stevedores. My God,
Dean, pack your trunk and flee to-night. This is the end
of all things. Have you dreams, ambitions, hope, courage,
youth? Abandon all who enter this profession!"

John remonstrated. There was the great opportunity of
forming character, surely it was a noble thing to teach the
young, to gain the confidence, if not the affection of boys,
to watch them grow in intelligence, to trace the operations
of their fresh minds slowly opening on a wonderful world?
Mr. Woodman listened patiently to John's panegyric, and
peered at him over the top of the gold-rimmed spectacles
he wore when correcting exercise books in the jumping in-
candescent light.

"Dear me! This is almost pathetic! Your innocence
moves me. I hope you will pardon my saying you must be
very young. Eighteen? Ah! that is a blessed age, but
you have yet to learn what boys are. Let me warn you
and save you much pain. They are devils incarnate. And
don't cherish any illusion about being a schoolmaster. We
are a race of pariahs. At forty we have no feelings left;
we are desiccated text books. At fifty we are old fools
haunting the doorsteps of the scholastic agents or short-
sightedly sitting on the prepared pins of our loving pupils.
Don't think you will receive any gratitude for your labour;
you won't. Your cheque at the end of term wipes out all
obligations. After three years' close attention, they are not
even your boys. They pass on to a public school and re-
pudiate you. Boys are sent to preparatory schools by lazy
parents who wish to get rid of the responsibility of their
offspring, or by upstarts who want to start the new genera-

tion in the grooves of social respectability. They will hold you in utter contempt because you cannot do anything better than bring up their children for them. Epictetus was a prince in comparison with the modern schoolmaster!"

Woodman's theory, nevertheless, was not strictly applied. He was firm with his boys, made them work hard and was a martinet in detail, but he was a sportsman and the boys responded to his sense of fair play. As for John, by the third day of term, he was devoted to them, although hating more and more the dreary routine of his life. It was fascinating to study this dozen or so of young lives given into his keeping, to note the amazing divergence of character which manifested itself so early. John found himself looking through them to the parents beyond. He had a perfect index to the home life and the characters that had influenced them. The generous boy and the greedy, the frank and the secretive, the imaginative and the stolid, the sharp and the dull, the graceful, the strong, the quick, the ugly, the slow, the boy of bright honour, and the boy with a tendency to deceit, the potential coward or hero—they were all here in embryo. Education after all was only a wind that could bend the branches, it could not change the nature of the plant.

II

At the end of the first week, John was in a highly nervous condition. The monotony of the work, the regularity of the hours, the seclusion in a small world, the absence of all friends and his isolation miles away from all who knew him and with whom he could talk intimately, preyed upon his mind until one evening he reached a point of frenzy. He banged down a pile of exercise books, kicked a cushion vigorously, and then swore at the wall, from the other side of which came sounds of a small boy practising Czerny's One Hundred and One Exercises for the pianoforte. Woodman watched this outburst of wild rage with amusement.

"Beat your wings, my poor little moth! You will soon tire and subside—we have all passed along that *via dolorosa*," he commented.

"It is unendurable!" cried John, flinging himself in a chair.

"The capacity of man to suffer the slings and arrows of outrageous fortu—"

"Oh, shut up!" snapped John. Woodman regarded him sympathetically. He had grown to like this bright lad, so freshly enthusiastic, and bit by bit he had learned his story. In exchange he had shown John some of the poetry which he wrote secretly. Strangely enough it was highly sentimental, the safety valve of suppressed romanticism.

"Come on to the lake," he urged. John followed. It was their favourite pastime. They had resurrected the old punt, and in danger of a wetting, they often pushed it along through the thick water lilies that bent under its prow, and slowly closed again on the track they made. Meanwhile, the rooks, watching them from the elms above, cawed loudly, and the water hens showed alarm. The two masters became incredibly young once they were in the punt. They rocked it to see how near shipwreck they could go; they sang in a loud voice all the absurd ditties they could remember. Had their young charges seen and heard them, it would have been an amazing revelation of the humanity of masters out of school. As it was, Mr. Tobin complained that some of their noise had carried across the lawns to the open dormitory windows. But they simply had to sing; it was their one outlet of pent up youth within them. They would punt about until the dusk had given place to darkness, when the elms seemed gigantic and a rising moon peered in between the branches and watched the rippling reflection of her light. Around them all was quiet save for the weird squeal of a weasel in the woodland or the melancholy hoot of an owl.

One evening John was more noisy than ever, and Woodman threatened to capsize him, but there was good reason for this exhilaration. The mail had brought an acceptance of a long poem from the Editor of the *British Review*. He had written in competition with Woodman, who urged him to send it to an editor. With no faith, but some hope, John obeyed. His surprise, when the acceptance came, was unbounded. It was a long satirical story in the manner of Masefield. John had feared it was too long, for it took twenty pages, and here were the proof sheets and the offer of three guineas for his work! Those proof sheets kept him in a state of elation for several days. He had never seen himself in print except in the school magazine, and here was a great review printing his work! John cashed the cheque and ordered one pound's worth of copies of the review when it came out, which he distributed among his friends at some cost. Then he must see the reviewers' comments, and another guinea went to a press-cutting agency, which sent all the advertisements containing his name, and one criticism, if the slightly disparaging dismissal could be termed a criticism—"Mr. John Dean contributes some verses of a satirical nature." The net profit on the transaction was five shillings and sixpence which John invested in paper and envelopes. He had tasted printers' ink. John had seen a way out. He subscribed to the *Bookman,* devoured the *Times Literary Supplement,* and enquired the cost of joining the Society of Authors.

By the middle of November, with its dark winter nights when the wind howled among the chimneys, swayed the leafless branches, scurried along the cold flags of the corridors and rattled the shutters of the school-room windows, John had reached a point of nervous desperation. One night he beat his hands on the walls of his room in mere foolish impotence of rage. Even the placid Woodman, swallowing blood pills and putting on weight, became alarmed. There was an intensity in John's despair that made him apprehensive. It was in vain that he encouraged his literary work and discussed the novel which John had begun as a distraction, but had now discarded. He dragged him out for long walks down the bleak country lanes, but could not get him to talk. He was thin, with rings under his eyes, and the rose-red of healthy youth in his cheeks had given place to a hectic flush. He had moments of hilarious mirth, as alarming and as unnatural as his despair, and one night he had aroused Woodman in his bedroom, declaring he could not sleep alone in his room any longer and begged to be allowed to sleep on the couch. Woodman assented gladly but he was awakened later by a sound of sobbing in the darkness. He lit a candle and leaned up on his elbow.

"Dean—my dear fellow—you must not go on like this—you'll make yourself ill."

He heard John clear his voice.

"I know—I'm a fool—I'm horribly ashamed of myself —but—but, oh, my God, I am wretched."

"Why, you silly old thing, this morning you were making your boys yell with laughter."

"And got snubbed by Tobin for it," retorted John. "Put out the light, Woodman—I'll behave—and thanks awfully."

Woodman doused the candle with the matchbox. In the morning John was normal again. Neither made any allusion to the scene in the night. It was a bad dream.

CHAPTER IV

THERE were now rapid phases to John's character. He was beginning to apprehend all the wonderful interests of the world, interests from which he was being boxed up. He longed for the sound of a woman's voice and a glimpse of beauty; a violent nostalgia seized him. The mention of Asia Minor in the geography lesson—and he was leagues away swinging his bare legs on a verandah shaded with almond blossom, hearing the singing of the stream down the gorge at Amasia, watching the light silver the waterfall as the moon came over the mountain cliff and flooded the valley. He recalled his father reading to him; he could hear the clatter of his pony's hoofs in the courtyard, hear Ali calling him out to play, Ali his bosom friend, whose last gift now lay on his chest, whence he had never removed it. Or he would be suddenly transported to Sedley by the sight of a familiar dictionary, and again sit working and chattering with Vernley and Marsh in their study. His longing for his friends increased with the passing days. Vernley wrote faithfully, chronicling doings at Cambridge, sometimes unconsciously causing pain by the enthusiastic mention of a new name, which John felt was taking the place of his own.

As anticipated, Marsh was a great success. In the freer atmosphere of the university he had blossomed into a man of power and influence. He had already made a brilliant début at the Union, and prophets talked of him as a future President—"Marsh says the office would be yours for the asking, there is no one here who could stand

182

up with you—and I agree; why on earth don't you come, you dear old obstinate Scissors!" John was almost persuaded, but pride held him back. He must work out his own salvation—a memory of Browning helped him:

"But after they will know me. If I stoop
Into a dark tremendous sea of doubt,
It is but for a time; I press God's lamp
Close to my heart; its splendour, soon or late,
Will pierce the gloom; I shall emerge one day."

Was he a coward? He had a fear of poverty, and an almost desperate fear of the future at times. He was immersed in the poetry of Shelley and Keats, and soon was longing ardently to die of consumption in Italy, long before he would be twenty-six. In another mood his ambition carried him to dizzy heights. Recollections of talks with Mr. Ribble came back. Downing Street was not such an impossibility after all. He could speak. What had Vernley said in his last letter? And Mr. Steer had written to him about his article on "The Rise of Naturalism in English Poetry" which had appeared in the Blue Review, and asked him to be sure to call when next in London, in order that he might meet "some of your contemporaries"! From that day on London began to call him. That was the battlefield. Woodman agreed. "This is a dead end," he said, "but useful for the future."

"Useful, how?" asked John.

"You're getting material to write about. Think what a story's here for you one day, when you look back. You'll smile then."

Gradually John's mood of desperation passed. The problems of life was yet to be solved or attempted, but he was young. He had intense ambition, good health, friends, and certain qualities which secured him notice. He became aware that he possessed what men call a personality; there was something that made persons ready to do him a service, and this asset was the latest of his discoveries. At the Vicarage, Miss Piggin had proved her friendship. She left him books; she knew something about art, having spent two terms at Newlyn; at least she knew the various schools of art, the names of the galleries in London, and the queer methods employed for achieving success.

For the first time he heard of the Vorticists and the mad young men of the Backyard Gallery, which specialised in chimneyscapes and exalted the hideous. She told him of energetic young James Squilson, one part artist, and two parts publicist, the one part being good, the others impudent. The good was at present carefully hidden, while his monstrosities had created sufficient of an outcry to make those beardless Jews, Messrs. Riverton, give him a one-man show at the Trafford Galleries. This exhibition, Miss Piggin said, was a great success. Society flocked to it and declared it unique. It bought enigmatical canvases at fifty guineas each, which were cheap, considering they were fashionable and provocative of discussions at dinner parties. Major Slade, a charming man, who liked having artists to dinner, bought several and felt like a connoisseur for six months, which was as long as he liked any sensation. Squilson's third exhibition cooled Slade's waning enthusiasm. The perverse fellow had become an artist. His paintings might have been accepted by the Royal Academy. When Squilson declared, to the horror of society, that he would not object to being accepted, Slade dropped him and gave away his works as wedding presents.

Miss Piggin was musical also; she played Bach and cultivated an enthusiasm for Scriabine. John found that his musical intelligence ceased after Debussy—Ravel was his breaking point, although Stravinsky's *L'oiseau de Feu* seemed to give him a prospect of a new land where the animals were articulate.

John became rather a frequent visitor to the Vicarage. Mr. Woodman was asked to dinner also, but he was asked as a companion, and was useful in occupying Piggin's attention. Miss Piggin, accustomed to the rôle of hostess since her mother's death, devoted her attention to John. Formerly on festive occasions she had asked her friend, the the doctor's daughter, to assist her. She decided that she could manage well enough with such obliging young men. Miss Piggin also found a new incentive to dress rather better than usual. The sleepy life of a country Vicarage had caused her to become somewhat lax in the past; it was no use being a fashion plate when there was no one to notice. Now, however, she made a surprising resurrection; even the village publican commented on it, as also poor little Miss Timis, called in to do the sewing.

Although Miss Piggin was well aware that nature had not been lavish at her birth, she knew that fashion has given woman a good frame for an indifferent picture. Short sighted, out of doors she wore spectacles, but these were discarded in the evening. She was troubled with chilblains on her hands, it is true, but she had a wonderfully fresh complexion for a young woman of nearly thirty. John in fact thought she was about twenty-three, though she seemed to have seen a lot in her short life. But she could talk and had an eager interest in literature, of which she was no mean critic. As an artist she was sufficiently good to merit her asking John to sit to her, which he did, getting an ache in the neck, while she made a very idealised drawing of him. It was a little trying, for the sitting which he had been told would require a few hours, ran into weeks. Miss Piggin seemed everlastingly taking out the next day what she had achieved with such elation the previous day. The eyes and the mouth caused the most trouble. These required several visits from the easel for close study. His hair was comparatively easy, for she could arrange it to fall as it suited her. She told John he had sensitive nostrils and a perfect, but sensuous mouth.

"Not sensual?" he said laughing.

"It might become that—yet," she replied.

It was good fun and he liked the little teas they made in the studio, with the aid of a gas ring. Afterwards he insisted on washing up while she dried the tea things. It was a domestic moment and it gave Miss Piggin a thrill; he looked so fascinating with his sleeves rolled up above the elbows. Once, when he dozed while sitting, she had hoped that he would fall fast asleep. She would just kiss his head as it lay, with its tumbled hair, on the side of the chair. But he aroused himself, and Miss Piggin was grateful that she was saved from being so foolish.

She held John from a nervous breakdown. She took him for long walks and encouraged him to talk. He found his idea of going to London to write, eagerly supported. What to write he hardly knew. Miss Piggin suggested journalism. She had met quite a lot of journalists near her rooms at Hampstead. They seemed very jolly and not hard-worked. It was true they had small private incomes or self-sacrificing parents. She gave John the address of a boarding house in Pimlico. If he went to London, he would find it cheap but not nasty.

It was on one of these walks one day an incident occurred that thrilled her with a revelation of the male in

action. They were on a narrow and muddy road when a
cart came into view, with a red-faced youth lolling on the
top of a load. Although there was no space for the two
walkers to stand in, he drove his cart forward, jamming
them up against the wall and spattering them with mud.
Miss Piggin gave a cry of despair at the sight of her
muddy skirt. With a quick movement John ran to the
horse's head, seized the rein and pulled up the cart.

"Why don't you look where you are going?" he shouted
angrily.

The lout blinked at him.

"Shut yer——mouth."

John flushed and tightened his grip.

"You'll get down and apologise to the lady," he said
firmly. Another flow of indecent language.

"Let go that——rein!" finished the carter.

"I shall not. Come down!" retorted John.

The carter raised his whip and brought the lash down
across John's shoulders and neck. The horse reared,
John started forward, seized the dangling leg of his aggressor, and brought him sprawling down into the muddy
road. He was up in a minute bellowing obscenely with
rage. John dodged the blow directed at his mouth.

"I'll fight yer! I'll fight yer, yer——" yelled the carter
stamping around. John slipped off his coat and waistcoat; the carter followed suit.

"Oh, Mr. Dean, please, please!" implored Miss Piggin
from the mound on which she had taken refuge.
John's answer was to fling his discarded clothes into her
arms. She looked around, meaning to shriek, but as no
one was in sight it seemed useless. Meanwhile the battle
had begun. The antagonists were as different in appearance as they were in method. The carter was a heavily
built youth of about twenty. He was sandy-haired with

a tanned face and neck. His arms were muscular, and the gaping shirt revealed a hairy chest. He was a fellow not likely to be knocked out, especially by the lightly built, slim youth, who looked almost delicate in contrast.

Could this determined, lithe fighter make any impression on an opponent so firmly built and muscular? Miss Piggin thought not, and began to think of intervention with her umbrella; but she might poke the wrong person. She was cheered to notice how quick her champion was. It was a contest between speed with intelligence and strength with obstinacy. Mr. Dean might set the pace, but would he wear down this bulwark of seasoned flesh?

They had both received blows, and the nose of the slim youth was bleeding. The other, however, was also bleeding at the mouth. Miss Piggin felt faint and yet thrilled at the sight of these flushed youths, their hair falling into their eyes, one breathing hard, and the other looking implacably fierce. It reminded her of a fight she had witnessed between two stags on Exmoor. There was something exhilarating in the spectacle, though horrible.

Considerable in-fighting followed which evidently distressed the carter. Although Miss Piggin could not determine who was getting the blows—they were bent down together—the carter was letting forth "oughs" and "ahs" either as expressions of satisfaction or of receipt. The carter had opened with a wild but weighty swinging of the arms, which the other cautiously avoided. One blow from those sculpturesque forearms would have rendered him hors-de-combat. He waited his opportunity, backing slowly until he secured a favourable opening. One fist landed over the carter's eye. He grunted but his progress was not impeded. The next moment they had clinched, for which Miss Piggin felt grateful. She would have left them in this harmless position, if she could, until she had returned with the village constable. She now stood with bated breath, for when they broke away some one would receive a blow.

Here John's small supply of ringcraft, gathered in Sedley gymnasium, came into play. He used the clinch to rest himself upon the bulk of the carter, who pushed him around, tiring himself. Then seizing a propitious moment, he threw off his assailant's arms, feinted to the left cheek, and swung in with a sharp upper cut with the right. It caught the carter neatly under the chin, lifted him and sent his head back. He went down heavily with a lost balance. John walked round till his opponent was ready to rise. His blood was up, there was a grim expression on his face, and Miss Piggin, catching a glimpse of his steely eyes, cold and fierce under the mop of disordered hair, changed in her alarm. She feared now for the life of the carter, raised up on his elbow and contemplating things.

"Oh, Mr. Dean!" she whimpered.

He continued to walk round as though he had not heard. The carter painfully rose to his feet, and then with a torrent of abuse, rushed in mad fury at the waiting foe. A right from the shoulder caught John on the chest, breaking his guard, and sent him down to his knees with its sheer strength. The carter had no code to obey and was ready to follow up his advantage, but in this he was unwary. John waited until he stood over him, and with a crouching spring came up under the raw fellow's guard, reaching his chin again with some force. Shaken and somewhat dismayed with this surprising return of an apparently beaten adversary, he began to retreat, and John, still full of battle, saw his chance. There was some swift in-fighting which Miss Piggin could not follow, because now the amount of blood visible on both antag-

onists made her feel ill. She turned her head away.
When she looked again, it was all over, John stood surveying the huddled up form of the beaten youth.

"Can you get up?" he asked coolly. The voice was almost cruel in its tone, thought Miss Piggin. Then John
stooped and pulled the sullen fellow to his feet. They
stood facing one another for a long interval.

"Will you shake hands?" said John, extending his.
There was no response for a moment.

"Yer. . . ." snarled the carter, his eyes still full of
battle.

"I'm sorry then," said John unrolling his sleeves.
There must have been something crossing the slow brain
of the carter. His eyes changed expression.

"Yer've won . . . boss," he said slowly. John heard
the changed tone and again held out his hand. The carter
took it.

But peace had left them both strange spectacles. The
horse even seemed a little afraid of its master, and turned
its head as he approached. He was wiping his
face, which had begun to swell, with a red handkerchief. John was doing likewise. The absurdity of the
whole affair was intensified in the process. Miss Piggin
now approached and offered a diminutive handkerchief,
which John accepted, for his own was soaked by a per-
sistent nose. The right eye was slowly closing up.

Without furthur comment the carter took his horse's
head and led it off down the road. As John looked up
and caught Miss Piggin's piteous expression, he could not
help laughing.

"I suppose I look a beautiful object?"

"Oh, Mr. Dean!" was all she could say. If only he
would faint now, all was safe! Her womanly instinct for

nursing the brave rose within her. She would dearly have loved to hold him in her arms and bathe his face, and tidy his hair. But romance gave place to the practical.

"You must come to the Vicarage first—you can't return like that."

"No—I can't—but I want washing now before it dries," he replied. There was a canal bordering the next field; the road led over the canal bridge. The Vicarage was two miles away.

"I'm going to swim in the canal!" he said.

Miss Pilgrim shivered at the idea. "It's terribly cold!" she cried. "You will get a chill."

"It's the tonic I want," he replied. "You stand on the bridge. I can strip underneath if you'll keep watch."

He led the way, and left her on the bridge. What an amazing man! A minute or so later she heard a splash, and shivered sympathetically in the cold November wind. She could not help just looking over the bridge a moment, and caught a glimpse of white shoulders, a dark head, and the strong arms thrashing the grey water into a foamy track. Then he turned and she looked away.

When he came up and joined her on the bridge later, he looked marvellously refreshed. It was true his eye had closed up but most of the horror of the battle had been the blood.

"But how have you dried yourself?" she asked, as he squeezed his hair with his hands.

He laughed at her with his merry eye—the right one, still visible.

"On my shirt."

She blushed crimson. Men had shirts, as she knew, but it was awkward to be told so by men. They walked home through the barren copse, burning red on the horizon

where the sun left the winter day. For one person these
were the woods of Broceliande, and her heart warmed towards the young knight fresh from the battle.

Mr. Woodman's expression, at the appearance of John
just in time for tea in the study, was a mixture of surprise and disapproval.

"My dear fellow—" he began. "You have not been
fighting? An assistant master! Whatever will Tobin
say? Don't eat all that toast—here's the fork, make
your own—he will want a full explanation of that eye.
What an eye!"

John briefly recounted the episode.

"I should leave out Miss Piggin," said Woodman.

"Why?"

"Tobin strongly disapproves of masters walking about
the country with young ladies, and as for fighting for
them like bulls in a herd . . ."

"Oh, stop ragging. What's the best for a black eye?"

BOOK IV

LIFE

CHAPTER I

I

TWO young men stood on a country platform saying good-bye to each other. One was bound for Cambridge, the other for London. Two trunks were in charge of the porter, but neither of these belonged to the bronzed young fellow who took his seat in the train. For although London was his destination, he had as much foreknowledge of his actual resting place in that metropolis as had Mr. Richard Whittington many years before him. The latter was supposed to have brought a cat with him; the young man in the carriage had no cat. He had health and ambition, also one hundred and twenty pounds in the bank. He had been able to save the whole of his salary for the second and final term at Chawley School, which he had left at Easter, to the sorrow of the boys, who had marked their adoration with some tears, and a presentation set of "Shelley's Poems." He had taken a bold step, highly applauded by Mr. Gerald Woodman. He had sacrificed an income of sixty pounds a year, with board, lodging and washing, for the uncertainty of London.

But there was no regret in his heart on this lovely spring morning. The song of the lark mounting to a southern cloud, the sense of budding things in hedge and tree, the sharp air, and the exuberance of his friend, Bobbie Vernley, all augured well for the adventure.

"You have given me a great time, Bobbie," he said,

looking on the good-natured face of his friend. "Don't forget to tell Marsh to write, and let me have all the news. I will write as soon as I get my rooms."

There was a slamming of doors, the screech of the engine whistle, a final handshake, a look in Vernley's eyes that told him much, and they were parted again.

John sat back in the seat and watched the familiar station glide away. Somehow this place always marked the beginning and end of things. When next he came how would he stand—a success or a failure? He had weighed anchor and was putting to sea. He had youth, one hundred and twenty pounds, and determination.

Opening a note book, he glanced through a list of addresses which gave him a little comfort. He knew a few persons in London. There was Mr. Steer, and a renewal of his acquaintance warmed him with joyous expectation. There was Mrs. Graham, to whom he was confidential, and who, looking in upon his dreams knew to what starry pinnacles he aspired. Muriel had insisted on an early call on Mr. Ribble, but John felt doubtful. A busy politician would find courtesy and kindliness heavily taxed if every stray youth seeing London rang his door bell. But he made one promise to call formally. There was a hope of companionship in the presence in town of Lindon, who had just left Balliol to study at the Royal Academy of Music, but a certain shyness still hung over his relations with that brilliant person. There was something he never quite understood, a reservation in manner, if not in speech, which told John theirs could never be an equal friendship. Somehow he always felt the debtor to Lindon, perhaps owing to his manner. Despite his cordiality, his obvious liking of John's company, the latter always felt diffident; perhaps now he would learn to know

Lindon better, relieved of the halo of a schoolboy's worship.

Interleaving his note book was Miss Piggin's card, and on it, in a pointed Italian hand, the address of a boarding house she recommended. "Mrs. Perdie, 108, Mariton Street, S.W." In his pocket, John carried another specimen of Miss Piggin's handwriting, on the flyleaf of "The Private Papers of Henry Ryecroft," calmly setting forth the inscription—"To John Narcissus Dean from Elsa Piggin, in memory of walks and talks." Some of the letters had run, Miss Piggin explained, owing to the dew dripping from some roses just gathered, on her writing desk. The warmth of her pillow overnight had somewhat crinkled the dried page, but this Miss Piggin did not attempt to explain. She carefully hid from all eyes that, with his departure, Romance died. Henceforth, she accepted Fate with gentle compliance. No more rebellions, never again the false hope of Springtime; even photographs were resolutely put away, John's included, but she permitted one small snapshot taken on the football field, to remain on her dressing table. He had such a handsome leg, and her soul craved beauty. For the rest she was unwearied in attention to her father. He found clean nibs in his pens, his note-books carefully dusted and replaced. She had a great scheme that afternoon for the Ladies' Sewing Meeting, which foretold long months of patient work—an altar cloth, embroidered with scenes from the life of St. John. Appropriately therefore, the opening lesson was read from the Gospel according to St. John. She began it with loving reverence. St. John was such a beautiful name, she thought.

And John? Alas! he too dreamed, of a fair face, the laughter of maidenhood, the sudden shaking of curls beautiful in their agitation. Those last moments in the hall, awaiting the arrival of Tod with his car, were painful almost. One by one they had said good-bye. Mr. Vernley, red faced, cheerful, friendly; Mrs. Vernley, motherly to the last, then Kitty, off for her morning ride, and Alice about to retire to her voice production; and then they were alone for a few precious moments.

"You will write?"

"Every day, darling," he vowed.

"I shall always think of you."

"Always?"

"Always!" she promised.

Their hands are locked—silence, and tears in Muriel's eyes.

"I shall soon be on my feet."

"I know."

"Muriel!"

"John, dearest!"

"London is nearer than Chawley."

"Yes, John, but—"

"But?"

"It is so new, such an adventure."

"That thrills me—our day draws nearer, *our* day, Muriel." There is another pause. Bobbie bangs the door open before approaching.

"Car's coming round, Scissors," he shouts. "Good-bye, Muriel, old thing! Remember me to the nuns!" He strides up and kisses her soundly on the cheek, sees tears in her eyes; she feels the reassuring pressure of her brother's hands upon her arms. And then they are gone.

As the train drew in through the panorama of chimney-pots, factory roofs and gasometers, it was her face John saw, over the wretchedness of the bewildering city. In the station he awoke to the reality of the things under the girders and glazed roofs. He carried only a bag; his trunk would be forwarded when he found rooms. He stood on the platform hesitating a moment. London frightened him. It was so vast and self-centred, so busy with people who had apparently solved the problem he had to solve. Where should he begin, and how would it all end? For the moment he had one rule, strict economy. He made his way slowly up the incline out of Liverpool Street Station, and asked a policeman the best means of reaching Mariton Street. "Where is it?" he asked the genial fellow whose robust countenance cheered him.

"Pimlico! No. 6 bus to Charing Cross, change to 24, that'll take you down to Mariton Street." John thanked him and clambered to the top of the bus. He watched the traffic, human and vehicular, streaming down Bishopsgate. At the Bank, he could not suppress a thrill as he looked on the restless tide surging into the vortex before the Mansion House. St. Paul's, lifting its sun-struck dome into the morning air, pigeon-haunted, floated away behind, and the short descent under the viaduct brought them to Ludgate Circus. There, narrow, mazed with telegraph wires, jammed with buses, cars, lorries, and hurrying humanity, rose Fleet Street. An incommunicable wonder stole in on the boy's heart. Here was the battle ground whereon he would throw down his gage. The roar in his ears might have been applause, or was it the laughter of ridicule? The gold-lettered sign-boards announced the tributary channels on either hand. Names familiar on the breakfast table; names of power and wonder leapt forth from these insignificant buildings, behind those walls sat the men who held the world in leash. The fall of empires, the death of monarchs, the ruin of men, the fame that sprang upon them; all these things found their historians here. Man-made, this world was hedged round with the divinity of power. Within those drab buildings beat the pulse of Time. Mercury, wing-footed, swept down those narrow stairways, and leapt forth from fourth-storey dwellings of the Olympian "We."

It was soon passed. The roaring bus soared up the gradient towards the Griffin and Shield at the City entrance of Temple Bar. Beyond, a widening way diverged in two crescents around the pinnacled church. High up on the right, the solemn solidity of the Law Courts, its clock hung from the tower far over the narrow street; a swerve and a new vista. The Strand leading onwards past the wedge of the Australia House, the pillared colonnade of the Gaiety Theatre, and the narrows, with hotels and theatres on either hand. Then the railed front of Charing Cross, a brief right hand glimpse of St. Martin's Church, and John descended. Around the corner broke the wonder of the world, Trafalgar Square, flanked by the National Gallery, white against the blue sky, cumulus-banked with summits of sunlit snow. Aloft, Nelson, dark and solitary, looking riverwards far over the head of the unfortunate monarch, superbly seated and orientated; the four lions, symbols of British solidarity and regal magnificence, in whose ears the song of the nation's traffic sounded by day and by night, guardians of the hub of empire; and listeners, perforce, to the revolt of humanity.

Long stood the youth, gazing upon this scene, watching the brilliance of the fountains with their scintillating jets, about whose spray naked urchins as if strewn from a garland of Correggio, shouted and splashed. Into his heart stole the magic of the place. Here was the visible pulse of the nation, the England in which he lived, an Englishman. Here was the dream, tangible, carried in the hearts of a thousand pioneers across the wastes of far places, the music accompanying the hymn of duty, the thought that built the empire imperishable in the love of her children. He looked on the Roman magnificence of the Admiralty Arch, caught a swift translation of a Venetian moment when a cloudless azure dome encupped the towered church; and then, with a start, he returned to the business of the day. A few minutes later one view crowded out another, until amid ecstasy and wonder, he seemed to be riding through history. Whitehall, broad, official, stately; the sudden leap to sight of Westminster Hall; the familiar homeliness of the Abbey; the tracery of the Houses of Parliament; the clock tower and the bridge, and ere the tumult subsided in his heart, followed the long cathedral-greyness of Victoria Street, ending in the vulgar rout of traffic about the railed courtyard of Victoria Station. John laughed to himself, swaying on the bus. Was he seeking lodgings or El Dorado?

When the bell rang for the fifth time that morning, Mrs. Perdie let forth a protest.

"Sure there's no peace in a basement kitchen," she moaned, wiping her hands dry after peeling potatoes for the evening meal. It was no use expecting Annie to answer the bell; she was on the fourth floor making the young gentlemen's beds, and lost that moment in contemplation of a gaudy pair of pyjamas. So while Annie speculated on the cost of a blouse made out of the same silk, Mrs. Perdie climbed the stairs and opened the door to another exquisite young man. But she had a trained eye, and the first words of enquiry told her that this was the genuine article, the product which Mrs. Perdie, proud of being a connoisseur by virtue of seventeen years' service in the best families, reverenced and made adjustable terms for. The mention of Miss Piggin's name immediately confirmed her impression. Warmly she invited the young gentleman into the drawing room, hastening to draw up the Venetian blinds and apologising for her appearance.

"I'm not like this of a night-time. You see, when they are all out I give a hand to the maid." Then she was silent a space, while she absorbed the vision of the young man seated before her. A visit from Phoebus Apollo himself—the original of the plaster statue on the shelf over the aspidistra—would not have silenced her so effectively.

"I knew at once he was of quality," she confided to Annie later. "His hands, gloves and shoes—you can never go wrong there. You can't be sure of accent. Some people are regular parrots. And he was that shy I could have hugged him. Didn't like to ask how much, he didn't, or what it included. Different to that brazen pair on the fourth floor."

The interview was indeed somewhat painful to John. He had heard warning stories of the rapacity of landladies, of their dirty rooms, bad food and subtle extras. The most familiar jokes were based on the experiences of unfortunate lodgers. He had expected to find Mrs. Perdie rat-faced, with a withered neck and untidy wisps of hair. This round-faced woman with the pleasant smile and a straight-forward air was not the original of the caricatures; moreover he saw no cringing cat. There was not even a bunch of wax grapes under a glass dome, which Tod assured him monopolised the mantelpiece in all boarding houses.

At her invitation he made a tour of the bedrooms, and heard as he mounted the stairs, the separate histories of the occupants of each room. She halted on the third

floor and led the way into a back bedroom. It was well-
furnished as a bed-sitting room. A writing table stood
under the window, which looked out on the wide expanse
of a factory yard. The sky was cut by a huge chimney,
belonging to the Army Clothing Factory, but this was not
unpleasant, for it bore a slight resemblance to the Campanile of St. Mark's, Venice; at least with a blue sky an
hour after sunset, the illusion was not impossible. There
was a large mirrored wardrobe, a bed with a purple eider-
down, a boxed-in wash-stand, a small table, an easy chair
and a gas stove.

"Gas is extra, sir, there's a shilling slot meter in the
recess so that you only pay for what you burn. The bath
room, with a geyser, is on the landing. This room and
board, is two guineas a week, laundry and boot cleaning
extra. There's breakfast and dinner in the evening,
with midday dinner and tea on Sundays. All our guests
have lunch out. I'm sure I could make you comfortable,
sir."

Looking at the woman, John felt sure too. He was
glad to have settled the problem so easily. Before he
went, Mrs. Perdie gave him a latch key—a sign of confidence in view of the smallness of his bag, and in return he insisted on paying her a week in advance which
caused her to say to Annie, "only a gentleman would
think of that—handsome-like. There's nothing like the
quality."

When she showed John out, he was reminded that dinner was at seven, and buses ran every ten minutes from
the corner.

"I don't know your name, sir," said Mrs. Perdie
finally, as the young man put on his hat.

"Dean—John Dean," replied John with a smile.

Mrs. Perdie smiled back as she closed the door.

"Bless 'im," she said to the cat, which then appeared. "I wonder what he does—and such nice teeth and manners!"

When Annie descended from her dreams of glory, with a few loose feathers in her hair, Mrs. Perdie was rubbing a serviette ring.

"Annie—there's a new gentleman comin' in to-night; set a clean napkin and this ring between Miss Simpson and Captain Fisher, and get the back bedroom ready. Take the best towel up."

II

When John returned to Mariton Street that evening, the beauty of London burned in his blood. He had given himself up to pleasant vagabondage all that day, abandoning the quest of livelihood. On the morrow he would begin that grim task. So after sending the address for his luggage to be forwarded, noon found him walking along the road by the garden wall of Buckingham Palace, towards Hyde Park. It was sunny, and the pleasant hum of traffic, the bright-faced messenger boys, the nurse girls with their well-dressed children, the crescendo of an approaching bus, the lovely elegance of the lady whose car went parkwards for an airing, the stately fronts of the houses, the sun-gleamed masses of clouds that backed the dark figure of the charioteer on the quadriga near Green Park—all these things were part of this wonderful song of life. It was almost incredible that he should seek a niche in all this splendour. Those people around him seemed so well established; had they ever begun, or had they been mere victims of circumstances?

He watched a couple of riders turn in at Hyde Park Corner; a fresh-faced young man, stolid with good food and no worry, accompanied a fragile girl, whose well-

tailored riding habit for a moment called up another
figure he knew well in similar attire. He followed in at
the gates and turned to the left, wondering if ever he and
Muriel would ride together down that glorious stretch.
He sat down on one of the chairs and watched the riders.
Children accompanied by grooms, elderly army officers,
a very stout lady who appeared to break down the fet-
locks of her mount, a tall girl in black top-boots, who gal-
loped, with splendid hands, and laughed back at two
young men who made desperate efforts to keep with her.

Then his attention was attracted by an elegant apparition, which alighted like a bird of paradise from a car
on the edge of the curb. It was a boy-officer in the
Scots Guards. He was very tall and languid, but held
himself stiffly erect as though there was a cavity between
his shoulder blades which he wished to keep closed. It
was difficult to know how he ever washed his face, so rigid
were the arms. His hat which had a brass peak and a red
and white diced band, half buried his face, the chin receding underneath a hairless upper lip, delicate and
curved. His painfully erect carriage seemed derived
more from mechanism within than from the operation
of will. His tunic suggested a theatrical tailor, so flawlessly did it fit, with an exaggerated waist-line that made
an hour-glass of a human trunk. And as if in fear that
it was just possible some one might mistake the young
elegant for an ordinary officer in an ordinary regiment,
the tailor had descended from fashion to eccentricity in
the cut of the trousers, which, receiving inspiration from
golfing breeches, bulged below the knees, where they were
caught up by puttees that wound about two stick-like
legs ending in enormous booted feet. The young man
was evidently delighted with himself. He turned round
three times in the sunshine, like a parrot on a perch.

Then it happened that a square-shouldered country youth, in a coarse copy of the same uniform, but with ruder brass embellishments, saluted and passed. The immediate effect was wonderful, if startling; a swift spasm, as of a Titan struggling with tetanus, galvanised the young officer into movement. By a terrific jerk, he succeeded in bringing his out-turned palm behind his right ear where it locked for a moment before being hurled downwards to its former rigidity, the disturbed flesh subsiding again into calm dignity. A few minutes later he was joined by a brother officer, an even more splendid figure wrapped in a long greatcoat of gorgeous blue, double-breasted and broad lapelled, with two vertical rows of buttons and a glimpse of scarlet lining within, where it gaped about his knees. The waist line was identical, a similar hat hid a similar face. One felt there might be a thousand of these in a box somewhere.

The Comédie Humaine continued. Two seats away from him a rather stout lady, accompanied by three Pomeranian dogs, seated herself. She was half-buried in furs above the waist, and half-naked below, but apparently suffered no discomfort. John could not help looking at her ankles, which were shapely, a diamond watch-bangle encircling the right. The lady noticed John's gaze and did not seem to mind, for she smiled. Slightly embarrassed, he thought it right to smile back, transferring his gaze to the Pomeranians, in suggestion that they were amusing. The exchange of smiles, however, made him aware that the lady was of indeterminable age, but had a very fresh complexion. The wind also told him that she liked expensive perfume. He continued to watch the horses and the people, and caught whiffs of conversation. He heard, from the young men, that certain things, he could not hear what, were "rather priceless" and "topping." One voice was ecstatic over Pavlova, "but Novikoff!" exclaimed an adoring feminine voice, "you've seen the Bacchanale?" Presently a long purple limousine drew up to the edge of the curb. The lady with the dogs rose and went towards it, the chauffeur opening the door. She was just entering the car when one of the leashes dropped from her hands. The dog immediately ran off in the direction of John.

"Naughty Topsie!" she called. "Come here!"

But Topsie welcomed liberty and sped on, John in pursuit. He soon retrieved the runaway and towed it back.

"Thank you so much," said the lady sweetly. "Topsie is such a rebel—I love dogs, don't you?"

"Yes," said John. He thought she looked critically at him.

"Have you got one?" she asked.

"No—I have just left school—it is difficult there."

"Oh—and are you starting business; I suppose you're quite thrilled!" She laughed again and John responded.

"I have not started yet—I have just come to London to-day."

"All alone?" asked the lady, arching her eyebrows.

"Yes."

"But how romantic! You sound like Dick Whittington, without a cat or a dog!" She laughed again at her joke. He noticed she had beautiful small teeth; a rope of pearls lay on her throat.

"Do you know London?" she asked again.

"No—I have never stayed here for any time," he answered. The chauffeur still waited with his hand on the door.

"This park is very lovely," she said, gathering her furs about her. "You should see it—will you drive through it with me?"

The invitation was so gracious and alluring John could not refuse; he followed the lady into the car, and with the dogs in their laps, they glided forward. It was a luxuriously appointed car. Three silver sconces held flowers whose perfume competed with that of the lady. The chauffeur in front wore a cerise uniform, with a broad green collar. Inside they were quite silent for a few minutes. John's shyness overcame him, while the lady, reclining on an air cushion, arranged her furs and played with the collars of the dogs on her lap. John knew that he was being closely scrutinised, and he resolved not to reveal any more of his personal history. This close contact showed that his companion's age was about thirty-five, and the fresh complexion had not been acquired in the open air. She made no secret of this, for she lifted her half veil, opened a vanity bag, took out what appeared to be a silver pencil, and raising a small mirror, carefully attended to her lips, which reddened in the process. John wondered who she was. There was a little pile of visiting cards in the wallet under the motor watch but they were upside down so he could not read them. She was evidently a wealthy woman, and in some respects reminded him of Mrs. Graham, who also had a green jade vanity bag. Mrs. Graham, however, on the one occasion when she used its contents, told him to turn his head away. The lady in the car, having completed her toilet, raised a lorgnette, looked out of the window for a few moments, dropped it, and addressed John.

"London can be a very lonely place," she said. "I know, because my husband is in India with his regiment."

John hesitated in reply. He could not just say, "Oh," and if he said "I'm sorry," it would be stupid. So he simply said, "Yes."

"Have you many friends here?" she asked. The question was kindly. He chatted brightly. Her first impression was correct, she thought, looking at him. He was a very handsome youth. When he looked down she saw how the long lashes swept his cheek, and when looking at her his eyes had wonderful depth. She liked the fine line of his profile, and the well-shaped, sloping ear; his hands too were fascinating, being strong and veinless. And in every movement and line, there was the symmetry of thoughtless youth, which was delightful. After a short time he, too, was admiring her intensely. She had an alluring voice—and he could not help noticing the ankles and small feet, so beautifully shod.

They turned and twisted, caught a glimpse of a sheet of water, an ornamental garden and bridge, then turned again, running parallel with a main road, whose roar could be heard behind the screen of trees. The watch hands pointed to ten minutes to one.

"I am lunching in Cumberland Place at one," she said. "Can I drop you on your way?"

He had no way, but did not care to confess it.

"At the gates will do, thank you."

When the car drew up near Marble Arch, she took a card from the wallet.

"This is my name and address. Since you are new to London, let me offer you hospitality. Will you not dine with me one evening at my house?"

He thanked her.

"Shall we say Thursday at seven? It will be quite *en famille*. You will be the only guest." She showed her beautiful teeth when he assented, and held out a diminutive gloved hand as he stepped out of the car.

"Good-bye," she smiled, as he raised his hat, a glance taking in the sweep of his brow with its clustered hair. The door closed, she leaned back with a parting glance, and as the car lurched forward, he replaced his hat. He looked calm enough, but there was tumult within. For a few moments he gave no thought to lunch. What a wonderful place London was! Then he became conscious of the large, neat-lettered card in his hand. "Lady Evelyn Warsett, 607, Queen Anne's Gate, S. W.," he read. Also he remembered he had not told her his name.

When John returned that evening to Mariton Street the dinner gong was creating pandemonium in the hall below, and there followed an opening of doors, a creaking of stairs and a babble of voices. He halted on the threshold of the dining room, dreading his entry into this strange circle. But Mrs. Perdie was waiting for him and piloted him to his place at the table, where she introduced him to Miss Simpson on his right, and Capt. Fisher on his left. The captain was very curt and ignored him throughout dinner. Miss Simpson was assiduous in polite attentions and small talk. When she discovered he had been in Asia Minor, life suddenly brightened for her. She had lived a year at Samsoon, with her brother, then the Consul, now a Governor in India. The Captain sniffed and fidgeted. He hated all his talk about Asia and India. He had spent most of his life on the Gold Coast, and knew it was not so fashionable.

When dinner was over the young men lingered behind.

"Perhaps you would like to have a smoke?" suggested Mrs. Perdie, going out and leaving John with the other boarders. He now looked more particularly at his companions. They had crossed to one of the windows where they began to bewilder the parrot by blowing smoke into its face. Presently one of them seemed aware that John was in the room. Pulling out a silver cigarette case he opened it and held it towards him.

"Have a gasper?" he drawled genially.

John presumed he meant a cigarette, and took one. The donor extended an elegantly ringed hand to light his own. There was an excessive length of cuff. John's eye moved along the arm, and noted the carefully knotted tie. The clothes were ultra-fashionable, the cut of the waist being much exaggerated. The trousers had a razor-edge crease and the patent boots, narrow and pointed, were topped by brown canvas spats. But despite the elegance there was something too pronounced in everything. The cloth was just too light in colour, too loud in check, the cameo ring too large, the pearl pin too pearly to be genuine. Even the hair was curled until it suggested a wig rather than a natural covering, and the skin had a curious poreless texture. But all these might have passed unnoticed by a less critical eye than John's, fresh to impressions after the plain severity of schooldays, had not the voice, and accent deliberately assumed, been so truly remarkable. It was a high-pitched voice, that rather sang than spoke. He turned from time to time to his companion, to whom, to John's amazement, he alluded as "my dear"—John wondering if that was the fashionable pet name in London. The friend was of similar type, but he talked less and giggled more. The teeth were profusely stopped with gold, and while they talked, he extracted a piece of washleather from his yellow waistcoat pocket and polished his nails. He was the younger by about two years.

"Mrs. Perdie didn't introduce us," said the elder—"my card."

John took the piece of pasteboard and read it. In Roman printed type it ran "Reginald de Courtrai. Greenroom Club, W. C."

"You are French?" asked John.

"By descent—my grandfather was a Courtrai de Courtrai."

"Oh—I'm afraid I haven't a card yet—my name's Dean."

"Have you come to business?"

"No—I have not long left Sedley."

The companion also held out a card. John accepted it and read, "Vernon Wellington, Greenroom Club, W. C."

"I bet Reggie at dinner you were a public school boy," said the donor. "Good old public schools we always say! Glad you've come. We are trying to put some tone into this house. Lord, it needs it, look at this!" He waved his hand derisively towards a red-blue-and-gold china shepherdess on the mantelpiece.

"Fine place, Sedley," commented Mr. de Courtrai, puffing out smoke, one leg crossed in the arm chair. "Eton,—Harrow,—Sedley—I think I should have chosen Sedley had I not been educated on the continent. There's a fine tone about Sedley, what do you say, old dear?"

The old dear agreed. "My people insisted on me going to a private school. Thought me too delicate. Always regretted it." He adjusted his tie carefully, glanced at himself in the mirror and smoothed his hair with a thin white hand. "You're new to London I suppose?"

"Yes—I arrived to-day—but I shall like it."

De Courtrai blew more smoke into the air.

"You must get some cards—really, my dear."

"And a club," added Wellington. "Every fellah must have a club. We'd put you up, but ours is for the profession."

"Profession?" asked John. He was eager to know what they were. He had never met any one quite like this.

"We're on the stage," replied Wellington.

"Oh—it must be very interesting work, acting."

"We aren't actors; we're in the ballet—the Empire. We're opening next Monday—'Scheherezade.'" De Courtrai stroked his ankle. "A superb spectacle, you must come."

John had never seen a ballet and he could not imagine the parts played by these young exquisites. He remembered two pictures by an artist called Degas, on which Mr. Vernley set great value. They were of ladies in short fluffy skirts with stumpy legs, on one of which they stood, stork-like. Bobbie said they were ballet-girls, and that Tod had once run one, whereupon John naïvely asked "Which won?" causing Vernley to collapse in shrieks of merriment. He had never heard of men doing ballet dancing. Perhaps they had something to do with the scenery. He did not care to hint at this, however, and said how much he would like to see the ballet.

"He'd better come on Wednesday, my dear," said de Courtrai, addressing Wellington, "when we're doing 'Carnival.' He'll fall in love with Harlequin, won't he?"

Mr. Wellington giggled and exclaimed—

"S'nice!"

"Is she very beautiful?" asked John.

They opened their eyes wide. Mr. Wellington again giggled, put his hand delicately on his hips, shook himself and exclaimed, "Chase me!"

"My dear!" exclaimed de Courtrai, dabbing his nose with a highly-scented handkerchief, "It isn't a she, it's a he!" They laughed again, in a high-pitched key which jarred on the young man, and they saw that he resented their mirth.

"You mustn't mind, old thing," de Courtrai exclaimed apologetically, touching John's arm. "You're really rather sweet."

John got up.

"I'm afraid I must go and unpack now."

"Can we help?" volunteered Wellington.

"No, thanks, I haven't much," he replied and went out. He could hear them giggling as he went upstairs to his room, and felt furious with them for making such a fool of him. How was he to know that Harlequin wasn't a ballet-girl? He would talk less in future, and not ask so many questions. But he disliked their manner although they had been very friendly.

Half an hour later there was a tap on his door. With his head deep in the almost empty trunk, John paused. The tap was repeated. In reply to his call Wellington and de Courtrai entered, the latter carrying a cup.

"We've brought you some coffee we've made in our room. Ma Perdie won't make it without a shilling extra."

"Oh, thank you," said John taking the cup. They paused.

"Won't you sit down?—at least, there's only two chairs; I'll sit on the bed."

They sat down and John sipped the coffee. It was made from essence and sickly sweet, but he had to drink it.

"You're very jolly in here," said de Courtrai thrusting his feet out towards the gas fire. "A nice warm room —we're at the top. You're getting your knick-knacks about, I see."

"Yes—just a few I've brought."

Suddenly from the other side of the room came a loud "Ooh!" It was from Wellington who had been walking round on a tour of inspection. He had halted at John's ivory brushes, with his father's monogram and crest.

"What charming brushes!" he sang. "Look, my dear,

aren't they just too lovely!" He carried the tray to de Courtrai.

The latter looked.

"Yes, I believe they're heavier than mine. But Welly, you mustn't be so rude."

"Oh, it's all right," said John weakly. The next exclamation came from de Courtrai, who suddenly saw the portraits on the dressing table.

"Who's this?" he asked picking up Vernley's portrait.

"My friend."

"What a sweet face!"

John could hardly agree, and he thought with a smile, what Vernley would have said if he had heard himself called "sweet."

"And this?" Wellington picked up Marsh's photograph.

"Another friend," replied John briefly. Next to it stood a portrait of Muriel. He didn't want them to probe all his secrets. He was a fool for putting it out.

But de Courtrai's eyes travelled over it without notice, to a Sedley group.

"Who's this with the ball?"

"Oh—that's Lindon, the Captain."

"What a wonderful figure!"

"Yes—he weighed twelve-stone-four. He was stroke in the first eight too," said John, "and he's a fine pianist."

"You can tell he's an artist by his eyes," exclaimed Wellington. "I never make a mistake that way; do I, my dear!" He giggled and sat down.

"Never, Welly—you've a gift for the s'nice and s'naughty."

"Go h'on!" giggled Wellington, dabbing his face. John stared, de Courtrai saw the wonder in his eyes.

"We must hobble off—we're in the way—we'll see you again."

"Don't forget Wednesday," cried Wellington in the doorway.

"Ta-ta!" called de Courtrai. The door closed.

What a pair! John didn't know whether to laugh or be angry. They were very vulgar and inquisitive, but also very friendly. He would not encourage them, however. He resumed his unpacking. An hour later he had finished, and was preparing for bed, when there was another tap on the door. This time he pretended not to hear; he did not want them in again. But when the tap was repeated, he went to the door and opened it. In the darkness of the landing, he could not see who it was.

Captain Fisher paused on the threshold. He had come out of the darkness and stood blinking in the light. John waited, for he seemed about to say something. There was a long pause, a clearing of the throat, then—

"Permit me to introduce myself, sir, I am Captain Fisher, Fisher of the 3rd Foot, sir. Twelve years China Station, twelve Malta, six Gold Coast—damn it. Glad to know you, sir!" he stammered, then bowed low.

Embarrassed, John bowed also.

"Those were days, sir,—days—days of—" he put a hand on the lintel as though the memory was too much for him. "Egad, sir, they *were* days. Fisher was a boy, sir, Lavington will tell you, sir—General Lavington, God bless him—ninety-two to-day, sir—we've drunk his health at the 'Rag' to-night. A great Speeeech . . . a wunnerful man . . . ninety-two, not much longer, sir, any of us. An' here we are, in a Perdiferous house—pardon me, it's a great night—with foreign meat, cats, parrots and a shilling in the slot. If any had a' known on China sta-

tion that Charlie Fisher would have been living in this
manag—menag—caravanserai, as Omar would say—
You've seen 'em, sir,—the blighted blossom of India! Ha!
Ha! An' the eunuchs—yes, sir, that's what they are!
Pouff!" Here Captain Fisher steadied himself from a
fitful gust of indignation. "Now there's a gel out
to-night—

Take a pair of sparklin' eyes
an' a—"

hummed the Captain. "You'll see her, sir, what a glorious vision! Wants breaking, sir! A high stepper like
her father's fillies, but what a head—what a—I'm a connoisseur too, in my day, Dandy Fisher they call me.
China Station twelve years, twelve years Malta, Gold
Coast—"

"So you said, sir," interrupted John, breaking the circle.

"You're a fine lad," exclaimed the Captain, looking at
him keenly. "Just such a lad as mine, God bless 'im.
What's y'name?"

"Dean, sir—John Dean."

"John—ha! so's mine—God bless him—dear ol' John
—dear ol' John." He swayed a little, as he surveyed his
waistcoat. "He was your age too, and his hair too—just
such hair—the gels loved him—dear ol' John."

"Is he—is he dead, sir?" asked John.

The old man straightened himself proudly.

"For his King and Country, sir—in the Boer War—
an' a V. C., sir,—a V. C.—God bless 'im." A tear
trickled down his nose. "The last to leave me—the
last. General Lavington said to-night—ninety-two, sir,
he is, he referred to John, he knew 'im—signed his first

papers, sir—dear ol' John. Come and have a drink, me
lad." Captain Fisher turned and put a shaking hand on
the banisters.

"Not to-night, sir, thank you, it's late."

"So 'tis—so 'tis. Good night, my lad. God bless you!"

"Good night, sir!" John waited until the broken old
man reached his room, and then closed his door.

With a last look round his little room, John swiftly undressed, stood pyjama clad and barefooted a moment after
brushing his hair, looking out on the bright moonlight
night, and the quaint caricature of the Campanile. Then
he turned off the light and leapt into bed. But not to
sleep. This was his first day, and he now slept for the
first night in the city he had come to conquer; so far
he had done little conquering, he thought, as he reviewed
the events of this day. The moonlight flooded his room,
making it still more unfamiliar. He watched the swiftly
fading glow of the gas fire, and his eye caught the portrait of Muriel, illuminated in a direct beam of moonlight
on the mantelpiece. Mastered by an impulse, he threw
back the clothes and put a foot on the cold floor, then
sprang out and took the portrait from its place. For a
long moment he looked at it in the dimness, then pressed
his lips to the cold glass, and was about to get into bed,
when he did what he had not done for a long time. He had
never given any serious thought to religion; perhaps he
was instinctively rather than formally religious. The
times when he had sat in school chapel had been irksome,
though occasionally a hymn, and the high fresh voices of
the choir had stirred him, aesthetically, not spiritually.
But to-night he felt very lonely, and just a little afraid.
Moreover there was a new faith in his fervent love for
Muriel, which somehow required expression. So quietly he
slipped down to his knees, buried his face in his hands,

and prayed in a somewhat disordered fashion for something which he could hardly define. Then standing up again, he looked at the photograph, wondering whether the head he saw, in reality lying on a pillow in a quiet country room, flooded with light from this same moon, would realise anything of what he had just done and said. He turned to replace the frame, then, on a thought, put it under his pillow and got into bed. Two minutes later, quiet breathing in a silent room told of a dreaming head, smiling for some reason, buried deep in the pillow. He was oblivious even of Capt. Fisher's deep bassoon in a room above.

CHAPTER II

I

HE had never experienced anything like this before, and after the dismal events of the day, the
exhilaration he felt was heightened by reac-
tion. The stall in which he sat was luxurious. It was
good to see around him so many prosperous, well-groomed
men, and smiling, richly clad, or half-clad women. Then
the lights, streaming on the gilding, the brass rails, the
tall proscenium, and the gaudily panelled ceiling, with
its naked nymphs, rosy limbed, floating from pursuing
youths on banks of fleecy cumulus,—all tended to awaken
the senses. But oh! the music and the ballet! that wild
spontaneous rush of thistledown feet and lovely limbs,
the glitter, the elaborately evolved design, the swift riot
of colour swimming on a sea of soft melody that poured
out over the darkened auditorium! From the white beauty
of "Les Sylphides," dreamlike, as a stirring of lilies on
a moonlit pool, they had passed to the happy flirtations of
"Carnival." John, in ecstasy, forgot the sick misery of
his heart, forgot those cold refusals, the reluctant opening of numerous doors, the frigid examination of self-
confident men, the waiting, the snubbing, the insolence of
office boys and porters; his deep hatred of Fleet Street,
his apprehension of fruitless days, all passed away as he
peered into these glades of music and loveliness. With
the blaze of prodigal splendour in "Scheherezade," the
swift change of music from revelry to terror, the hurrying

220

and scurrying of silk-clad women, the stern dignity of the departing Sultan, John's head swam. He almost forgot to look for Wellington and de Courtrai in that rapturous release of the captives and the licentious abandon of the women on their entry. It was with difficulty that he penetrated their disguise, for the effeminate dandies of Mariton Street were half-naked dusky men with muscular torsos who leapt and danced with fierce exultation before their adoring lovers. John could hardly realise that these superb athletes, masters of rhythm and gesture, were the two vulgar youths who, despite his coolness, had shown him nothing but kindness, with such insistence, that he had accepted their pressing invitations to this performance. And his amazement passed to unbounded admiration when de Courtrai died from a stroke of the Sultan's scimitar, in a magnificent somersault that laid his body prone at the feet of his terrified mistress. The curtain fell to a tumult of applause.

The long interval enabled John to explore the promenade at the back. He stood in a corner and watched the parade, and wondered if it was always the same, night after night—what kind of lives these people lived, where their money came from, their nationality, for there were overdressed young Jews with patent-button boots and silver-topped canes, elegant dandies with waisted coats, girlish-looking youths that smirked and simpered, heavy-jowled men with pendulous stomachs and evil gloating eyes under bald, shiny heads. The women too, French, German and Russian, dark, fair, loud-voiced, high-heeled, arrayed in furs, small-footed and mincing, they passed, with quick eyes and mechanical smiles, or sulky stare and—

"Penny for your thoughts, dearie," said a girl in a large white stole, as she laid a kid-gloved hand on John's arm.

He started more in fear than surprise.

"Lord love us—I shan't bite yer!" she laughed. "So shy! and a pretty boy too," she added, giving her fur a twitch while she looked audaciously into his eyes with a frank stare. "How do you keep your complexion, lovey? That ain't Ligett's one and six in cardboard boxes, I know."

John smiled, almost unintentionally. She could only be about eighteen, and despite the hard mouth, she had innocent, kind eyes.

"That's right—you're a regular Adonis with that showcase smile," she exclaimed. Several persons were watching them. John coloured with self-consciousness.

"Gawd! I wish I could do that—an' I did once, dearie, before the dirty work on the cross roads. But I don't mind a Martini before Strumitovski waves his stick again."

What could he do? To say "No" might provoke an outburst. He moved towards the bar, her hand still on his arm. He felt a thousand eyes turn on them, heard a thousand whispers. He was sure the bar-maid smirked satirically when he ordered two Martinis. He had never had a cocktail in his life, and didn't know whether to drink or eat the red cherry in the amber liquid. His companion led the way and he saw she expected another, although he had not swallowed half of the bitter stuff. He ordered two more, and while they talked a warm glow crept over him, and with it a feeling of distance. He seemed to be talking to her down a corridor. There was a loud ringing of a bell above the babel.

"Where are you sitting?" she said, propelling him out. Before he could answer some one called "Dean!" rather excitedly. The voice was familiar, and turning, in the crush at the door, he saw Lindon.

"What on earth are you—?" began Lindon joyously.

Then, suddenly he saw the gloved hand on John's arm and swiftly glanced at his companion. Lindon winked expressively. "See you later, Scissors," he called. "I'm at Jules, Jermyn Street," and then disappeared. Utter confusion fell upon John. He strode fiercely along.

"Lord! do you owe him a fiver?" simpered the girl.

"No—certainly not, it's you!" he returned fiercely.

She did not flinch, accustomed perhaps to such remarks. John, although slightly drunk, was aware of his cruelty and felt penitent.

"Don't flare, dearie," she said quietly.

He halted at the corner where he turned for the gang-way.

"Good-bye," he said, somewhat ungallantly, to which she responded by detaching her arm.

"Aren't you coming home with me, boysie?" she asked plaintively, her eyes very serious.

"No—thanks, not to-night—I don't—I—" but he could not say it. She divined it, however.

"I know you don't—and I'll not be the first. You shy darling!" she cried impulsively, taking his face between her hands and kissing his mouth. A moment later she had gone, leaving nothing but a faint odour of stale scent. Pale now, John leaned on the wall while the blood surged to his brain, then, with a heart thumping tumultuously, he found his way back to his seat. The rest of the ballet passed unheeded; his mind was tracking that plaintive little face through the dark house.

When the curtain fell on the final divertissement, in accordance with instructions John found his way round to the stage door, in a dark back street, where stood several luxurious motor cars, a small group of young men and women, autograph hunters chiefly, a tout or two, all kept outside the stage door, blazing with light, by a hoarse-

voiced man in livery, to whom in turn, each member of
the company called "Good night, Billy." At last Wellington and de Courtrai appeared and with them, three young
ladies of the ballet, called Fluffy, Pop and Pansy respectively. On the programme they had Russian names, as
had his two friends, but their accents betrayed familiarity
with Balham. They were pupils in the *corps de ballet,*
and for ten minutes—during which they all walked
towards Piccadilly Circus, there was an animated discussion of the performance, its errors, and the wickedness
of the conductor who had taken the last score through in
six-eight time, causing a collapse of the principals the
moment the final curtain had fallen, whereupon he had
been summoned to the wings by Lydia Lamanipoff and
had his face well slapped for his insolence. Pop declared
that it would end that "affair" which had been a subject
of current gossip ever since Lydia had thrown over Ta-
manski for biting her shoulder in the "Bacchanale."

John was swept along in the crowd, his own little group
noisily laughing and talking, Pansy hanging on his right
arm, while her other fondled a Pekinese dog with an
enormous blue bow. They turned in at a restaurant on
the corner of a street, descended some marble steps that
wound round a lift, and suddenly John, pulled through a
couple of swing doors, halted amazed in a marble panelled
room, over-lit, with innumerable small tables surrounded
by men and women. Wellington made his way down the
centre of the room, glancing at himself in the large mir-
rors on his left and enjoying the sensation their entrance
caused. He commandeered a table down at the bottom,
near the noisy waitresses' buffet; above the babble of voices
rose the discordance of an orchestra on a dais. Its
chief function appeared to be that of creating as much
noise as possible, including antics at the piano and on a

small drum and an organ. Wellington and de Courtrai appeared to be well-known, for several dandified youths, distinguished by spats, cuffs, side-whiskers or monocles, came over to speak to them, and all were very convivial, ending their remarks with, "Won't you introduce me?" Handshaking was a great ceremony, accompanied with "How d'ye do?" to which was allied its inseparable bromide, "Pleased to meet you."

Pop distinguished herself by ordering steak and chips and a bottle of stout; Pansy had a more delicate taste, ordering sardines on toast, which de Courtrai declared was a specialty in this hall of many tables. Bewildered, John ordered the recommended dish, refused a cigarette from a pale gentleman who insisted upon talking across Pansy to him, and was suffocated with the heat and tobacco smoke. The conversation was still of Lydia and her loves, punctuated by long stories of the ladies, and other ladies' furs and "fellahs." John, desperate for a theme of conversation, began by praising the Pekinese, and then narrated his experience with the lady and her three dogs in the park. To his surprise it awakened immediate and deep interest. At the end, the girls giggled and Wellington exclaimed, "Chase me!"

"It's thumbs up," said de Courtrai, wisely.

"What a cheek!" asserted Pansy, rolling her eyes; Pop declaring, "It's a shime to lead awy the young,"—whereupon there was loud laughter.

"Mind what you drink," said Fluffy impressively.

"I should take Welly as chaperon," advised Pansy.

John, getting redder and redder, partly in anger at his own naïve foolishness, partly at their insinuations, declared he was not going at all.

"What!" they all screamed in amazement.

"Wish I'd the chance," commented de Courtrai, adjust-

ing his tie. "I want some one to take a motherly interest
in me."

There was another bellow of laughter. All eyes were
turned on their table. John wished he could get away.
But they sat on until the lights began to go out, and when
at last they were in the street again, John discovered, to
his dismay, they were not bound for home but for Pop's
flat off Jermyn Street. He suggested going home alone.

"Rubbish, the fun's just beginning," cried Fluffy, taking
his arm. He was swept along with them. Pop led the
way, herded them into a small lift that ran up out of
a dark hall in the street. It halted on the fourth floor,
where they all emerged.

"Wonder if the Colonel's in," said Pop, turning the
key. They all followed and the question was answered in
the diminutive hall by the emergence from a brilliantly lit
room of the Colonel himself. He was big fat man, with a
treble chin and thin lips. His eyes were beady and their
sockets were sunken and baggy. On his enormous
stomach he displayed a heavy gold chain, and as if to
augment the size of the foundations of such an enormous
superstructure, he wore white spats. A diamond glittered on his finger, six black hairs trailed across his gleaming head, and his teeth were stopped with gold. Anyone more unlike a colonel, John had never seen. When
John, later, asked de Courtrai for his regiment, the wise
young man laughed.

"Oh—he's one of the Nuts," answered de Courtrai.

Certainly he was. He kissed the three girls in a
fatherly way, poured for them all a whiskey and soda, offered John a cigar, and finally sprang amazingly on to
the lid of the baby grand piano, where he dangled his
enormous legs. Pop disappeared into an adjoining room.
Then it *was* her home thought John, for she emerged a

few minutes later in a kimono, with slippers on and her
hair down. She curled up on a cushion by the fireplace, lit a cigarette, and looked up admiringly at the
Colonel. He had now dismounted, to permit Fluffy to
sing, Wellington accompanying, after which the latter
played with a skill and touch that surprised John. When
Pop had contributed, "Keep on loving me," to which re-
frain the Colonel pursed his lips frequently, they called
for John to perform. He pleaded excuse, but they would
not listen.

"I don't know anything, really," he urged, but they
forced him down to the piano.

"What is it?" asked Fluffy as he played the opening
bars.

"*O Lovely Night.*"

Pop looked at Wellington.

"My—he's rapid, ain't he?" she said, but John did not
hear.

There was a strange stillness as he sang. Even Fluffy
stared into space, her pretty little face, under the rose
shade, pensive. "Makes me all shivery," she whispered,
between the verses.

Why did he sing this, John was asking himself. It
was quite out of keeping with the atmosphere. He was
a fool to court failure like this, but he struggled through.
No one spoke when he finished. Finally Pop asked for
another cigarette.

"You've got a lovely voice," said the Colonel. "Wish
I could sing like that. Could once, when a kid—in a
choir," he said with a wry smile, pouring out a whiskey
and soda.

"Lor—you in a choir," smirked Fluffy, pushing a thin
finger into his pendulous stomach. The Colonel resented
this familiarity.

"Yes, my gal, me in a choir—and solo tenor too, don't you forget it!" He gulped down his drink and sighed. Pop put her arms round his neck and kissed his bald head.

"Did 'ums den," she crooned, and they all laughed.

Soon afterwards they left, Pop and the Colonel standing in the doorway until the lift had gone down. Later, walking down Mariton Street, after they had parted from Fluffy and Pansy, de Courtrai discussed the girls.

"Orl right, of course, but, as you know, not ladies."

"Is the Colonel Pop's father?" asked John.

His two companions halted and stared at him.

"My dear child—" began de Courtrai.

"Dean's my name."

De Courtrai gaped.

"Really if you resent our—" Wellington drawled.

"I do resent being made a fool," said John, hotly.

The conversation was strained for the rest of the walk home.

The Viennese clock in the drawing-room struck three as they lighted their candles in the hall.

II

The following morning, in a contemplative hour in bed, John was conscience smitten. He was on the road to ruin, exactly as in the books he had scoffed at. Flashy companions, the stage, the stage door, actresses, fast places of resort, doubtful flats, men of loose morals, and drink—yes, three drinks, two in the bar—the bar!—and one at the Colonel's, and then, as ended all vulgar affairs, a quarrel on the way home. What would Muriel think if she knew? Was this the way he was winning through? He had been in London four days and was on the downward path. Penitent, he sprang out of bed, and

to strengthen his will, denied himself even a dash of
warm water in his bath. At breakfast de Courtrai and
Wellington were missing, for which he was grateful. It
was good to talk with the Irish girl, enjoy her bright
laughter and the fresh look in her eyes; what a contrast
to those bedizened ladies of the ballet. Mrs. Perdie was
in her most motherly mood; she came up specially from
the kitchen to have a look at Mr. John.

"I wondered if you were coming in, Mr. Dean—I was
awake with my lumbago—but there you are. It's a
strange young man who can resist the night air of
London!"

He felt inclined to resent her comment, but it was so
good-natured that he laughed in reply. The real mother
emerged half an hour later when she met him alone in
the hall, where he came to enquire after his laundry.

"You'll soon lose that lovely colour of yours, Mr. Dean,
in this whirlpool, if you deny yourself proper rest. I've
seen many a bright young gentleman go dull through
coming home with the milk. Perhaps I shouldn't say it,
but lor, Mr. Perdie always said I was mother-mad, an'
p'raps I am. You'll not wear yourself out chasing the
moon down, will you?"

Her good-natured face wore an anxious look.

"An' it's not for me to say really, but them young gentlemen upstairs are not your kind, and I'm sorry if I'm
presuming, Mr. Dean," she said, wiping her hands on
her apron.

"Not at all—I appreciate your anxiety, Mrs. Perdie,"
answered John. "I shan't use my latchkey very often,
you'll find."

"There, sir, I felt I must say it, seeing you might ha'
been my own son, sort of fashion, an' I'm easy now."
She disappeared suddenly below.

At ten-thirty that morning, John sat in the office of the *New Review*. He had with him a letter of introduction from Mr. Vernley to Melton Cane, the editor. For one hour he sat in the waiting-room overlooking Covent Garden, while he listened to the whirr of the typewriter in the next room. A door on his right opened into the editor's den, wherein sat the assistant editor reading manuscripts, which he took ceaselessly out of a big tin box. The reader was a tall heavy man, with sandy hair and a fresh complexion. He had chatted pleasantly with John and told him poetry was a drug on the market, and they were choked with it.

"Ever since we discovered Mayfield's narrative epic, we've been inundated with plagiaries of his work. I wade through them until I sink in despair."

"But I haven't brought any poetry," explained John. The big man gave a sigh of relief.

"You look like a poet—which made me think there was no hope for you—all those who look the part write dreadful rubbish. You saw that schoolgirl's-dream come in a few minutes ago?" He alluded to a magnificent, leonine-headed youth with flaming tie and dark cloak whom John had taken for one of the great on earth. "Here's the stuff he's left—without a stamped addressed envelope for return—

My soul is bitter within me,
Long nights have I contemplated
The ego that is mine
And questioned to what immortality
Destined I go—

I can tell him at once—the waste paper basket."

The offending manuscript joined the pile of the rejected.

"You *do* write?" asked the assistant editor.

"A little."

"Prose or poetry?"

"Prose."

"Ah! there's some hope, but not much. Are you aware, my dear boy, that only three out of every hundred novels bring their authors royalties, and that only one of those three provides a decent income? Do you know that editors rely on big names, their directors' literary shareholders and occasionally, when they have been out of town too long and must go to press, the literary agent?"

John did not know this. The assistant editor stood up and yawned. "One day I'm going to run a school of authorship. Having been a hack for ten years with the income of a typist, I shall tell the aspirants how to become authors, and get testimonials from all the editors in whose papers I shall advertise my prospectus. Have a cigarette?"

John took one. They smoked in silence for a while. The assistant editor pointed to a portrait on the wall. "That poor devil committed suicide in Brussels last week. He had a net income of £4 per month from this *Review*. Why do people write poetry, why do they write at all? Literature is not a profession, it's a form of vagrancy."

"You've been a vagrant?" said John.

"How did you know?"

"I read your travel books and liked them."

"Oh—well, I'm off for good this time. I'm going to Capri where I shall sleep all day and talk all night. Been to Capri? No? Well, it's a good place to fade away in. Are you going to wait for Cane?"

"Yes."

"He'll come in with a rush and go out with one. He's lunching with the Irish Secretary. He's in such a hurry that he's never sure whether he is in Constantinople, Berlin or Paris. His pet theory just now is the German menace; have you anything on the German menace?"

"No—I've—"

"That's the line at present. Last month we were Malthusian, this, we are standing for strong language in modern verse, next the German menace—we don't know what after that; the menace may run to two numbers. You will notice I am discreet. That is half my charm. It's now twelve, I think you'd better wait half an hour, and then come out to lunch with me."

"Oh thank you, but—"

"No, it's not kind of me, as you think. You keep me from being bored with myself. Presently you shall tell me all the ambitions of your white young soul, all the sinks you are going to flush with your flood of zeal, the heights of fame you will scale, the way you propose to pay for board and lodgings, how you'll persuade the publisher you are the infallible boom he is waiting for. But you shall not read me any of your poetry."

"I don't write poetry. I told you I didn't," began John.

"Almost I am persuaded," said the assistant editor. "But you will; the symptoms are there It is a mental measles you cannot escape." He stacked up the unread manuscripts. "There are poets in that pile who can write like Keats, like Shelley, like Byron, like Wordsworth, and they do it just as well. They've been born too late. What they can't do is to write like themselves. There are over thirty Swinburnes here, and enough suggested immorality to poison the Vatican library. Most of it is written by young ladies."

At this moment Mr. Cane came in. He was a little man, going bald, with scrubby moustache. John was about to retire, but he bade him stay. Rapidly he glanced through half a dozen letters on his desk, dictated social acceptances to his typist and then turned to John.

"Now—what can I do?"

John presented his letter. Cane read it quickly.

"You want work, I see. There's none worth having in the literary world. You're well informed, I'm told. Do you know Elverton Thomas?"

"I've heard of him."

"He wants a secretary who can get points for his speeches. If you like, I'll give you a letter to him at the House of Commons."

"It isn't what I want, thank you," said John.

"We don't always get what we want," snapped Cane. "I can't do anything else for you," he added with an air of ending the matter.

"You can if you will, Mr. Cane, please. You know Mr. Walsh."

"Well?"

"I want to see him."

"Newspaper editors are very busy men."

"They've always time for good business," urged John.

"H'm—how old are you?—you can get what you want, I see."

"Nineteen, with lots of drive in me."

"You want to get on a newspaper?"

"Yes—I'm determined to."

"I'll ring up Walsh. Go to his office at five to-day. He'll be in then."

"Thank you very much."

Cane stood up, buttoned his coat, put on a glove.

"I'm going now," he said to his assistant. "I'll sign those cheques this afternoon. Send back Professor Railing's articles on Shakespeare—there's nothing bar his resurrection could make a noise for him." He strode to the door.

"How's Mr. Vernley?" he asked John.

"Very well, sir, thank you."

"And Muriel?—a bright child that!"

A light leapt in John's eyes. The other man understood at once and gave him the first warm human look.

"Oh—she's very well, sir."

The door closed, he was gone.

"There! what do you think of him?" asked the assistant, somewhat proudly, John thought. "He'll play bridge at the Reform until four, dance at Murray's during tea, and rush back here before dressing for the opera. And those simpletons," with a wave towards the pile of the rejected, "think he spends his time discovering them for the next number. Our next specialty in verse—is a mechanic poet. There have been navy poets, tramp poets, fishermen poets, postmen poets, porter poets, but no one's found a mechanic poet. I have, and strange to say he doesn't write about lathes, cams or beltings. He's gone back to pure Greek. Here's 'Iphigenia in Balham.' Victorian bricks and mortar mixed with ancient Greece. We've prevailed on the Bishop of London to quote it next month. That'll start the *Church News;* an interview in the *Daily Mail* with the new poet, and we are well into a second edition. Now let's go to lunch. I don't know your name. I'll call you Narcissus—listening to my echoes."

"That's a lucky shot," said John. "That is my nickname. Dean's my name."

"Ha!" said the assistant editor. "You are a reincarnation. I must take you to a lady friend of mine. She will see the aura of a chlamys under your flannel shirt. My name, too, is strange—not what you would think for a moment. Not poetical or suggestive, scarcely practical even—just Smith—you start at the revelation. It is distinguished only by having neither a 'y' nor an 'e'. We belong to the original Smiths—the blacksmiths. Ready?"

Crossing the Strand, John began to wonder if this was the inevitable end of all attempts to do work in London. It was good-natured of this stranger to take him out. He was amused at his torrential witty chatter, but it was not solving the all-pressing problem of getting a living.

After lunch they parted in the Strand, John promising to take Smith the short story which he confessed he had written. It was now a quarter past three. He walked slowly down towards Fleet Street. Would Cane fulfill his promise and arrange his interview with Walsh? He particularly wanted to join the staff of the *Daily Post*. He had read it regularly at school. Three times they had published letters of his, and they had taken two articles.

He found the Square, lying back from Fleet Street, in which the offices of the *Daily Post* were situated. Through the swing doors he came to an enquiry office, and asked for Mr. Walsh. Had he an appointment? He thought so, through Mr. Cane. The uniformed attendant noted the fact on a slip of paper with John's name. He was then led into a small waiting-room. It was opposite the lift and contained a bare table and four chairs. The walls were hung with portraits of former editors and directors. John waited, standing. His heart was beating with suppressed anxiety; he felt he was on the fringe of things.

A long wait, then a page boy asked him to follow. He entered the lift, rose several storeys, walked down a long white-bricked corridor, turned a corner and found himself in an oval hall, with several doors leading out of it. John was asked to wait. Behind one of these doors sat the great man. There was much coming and going of clerks, and possibly reporters. Half an hour dragged by. John stood up and paced the floor. Then three quarters of an hour, and still no summons. Through a glass door he could see a young man writing under a shaded light. He tapped the door, and the writer came to him.

"Is Mr. Walsh disengaged yet?"

"I don't know—have you an appointment? What name?"

John told him. The dark young man disappeared through another door. He came back in a few seconds.

"Mr. Walsh is sorry, but he cannot see you."

Dismay covered John's face.

"But I have been kept—"

"He is very busy to-day."

"Surely he knew that before?"

"Perhaps—but he can't see you."

"Then I shall sit here until he can."

The young man smiled.

"This office never closes," he said.

"But that door opens," retorted John, nodding at a door.

It was a lucky guess.

"His secretary won't let you in—it is quite useless, really."

"We shall see," said John, now enjoying his obstinacy. A door close by opened, and a small clean-shaven man, of middle age with gold pince-nez, stood by listening to the debate. He suppressed a smile as he looked at the flushed youngster, then came forward.

"What do you want?" he asked.

"I want to see the editor, sir, and if he's a gentleman— he'll see me after waiting for him an hour."

The man peered at him through his eye glasses.

"I'm afraid he's not a gentleman, but you can see him."

"Oh, thank you, sir."

"Come along," he said and showed him into a large room littered with papers and books. He motioned John to a seat.

"Now what do you want?" he asked, standing with his back to the door.

"I want to see Mr. Walsh, please."

"On what business?"

"It's personal—" began John.

"Perhaps so—but he must know. You want to write for the paper I suppose?"

"You've guessed it, sir,—but do let me see him," John pleaded.

"He's engaged with the chief reporter at present—but he will see you soon, if you're patient."

He then left the room by another door.

John looked out of the window, down across the flat top of temporary buildings, and saw the traffic surging along Fleet Street. He was engrossed in the spectacle when his benefactor re-entered and seated himself in the revolving chair before the littered desk.

"The editor will see you now," he said.

John jumped up.

"Oh, thank you sir," he cried, and walked toward the door.

"In here!" said the man, waving a hand for John to resume his seat. "I am Mr. Walsh—though you may have expected a gentleman."

"Oh!" cried John, and collapsed in confusion.

"Mr. Cane tells me you are an enterprising young man. I see you are an obstinate one. They are both qualities required on a newspaper. I'm sorry we've no vacancies. The principle on which a newspaper is staffed is that we always have more men than we can employ—for emergencies and for weeding out. You have no experience?"

"No sir, but I—"

"Don't worry, experience is unnecessary to any but duffers. You look sharp. Leave your address with my secretary. If a vacancy occurs—"

"But it won't sir."

"How do you know?"

"I know that's the way every unsatisfactory interview ends," said John, grimly, more desperate than insolent.

Mr. Walsh got up and crossed to the mantelpiece.

"How old are you?"

"Nearly twenty, sir. You see, I must earn a living, my bit of money won't last long. That has nothing to do with you, but I know you will be glad to have me when it is too late."

The editor smiled.

"You believe in yourself, and you'll succeed. But I can't take you on. I'll attach you, however. You can do a few theatres, and art galleries and perhaps the literary editor can give you a little work."

"Oh, thank you sir."

"And one day we may be able to put you on the reporting staff."

"On what basis am I paid?" asked John.

"For what you do."

"And how much is that?"

"Depends on the chief reporter. It's all I can offer you, it's a chance."

"I'll take it, thank you."

John rose.

"See Mr. Merritt before you go." He held out his hand. "And I wish you luck."

John was dismissed. Outside the door he took a deep breath. He had won the first round. All now depended on Mr. Merritt, who, he learned, was out. John left word to say he would call the following afternoon. His next job was to go into Philip's shop, and buy a map of London. At tea, in a Lyon's shop, he read down a list of amusements. Dramatic critic for the *Daily Post*—he murmured to himself. It sounded splendid. And what a shock for Wellington and de Courtrai! That evening he wrote to Vernley, to Muriel and to Marsh. He also sent a letter to Mrs. Graham and Mr. Steer, saying he was in London, and asking if he might call.

CHAPTER III

I

IN the entrance of the Circle Theatre there were already
several loiterers awaiting friends with whom they
were going to see the new play. Among them John.
There was of course, nothing unusual in his appearance;
the gallery queue which had filed past the main entrance,
after its long vigil, would not know he differed from any
other of those fortunate fellows who, well-groomed, drove
up in taxis and cars and walked to their reserved seats,
carrying the undigested peacock to the stalls. It was all so
new to him, this animated scene with its types of humanity. Merritt, a thoroughly good fellow who had immediately shown a kindly disposition to the new man, had introduced him to Bailey, the dramatic critic of the *Echo,*
who now accompanied him. Together they stood by the
portrait of a famous American actress and scrutinised the
arriving audience. There were Jews, of course, little men,
with semi-bald heads and black curly fringes; they all
wore patent button boots, and very fancy dress waistcoats.
The cut of their clothes was ultra-fashionable, and there
was a glint of gold and a flash of diamonds at many points
of their ostentatious persons. Gold-mounted walking
sticks and cigars were noticeable.

"These are the inner circle of the dramatic world," said
Bailey. "That's Reinstein; he owns six theatres and a
chain of restaurants; you eat his dinners and then try to
digest them and his plays in his stalls. I've seen great

240

dramatists, men who can make you weep with their beautiful sentiment, run across the street to speak to him."

"That's an awful looking beggar," said John, catching
a vile leer directed at an under-dressed young woman who
waved an ostrich feather fan as she passed, on the arm
of an old man.

"A clever fellow—nine successes this season. That's
Wentz, his scout, a word from him will make or mar an
actor or actress."

"Who's the man he's talking to?"

"Ah—that's Lewis—he's one of us," replied Bailey.

"Us?"

"The most aggressive, the most feared and advertised
of us all. His column every Sunday is said to be the only
thing that Reinstein and his crowd worry about."

John looked at him. Hook-nosed he wore an igra-
tiating smile and his voice purred as he spoke; when he
laughed he emitted a high falsetto note. John's observation was broken by the entrance of an amazing spectacle into the charmed circle. A man, so diminutive that
his dress shirt dominated him like a plate on a plate-
holder, was shaking hands with Lewis. On his fat nose he
balanced, precariously, a pair of pince-nez through which
he peered bemusedly. The tips of his chubby hands
just emerged from two prominent cuffs, his legs being
wholly lost in corkscrew trousers falling over the feet.

"Good heavens!" cried John, "just look at—"

But another apparition joined the circle. Nature had
created him as an antidote to the little man. He was
huge; a behemoth. His heavy jaw, the massive head, the
long teeth, made him a perfect ogre, and in fulfilment
he scowled at his companions. His large hands hooked
themselves by the thumbs on to the pockets of voluminous
trousers

"They belong to us," said Bailey, enjoying the shock he administered. John's pride in his vocation had been too obvious not to afford amusement to a confirmed cynic who had sat in the stalls for twenty years, and had never betrayed the weakness of enthusiasm.

"But—but surely," said John, "the newspapers don't send people like these—what about their dignity?"

"Dignity! There's no such thing in journalism. That belongs to the leader-writer—in print."

"Are they all like this?"

"Most of us," replied Bailey, lighting a cigarette from the stub of another. "We're working 'subs' by day and deadhead gentlemen by night—the more respectable are civil servants—and they are the least civil critics. Still —there are a few presentable ones; we have the Grand Old Man—he's not here yet. He is a perfect contrast to the Nut-food man—they'll be here later."

A curly-headed young man in a fur coat strolled in. He gave himself a side glance in the long mirror, approved of his classic beauty and passed on. Everybody nodded to him and he acknowledged their homage graciously. Several elderly ladies and a flashily dressed actress hurried after him into the theatre.

"That's Ronnie Mayfair—the actor. Freddie Pond will be here soon. I've never known him to miss a first night."

Just then, John's attention was attracted by a swift glimpse of a passing head. Its unusual beauty arrested him, the dark vivacious eyes flashing under a head of black bobbed hair. She could not be more than twenty, he thought, she was so slim. The extreme simplicity of her dress, falling without any decoration from shoulder to the knee, emphasised the lightness of her poise. She was a swift darting creature, with a sensuous mouth, crimson and pensive. But there was determination. defiance almost, in every movement of her body. Passion merely smouldered: she could be a creature of sudden contrary moods. She threw John a quick but searching glance as she passed, conscious of her power to attract, and the weakness of all his sex to respond, and yet it was not a challenge so much as a half-contemptuous provocation of his nature. Bailey, observant and detached, did not fail to see the magic fire that had leapt from one to the other. He saw this youth quiver with a sudden agitation, saw the answering challenge of the lithe form that flitted by, sure of the spoil if it cared to possess.

"No," said Bailey, laying a hand on John's shoulder, amused at his false assumption of indifference, "don't be another moth. There are too many singed already."

The boy laughed, then, with a careless tone—— "Who is she?"

"The Chelsea Poppy—she's Hoffmann's famous model."

He knew then in a moment. So this was the Chelsea Poppy, the much sonneted model of Hoffmann's famous heads. He loathed this forceful Jew's sculpture—its deliberate accentuation of the ugly, its cult of the repulsive, its coarse workmanship, apologised for as the new art. Like others he had wondered how foolish Society women could make themselves so extravagant over this ugly little man, the jerseyed king of the Café de l'Europe, with a court of disorderly disciples. The head of Poppy was famous. In the marble he had loathed its sensuality, the ugliness of the contorted face. But there was a repulsive similarity to the original; it was a cruel travesty of the flower-like beauty he had just seen.

"She's—amazing," said John, not trusting himself to say more.

"In many ways," added Bailey. "Here's Freddie. It is a perfect first-night, if the Grand Old Man will come."

"Curtain up!" came the call. The lounge emptied into the darkened house. The dramatic critics became very serious.

II

The end of the first act gave John another glimpse of the Chelsea Poppy, a less assuring glimpse. She was talking, at the entrance to the bar, to a cadaverous fellow who leered at her, and an involuntary shudder passed over John as he noticed the possessive look in the eyes of the man; he resented the fact that the girl seemed in no way perturbed. Probably she was at home with that kind of man; certainly she talked with absolute familiarity, and her hoarse little laugh jarred on the ears of the youth ready to adore. Twice she winked at a pair of young cavalry officers who sat on a lounge opposite, partly to display their seamless boots, partly to catch the girl's eye. Snatches of their conversation floated over to the youth who stood alone under the mirror. They were enjoying themselves at the expense of the promenaders. The diminutive fat man provoked their scorn.

"How do such people get into this part of the house?" asked the pink and white youth, twisting an auburn moustache.

"Can't say," drawled the pride of the regiment, regarding with satisfaction his thin thighs. "The fellow's a reporter I suppose!" They yawned and then watched a girl's ankles until she drew near, whereupon they coldly looked at her from head to foot. She seated herself on the lounge. When John turned away she had taken a cigarette from the proffered case. They did not rise with the call of the curtain. In the interval after the second act, John let Bailey point out more celebrities. There was a distinguished looking Jew, with dilated nostrils, iron grey hair and a stoop, handsome in the manner of his race, bearing the impress of intellect.

"That's Luboff the novelist!"

The famous portrayer of Jewry passed; his face, despite its lineal coarseness, had an amazing beauty in its character. A few minutes later Bailey was talking with the novelist and introduced John, who found himself magnetised by an intense personality with great charm. He was a man with a hundred fights against poverty, prejudice and ill-health, but he had triumphed nobly. He had interpreted the Jews to a scornful world, displayed their poverty, revealed their poetry. As a dramatist he had assumed the rôle of a reformer; he entertained the crowd, but he lectured it. After a few minutes' chat he left them to speak to Lord Rendon, who, despite his elephantine exterior, had a nimble mind versed in the subtleties of politics and philosophy. At this moment John's attention was arrested by the re-appearance of the girl in red. She was talking to an astounding man whose hair straggled in disorder down to and over a soft brown collar. He wore a pair of black metal pince-nez, smoked a stubby pipe, the bowl of which he pressed from time to time with fingers that scorned the need of the manicurist. The Socialist was written all over him; there was sabotage in his eyes, repressed defiance in his gestures. He wore, to accentuate his untidy eccentricity, a faded brown sports coat, the pockets bulging with papers, and most of the buttons missing.

"Ah," said Bailey, "now you've seen the nut-food man —that's Adams of the *Argus*—clever chap, but thinks untidiness is a sign of intellect."

"I see he knows the model—he's a Bohemian?"

"Yes—at least he hopes so. We haven't any real Bohemians in this country. They live on the Continent.

When Englishmen try to be Bohemian they only succeed in being lazy or noisy. You'll find that each of them is regarded as a rising poet, a rising novelist or a rising dramatist. They're always rising until they are middle-aged, when they disappear somewhere. Really, Bohemians are the dullest persons; they've no topics but their egotism. Avoid them, Dean—they're never hygienic. I can enjoy a third-rate artist who is ornamental, but these people are merely extravagant."

"But he looks interesting," urged John.

"So he is—you want to meet him?"

"Well—" He was desperately anxious to know Adams, for Adams knew the girl. He must speak to her before the play ended. Bailey guessed the hope and buttonholed Adams who shook hands.

"This is Mr. Dean. Tilly," he said, turning to the girl who had drawn aside.

"Miss Topham," he informed John. The girl looked at him casually, and merely exclaimed, "Oh!" It was a shock to the eager youth and for two or three minutes she ignored him. Then—

"You're new to London?" she said coldly.

"Yes, but who told you?" answered John.

"No one,—I could see you were by the way you've been looking at people."

This was a set back. John gave her a frightened look and she was pleased by this success.

"Have I—I hope I don't appear—" he stammered.

"It doesn't matter—they like it; that's what they come here for."

John was a little uncertain who "they" meant. It seemed to include every one but herself.

"Have you a cigarette?" she asked, abruptly.

The boy's heart sank.

"I haven't—I don't smoke. I can get some."

"Don't bother." She looked at him curiously. "You don't smoke—you're a queer kid." They stood alone now, for Adams and Bailey had strolled on. He noticed how transparently thin were her hands, which she tucked in her belt. Her neck had a lovely line in its perfect sweep from the throat down.

"You are an art student?" she asked, with a faint smirk.

"Oh no—I'm on a paper—why?"

"You examine like one."

He flushed with the detection, and she gave a little laugh of triumph.

"Sit down and tell me all about yourself—you puzzle me," she said. "You look as if you'll do all sorts of wonderful things, but people who look like that hardly ever do anything."

He was easier now. They sat side by side on the lounge.

"There's little to tell, Miss—"

"Oh, drop that, I'm Tilly to every one."

"Tilly then,—you see I haven't left school long."

"I can see that—the down's on you yet." The remark hurt him and she saw it, swiftly.

"Don't mind me," she said quietly, putting a hand on his arm. "You see I'm used to men that gloat and want rebuffing."

She laughed at the surprise in John's eyes.

"Don't look like that or I shall melt. You're a nice boy, and I'm afraid of you."

"Of me?"

"Yes—you make me think of lots of things I've given up thinking about. Harry must ask you to tea."

So she was married! Of course she was married, he

reflected, he was a fool not to have known from the first.

"I should like very much to come."

She looked at him again, until he looked away, and with a little laugh jumped up. "We must get back now. I'll see you soon. Good-bye!" and she was gone. What an off-hand creature! He was annoyed at her manner. She had treated him like an infant. She had laughed at him. He had let her see too much. When the play was ended and he stood in the crowded vestibule with Bailey, amid the crush of fur-wrapped women and black-coated men, he was still thinking of her.

"You've made a hit with Tilly," said Bailey.

"I!"

"Yes—and she doesn't pay compliments—but don't let her play with you; she doesn't take any one seriously."

"I'm not likely to do that," replied John shortly.

"Come along then—we've to get our work done."

III

Merritt, chief reporter of the *Daily Post,* was a remarkable little man. He was quite aware of this and retained his reputation with ease. The life of a chief reporter is a desperate one. The most amazing news scoop to-day is dead twenty-four hours later, and a big reputation can be lost in a day's idleness. Merritt showed no signs of anxiety. He sat at his desk in the stuffy little room adjoining the reporting room, whence he would dart out to send a man speeding across London or to Aberdeen. His totally bald head gleamed with vitality. He could be very rude and very rough, but men had rushed to Ireland at his behest and accounted themselves rewarded when he smiled and said "Good!" He was part of the *Daily Post* and could not conceive how a man could wish to live for anything else. No one ever saw him

go home and no one ever saw him come; he was the first
and the last, and when he had gone, he was not at rest.
His voice often spoke over the wire from Brixton, dis-
turbing the early morning rest of a jaded reporter. A
fire at Muswell Hill, a murder in Camden Town, a bur-
glary in Knightsbridge or an assault at Tottenham—he
knew of it first, scented the clue, despatched the sleuth-
hounds.

It was rumoured that he was married, but for years
there was no evidence, until one day he disappeared and
returned wearing black. He had buried his eldest boy
of twelve. The senior reporter to whom he mentioned
this was about to make a remark, and he saw Merritt's
mouth twitch, but the next second he was being told of
an entry on the diary. It was work, work, work. Other
men fell ill, became nervous wrecks, took to drink, were
promoted, or left. Merritt remained chief reporter,
known from one end of Fleet Street to another, perhaps
from one end of the world to the other. He never went
out, save at four o'clock for an hour, when he would be
seen in a bar near by, within sound of the buses, and he
went there for news. He knew every one. Men in the
Lobby of the "House," on the Stock Exchange, in Whitehall or at Epsom would ask "How's Merritt?" He was
the link to publicity. He knew enough about the lives
of men to equip a squad of blackmailers; and K. C.s consulted him when accepting briefs. He had saved a king
from assassination and rescued a bishop from a charge of
being drunk and disorderly. He had witnessed a succession of editors. Merritt stayed, for Merritt was the *Daily
Post*.

But above all, this stout little man of fifty knew men.
It was he who discovered Burton Phipps, their star descriptive writer, had sent him off to Norway to inter-

cept and expose the sham explorer of the Pole. Jane, the finest parliamentary sketch writer in England, was trained under his hands. Merton, the editor of the *Morning Telegraph,* Layman, the President of the Board of Trade, Reddington, chairman of the United Banks—all had groaned in their youth under his merciless yoke of discipline. Loved and feared, he spared no man, and he never encountered rebellion because he never pitied himself. "Merritt's a devil," every one said—"but a wonderful devil," they added.

He took John in hand. He made him compress a column of wonderful writing to fifteen living lines. He made him re-dress a plain narrative in a style that "tickled." He told John to use words of as few syllables as possible. "All sub-editors are ignorant and full of malice," he said, with traditional jealousy. He was never to worry about what the public thought of this or that. "The public don't think, they follow." It was a heartbreaking apprenticeship. The fine column on the Kennel Show went into the waste paper basket. "There's two murders come in and the subs say we're overset." He ridiculed a "special" on teashop girls with rapier wit, told John he wrote too fast to write well, and was as guileless as an infant in arms. Once, with a brusque committal of a much-esteemed article, he brought misery to John's eyes, saw it, and growled,

"You're a journalist all right, but your stalk's green," and with his wry smile brought a lump into the youth's throat.

"Am I—am I giving satisfaction, Mr. Merritt?"

The chief reporter looked over the top of his glasses—

"The Chief sent you to me for occasional work. You've done a banquet, a dog-show, four police courts, three inquests, two plays, a poster show and several special enquiries. You've been running about like a hare for ten days—you've not been an occasional, but a daily event. And I don't waste my time!"

It was true, John was worked hard every day. Each night the diary had the initials J. D. with a cryptic assignation following. Sometimes he accompanied a senior, a note-taker, and looked out for a descriptive paragraph; more often he was alone. On the night that he had returned from his first play, after he had sent in his pencilled copy to the subs room, he looked at the diary and almost jumped in exultation.—"J. D. 7.15., Artists Union, Chelsea Theatre, half col." Here was his chance!

IV

The members of the Artists Union were certainly artistic. A novelist who specialised in love and divorce in the Sunday newspapers and was dignified with the title of 'publicist' made a long tirade against the ignorant but prosperous industrial classes. A young man followed this, very nerve-racked and bordering on hysteria, with an oration proving that hunger and genius were inseparable, whereupon a stout lady at the back of the diminutive theatre rose up and declared that all artists, musicians, and authors should be a direct charge on the Government, a sentiment that was applauded loudly. Thoroughly enjoying himself, John sat next to a young lady in a gaudy kimono who was busy sketching the speakers, while a young man with a red beard that half hid a very weak mouth, drank tea out of a thermos flask. A wealthy lady, interested in art, occupied the chair, which must have been very uncomfortable, for most of the brilliantly insulting things said applied perfectly to her husband, a wholesale grocer, who, to atone for disfiguring England with placards inciting the public to drink Tiffinson's Tea, bought preposterous modern paintings at well advertised figures. John discovered it was a gathering of minor notabilities; there was Mr. Shandon Gunn, the cubist painter who laboriously disguised the fact that he had ever studied at the Slade School, or knew the meaning of perspective. When slightly drunk, he was reputed to be epigrammatic. His speech was cheered vociferously for its cleverness in conveying absolutely nothing to the audience. He was followed by Mr. Leslie Bumbo, a pallid fellow, the apostle of art with an ego, who wrote art books, and kept a book shop in a slum, which revealed a knowledge of business, since the bookshop kept him. Moreover, he led a culture movement for leisured ladies, who gathered every Wednesday in a shanty at the back of his house, where, in a dim light and a dim voice, he droned out his latest discourses on art. It was remunerative if mournful, for the ladies paid a shilling for admittance, bought the discourses and went home feeling gloriously advanced. His speech this evening was confined to an embroidery on "The Ugly as an incentive to Murder."

John was indebted for personal details to the young lady in the kimono, who called him "kid" and smoked incessantly while she drew. Towards the end of the meeting she waved her hand to a girl who had pushed forward in the crowded doorway. John looked and, with a slight thrill of pleasure, recognised Tilly. In the conversazione that ensued when the formal meeting ended, they sat in a corner together and drank coffee. She knew everybody and introduced him freely as "Scissors." When the company was going, Tilly, who had collected a small crowd, caught hold of John's arm.

"Come along, Scissors!" she cried, propelling him towards the door

"Where?" he asked.

"To my studio—we're having a romp."

"But I can't go—I've to get my copy ready for the office."

"Oh damn!"

He wished she hadn't said it. Perhaps he was old-fashioned, but somehow, a girl who used that word was a little—er? That was what John could not precisely say; he had been trying to since their first meeting. He did not want to appear a prig, and yet—. He knew Muriel would not approve, but he laughed at the thought. A speaker had been attacking the Victorians for their smugness—well, he was being very early Victorian.

"Come on, kid," cried the young lady in the kimono. He stood between Scylla and Charybdis. A vision of Merritt nerved him to resistance.

"Then come after, we'll go on till three or four." Weakly he declined and weakly he surrendered. He took the address and promised to return as soon as he could. It was half-past one when his work was done, and he knocked at the door of Birch Lodge Studios, No. 4, off the King's Road. There was a great noise of revelry within. When the door opened, he found himself in a large room, with a half-roof of sloping glass through which the moon peered down. A dozen Chinese lanterns illuminated the room and were reflected in the polished floor whereon about twenty couples were dancing to the music of a gramophone.

"Scissors, you dear!" cried Tilly, as he entered. "I didn't think you'd come."

"But I promised," he said, as she took his overcoat. The next moment she had taken him in her arms and they were whirling through the maze of the dance. She was hot and the studio was stuffy, and there was a lan-

guor in the manner in which she hung in his arms that
was half-trustful and half-seductive. At the far end of
the room, where the candle of the lantern was guttering,
it was almost dark as they danced round. She gave a
little laugh as the candle went out, her mouth provok-
ingly near to his, her eyes softly luminous in the moonlight falling through the glass. The rhythm, the warmth,
the music worked upon him; he was whirling, he knew not
where. For a moment he hesitated, then laughed as she
laughed, and the next moment quenched his boyish thirst
on her lips. Convulsively she clung a moment, then collapsed softly in his arms, and he experienced a strength
that was weakness, a tenderness that was cruelty. He
paused, floundering in a sea of the senses.

"Go on," she whispered, for the other couples in rota-
tion were crowding upon them. She pushed him round,
but not before the girl in the kimono swirled by and
laughed out.

"Caught you that time!"

The tone was vile, the accent inexpressibly vulgar; it
jarred on the excited youth who danced dizzily. Tilly,
more acutely alive and now self-possessed, felt her part-
ner give a shiver of disgust.

"Let's sit this out—I don't want to dance any more—
please."

They sat on a camp bed along the main wall, in silence.

"You're angry," she whispered looking at him coyly.

"I'm not."

"Oh, yes you are—look at me, you sulky boy."

He looked into her mischievous eyes, and he had to
laugh.

She twined her fingers with his.

"That's sensible," she said. "We're only young once,"
and she let her head rest on his shoulder, her soft hair

warmly clouding his cheek. The next moment he was
holding her with all the strength of his lissome young
body, and laughed delightedly when she winced at his
ardour. Yes, he was only young once.

"—way down in Tennessee,"

whined the gramophone. Only a few were dancing now.
Little bursts of laughter and chatter came from dusky
groups around the studio. It was all rather unearthly in
that aromatic atmosphere. Some one wound up the
gramophone and put on a new record—

"While shepherds watched their flocks by night
All seated on the—

"Oh, stop it," came a voice, and there was a laugh all
round.

"Got 'em mixed," responded another. "Here's 'In Ala-
bama'—how's that?" The gramophone whirred on, and
the dancing began again.

It was nearly three when the guests began to depart.
John knew none of them. He had not seen their faces
clearly all the night, but they somehow knew his name
was "Scissors," and treated him familiarly. Most of the
men were about his own age, the women a little older.
The humourist of the party, whom they called "The Doc"
was about forty-five and seemed to father the assembly.

"Don't go yet," said Tilly as she stood by the door.
"I'm not a bit sleepy and I want to talk." He stood aside
and let the others go. At last only one girl remained.

John came back to earth abruptly.

"Where's Mr. Adams—I haven't seen him all the evening."

"Harry?—oh, I don't know—he comes in when he likes,"

replied Tilly, drawing up a chair to the anthracite stove. She began talking to the other girl Fanny, who presently rose and said, "Good night," disappearing into another room.

"Is she staying with you?" asked John.

"Who—Fanny?—no, we live here together. She's getting married next week, poor kid, to a little blighter. Lord knows why she picked him—or why any girl marries at all."

"But—you're married!" said John, surprised.

She stared at him.

"Married—whatever makes you think that?"

"I thought Mr. Adams—"

Tilly interrupted him with a short laugh.

"You've been listening to gossip. Everybody says I'm going to marry him—but I say not. I'm not going to keep any man, and that's what marrying a man of genius means."

But John cared nothing for the philosophy. He was relieved, for the last two hours he had felt an unmitigated bounder. A new cheerfulness swept over him, and Tilly noticed it.

"Why, you're waking up—you've been like a bear with a sore head!"

"I'm sorry," he said, simply.

"All right, Scissors!" She slid on to her knees at his feet. "And kissing's no harm," she sighed, looking up into his face. "And oh, I'm so lonely at times!"

She pulled his face downwards with her tiny hands, and ran her fingers through his hair. The sensation made him laugh as he slipped his arms under hers and drew her upwards until their lips met. In the darkness he could hear the beating of their hearts, and the silence singing in his ears.

CHAPTER IV

A NNIE had been upstairs three times that morning
to see if Mr. Dean's shoes had been taken inside
his room. But the door was still closed and the
shoes on the mat outside. At last she gave away her secret
hero.

"Mr. Dean's not up yet," she said reluctantly to Mrs.
Perdie, as she came downstairs to the kitchen. "Shall
I keep his breakfast 'ot?"

"What?—not down? Why it's half past ten! Have
you cleared away yet?" cried Mrs. Perdie, emerging wet-
handed from the scullery and a brisk encounter with sauce-
pans. "We can't keep breakfast going into lunch time."

Annie halted, she did not expect an order that would
deprive her favourite of his breakfast.

"You'd better take it up on a tray to his room," said
Mrs. Perdie, relenting—"and I'll speak to him when he
comes down." She disappeared again into the scullery
where she thought long on the ways of young men and
how cruelly the wicked city corrupted them. Lying in
bed late had been the first sign of Mr. Perdie's breakdown.
Once a man began to lie late, his backbone went, of that
there was no question. She tolerated such a thing with
de Courtrai and Wellington on the top floor. It was in
keeping with their characters. Weedy young men in a
fast profession might be expected to lie in bed in the
morning, even at the cost of losing breakfast.

Strange to say, the one who suffered most, Annie, who
carried up the breakfast, grumbled least. She tapped

gently at Mr. Dean's door, to absolve her conscience, but not to wake him, then she tiptoed in. He was fast asleep—though she could see very little of him, with his head buried in the pillow and the sheets hunched up round his shoulders. Cautiously she drew up the blind and flooded the room with light. Then she placed a small table at the side of the bed. Still he slept. For a few moments she stood in romantic contemplation of his tousled head, with its ravelled locks. How lovely he looked, with his boyish colour and his strong throat. His pyjama jacket, unbuttoned, gave a glimpse of a strong chest. Greatly daring, she leaned forward. Just once she would do it—she might never have the chance again —and oh, she had wanted to, so many times. Often she had longed he would just come and put his arms round her and kiss her fiercely—she wouldn't have minded if he had been cruel even. She stooped and very lightly kissed his hair, just where it fell in a mass to one side of his brow, and she felt her very heart would betray her. But he slept on, unconscious of all the love poured out over him. Softly Annie went out. She halted on the threshold with the tray in her hand, flushed and trembling with excitement.

"Lor—I'm daft!" she thought, and then walked loudly into the room and deposited the tray on the table with a bang.

"Here's breakfast, Mr. Dean. It's half past ten and missus says she can't keep it any longer!"

He was awake in an instant.

"Good heavens—I've overslept!"

"I should think y'ave, Mr. Dean—that's being up 'o nights at them dances."

John laughed.

"Captain Fisher's been asking for you, Mr. Dean.

He's very excited at breakfast about something in the papers. He says you're a remarkable gentleman. He was so excited."

"But what about, Annie?" asked John stretching.

"I don't know that, sir, but he wants to see you—come in drunk last night 'e did, and was 'orribly rude to Miss Simpson, on the landing. Said he hated damn gramophones grinding hymn tunes over his head. He apologised this morning and now says he's been grossly insulted because Miss Simpson didn't say anything, but gave him a temperance tract. The missus had to speak to them both and the Captain gave notice."

"When does he go?" asked John, cracking his egg. The gossip of this caravanserai amused him.

"He never does go; he always gives notice when Mrs. Perdie says what she thinks," replied Annie. " 'Ow could he go anywhere else when all know 'is little 'abbits? But I've got a lot to do. The tea orl right, Mr. Dean?" she said, moving to the door.

"Quite, Annie, thank you," he replied smiling at her. She closed the door on her hero with a resolute sniff.

Drinking his tea, with a head clearing, John became reflective. This would really not do. Half of the morning gone, and he was due at the office at twelve! Then his mind went back to the night before, and to Tilly. It had all been rather hectic. Now he thought of it, he had been a decided fool, sitting there until the early morn, just holding in his arms and kissing a girl whom he had not known six hours, and who called him "a dear kid." Why had he behaved like that? He was lonely perhaps—and he had amused himself, that was all. He didn't, couldn't love her, and certainly she had never for a moment thought of him in that way. Turning to pour out some more tea, his eyes fell on a framed photograph on his dressing table.

Yes, he had been a bounder—he couldn't tell *her,* she wouldn't understand, for even he did not. And yet, if he met Tilly again—he dismissed the idea deliberately, but remembered in doing so that he *would* meet her again. There was a dance at the Studio next Friday. No,—he must not go there again.

He slipped out of bed, and bath towel in hand, surveyed himself critically in the glass. Did he look a rake? Was dissipation stamping its marks upon him? But the vision in the mirror was that of youth, flawless in careless health and grace.

When he appeared in the hall downstairs, and Mrs. Perdie hurried forth to give a little motherly advice, he looked such a slim picture of radiant youth, his dark eyes shining, his face gleaming, with high spirits bubbling over, that she lost the opening words of her prepared overture, and worshipped for a moment, after which her chance was gone, for Captain Fisher emerged from the drawing-room, newspaper in hand. He flourished it in John's face.

"Egad, sir, it's great—I've not laughed so much for years—you've got the real touch—I always thought those Bohemians were mad."

He touched his forehead with the rolled-up copy of the *Daily Post.*

"May I look a moment?" asked John, a little bewildered. He opened the paper on the third page and saw his name in black type. The editor had put it to the description of the Artists Union meeting. John suppressed a shout of triumph. There was his name true enough, "John Dean," with three quarters of a column of close print following! Of course, the House of Commons was not sitting, so space was plentiful; still there was his name, for all the world to see!

The omnibus that carried him on its top that gay spring morning as it wound its way past the Victoria Station down Victoria Street, under the grey front of Westminster Abbey façade, on up lordly Whitehall, might have been the steeds of Apollo the sun-god, so radiantly rode youth through the world, all civilisation singing about him, organised for his delight. He remembered hearing an odd remark of Merritt's one night.

"The first time you hit a bull's eye with the Chief, he gives you credit for it—there's your name on the target —but you've to be a marksman for that to happen." And it had happened. For the first time he experienced confidence, he was now conscious of approval. Before, it had been like dropping his articles down a drain. They disappeared for ever.

Merritt said nothing to him at the office, but in the afternoon, as he sat writing a letter in the reporters' room, the door of Merritt's little office opened. There was a sound of laughter within, and John caught sight of Phipps, who had just returned from a conference at Vienna, on which he had been writing with customary brilliance. John had never spoken to their leading man, who was as dizzily remote from his humble inquest-police-court haunting orbit, as the Pleiades from the sun.

"Dean," called Merritt, putting his head round the doorway. John went in. "I want to introduce you to Burton Phipps," he said. Phipps rose and held out his hand to him. John could not see him clearly in the sensation of the moment. Why was he so ridiculously sensitive that his eyes watered, whenever something really wonderful happened? He gulped and heard Phipps praising and laughing about his article.

"Are you doing anything?" asked Phipps.

"No, sir."

"Come out and have tea with me then. Good-bye, Merritt."

"Good-bye—Phipps."

John followed as in a dream.

Outside they crossed the square, plunging into the five o'clock traffic vortex below Ludgate Circus, walked a short way and then turned into a narrow entry. Through a couple of swing doors they found a hall, whose walls were plastered with notices, and then a lounge with small tables. A few men nodded to Phipps, the diminutive waiter smiled as on an old friend when taking the order for tea.

Now for the first time John was able to look critically at his new friend. It was a face and head of arresting dignity, beauty almost. Of small build, he was a slim, compact man of about thirty-five with a boyish expression. He was pale, his eyes a steely grey, very intense, with points of light in the pupils, glowing and alive in contrast to the general pallor of the brow. His hair was short and slightly wavy, the nose arched and Roman. It was a chiselled face, that of a man of thought, into whose lines had passed the experience of emotion, suffering perhaps. It was, in a curious way, a face, ascetic and carven, that suggested sorrow, sprung from contemplation rather than life's trials. And the voice was in accordance with this impression, for it was deep, with notes of rich melancholy, the voice of a great preacher. To John, he seemed much as he would have expected to find one of the knights of the Round Table, a strong, handsome personality—yet human, and sensitive to the beauty of life as well as its ugliness. There was a quick nervousness in the shape and movement of the hands, the right fingers being stained with nicotine, for he was an incessant smoker of cigarettes. In his talk he had a sense of humour which seemed to belie the seriousness of his expression, but that may have

been due to his subject, for John had got him to talk of
his famous adventure at a Grand Duke's wedding when he
had figured as a foreign statesman and given Fleet Street
an "inside" story that kept it talking for twenty-four hours
—a long time for Fleet Street to discuss any subject.

Then he told John something of his experiences as a
war correspondent in the Balkan War.

"A bloody, horrible business. I can hardly forgive the
folly of men, Dean. There are people here talking about
our next war—with Germany. What insanity—and what
wickedness! If only they had seen and not read about
war. I don't think there's any war worth fighting."

"Not for honour?"

"Were they ever fought for that?" Phipps looked at
him piercingly.

"I suppose not," assented John.

"And in future, there'll be no war worth winning," he
said in his deep voice. "The price of the effort will out-
value the prize. Well, if another war comes along, thank
heaven I shall be too old for sending telegrams to the
British Public about its picturesque bloodiness."

When they had parted John felt he had made a new
friend. That was the marvel of London. You met the
men who did things; you were at the hub of creation, their
names and faces were familiar with the day. Steer,
Ribble, Phipps—what would some men have given for his
good fortune?

When he arrived back at the office, word came that the
Chief wanted to see him. He went through to the Secretary's room.

"Oh—Mr. Walsh's just going—I'll ask if he'll see you."
He came back a moment later and ushered John in.

Walsh sat at his littered desk.

"Sit down, Dean. Do you know French?"

"A little, sir."

"Do you speak it?—can you be understood and understand?"

"I—I hope so sir."

Walsh smiled.

"And how much Danish?"

John looked surprised. "Danish, sir?"

The editor laughed and then got up, putting his hand on the youth's shoulder.

"Don't let that worry you—England was proud of possessing a Viking's daughter as queen, but few of us know a word of her language. On Friday, I want you to go to Copenhagen to an international telegraph conference. It will last a fortnight. Merritt will tell you what we want, and our man in Copenhagen will look after you. You will go to Harwich and cross to Esbjerg. The cashier will give you the necessary money. I hope you'll enjoy the trip. Good-bye."

He touched a bell, his secretary came in, John went out. Dizzily he walked back to his room. Travel! And he was a special correspondent! He could envision the italicised words, the magic words he had seen under Phipps' name. *Our Special Correspondent.* To Merritt he stammered out the news, but the unimpressionable Merritt seemed to know all about it.

"Keep your mouth shut until you go—or others will be green with envy. They can't help it, poor fellows. Half of them are plodders, and you don't work for all you do—it's just in you, that's all. That's half the tragedy of life —to the plodders. You needn't come in to-morrow. I'll look up the boats and trains."

Outside, in the street, John stood for a moment, while the world went by him. A queer fellow Merritt. How he had humbled that triumph—"half the tragedy of life—

tc the plodders." Somehow it made his exultation seem
childish and mean. They were such good fellows too, full
of kindness, and a spirit of give and take, and he, the
newest among them, the cub, was racing ahead. It must
be bitter. They filed before him—merry little Bewley,
daring and audacious, Lawton, the dreamer and writer
of rejected verse, Russell, the ponderous, saving hard for a
home and sentimental about children, Johnson, who longed
to retire on a farm—name after name, each coupled with
hopes and ambitions.

And now his chance had come. He must tell some one.
He went back into the clerk's office and rang up Mrs.
Graham. Yes, she was in and would be delighted if he
would dine with her. At the Temple Station he booked
for Sloane Square, his nearest point to her flat in Cheyne
Walk.

CHAPTER V

I

THE success that fell upon John Dean did not delude him. He had been unnerved too young to feel trustful toward life. While everybody called him lucky or blessed by the gods, and prophesied the dizzy heights to which good fortune would carry him, he was, nevertheless, suspicious. Twelve months had gone by since he had secured his position with fine work at Copenhagen. That mission, which from an incident had developed into an important European situation, he had handled in a masterly manner for his years and inexperience. Some men in Fleet Street called him precocious, others, less complimentary and less successful, brazen-faced. Phipps, with whom a warm friendship had grown up, called him "an amazing child," and laughed good-naturedly over the adroitness with which he had got his despatches through ahead of his colleagues. They had met, about mid-June, at Warsaw, whence Phipps was bound for Constantinople to report on the Young Turk party and the revolutions. It was the following Spring when they met again, and greatly to John's delight, Phipps had hunted up Ali, at college in Constantinople, and had brought back news that the finely grown young Turkish gentleman, now a keen follower of Enver Bey, had talked rapturously of John and the early days at Amasia.

"You must be one of his gods, Dean, by the way he spoke of you."

"We were great friends, I remember. I often wondered if he still recalled me. We have ceased to write—how strange to think he is now a big fellow—he used to be so shy."

Phipps had brought a letter for him. Later, in his own room, John had broken the seal and read it. It was a strange epistle, one moment full of the formality of the Orient, and then suddenly passionate, breaking into ornate declarations of eternal friendship. But it was Ali, as of old, and as John read, there were the old scents of that gorge in his nostrils; he could hear the tinkle of the Yeshil Irmak as it ran down, moon-silvered, over the stones, and, as the moon peered into the dark ravine, the distant-drone of the drums in the valley. The old thrill was still in his blood.

"O sworn brother, I clasp your hands and look into those wonderful eyes of yours. Still am I Ali, your proud servant, still would I follow you, John effendi. Often I think of you in the night time when the caiques are at rest by the Galata Bridge, and the moon floods the cypress groves. Often I wonder if still that gift of mine is with you. Your friend tells me that you prosper, that you are fair to behold, a leader among men. It is well. I knew this would be, of old. Sad that manhood is upon us and that we hear not the voice of each other. Still in my heart you linger. In time, it may be we meet, and oh, beloved friend, the joy that shall fall upon us, Insh'allah."

On the night he received the letter, John went round to Lindon's flat at Battersea, which overlooked the river and Chelsea on the opposite bank. It was a grey Spring evening, and the great flood ran linked with lights reflected in the stream; the beauty of melancholy was on the face of things. John stood staring out of the window. Lindon was playing by candle light; now grasping fame as a pianist, he was attractive and forceful as ever. John watched his splendid head between the candles on either side, as it moved. with the rhythm of a Brahms waltz. Suddenly the player stopped.

"A penny, Scissors," he said, seeing the deep gaze. John laughed and looked out of the window again.

"They're not worth it—only—I often wonder, Lindon, if ever we quite realize the whole wonder of life—of this—of friendship, of youth? It's all slipping by and it's so good, and we make so little of it."

Lindon rose, walked across to the window and put his arm in John's.

"Scissors, you're quite an old sentimentalist. Of course it's good—and we enjoy it, at least I know I do."

They watched the sunset fade in silence. When a last line of flame had died into the grey bank of cloud, John spoke. It was evidently the end of some thoughts.

"It will have been worth it—when it all ends and we look back. I've been lucky."

"Ends? What a morbid fellow you are! Why ends? It's all just beginning, Scissors! Why we've got the world at our feet!" Lindon laughed. It was so hearty and infectious that at any other time, John would have laughed too. Ali's letter had upset him a little. He shivered in his chair.

"You know, it's silly, Lindon—but I feel there's a tragedy coming. Life's just too good—it won't behave always like this. It waits and then pounces and you are in its grip."

"Rot!—Scissors. Let's have the light on, it's getting creepy."

"No—I want you to play—"

"What, in the dark?"

"Please—play that Brahms again—I can see all kinds of pictures."

For a moment, Lindon hesitated and then, seeing the earnest appeal in John's eyes, shook him playfully and went over to the grand.

"I shall have to feel my way, Scissors."

But he played very softly and with great feeling. John sat in the window and let the rich music flow over him in that growing darkness. It was of Ali he thought; and then he was a little boy on the verandah, in the arms of a grown man; suddenly he was standing with him under an almond tree in blossom, and the man's head was bowed in grief; out of the dusk came face after face; what did they here in this scented Eastern Garden? He caught the swift animation of Marsh's glance, about to speak; there was Vernley, the old poise of the head he knew so well; and, somehow, Mr. Fletcher was with them. How wonderfully Lindon was playing—and how insistently came the muffled pulse of a drum, perhaps down the gorge in the old deserted Khan. He must follow it—how it beat through his brain, insistent and full of wonder. He was going towards it, strangely elated.

It was quite dark when Lindon struck the last chord and let the sound flow through the room before the pedal-release curtained the room in silence.

John started, as if rudely awakened.

II

It was a London he knew now. He had followed the long social programme reaching its climax in June. He watched the fashionable crowd at Burlington House on private view day; the smaller, but more interesting gather-

ing at the Grosvenor Galleries when the International
Society's show opened; concerts at Queen's Hall, first
nights at the theatre, garden parties, polo at Hurling-
ham, the Derby and Goodwood,—all these things occupied his days. It was a vivid, everchanging experience,
this life of the journalist, and with it all he touched many
circles and found new friends. The cranks, the idealists,
the hard relentless men of affairs, the propagators of creeds,
—he met them all, and from them learned something.
There was a soft spot in the heart of most men if you
could touch it; they were very human in one aspect,
though he stood appalled at the pace humanity set itself
in the mad race to success. How many of these hectic
men and women ever realized what life was? They dared
not stop to contemplate. On, on, on, lest the horror of
their own entity should frighten them. They feared
themselves, they must never be left to themselves. Solitude meant madness—there was forgetfulness flowing
down the crowded thoroughfares.

"Only artificial people praise the country—they feel so
superior to it," said Harry Merivale, brightly, as he sat
at lunch in the Union Club, where John was the guest
of Major Slade. The company laughed at this statement;
it was the applause that always spurred Merivale to further efforts in the preposterous. At thirty he had been
considered a wit and a man of promise. Now at forty cautious men shook their heads and looked suspiciously at
the flippant monologue-artist. Merivale was an advanced
revolutionary on five thousand a year. Three years as
private secretary to Lord Eastbourne had filled him with
contempt for those who did not decorate their titles. Merivale, who developed his sense of the theatre assiduously
and derived pleasure from the fact that persons thought
he must be descended from the famous historian of the

Roman Empire, was a precisian. He pronounced his words, despite the pace of an utterance made to prevent interruption, with unction; he was as careful about their use as he was careless about their meaning. He would have sacrificed his grandmother for an epigram.

His attire was as precise as his small flat in Mayfair. He hoped he was the last to preserve the traditions of the Augustan age. He read Locke "On the Human Understanding" in a room hung with choice examples of Signorelli, Lippo Lippi and Angelico. His furniture was Chippendale, his books were all leather bound. Sometimes in a long monologue on the bad government of the age, he quoted John Stuart Mill. He refused to recognise any novelist since Fielding, any musician since Handel. The last statesman died with Pitt the younger. The only persons he really respected were his valet and his banker. They both moved in the best circles. Major Slade collected his epigrams and performed the office of an enlarging mirror. He spoke of Merivale with a note of melancholy as of a man who could have been great had it not been vulgar. Merivale himself found comfort in this reflection; after all, he was, among the crowd, the one man self-possessed.

His day was perfectly ordered, his trousers perfectly creased. A vellum bound copy of "Marius the Epicurean" always lay on a bedside table. He had a model bachelor's rooms, and kept a full diary. He envied the poor their indifference to dirt and despised the rich for their contempt of brains. He had a beautiful voice, an unfailing eloquence and a safe income; few men had attacked the dinner tables of Mayfair with more perfect, if restricted, assets.

John met Merivale at the Phyllis Court Club, where he had been staying for Henley Regatta. Marsh was rowing for his college, Vernley and his people were also at the club. Merivale was known to Mr. Vernley, who delighted in pairing him with Marsh, now a brilliant extempore antagonist. Those had been great days at Henley. Marsh was radiant. Never had John seen him more audacious, more triumphant. Merivale, disconcerted, admired, and, being an astute tactician, adopted Marsh as his pupil. Their dinner table was the noisiest, their little set the most conspicuous. They all registered a vow to spend August together on the East Coast.

These were days of supreme happiness. Evenings in Mrs. Graham's charmed circle, the intellectual stimulus of a supper gathering at Mr. Ribble's house, the glimpse of home, obtained at Steer's, where the nursery woke to riotous mirth with the advent of "Uncle John"—or those marvellously perfect dinner parties at Slade's house in Braham Gardens, with guests as carefully chosen as the menu; the air of self-possession and quiet mannered ease, the atmosphere in short which is the inseparable adjunct of the Wykehamist the world over—or, turbulent and youthful, the late dance-parties in Tilly's studio—with Tilly, deep in love this time with the attractive young pianist whom John had brought along one evening—yes, it was a splendid life, with every hour booked ahead, and heights of glory for youth to scale.

But, in all these things the most ardent, John turned aside at moments and his thoughts were far away. If Muriel were here among his friends, to share this wine of youth! At night-time, often in the stillness of the long stone streets, so solemn at mid-night, as he walked home, he would wonder just how she lay pillowed in her bed in a room he knew not in the Convent of the Sacred Heart. A momentary glimpse held him in the spell of recollection—the way her little hand tucked away a rebellious curl behind the ear, even the way she had of nibbling at a concert programme! And to see her run up a flight of steps—up the terrace at "The Croft," and then turn at the top, breathless and flushed, her eyes shining! Why was she exiled from him? It was cruel to waste the ardour of their youth in this senseless fashion.

On his last visit to the Vernleys, he could no longer keep silent upon his dream. Quickly, bluntly almost, he poured out his whole heart before Mr. Vernley, who listened to him with a kindly tolerance. It might end everything; he would have to leave the house, of course, but this dual existence was intolerable. To his surprise Mr. Vernley just placed his hand on his shoulder, and said very kindly—

"You must be patient, my boy—you are but boy and girl yet. Twenty-one—and so much before you yet. Just wait, John, and then we'll talk seriously."

"But I'm very serious, sir."

Mr. Vernley smiled in his kindly fashion.

"That is why you should wait. Come, John—suppose we talk of this in a year?" He looked at the intense young face before him.

"Then you—you don't forbid me, sir—I mean I may hope—" he stammered.

"The verdict is with Muriel, John. She will know her own mind soon, and when she is home and has been presented, then you two can decide. I am not so old-fashioned as to think a father can do other than advise. If I say 'Good luck' to you, will that suffice for the present?"

"Oh, thank you, sir!" cried John, gladly.

So ended the overture. It was a phase successfully passed. The young lovers breathed freely again. Time was the enemy now.

The summer wore on. There were visits to the Fletchers and to Marsh's.

"Mother's another 'ism," said Marsh, meeting him at the station. "They come and go like Dad's pipes. She's a Sunphoner this time—all gladness and love is transmitted on rays of light. To smile is to love. Clouds, which obstruct sunshine, are agglomerations of sin. When you frown you are abetting the devil. Mother carefully cultivates the gladsome wrinkles of the sunphoners. Dad calls it the Cheshire Cat Society."

John found her as sweet and gentle as before. Always in her hands there seemed to be flowers, and the birds sang louder in her garden. Were any evenings, anywhere, more restful than those around her lamp? Mr. Marsh came and went from the study. His hair was a little whiter, his belief in the *Nation* even more unshakable. As for Marsh, was there any one in the world quite like this tall, perverse, quick-spoken humourist? Mrs. Marsh sat and worshipped, her hands ever busy in his service, and John thought he treated her like a fluttered bird, something to be petted and soothed.

"It is splendid to watch over your success, John," she confided one evening. "But please don't let success harden you."

"Am I hardening?"

"No—perhaps not—it's youth changing, I suppose—I would like to keep that first glimpse of you—when Teddie brought you here—so nervous."

John laughed happily, and held her hand which, somehow, had found its way into his.

"What a silly little woman I am," she whispered.

"I think you're a darling," he responded, "and Teddie's a lucky boy."

It was good to fall asleep in that little chintz-curtained

room, to watch the moon climbing through the elm-tree branches, to hear the owl screech and the church clock strike in the dead of night, or to wake with bird song in the cold freshness of the country morning. Then Teddie would bang about, pyjama-clad with tousled hair, uttering some fantastic epigram, or a new plan for exasperating the conservative-minded.

It was he who, one morning in Grafton Street, saw in the shop window of an antique dealer, a small bronze statue labelled "Narcissus listening to Echo."

"Scissors!" he cried, clutching his arm. "There's your namesake, minus tailor's trimmings!"

In a moment he had rushed into the shop. A fierce discussion ensued with the bespectacled Jew, who began a recital starting at Herculaneum B. C., but was interrupted in the Italian Renaissance by Marsh, who calmly offered him half what he asked. They haggled and scorned each other while John wondered which traced his ancestry to Judæa; then Marsh conquered at his original bid.

They bore it home, swaddled in *The Times,* to John's room. John protested, he could not let Marsh pay so much for a present, but all his protests were over-ruled.

"Of course you must have it—and offer libations to your great ancestor. What a leg he's got—he could do with more meat on his torso and less on his toes, while you could—"

"Don't be rude," interrupted John.

"It was a trick of the Phidian period of sculpture to lengthen the tibia to ensure—" on went the dissertation. Mid-way through a comparison of Michael Angelo with Benvenuto Cellini, there was a sudden explosion.

"The old devil!" cried Marsh, looking closely at the statue. "He's swindled us—it's cracked over the thigh—look!"

John looked. There was a fissure in the bronze about an inch long.

"An appendicitis operation," said John.

"I'll take it back," cried Marsh indignantly.

"Don't—I like the lad better for his imperfections—he's more human."

So the statue remained, raising its finger in a listening attitude on the bookshelf, recalling with an antique grace an artist's triumph in a dead civilisation. It revived, indeed, a pagan creed in the Perdie household. True, Mrs. Perdie was shocked by "that 'eathen thing without its coverings," and Annie simpered whenever she swept the feather brush over it, but Miss Simpson's eyes watered when she saw it, for she recalled how her dear brother, the Governor, had shown it to her in the museum at Naples—"when I was quite a girl, and Lieutenant Ranson, a charming young gentleman, was going to buy me a copy, but—"

John had seen his portrait on her table, and had looked silently at the laughing face of the lover, drowned a week after it was taken.

Wellington and de Courtrai borrowed "Narcissus" for a tea party they gave, with great success, to a crowd of ladies and gentlemen from the theatre.

"Yer can't see fer face powder in the air," commented Annie, after taking in the tea. John was a guest. He enjoyed hearing them lie so magnificently to each other about the salaries they earned and the promises made by managers. Yet they were good-hearted backbiters, loving the venom for the chameleonic skill with which their tongues struck the victims, intending no permanent harm to any one. They all showed the worst side to the world and kept their private griefs smothered in the dreary back rooms of dingy lodging houses. For all their cheapness, Wellington and de Courtrai had hearts of gold. They had nursed him through a bad attack of influenza, with unwearying devotion, and no woman's hand could have ministered more skilfully and patiently. Their artificiality was on the surface, their feminine air companioned a feminine tenderness to each other—and on this occasion, to John. Even Captain Fisher, when they cooked his breakfast, on the sudden collapse of Mrs. Perdie and Annie with influenza, declared they were born batmen.

"If they'd take a cold bath every morning and crop their hair, they might pass as men," he growled. They would have won him completely by their attentions during those influenza days had they not called him "dear," in conversation on the third morning, whereupon Captain Fisher spilt his coffee in an apoplectic rage.

III

It was during those weeks of July that Lindon arrived at a condition which to John seemed hysterical. Ever since he had taken him to Tilly's studio he had haunted the place like a silent ghost; that he was madly in love with her he made no attempt to hide, and she, no less than he, found the day dull when he was absent. He vowed that Tilly was necessary to his music; he could not work without her, there was no quality in his playing unless he played to her. One night, after John had dined at his flat, Lindon walked up and down the room, pouring out his agony of mind. His people had refused to allow him to marry yet. "I'm tied up with an allowance, Scissors—and I can't go on—we can't go on—it's hell!"

"We?—is Tilly unwilling to wait?"

"Yes, to wait—like me—why should we lead this miserable divided life, when we belong to each other, when there's no existence apart? I tell you it's immoral! Why

shouldn't I marry—in the vigour of youth, with a girl in
a million. It's natural, it's right—and we're told to wait
—for what? Till we're wiser, if you please. Wiser!—
oh my God! Madness, that's how it'll end!"

Suddenly he turned upon his heel and looked at John,
who sat quietly in a chair.

"Scissors, sometimes you make me want to kick you—
you agree with 'em! Have you got an ounce of passion in
you? Do you know what sex means? I doubt it. Why,
there are nights I can't sleep, when I think such things
as—but you never seem to be aware of anything. I have
seen you dancing with girls, your face like a wax mummy.
Why when I take hold of them, sometimes I want to make
them cry out in my grip, and when their hair touches my
face, I—I—"

He halted then, and caught John's wrists in a vice.

"I don't believe you've ever felt like crying about a girl
just because she's been pleasant to another fellow, or
wanted to gather her up in your arms and carry her off
to a secret place."

The younger man broke away from the frenzied grip.

"Lindon, I shall think you are mad in a minute."

"I am—do you wonder? Here am I, a vigorous man,
with abundance of life singing through every vein, all nature crying out for me to express myself, and night and
day I fight the desire down, hold myself in leash, shut up
in these four walls—you must know what it means, you're
no longer a kid. Nature never intended this, she meant
us to break the barriers. We're all defying her; I am,
you are, Tilly is—and it's all wrong!" He looked desperately at John.

"I don't think love is a thing that you can talk about
in this way," said the other quietly.

"For you—perhaps not—you're not hot-blooded like

me—you're self-contained. But I'm not like that, I must have somebody I worship. Why, do you know at Sedley, it was you—there, now you know I'm mad." He laughed bitterly.

"I knew," said John, looking out of the window.

"You knew that I cared about you?" asked Lindon. They heard the clock tick in the long interval of silence.

"Yes—I could see you liked me very much, and I was afraid of you—I was told you were very jealous."

"By Vernley?"

"Yes."

Lindon laughed rather grimly.

"You see how I torture myself—I don't suppose I'm normal," he added bitterly.

"No one in love is," added John, half to himself.

Lindon looked at him keenly.

"How do *you* know that?"

"You're not the only lover, I suppose?"

For a moment Lindon stared at him; there was such a depth of feeling in those simple words. Impulsively, he linked his arm in John's.

"Scissors, old thing, forgive me. I'm a selfish beast— why do you let me carry on in this childish way?"

John half smiled in reply.

"Because I've often wanted to myself. After all, you know, you should be grateful—Chelsea's nearer than Belgium."

IV

The last week in July saw a great re-union. The Vernleys had taken a house at Mablethorpe, on the East Coast, for the summer. Its chief attraction was that it possessed no distractions. There were neither pierrots, promenades, theatres, nor any of the other feeble forms of amusement with which people in search of a holiday disguise their boredom. And to increase the solitude of their retreat, the Vernleys' house was a mile out of the village, snugly ensconced behind the high sand dunes with which early settlers had fought the encroaching sea, and kept for themselves a lowland intersected with dykes and devoid of trees. Bobbie grumbled all day long at the obvious insanity of his people in choosing such a place. A lover of the flesh pots, he contemplated the house and surrounding country with supreme disgust. His disapproval was obviously artificial, however. They had brought their horses with them, with which to explore the Lincolnshire lanes. A short car journey took them to Skegness, "which is Mablethorpe, only more so," commented Bobbie. Kitty found great excitement in riding her mare down the sand dunes, until the authorities protested against the breaking down of the sky line and Mablethorpe's one claim to singularity. But the tennis and the bathing were without fault. Even Bobbie was silent upon these, and his frequent indulgence in both betrayed almost enthusiasm. Mrs. Vernley had chosen the place for the air, although Mr. Vernley swore that it was because no friends would come there to visit them. He was consoled somewhat by the discovery of a radical parson in a near village, who knew all the quaint little inns and the merits of beer.

For the greater part of the day they all lived in bathing costumes since, as Marsh expressed it, the weather was hot and as perversely pleasant as the landscape. Lindon was with them, Lindon dwelling in a wonderful July heaven, for diplomatic John had contrived for an invitation to be sent to Miss Topham, whose pleasure coincided with the business of painting Kitty on horseback. Their open delight in each other supplemented the mirth of the party, though perhaps John felt lonelier in contrast, for Muriel was visiting the home of a school friend at Liége until the second week in August. John's sky had just a little shadow in it, but with Marsh and Vernley at hand, there were no silences for self-commiseration.

They breakfasted at seven, with the sea wind blowing through the room. It was Mr. Vernley's great complaint that there were neither letters nor newspapers until eleven o'clock. A great strike was threatened, and he watched it carefully day by day.

"Have the silly beggars struck yet?" asked Bobbie, one morning as they all lay, after bathing, on the slopes of the sand dunes facing the sea and the wide flat beach. As he asked the question he was industriously trickling sand down John's bare leg.

"No—the Prime Minister receives a conference to-day. There seems to be more trouble over the Sarajevo incident."

"What's that, sir?" asked Vernley.

"One of the Hapsburgs potted at by a Serbian—those blighters are always shooting one another in the Balkans," interrupted Marsh.

"There's a report from Copenhagen that Russia's mobilising," said Mr. Vernley.

"Oh, you must never believe reports from Copenhagen, sir," cried Lindon, looking sideways at John. The next moment he just escaped a shoe by ducking.

"The Kaiser says that Austria must have guarantees from Serbia, with penalties, and that Russia must acquiesce."

"I wish somebody would have a shot at that idiot," said John.

"Well you can, when he's had one at us, as he intends," replied Vernley.

"Oh, bosh!" cried Marsh, "every half-pay major who wants conscription and has had a week's holiday in Berlin, propagates that yarn. The Germans would no more think of fighting us than the Chinese—they wouldn't have a dog's chance."

"With twelve million disciplined troops?" queried Mr. Vernley, over the top of his glasses.

"Why, sir, we'd never meet 'em on land. How would they get here—with our navy?"

Vernley got up and shook the sand off his legs.

"Come on, Scissors—let's have that tennis four—if we let Lindon and Marsh go on there'll be war in England; I can see Lindon's gorge rising at the little Englander!"

"Little Englander—why of course! We are the wealthiest race on the earth, have the greatest possessions, and the worst slums!" cried Marsh. "What good is the wealth of India when there's Sheffield, or the possession of Egypt when it can't wipe out the slums of Lancashire—we have the largest national debt, the heaviest taxation! And there are idiots banging the big drum, raising the German bogey, because they want to go and grab more countries, when we can't manage what we have got!" Marsh was flushed and the wind had blown the hair down into his eyes.

"But we do manage it—and well," asserted Tod, usually silent, and just appointed to a commission in the Guards. "We have civilised India, brought justice and liberty to its people as well as health—"

"And Christianity," added Mrs. Vernley.

"Yes, and thrown away hundreds of lives and millions of money on South Africa—only to realise we had no right there and to give it back again," retorted Marsh.

"You must admit, Teddie, we have a genius for government," said John.

"Not while we've Ireland threatening insurrection every minute," flared Marsh, his blood up.

"I think you boys had better play tennis," called Mr.

Vernley, from behind the newspaper. "You'll get hot to some purpose then. But unless I'm mistaken, this old country will be in the balance soon. Austria has attacked Serbia, and is bombarding Belgrade. Russia has sent an ultimatum on behalf of her ally, and the Kaiser is hurrying back to Berlin."

"That idiot will only stir up the mess," said Bobbie. "What's it all about, Dad?"

"The Austrian Archduke was assassinated at Sarajevo. Austria demands penalties and will not accept Serbia's offer. It is reported Germany is strengthening Austria's hand, and Russia stands behind Serbia. Sir Edward Grey has offered his services as mediator."

"Oh, he'll settle it!" cried Bobbie. "Clever dog, Grey."

"It looks to me like a European conflagration unless great tact is shown," said Mr. Vernley. He turned to his wife, "I think we ought to wire for Muriel to come home."

"But why? Belgium is not affected."

The whole circle looked at Mr. Vernley who took off his glasses and tapped the newspaper.

"It may mean war for us."

"For us!" They all echoed.

"We've too much sense, sir, to be messed up in these ludicrous Balkan squabbles. The blighters are always nibbling at one another's ears. Well, here's one who won't join in. If every man thought and acted as I do, there wouldn't be any wars!" declared Marsh.

"Why?" asked John. He had never seen Marsh quite so excited before.

"Because if there were no feeble fools willing to be made into gun fodder, there'd be no wars. You can't have wars without soldiers."

"But supposing Germany declared war on us," began Tod.

"Oh, bosh!" interrupted Marsh.

"Germany will not declare war on *us*," said Mr. Vernley quietly, "but if this unrest spreads, she may declare war on France—and that would involve our honour; we should have to help France."

"It seems a terrible mix-up, all these entangling alliances," sighed Mrs. Vernley, "and it is unthinkable that the world's rulers will let us slip into war. To-day war would be terrible with all the science and inventions of this age."

"It would be insane!" cried Marsh loudly. "We must refuse to be pushed in by the financiers and land-grabbers. Think of the millions it means, the homes ruined, the sons and fathers butchered—why it's incredible!"

"But if our honour—" began Tod.

"Honour be damned!" snapped Marsh. Then quickly, "Oh, I'm sorry, I didn't mean that. But it's wicked to think of war. I refuse to think of it."

"We may have to, Marsh," said Mr. Vernley.

"I won't."

"If we had to fight, wouldn't you?" asked Kitty.

Marsh stood up, looking very handsome in his flushed indignation but John noticed how his lip trembled as he paused before answering, and looked out to sea.

"No," he said quietly.

Mr. Vernley looked at him steadily.

"I'm afraid, Marsh, you would be—" he began to say.

"Called a coward, sir—I know. But war's insanity, and only the corrupt, the insane and the ignorant will allow it. I'll consider it my duty to refuse to condone it at any cost."

"Oh—you're—you're impossible," muttered Tod.

"You're—you're a professional soldier," retorted Marsh, and the moment he uttered it, turned white in the face.

"Oh—Tod—please I didn't mean it like that—I didn't really." There were tears in his eyes as he turned appealingly. Tod put his hand on his shoulder and smiled at him.

"It's all right, Teddie—you were always volcanic. I believe you're the kind of fellow that would win the V. C."

"I think," said Mrs. Vernley breathing freely again, "that it is very silly to take things as seriously as this—there won't be a war."

"Grey'll settle it," said John.

"We hope so," added Mr. Vernley, folding up his paper. "But I shall go to town to-morrow to be at the centre of things and I shall wire to Muriel."

"But she will be home in a week, father," cried Mrs. Vernley.

"And she's quite safe in Belgium," declared Bobbie.

"Perhaps—I hope so, but it's too near the storm centre," replied Mr. Vernley. "And now, my dear, what about lunch?"

Walking back to the house, John expressed fears about Muriel to Bobbie.

"Oh, she's all right," he replied, confidently. "The guv'nor always takes a serious attitude to things—it's a parliamentary habit, Scissors—and Muriel can look after herself." Marsh walked silently with them. He seemed depressed. The sky was blue, the sun shining, but John felt the air was heavy. He slipped his arm through Marsh's.

v

Rumours followed rumours, and one morning as John came down into the hall before breakfast, Tilly met him. She looked very attractive and girlish in her white jersey with its blue collar encircling her pretty neck. John could

understand Lindon's infatuation. He had watched her
slim figure in the water, a graceful sprite, so light and
vivacious that she might have been a fairy's child. Her
cream skirt this morning was short, revealing two shapely
legs in white stockings, and he could not help looking intently at the little bare patch beneath her throat, red with
the sun, running down to a channel of milky whiteness,
dimpled by the suggested proximity of her breasts. She
noticed his admiring observation, and placed her hand,
light as a bird on his arm.

"Scissors, what do you think—Tod's going to town with
Mr. Vernley this morning! I tell him he'll spoil the
men's four we arranged to play the doctor's friends."

"To town, whatever for?"

"I don't know, you persuade him to stay."

"Righto—where is he?"

Tilly nodded towards the dining room. John walked
in, and as he did so, he realised something.

"Morning, Tod!" he called brightly. "I hear you're
going to town."

"Yes, Scissors—I've got to see a few friends."

"Oh—you'll be coming back before I go?"

"Oh, yes—"

At that moment Bobbie burst in.

"I say, Tod, what's this nonsense about going to town!
You simply can't, you'll bust up the—"

He caught a glance from John that checked him.

"I must see some friends," said Tod. "I'll be back in
a few days."

"Oh, very well," assented Bobbie, lamely. John had
gone out. He followed quickly, overtaking him in the
hall.

"What on earth did you look like that for, Scissors?" he

asked. John drew him aside from where Mrs. Vernley stood watering a flower pot.

"I thought you did not realise."

"Realise what?" asked Vernley.

"Why Tod's going to town—it isn't to see friends." Then seeing the mystified expression on his friend's face, "I'll bet he visits the War Office to find out whether his regiment's likely to get orders."

"Good God!" exclaimed Vernley, "but—surely we're not going to war!"

"I don't know."

"We must keep this from the mater," whispered Vernley. Then, to John, "You're a wise old bird, Scissors—I'd never have guessed."

Immediately after breakfast Mr. Vernley and Tod left for London. Their going brought one little hope to John. Muriel would be here now in a few days. This was the last week in July—Tuesday. He had to return in a week, the Tuesday following Bank Holiday, on August the fourth. Muriel would be here by the 1st at the latest. They would have a few days together before he could come back again, early in September. On the fifth he had to leave for Paris, to relieve Phipps, who was there on a special mission.

Those jolly days went quickly. They bathed, boated, played tennis and lolled on the dunes. Marsh made frequent excursions into Mablethorpe, where he had contracted a mania for shooting at bottles in a booth, returning with a cocoanut and a German watch as prizes. He was elated with his great success as a deadly shot.

"I'm surprised you should like shooting," laughed Mrs. Vernley when he presented her with a cocoanut, and pinned the watch on the cook's blouse.

"But at bottles, not human beings, Mrs. Vernley!"

"Same thing as soldiers," cried John.

"How?"

"According to you—green and empty."

There was a laugh all round and Marsh shied the cocoanut at John, who split his white ducks in performing a somersault. That afternoon he infected Lindon and Tilly with his craze and dragged them off to Mablethorpe.

John dozed on the lawn, Bobbie was engrossed in a novel, Mrs. Vernley was taking her siesta. Only Kitty was alert. She had been writing to Alice who was singing on the morrow at Manchester. Suddenly she put down her pen.

"Bobbie, I say, just look at Teddie tearing along—has he gone mad?"

She pointed and they looked in the direction of the Mablethorpe road that ran between a deep dyke and the sandhills. He was running breathlessly, his shirt wide open at the neck. He was a lonely figure on the road, but, catching sight of them on the lawn, waved a paper in the air. John woke up.

"He's won another prize!" he suggested.

"But where's Lindon and Tilly?" asked Bobbie.

Then John started up and went across the lawn, and Marsh, now within hailing distance, shouted—

"Special out—Germany's at war with France—threatening Luxembourg!"

A minute later, panting, he reached the gate, where they ran to meet him.

"Hoo! I'm blown—there!" He thrust the paper into eager hands. "Tilly and Lindon are coming—I've run all the way. It looks like business, doesn't it?"

They read down the column. It was brief, with

messages from many sources, none authoritative, but the
fact was clear—Germany and France were at war.

"Germany has delivered a request to Luxembourg
asking for the free passage for her troops to the French
frontier; her neutrality will be respected in the event of
acquiescence," read John aloud.

"Neutrality respected—after walking across them!"
snorted Bobbie.

Suddenly John gripped the paper.

"Brussels. From our special correspondent. It is
rumoured that a demand for the free passage of German
troops, as in the case of Luxembourg, has been made to
the Belgian Government. No official statement was made
at noon, but the Belgian army is being mobilised as a pre-
cautionary measure."

And Muriel was in Belgium!

At tea they had a thousand hopes, fears, views. All
the evening Marsh walked about muttering, "It's incredible—the twentieth century, and civilisation to come
to this! But it'll all be over quickly, there's that in it."

"Quickly, why?" asked Bobbie.

"The Germans will be in Paris in a fortnight!"

"They won't!" said John grimly.

"Why not?" asked Kitty.

"We shall stop them."

"We?" echoed Tilly.

"Yes—France is our ally, we must stand by her."

"There's no definite treaty compelling us," said Mrs.
Vernley.

"It's not a matter of compulsion—it's a matter of
honour," asserted Lindon.

"Honour!" cried Marsh. "Honour—and spread the
massacre!"

"The French are our allies. Germany knows that, and has thrown down the gage. We are challenged," said John grimly.

"Then—it—it means war for us?" asked Mrs. Vernley.

"Yes,"

"Oh dear—oh dear—oh dear!" she murmured, clasping and unclasping her hands. Marsh sat silent with the rest. The net was closing. Not one of them mentioned Muriel's name, chiefly because she was in all their minds.

That evening a wire came from Mr. Vernley. The Belgian Legation refused to issue passports. He had wired Muriel to return at once. He was coming down in the morning. Charlton, of the Foreign Office, said there was every hope that they would keep out of the war.

Mr. Vernley arrived in the morning, and with him came the news that Belgium had refused Germany the right of access across her territory and Germany had declared war and was hacking her way through the country.

"That means we are all in," said Lindon.

"We shall know soon. England has sent an ultimatum declaring she will defend Belgian neutrality according to the treaty."

Those were hours of suspense to the Vernley household, all their thoughts turned to Muriel. Where was she? Mr. Vernley was sure she was on her way to England; she had had ample time to reach Ostend.

"Just think, all of these people in a few days will be living in apprehension—and every one of us shouldering a gun!" said John, looking at the crowd on the shore. A group of red-faced youths sauntered by, hatless, in vivid blazers.

"There goes gun-fodder," muttered Marsh. The strain was telling on him; he had lost his buoyancy.

"You pessimist—youth's going to have the time of its

life—action, a world in the making! Why Marsh, it's our age, this. It means the old men take a back seat!" cried Lindon, laughing at Tilly, who hung on his arm.

"And what of us?" she asked, a little jealous.

"Nurses, all of you."

She shivered slightly.

"I should be ill at the sight of blood."

It was evening when they sat on the sandhills and saw the wide-winged sunset spread across the fen-land. Suddenly a cry from Bobbie made them turn. There, on the grey horizon, where sea dissolved into approaching night, they saw a twinkle of lights, flashing through the greyness. The slim forms of ships were just discernible as they slipped northwards into the gathering darkness.

"Warships!" cried Lindon. "We're ready and watching."

It began to rain. Bobbie and John were the last to enter the house. They halted for a moment in a cutting of the sandhills and looked over the dark expanse of sea. That slow procession northwards of ships had given a sudden reality to the rumours.

John took Vernley's arm as they walked on in silence.

"I wonder where we'll all be next year at this time," said Vernley. "I suppose this is the end of things—well—we've had a good time—haven't we, Scissors?"

John could not speak. The great drama rendered him speechless. Out there, across the North Sea, lay Germany. In millions of homes, their windows bright in the dusk, mothers and wives were saying farewell to their loved ones; in Austria too, in Russia, thousands of leagues across the Balkans, from the Bretagne coast to the sunny Riviera, the hand of Mars knocked on the door of castle and cottage. Already the sky was stabbed with flame, the silence of the harvest fields broken with the battery of guns.

John looked across the peaceful fenland. Here and there a light shone in a farmstead; the silence was broken only by the low sighing of the sea, fitfully borne inland. England, his country, sinking to sleep, guarded by her inviolate seas. A great love of this land rose in his heart. God keep her secure!

"Dulce et decorum pro patria mori," he half murmured to himself, but Vernley heard him.

"Yes, and there's one thing, Scissors—we're all in it together, that'll be the good part of it."

They walked on, arm in arm.

So passed Tuesday, August the fourth; the suspense of the ultimatum, and then the fifth, with *"WAR"* flaring in great letters on the bookstall posters. The station was crowded with the general exodus. All the Vernley household were going up to town. The platform was a scene of good-byes. Hatless lads were bidding one another cheerful farewells, the girls, jerseyed and laughing, hung on their arms. There was an air of suppressed excitement; they might have been going to a picnic, but deeper observation revealed a nervous tension. At Boston, Marsh left them to go on to his people. He had been very silent for the last two days. He said good-bye gravely. Only to John did he unburden himself in the last minute.

"This is the end of us all, Scissors. This war will go on for years. We shall be worked up into a fierce hate. The Press will keep it going, it'll get bloodier and bloodier —and no one will win in the end. There'll be nothing but widows and cripples, famine and debt. Good-bye, Scissors, write to me at home."

They shook hands; neither dared say more. The next minute, the train moved out, leaving Marsh standing amid his luggage, raising his hat to them, a graceful figure of youth, outwardly calm.

Intensity increased when they reached London. They all parted hurriedly. Bobbie was going to enlist at once, Tod had received orders. Lindon hoped to get out as a despatch rider. John, what was he going to do? He did not know, he was bewildered. In his head there was only one idea, to get to Belgium at all costs, to find Muriel, from whom no word had been received.

At his rooms he found a wire from Merritt, bidding him call. Walsh saw him at once. His wish was miraculously fulfilled. He was to leave immediately for Belgium as special correspondent of the *Daily Post*.

BOOK V
THE NEW WORLD

CHAPTER I

I

THE crowded steamer from Folkestone reached Ostend in the last glow of the sunset as it fell on the straggling Digue, domes, hotels, casinos, verandahed houses, the pleasure haunt standing inviolate on the edge of the plains, that beyond, were now drenched with blood. A fortnight had elapsed, full of irritating delays. There were interviews at the War Office, where every obstacle had been raised, frantic journeys to the Foreign Office, the Belgian Legation, the offices of the Newspaper Proprietors Association. Nobody wanted war correspondents out there, except the papers. Then more delay while John bought a car, a rare thing, for every one had been commandeered by the War Office; and with all this work he had made desperate attempts to get into touch with the *Daily Post* resident correspondent at Brussels, beseeching him to ask for Muriel at the Convent of the Sacred Heart. But all was chaotic at the other end of the wire and day after day he had to return to poor Mrs. Vernley with no news. Then, the last day, at the last minute, news came from Muriel herself. She had joined the Belgian Red Cross; the convent had been turned into a hospital.

The steamer was warped in at Ostend amid amazing scenes. The harbour was crowded with refugees, pitiable objects, sitting on their small bundles hastily gathered before flight. The moment his car was landed, John pressed on towards Bruges. Again and again he almost told his chauffeur to turn round and pick up the wretched people straggling along the road towards Ostend and England. Tired women trudged the long roads, carrying infants in their arms, while small children clutched at their skirts. There was no crying, no complaining, only dull, voiceless despair on every face. Old men and women went by, pushing their worldly wealth, bedding for the most part, on barrows. Yes, they had seen the war, out there. The German bombardment was terrible. They were destroying everything. The gallant army resisted every inch, but what could they do, little Belgium, against these hordes? John ran into Bruges soon after dusk.

At daylight, he was on the crowded road again, this time towards Ghent, where the other correspondents had established their headquarters. There had been one topic at Bruges. The wonderful English army was over and fighting! It had all been so swift and silent. The Germans were furious and amazed. They had orders to wipe out the contemptible little army. Nearing Ghent there were signs of war. Ambulance vans swept by, in them inert swathed figures, mud-stained and pallid. The environs of Ghent were choked with cars, lorries, refugees, detachments of men on the march.

John found his colleagues at the long low Hotel de la Poste in the Place d' Armes. There was Tompkins of the *Standard,* tall, lean, and depressed with the hopelessness of it all; and V. E. A. Stevenson, the veteran, who had seen ten wars, and hated them all. He was a cynic, a pacifist and a revolutionary. He derived grim satisfaction when ardent Belgians mistook him, with his red, weather-beaten face, trim beard and white hair, and breast blazing with war ribbons, for an English general. He suffered them to embrace him ecstatically, and sighed for his home at Hampstead,—"built out of the blood of the Boers," he explained grimly. Trevor of the *Times* walked about morose and self-important; the heavy brow of Willing of the *Express* was seen towering above every group of Belgian generals. He had a miraculous knowledge of the disposition of the armies, and they consulted him as a general staff. Also, genial, and an optimist to the core, Riddings of *Reuter* walked about the lounge in carpet slippers. He refused to go out. What was the good of running about the highways and the byways? Every general and person who was somebody came to the hotel. He picked their brains—"very poor rubbish heaps"— gathered up the gossip and at tea-time had such a store that the weary, muddy colleagues were glad to barter news. He was more eloquent, despite an impediment, with the poker in his hands, when, with the cinders, he would show why the Germans could not possibly get to Paris.

On the third day after John's arrival, Phipps turned up. He had been in the thick of it, at Termond and Alost. He had had no food, was nervy and on the verge of a breakdown. His eagle features were sharper than ever, and his brain wonderfully alert. His despatches had created something of a sensation in England, not only for their news, but also for the humanity, the tenderness running through his vivid epics of suffering and incredible heroism. He was in Paris when the war broke out, moved up with the French armies, had been with the British Army in its great stand at Mons, had dragged back through that dogged retreat, "a bloody terrible business, Dean—walking on torn flesh all the way,"—and had passed on into Belgium.

"God—how I hate it—it's insensate, blowing all these splendid lads to atoms, for what?" he cried.

"For England," said Trevor, with disapproving dignity. "England! Rubbish!" snapped Phipps. "They're giving the same reason in Germany, Russia, Austria, Serbia —the same fierce old women are brow-beating every timid lad, and the same stupid, red-faced Generals are sitting at mess while their puppets are pulverised with something they can't see, which doesn't give them a dog's chance before bespattering the turf with their brains! If this is civilisation, why—" he broke off as though realising the futility of everything. "I suppose we shall have to go on writing as if it were a football match, and be censored every time we hint at such a thing as spilt blood or a nasty mess."

He walked out, even more pallid, and went up to his bedroom where he hammered out a long despatch on his "Corona." Eight other correspondents were doing the same thing in other bedrooms. For an hour there was a rapid clatter of typewriter keys. At five o'clock the despatch rider left for the Signal Station, whence their despatches crossed the wires overnight, in time for the Englishman's breakfast table. Curiously, those at home knew more than these correspondents. They explored a corner, oblivious of the fate of the world beyond. In England every morning the public watched the ugly black snake marked on the map, as it slowly curled its way towards Paris. In a top left hand corner another black line closed in upon Antwerp and crept along the coast towards Ostend.

"We shall have to move out soon," said Riddings. "The streets are choked to-day with ambulances—that's a sure sign." Every night sleep was broken by the incessant roar of guns, and the night sky flickered and quivered. Those were the days when the name of Liége was on every tongue. Could General Leman hold out? Then came news of a terrible massacre at Malines. The name sang in John's heart like a bell. Muriel—was she there? Had she remained and met the German invasion, or where was she? He wired to the Vernleys' beseeching news. That same day a shell fell into the town. The British had marched through St. Nicolas; the fate of Antwerp hung in the balance, the black snake was closing in on Ghent and curling upwards towards the coast.

"If we don't move soon, we're luggage for Germany," said Riddings. "The generals have all gone and they know when it gets chilly as well as the swallows."

Walking down the Grande Place, John suddenly clutched Phipps' arm. The next moment he had seized a car standing outside a shop and was driving madly down a side street. Phipps watched him go in silent amazement, but John, half-crazed with fear that the car ahead would give him the slip, drove furiously, without heeding the traffic through which he miraculously raced. For in the car ahead, he had caught a glimpse of a face that had made his heart jump. Muriel was in it, a Muriel he knew despite her nurse's hood and cape! He was gaining on it now; it paused in front of a building. He alighted on the pavement simultaneously with the slim nurse.

"Muriel!"

She turned, then rushed into his arms.

"Oh, John!"

Two ragged children lifted their caps and yelled "Vive les Anglais! Vive l'Angleterre!" but the lovers stood there alone in the world.

"Why are you here?" he asked.

She laughed, her fingers playing with the button of his tunic.

"And you?"

"Our headquarters are here—Hotel de la Poste—until to-night," he replied.

Her face shadowed.

"I have just been fetched. Tod—he is here—dying."

"Tod!"

"Yes—he came out with the Antwerp expedition—I am just going in to him—come!"

She clasped his hand and they entered the gloomy porch together. The place had been a school—desks and chairs were piled up in the lobby. A Belgian soldier saluted and conducted them to the matron, a pale little Belgian woman. Lieutenant Vernley? Yes, he was here, but he could not be seen, M'sieur was ill, very ill, "a la morte," she added, raising her hands helplessly. John explained.

"Ah!—his sister?—pardon! We expected her. Yes, come! You shall go in."

They followed down a long ward, with dozens of beds, and groaning shapes beneath blankets, and entered a small room, very dull. In the corner was a bed and on it the figure of a boy. His shirt was open at the neck. His unshaven chin was growing a sandy beard, which contrasted with the green-grey pallor of his face; the hands which lay over the brown blanket, were red and soiled. Muriel slipped to her knees at his side.

"Tod dear!" she whispered, taking his hand in hers. But he lay without response, his leaden head deep in the pillow. John stood in the doorway.

"In the stomach, m'sieur—a shell splinter," explained the matron. "He has been delirious, 'Muriel,' that was all he cried, 'Muriel.' We found a letter from Madamoiselle in his pocket, and sent for her yesterday."

"He doesn't know me," said Muriel, turning pathetically, but a pressure on her hand told her she was wrong.

"Oh Tod, darling, I've come. I'm going to nurse you."

A glimmer of a smile faded across the lad's face.
John left her then, he would be back in an hour.

When he returned, Muriel, very quiet, was sitting in
the matron's room. He knew in a moment it was all
over. Very gently he took her into his arms, and let her
cry, with her head on his shoulder.

They buried Tod the next morning. Phipps was there,
and an English Army Chaplain, and two Belgian generals,
carrying wreaths from the town authorities. Thus another
Englishman was committed to the soil for whose defence
he had gladly given his young life.

After the funeral, they had to hurry away. Shells were
falling into the town. Melle had been heavily bombarded
and the Town Hall was a heap of ruins. Half the inhabitants of Ghent seemed to be streaming along the road
to Bruges. The inevitable moment of parting came for
John and Muriel. She was rejoining her unit, now at
Bruges.

When would they meet again? For a long moment
she clung to him in the desperation of love.

"We will get leave together and be married, Muriel,"
he urged.

"Yes, John but not now—we must go on, these poor
things need us. I am almost happy here. I could not sleep
in England, knowing what happens day and night!"

"Muriel—promise you will take care, I shall be anxious for you."

"And you—you are running all the risks. Oh, John, we
must come through! Life is going to be so wonderful
even yet."

He kissed her hungrily, wrapped the rugs round her
in the car, and saluted as it carried her away. He waited
until the traffic blotted her from view. Then he joined

Stevenson who was waiting with his car at the hotel.

It was burdened with their luggage, the precious type-writers precariously balanced on the top. They were go-ing south into the British lines and the welter of blood. Antwerp had fallen; nothing could now stop the Germans reaching the coast. And England perhaps. But that was an incredible thought to John. England could not know ruin like this. He looked up at the moon hang-ing serenely over the flat Belgian countryside. The same moon peered down on English homes and in silent glades where the birds slept.

II

So ran the drama, act by act, in those epic days. While England waited breathlessly, the terrible tides of war, now sweeping onwards, now refluent, devastated the countryside of Europe. The little fire, lighted in Sara-jevo, spread outwards until it lapped countries and cap-itals and nations in its lurid glow; until the windy plain of Troy, the desert slopes of the Holy Land, the forests of the Caucasian mountains, and the shores of the Tigris and Danube shook with the tramp of men. Month after month, the war spread its leprous hand across the face of splendid courageous manhood. Sometimes, in the agony of his soul, when coming from dressing stations where men held in their entrails, by pools coloured like sunset with the blood and limbs of men and horses, John cried out against the monstrous infliction of pain. Was it not better that the world should crash into another planet, and find the peace of obliteration? And to heighten the useless agony of this drama, came the reports of official squabbles, the blunders of statesmen, the rhetorical re-criminations of politicians, hurled from nation to nation

with cheap victories of words, while men struggled with
mud under a murderous hail of iron.

For fifteen months John rushed about the fringe of war
in his great car. They were days of terrible strain, but
his efforts seemed as nothing beside the herculean labour
of those wonderful boys who tramped along the tree splin-
tered roads of Flanders, singing in defeat as in victory,
dropping swiftly by the roadside in a convulsive cough as
death fell upon them from the air. He was up every
morning at five, astir before daylight in the cold wintry
air, with a long motor journey to the lines, there to watch
the coloured panorama of a bombardment, the unearthly
silence of "zero" when the barrage lifted, to wait in those
minutes when youth leapt forward upon death; and then to
visit the clearing stations where men who had been splendid to look upon, so full of the vigour of youth, lay torn
in ribbons, demented, delirious. Month after month he
went through the hideous routine when suddenly, one
night, after writing his despatch, he fell forwards upon
his typewriter. They found him in a dead faint.

"I've seen this coming," said Riddings. "He's worn
himself away—and he'll have company soon," he said,
turning to Phipps, "if you don't write and smoke less."

A week later John was at the Vernleys, lying about in
their rooms, and talking as though all those months had
been a nightmare. It was not the same house; Kitty was
nursing in London, Alice was on a farm. Bobbie was back
home with a wound, hoping to be released daily from
a luxurious private hospital in Sussex, "where the chamber-
maid's a countess and the matron a snob." Muriel—the
saga of Muriel, they all called it. She had contributed
to history. The story of her stand at Lens had made all
England ring with her fame. She had been mentioned in

despatches for her heroism under fire. John had not seen
her since that memorable day in Ghent, but letters came
and went. She wrote vividly of her experiences, and he
began to be a little in awe of her obvious efficiency. News
of one, he could not gain. There was no mention of
Marsh among any of his friends. Bobbie had been curtly
silent when asked. "Never heard of him—don't expect
he's wounded." Was that a sneer? thought John. Even
Mr. Fletcher, forwarding parcels from the boys of his
House asked, "We can't trace Marsh—do you know his
regiment? He does not reply to letters."

With quiet, and Mrs. Vernley's assiduous attention, John
quickly recovered. She had aged much since the death
of her eldest boy, and sorrow had rendered her more
gentle and self-effacing than ever. These were lonely
days for her, with Mr. Vernley away as a Director in one
of the Ministries, her daughters all on war work. They
had long talks at tea time, when John read the pages he
had gathered together of a book of despatches. He was
a famous man now, and he rather enjoyed the experience.
There was nothing elating in being famous, just because
every one was glad to shake you by the hand or because
your name was a password whenever and wherever it was
uttered; it was indeed wearisome to be pestered with peti-
tions for your support of all kinds of fantastic charities,
to be expected to speak here, there and everywhere, or
to be an afternoon's attraction at an ambitious lady's
drawing-room party. What he enjoyed was the free-
masonry in which he could now move among the men and
women of the earth who did things, and were great,
simply because their natures were rich in character and
prodigal with varying gifts.

After his sojourn at "The Croft," he spent a fortnight
in town looking up old friends. It was a London

strangely, terribly changed. It was, in one phase, a London more interesting. Down its pavements in great variety of uniforms, passed the young men of all the earth; youth from the plains, the jungle, the prairie, the veldt, the backwoods and the ranch, youth in splendid careless vigour, snatching hectically at joy, not turning to see the shadowy spectre over their shoulders. It was strange to stand in Piccadilly Circus, dimly lit, and watch the theatres pour out their festive crowds, to sit in the busy restaurants, to see mankind, strained, feverish, but debonair, trying to laugh in the face of ruin and death. It was a London of extremes; the wounded silently borne from Charing Cross, the beautiful living swept out in the deadly maelstrom at Victoria Station; the painted women gaily surrendering to the rabid hunger of youth in arms, full-blooded and reckless; the air of intense expectation of fresh development, the swift rise and fall of national heroes, the craving for a strong man to lead the nation to victory; the silent evidence of the wreckage in those endless hospitals, the fierce old women full of hate, and the beardless boys drilled and transported like sheep under the charge of hard-voiced blasphemous sergeants,—all these things revealed a nation at war, a nation unnatural in its hopes, fears, suspicions, enthusiasms, yet heroically treading the inevitable path through chaos to some kind of ending, either of victory or defeat.

It was while watching the crowd surging into the Piccadilly Tube entrance, that John's heart suddenly leapt up in surprise. Surely—yes, it was the undisguisable Marsh —and yet! John stared a moment. A tall, sun-browned youth in kilts, with the black and red hose of the Black Watch, was laughing down into the face of a girl whose hand rested persuasively on his arm. She was pursuing her profession, the oldest under the sun, with all the usual assets, the flaunting white stole over the shoulders, the large beaded vanity bag, one hand gloved, the other thin, manicured and nervous, glittering with rings, too large to be genuine. There was something pathetically obvious in the loud declaration of her clothes, the challenge of her carriage, the provoking tilt of her hat over large observant eyes. She had found her object of a night's passion and pay—the human agent of bread and rent. Here was another youth, beautiful in his strength, snatching at a brief expression of manhood as a pleasurable anodyne for an approaching ordeal.

She turned and the young officer half hesitated. John moved forward.

"Marsh!" he said quietly. A malevolent look glittered beneath the dark hat, the tall youth peered at the intruder half-resentfully; even then he seemed confused. With a shock, more of pain than disgust, John saw that Marsh was not quite sober.

"What are you—" began John, when Marsh's senses cleared.

"Scissors, by God, this is great!" Then, awkwardly, he grew conscious again of his company, insistently standing by him—

"This lady is—is—"

"That's all right, Marsh—where are you going?" asked John.

"He's coming home with me," said the girl sullenly.

John put his hand in his pocket and pulled out a note.

"This is an old friend I've not seen for a long time—I want to talk to him," he said quietly, putting the note in her hand. Defiantly she thrust it back, and her mouth, hard and unpleasant, curled malevolently; she was baulked of her prey.

"Keep yer bl—— money, I'm not depending on missionaries," she snarled.

John looked at her calmly.

"I'm sorry, I did not mean to offend you. Then you
will join me at supper with my friend?"

There was something so kind and disarming in his voice,
that she suddenly melted. Her eyes assumed a tenderness surprising and almost pathetic.

"I'll go—he's your pal I see, and you poor boys may
not meet again." She turned away, but John put a detaining hand on her arm.

"I really meant my invitation," he said quietly.

Then (God! the horror of it!), she momentarily mis-
interpreted his insistence, and involuntarily her professional air returned, only to be dispelled again by the kind
cleanliness of the young man's eyes.

"No—kid, thanks, I guess I'll pick up a boy."

John put his hand in hers.

"No—in memory of our meeting, have a—holiday," he
added lamely. This time she let the note rest in her hand.
He thought she was going to cry, but suddenly she turned
and was lost in the passing crowd. Marsh stood there,
silent, bemused. John said not a word, but called a
taxi, and pushed his friend into it. In the darkness
Marsh sat huddled up. They were speeding down Piccadilly and turning by Hyde Park Gate when he seemed
conscious that he was being carried away.

"Where are you taking me, Scissors," he asked in a
dull voice. (Could this be Marsh, the debonair, the ir-
repressible?)

"Home," John replied laconically.

"I'm leaving Victoria at four a. m.—for France."

John started.

"But you—you were—" he began.

"Going to spend the night with a gay woman, like the filthy cad I am. Oh, I know what you're thinking! Well, I was—I'd have been one of those deserters you see under escort."

"You're drunk, Teddie," said John.

"That's no excuse—in a court martial."

There was silence again. It was now half-past eleven. He would get him home and make him rest for the few intervening hours.

Mrs. Perdie was up when they arrived. Fortunately Marsh pulled himself together, and was his graceful self, but when he gained John's room, he collapsed on the bed. John went below to ask for coffee, a little apologetically. But Mrs. Perdie was in a delightful fluster.

"The bonnie laddie—oh, I want to cry when I see a kiltie. His mother must be proud of him. An' the Black Watch! Many's the time in Edinburgh I've seen—"

John left her in ecstasies. He wanted to pull the bonnie laddie round, for the credit of his dear mother and himself. But Marsh had recovered and was sitting upright in a chair. He had been brushing his hair and straightening the thin khaki tie.

"I suppose you're thinking—" started Marsh, bitterly.

"What a stroke of luck it was—Jove, Teddie, it does me good to see you! But where *have* you been?" cried John. And the other, seeing he had no intention of alluding to the circumstances of their meeting, took the hint.

"This is the end of two years' resistance to the folly of mankind," said Marsh in a laugh that had no mirth, as he stroked the sporran over his knees. "It's been a long disagreeable story! Let's see, we parted at Boston in August 1914—Lord, it seems ages ago. I went home, and then the battle began. I didn't believe in war—I don't believe in the war," he added with emphasis, "and I've gone through hell for my belief. I'm not going to give you a recital of it all. The badgering of one's relatives, the sneers, the fierce old ladies who asked if I didn't think I ought to go. And the mater's had it too. They made it so unpleasant for her that she never goes out now. Well, I've stuck it out for two years, and hell every minute of it. Scissors, I'm just nowhere at all. I went to some of the meetings held by the conscientious objectors, but they made me ill. Most of 'em are long-haired fanatics, living on vegetables and cram full of isms. They've got courage, there's no denying that; it takes more courage to stay out of this war in face of public opinion and calumny, than to go into it—but they seem to enjoy their persecution and welcome it. I can't—it's misery not to be along with all the boys, but I've stuck to my belief until—until—oh, Scissors!"

He bent his head forward, burying his face in his hands, and cried like a child. John moved, and sat beside him on the arm of the lounge chair, placing an arm across his shoulders.

"Teddie, old man—I know it must have been awful —you needn't tell me."

Marsh lifted his head again, and blew his nose very hard.

"Until, •Scissors—" he continued determinedly, "one day, a year ago, I was at Paddington Station, and saw Bobbie coming down the platform. He was in khaki, looking very fit. I hadn't seen him since our holiday. You can guess what a joy it was. I just rushed up to him— and—"

Marsh's knuckles whitened as he gripped his handkerchief.

"Scissors, he cut me dead—he didn't even acknowledge that he heard me—but he *saw* me—he looked right through me, and went on, leaving me like Lot's wife. I'd had a hellish time—that just finished me. A fellow can't go on fighting the world when his best friends quit him. I just went home and buried myself. I didn't write to you—or to any one; I wasn't going to risk a second incident like that. I kept in,—but—I've been in the war every minute. I've gone up and down those casualty lists, Scissors. They're all going; there's hardly any of the old set left. Fletcher's House has been wiped out—a whole bunch at Neuve Chapelle, and I'm going now. I don't believe in the damn war. It's mad, it can't bring anything but indemnities, starvation, hatred. Every day I am more convinced of the insanity—the beastly, selfish filthiness of it, with all these horrible old politicians making speeches out of it, the business man 'doing his bit,' as he calls his plundering, the fierce old women lapping up German blood like vampires. I've deserted, Scissors, I've funked the battle against it—I can't carry on this lone fight any longer. I enlisted a few months ago—been training at Salisbury and here I am, a tailored product of Scott Adie, Highland outfitters, and one of our 'darling brave lads' ready to die for his country."

He laughed bitterly at the wry humour of his position.

"I'm going to disembowel some mother's son I've never seen. They have been working us up to blood fury on stuffed sacks. I've learned how to draw out my bayonet with a twist, and when I've blotted out the light of life in half-a-dozen mother's hearts, a more expert pig-sticker than I am will blot out my mother's happiness. And it'll go on and on for years, till there's hardly a sane, able-bodied fellow left, and then one side will crack, and the political and financial ghouls will gather over Europe's corpse and exact terms and wave flags of victory."

Marsh stood up and paced the room.

"Where's the sense of it?" he cried, stretching out his hands. "What has victory to do with justice—the strongest wins!—but it doesn't follow the strongest is right!"

His eyes softened.

"And, Scissors, those kids in my platoon—there's not one of them eighteen yet; they're just babies and I mother 'em night and day. You know how puppies are, with clumsy paws and trusting eyes?—well, they're just like that, Scissors—and when they're—they're sent into the line—"

Here his words choked him. Mrs. Perdie entered with the coffee, and with further exclamations of delight offered all kinds of service. With many thanks and refusals, John got her out of the room again, but not before she had asked to give the young gentleman a kiss, "as if I was your ain mother, bless her—and God keep you safe," she said, retreating to the door with tearful eyes.

Marsh seemed better for having unburdened himself. John wanted him to have a nap, but he would not.

"Let's talk, Scissors, till it's time. We've such a lot to say and you never know, we may—"

"Oh, rubbish, Teddie."

So they talked, and the old days with their golden careless hours all came back again. Remorselessly the clock crept on. At three, Marsh said he would have to go. He had his kit to get at the luggage office. John went with him. They walked along the silent unlit streets. At Victoria there were signs of life. Figures in khaki loomed out of the darkness; for a moment they halted, the sound of marching feet came down the Buckingham

Palace Road. Ghostly they sounded in the night hush;
a little group under the flare of the coffee stall watched
them pass a thousand strong, burdened with kit, obscurely
leaving the homeland many would never see again. Marsh
and John watched them pass, grim faces, pallid in. the
dim light, a few whistling out of bravado, but apatheti-
cally silent, most of them. They followed the detachment
into the lighted station, passed the barrier at the departure bay. Marsh found a carriage full of other officers,
some half-sleepy after long night journeys, two saying
farewells to their lovers, one very drunk, alternately blasphemous and maudlin, kept in control by a friend. The
doors slammed, a shrill whistle cut off the useless scrappy
conversation.

Their hands met in a firm farewell clasp. They could
not trust themselves to speak. The train moved. Marsh
with a final forced smile looked at Scissors, equally mechanical in response. A yard now apart—two yards—the
train diminished, the carriage faded—then two red lights
receded in the girdered darkness; after that a mist and
the heart's desolation.

III

The next morning, the *Daily Post* rang up, asking him
to call at once, and the same voice told him that news had
just come of the death of Ronald Stream. It was difficult
for John to realise that the death of one so exuberantly
young was possible. He had a vision of a night in a room
at Cambridge when he had talked there, so radiant and
intensely interested in anything, and so much the young
god in his beauty and zest, that John had felt shy of
approaching him. And now he was dead, in the far away
Dardanelles. Fame too had touched him by his legacy
of a few immortal sonnets, in which beat the heart of

young England. Death seemed impossible to that pard-
like spirit, swift and beautiful. For a space, John thought
of his friend Freddie Pond. He had encountered him
only two nights ago as he leaned against the box office
in the vestibule of the Court Theatre, during an interval.
John thought he had aged and looked sad and tired, perhaps the act of watching the swift passing of so many of
the brilliant spirits he had herded, was wearing him. In
some respects, waiting at home was worse than the struggle
at the front.

He saw Merritt at the *Daily Post,* busy and tireless as
ever.

"Don't know what the Chief wants—are you better?
You're looking fit. Just heard young Bewley's won the
Distinguished Service Cross for bombing Bruges docks
—a bright kid always."

Walsh rang for John and he went in.

"You're fit, I see," said Walsh. "Would you care to
tackle a naval job?"

"Anything," said John, "rather than be out of it."

"I'm sending you to the Dover Patrol. I know little
more, how you'll live, on board or ashore. I'll give you a
note to Blackrigg at the Admiralty, he'll tell you. Good
luck to you, Dean."

He was outside again. This time the sea!

John called, in the afternoon, on Blackrigg and got his
orders, then he made his way to Gieve's in Bond Street
for a ready-made uniform; he was leaving for Dover the
next day. Outside the Admiralty Arch he heard his name
and turned.

A girlish figure in grey was calling him.

"Tilly!" he exclaimed in glad surprise, "wherever have
you sprung from?"

"I think I must ask that!" she laughed softly.

She was looking very beautiful and he wished he was not in such a hurry; he had much to ask her and she came out of a happy past.

"Are you in the same studio?" he asked, in a string of questions. She was thinking how big and strong he had grown, the boy had disappeared in this rather stern looking young man. But he had seen things and was a name in the world.

"Oh—no—I'm at our flat," she replied. Then, seeing the enquiry in his face—"Oh, of course, you don't know— we were married a month ago—I'm Mrs. Lindon now."

She saw his face brighten with sudden pleasure, and as he expressed his wishes, she could not restrain the tears that gathered in her eyes.

"You are—are not unhappy?" he asked, suddenly. "Lindon's all right?—where is he?" he added anxiously, as the tears trickled down her face. She choked, and he took hold of her arm to draw her aside from the inquisitive glances directed to them.

"He's—he's not killed?" whispered John hoarsely, apprehensive of the common answer of these days.

"No—no," she replied, in a quiet nerveless voice— "worse."

"Worse?" he queried.

"He was wounded four months ago—his right hand shot away."

They stood still, while the traffic roared about them. Strangely detached from the scene, John watched the confluence of the traffic around King Charles' statue, as it poured out of the Strand, Northumberland Avenue and Whitehall. He saw the pigeons fluttering down upon the placarded base of the Nelson plinth in Trafalgar Square, and over it all, his brain was repeating an awful echo,

"His right hand shot away," the hand that had threaded those swift passages of Beethoven, Chopin and Debussy on many memorable nights, one of the hands on which rested his future fame.

"Tilly, my poor girl!" he said quietly, as she stood there, frail and tearful. "Let's walk down the Mall—I want to hear all." He took her arm, and led her away from the traffic's vortex. For a space she did not speak, then she smiled wanly.

"Oh, I have him with me—he is so brave, and pretends he never misses it—ties his own tie and is so proud when he gets it straight—but I know all he's suffering. Sometimes I have seen him looking at the closed piano as if his heart would break." She said no more, and they walked on. Then abruptly John stopped and looked down into her face.

"Tilly—you have been married *a month*—then his—"

Her eyes met his and answered him simply.

"Oh, you poor brave child!" he cried, his own voice trembling this time.

"He needed me so, Scissors—and it makes no difference to me; at least I have him safe now. But for him—"

They walked on in silence. At the Marlborough Gate he left her, with a promise to call on his next leave.

CHAPTER II

I

THE months slipped by, months of peril, of thrills, of human drama and comradeship. On Christmas Day, as they entered Dover Harbour, John looked forward to the leave he had obtained. It had been a dreary, nerve-wracking experience, a life in which monotony gave place to unexpected activity. But the moment they reached the harbour, he was told to report at the Admiral's office, and half an hour later was under orders to proceed to Scapa Flow, the other extremity of Great Britain, there to join H.M.S. Fanfare, of the Grand Fleet. Hastily collecting his things, including a bundle of letters awaiting him, he bade hurried and warm farewells to his shipmates, good fellows all of them, despite the fact that they growled night and day about the Service, knowing well they would be broken-hearted if they had to leave it.

On the evening of the same day, he was in the night express to Edinburgh. He had had a few hours in London and had made three calls—first at Mariton Street to deposit clothes and get fresh ones. Here he found Capt. Fisher in a state of high prosperity, as something in the Ordnance Survey Department. He was enjoying the war tremendously and prophesied that it would last another five years.

"It has revived British character, sir—the tonic we needed!" he said, blithely indifferent to the holocaust of

318

youth. Miss Simpson, too, at the tea-table showed an indomitable spirit. She had been visiting the dear brave boys in a local hospital, and related with gusto a story told her of a Ghurka soldier who carried eight Germans' heads in a sack, which he had refused to give up. "That's what should happen to all the Germans," she added.

"It's very horrible!" said John.

Miss Simpson opened wide eyes in surprise.

Then he called on Mrs. Graham, for he remembered that her boy was a midshipman stationed with the Grand Fleet; perhaps they could meet. Her flat, with its exquisite taste, cast the old spell upon him, even before she came into the room. There was something so intimate in the books, cushions, curtains, rugs and china, something that revealed the hand of Mrs. Graham. She greeted him with great pleasure, made him talk, and as he did so, he sat wondering at her beauty, the lovely order of her hair, the music of her voice. She had just had a letter from Muriel. That opened the flood-gates and for an hour a wonderful little nurse near Amiens was the sole topic of conversation.

"It's more than a year since I saw her," he said, "and I am getting more desperate every day."

"You poor thing!" smiled Mrs. Graham. "This war is very hard for young lovers; I pity them most of all. But she writes?"

"Now and then—and wonderful letters too. I'm going to make extracts and publish them."

"You mercenary man!" she laughed.

The hour fled. He had to go. She pressed a little autographed copy of Flecker's Poems into his hand. He could smell the particular perfume she used, for an hour afterwards.

It was not until John was seated in the train, speeding northwards through the night, that he had time to open his lettters. There was one from Marsh, in a base hospital, wounded but cheerful and recommended for the M.C. "for conspicuous bravery in attack."

"Just fancy how all the 'brave lad' stick-at-homes will be writing to congratulate me on coming to my senses and showing my courage! Ough! Scissors, it makes me sick. One hundred glad-eyed youngsters were minced by steel in that attack—we gained eighty yards and lost it all an hour afterwards. What idiots we humans are!"

A very short letter from Muriel. She was resting after a nervous breakdown. How long was the war going to last? It was very wonderful being in the midst of things, but sometimes she wanted to cry out; was Europe quite indifferent to all the suffering?

"Oh, John, if only we could just romp into tea at 'The Croft' as in those old days, with Dad and Mr. Ribble discussing the Insurance Bill, and poor Tod banging in, covered with motor grease, and you and Bobbie eating up all the bread and butter. It is awful to think it will never be like that again...I feel ages old...If this—"

Here came a break in the letter.

"I've been called away for half an hour—a poor fellow in my ward who kept asking for me. He's only twenty-five, and so young and strong, with the dearest funny little smile. He's so helpless. I feel just like a mother, with all these big babies around me—and they're quite as troublesome, but very dear. I begin to realise, John, that I had never really lived. I see things quite differently,

*and you'll probably find me another kind of Muriel al-
together. I expect you've changed also—haven't all
values changed these days? We lived in a very little
world once, and thought too much of ourselves."*

He dropped the letter, a chill had come over him.
Was it envy of those big babies, and particularly the one
"with the dearest funny little smile?" Changed!—what
did she mean by that? He hadn't changed, why should
she? True, they hadn't met for a year—and she had
not written lately. Why had he not insisted on their
marriage? He laughed then, a little uneasily at a thought
that said, "You're jealous!" and read on—

*"It was very wonderful when you wrote about our set-
tling down when it is over—if ever. Somehow it seems
too much to hope from life. Things were getting very
crazy in 1914 and I feel this war is putting our relations
on a more sensible basis."*

A more sensible basis!—what on earth did the girl
mean. Was she getting unnerved? He read the sentence over again. Yes, he must insist on their marriage.
She wanted a controlling hand; this war was too much
for her. With this resolve, he read on again, and became
easier in mind.

*"John, I couldn't leave this now, like this, with all this
life going on. It must be terrible for women to sit and
wait at home. Poor things. I read some of their letters
to the men here and I nearly break down. I am feeling a
little shy of you, John, you are so famous now. The
nurses here bring me cuttings about you, and in the mess
room, there's a Sphere photograph of you coming down
a gangway. I love the naval uniform, and to think that*

I've never seen you in it! Be kind to all those dear little middies, they must feel so lonely on that big dreary sea."

John smiled as he put the letter away. At that very moment, one of those "dear little middies" lay with his head fast asleep on John's shoulder, where he had slipped over. He would have to tell Muriel that they detested being called "dear," "little," or "middies," and that the average "snotty" could be entrusted to look well after himself. There was another letter from Bobbie. He was not fit for foreign service and he had been given a post at the War Office. Miss Piggin sent a pair of woollen gloves she had knitted in "desperate moments," for Chawley School was now a hospital for the wounded, with Mrs. Tobin as commandant, "very successful, her firmness keeping the men in order." Mr. Tobin was a chaplain at the front. She had had a piece of Egyptian pottery sent by Mr. Woodman, who was a lieutenant in the Yeomanry stationed near the Suez Canal.

Having read his letters John surveyed his carriage, thinking of sleep. He had been unable to get a sleeping berth, but there was only the "snotty" and himself in the compartment. That young gentleman had been solacing himself for his departure from home-worship and civilisation, with a copy of *La Parisienne* and the semi-nude madamoiselles therein, all of whom appeared to spend their time dressed only in chemises, sitting on the knees of officers. John reflected on the necessity of a press censor for the safeguarding of "snotties'" morals. The immediate problem was how to dispose of this lad without waking him, if possible. John looked at the face on his shoulder; it might have been a baby's, so fresh and unwrinkled, with a little red mouth through which a row of white teeth just showed.

Very quietly he lowered the lad until he was reclining on the full length of the seat; pulling his legs up entailed risk, but it was done, and the Navy slept soundly. John made himself comfortable and dozed off.

II

He was awakened by a ray of sunlight striking his eyes. The train was standing in a small station. Looking out of the window, he saw a group of houses, all brightly yellow in the morning sun. A slight mist and a chill air told him it was early morning and there was the smell of the sea in the air. A great range of blue mountains loomed in the distance, with a flat estuary between, and the tide out. He was alone in the compartment, but in a minute or so his companion returned along the platform, fresh-coloured and bright-eyed in the nipping air, bearing two cups of steaming coffee.

"Will you have one, sir?" he asked. "I'm awfully sorry I went to sleep on you last night—did I push you off the seat, sir?"

John laughed and explained.

"Where are we?" he asked.

"Bonar Bridge—we're on the Highland Railway now, sir. We've passed Cromarty Firth—we've got a dummy fleet in there to diddle Fritz—then through Sutherland-~~shire~~—jolly wild and desolate over those moors all the way to Thurso. We'll be there by tea-time, sir."

The boy chatted away brightly. This was his second journey, he was proud of being a veteran. He had been in the Jutland Battle, blown into the sea and picked up from a grating by a submarine, along with five survivors of a crew of eight hundred.

The day drew on; noon passed; still they climbed north-wards. They were in desolate regions now, with tiny hamlets set in the wild moors. There was a feeling of great space and the silence was broken only by the cry of a bird. They passed Dunrobbin Castle, standing high and lonely on its promontory overlooking the desolate sea. As prophesied, they reached Thurso at tea-time.

A motor omnibus took them along the coast from Thurso to Scrabster, the point of embarkation. Here John parted from his young companion, who gave him the smartest little salute, bestowed on admirals and admiring young ladies only. John boarded a destroyer. Half an hour later, entering a gate made by two drifters which lowered a boom, he saw the Fleet. There it lay, enormous, like floating animals asleep on the water, glittering with the afternoon sun. Here was the strength of <u>England.</u> It *BRITA* was a sight to quicken the heart. From his place on the bridge, to which the skipper invited him, John surveyed this grey steel city of the brotherhood of the brave. The sea mist seemed to cloud his eyes.

That night he met his fellow officers, walked over the ship, a new model of the Dreadnought class, installed himself in his cabin, saw his office with typewriter, clerk's desk, and telephone to the wireless room. He interviewed his marine orderly, a stocky little Cockney youth, shining all over like the breach of a gun. He slept soundly that night, awakened early by his orderly with a hip-bath, hot water can and carefully brushed clothes. At ten a cutter came to take him to the flag ship to present his much-examined credentials. A smart flag officer met him at the top of the companion way and conducted him below. The Commander-in-Chief would see him in a few minutes. John waited on the deck flat. Rear-admirals entered and emerged from the white-enamelled, brass-handled door on his right. There seemed to be a staff of flag officers in attendance, all young and alert, with their gold lace and showy aiglettes drooping from their shoulders. Half an hour passed, John growing more nervous every minute. Then the young flag officer called his name and ushered him into the presence.

It was a large room, with a fireplace and the far end completely windowed, bow-shaped, under which ran a verandah round the stern of the ship, where grew potted geraniums. In the sunlit air above the wind-flecked water, small seagulls cried and hovered. The water threw a shimmering reflection on to the white ceiling. By a table, on which stood a silver portrait frame, a small bookrest holding novels, a "Who's Who" and an "Army Guide," was a baby grand piano. A red carpet covered the large floor up to the pilastered fireplace. All this John saw in a glance before looking into the face of the man, who stood, his back to a large flag-dotted map of the North Sea, holding out his hand, his face puckered in a pleasant smile.

He was a small man, with dark penetrating eyes, a thin-lipped wide mouth, with corners that suggested a vivid sense of humour. The nose was slightly hooked, and John immediately recognised the striking resemblance to his brother, a Hampshire vicar who had stayed with the Marshs. But if the great position and fame of the man before him made him nervous, it was immediately dispelled by the kindness of the voice, and the charm of his personality. For twenty minutes they talked, their conversation touching many points of common interest, and on this occasion only briefly upon the work of the new correspondent. Every minute an anxious officer looked into the room, but the Chief ignored his hint of fretful persons without. At the end, another warm handshake and John passed out. Back on his own ship again, he was assailed and made to satisfy the general curiosity concerning "the Old Man."

Thus he entered upon a new era of experience, and watched Spring give place to Summer in the chilly northern waters; and upon the precipitous cliffs of the lonely islands saw the bird life, indifferent to mankind invading its hitherto unmolested domain.

III

The tranquillity of his new life, despite the atmosphere of constant vigilance, brought a great calm to John. He had been a silent sufferer in the appalling devastation, human and material, he had witnessed in Flanders, and under the fearful strain of the Dover vigil. Life on board was industrious but regular, and with the cheerful companionship of these well-balanced philosophers around him, he began to feel less acutely sensitive to the tragic action of the world drama. In a way he felt uneasy. He was not quite taking his share of the burden laid on the shoulders of youth. He would have liked to stand by the side of Vernley and Marsh and a dozen others. Here he was a spectator, waiting for something that might never happen, something which he hoped never would happen, for the event was fraught with immense and appalling possibilities. Often John stared, hypnotised by the sleek quiet power of the long guns, that moved so slowly in the morning air, like cautious antennæ. Yet swift destruction could pour out of those harmless nozzles under the obedience of hidden forces within the turrets. It seemed incredible that floating mammoths such as these ships might dissolve in air under the battery of similar guns.

But as the weeks wore on, eventless save for rumours and the variations of discipline, the idea of war receded, though occasionally incoming destroyers or drifters brought grim little stories of short encounters outside their tranquil anchorage. They read the newspapers and closely followed the vicissitudes of the war, now spread to many fronts, in many climes, and affecting almost all races on the earth, either directly or indirectly. And the incredible was happening, the successive war prophets, the weekly commentators, fell into oblivion, for this war went on despite all the carefully enunciated reasons why it could not go on. According to statistics, the German legions had been wiped out many times over, but still they pressed hard the defending line, changed from the defensive to the offensive with astounding virility for an army pronounced exhausted and emaciated.

Letters from the front brought John into close touch with realities. Muriel now wrote less frequently. Her hospital work grew heavier; he could discern the heartache underlying some of her words, sometimes an impatient note of protest against the politicians gaining wordy victories, while wrecked humanity poured into the hospitals to be botched up and start out again, until the human shuttlecocks fell, never to rise. Then one day, a rare event, a letter from Vernley, a poor writer, yet one whose disjointed chronicles were eagerly read. John opened the letter in the messroom where he had been talking with the ship's doctor, and read through it slowly; then on the fourth page his heart seemed to stop.

"Poor old Marsh! I suppose we'll all go West sooner or later, but somehow Scissors, I can't think of him as dead. He was so full of life, such a tireless beggar and such a fund of fun in him. I'm tormenting myself with the thought that I once behaved rather silly—I cut him on a platform one day, before he joined up. I know it hurt

—I wanted it to—he told me so later when I ran across him here. Thank God we put it right. Still, I hurt him, Scissors, and he was too dear a chap for me to behave like that, and I'm coming to think he was right,— the more I see of this bloody mess, with no end to it, and all of us wondering why we stand it."

John put the letter down, numbed. He watched a destroyer through the porthole, passing on, saw a gull wheel and turn, with a silver glint as the sun caught its wings, heard the siren of H.M.S. Oak, speeding on its message-delivering mission; all these things went on about him, yet they were in a picture; only he was the unreal thing. Marsh gone! How could that be with the morning so fresh and active, with so much life about? Surely he would walk in here, and with a laugh, clap him on the shoulder, with something thoroughly absurd to say. Dead? Why—fellows like Marsh could not die!

His thoughts flew away to the rambling vicarage. He saw Mrs. Marsh sitting at the piano, under the lamplight; saw Mr. Marsh in his study, pipe going, the *"Nation"* in his hands. Could life go on and Marsh not be part of it?

Hours passed before the significance of it became clear to him, but a week passed before he was able to take up a pen and write to Mrs. Marsh. That terrible task performed, he felt now prepared for anything. The world was falling to bits; nothing could be saved. The bad news from the front affected him little. He wondered at the gloomy faces of the men around him. Why be affected by the inevitable? It would all be enacted as relentlessly as in a Greek play. Another blow would come yet, of that he was sure; life was to be wholly disintegrated.

But the weeks went on and nothing happened. Letters

came, curious restrained letters, at longer intervals from
Muriel. Vernley, as if conscious of the lessening circle,
wrote more frequently. Lindon, in a big boyish left hand
sent the town gossip; he had found a consolation, he was
composing, and Tilly was wonderful. June came, with
warmer and longer days in those northern waters, and
with it a hurried note from Muriel saying she would be
in London in a week; could he meet her, as she wished to
see him? Her wish was a command that found him
eager to obey. A few wires, an interview, and he was
released; his leave was overdue and the *Daily Post* offered to send a temporary substitute at once. John
waited impatiently four days and almost embraced his
successor when H. M. S. Oak brought him alongside.
He wired to Muriel asking when and where they could
meet. On Friday night he was back in London, more
wonderful, more beloved than ever to the exile, and found
a reply at Mrs. Perdie's bidding him meet her in the
lounge at Claridge's on Saturday evening at seven. He
pictured her, waiting for him there, in a chic nurse's
uniform, and to be worthy of her and in celebration of
the great occasion, he put on his best service jacket.

He was there at five minutes before the hour, and to
his surprise she was already waiting for him. He rushed
towards her with impetuous boyish joy, that raised smiles
on many observant faces around. Her greeting was more
restrained, and her calmness steadied him. How splendid
she was and how lovely, he thought. She had changed,
of course, but she was the more Muriel for all that.

"We've a private sitting room—let us go upstairs," she
said, when he had let her withdraw her hand.

"You're staying here?" he asked, surprised.

"Yes," she answered. There was nothing said in the
lift. He could only look at her, but once the door had

closed upon them in the small hall opening on the tiny sitting room, he put his arms out to take her into them.

"Darling," he whispered, but she seemed too agitated with nervous joy to respond, and led the way into the room, where she immediately sat down. Even then he did not see that she was slightly unnatural, as under a strain. The first indication was her voice as she pronounced his name. He looked at her more observantly; a dumb pain in her eyes, which met his with a quiet strength, caused his heart to sink a little.

"Muriel—there's nothing wrong?"

She looked down at her hands a moment, and then up at him as he stood over her. Something in her whole attitude struck him as piteous. He sat down opposite her.

"John—dear—I am going to hurt you terribly. If you cannot forgive me I shall understand. I am no longer Muriel Vernley—I am Muriel Harvey."

He looked at her. What was she saying? She was unnerved, he could see that; this strain had been too much for her. But in that brief silence she saw by the kindness in his eyes that he had not understood.

"I am Mrs. Frank Harvey, John—I'm married." And to make her words clear, she held out her hand, with its ringed finger.

Even then he just looked at her, and she saw that his eyes were those of a troubled child.

"Muriel—you can't mean it!—how can you be married!" he cried, in a low voice.

This time she could not look at him, she did not want to see the agony that was coming.

"I cannot ask you to forgive me, John—I know that, and if you think hardly, perhaps I deserve it—but oh, I don't want to hurt you—I don't, John, I—"

He had risen now and had gone over to the window, his face turned from her, looking down into the well of the building. What was he thinking?

"It's incredible!" he said huskily, after a pause. "You cannot make a fool of me like this, Muriel, you can't—why, it's impossible!" he burst out, turning and spreading his hands wide; and then seeing her face clearly for the first time, he knew it was true.

She was talking now—words, words, words. What could a woman say worth listening to by a man thrown on one side like a discarded doll; and he knew it all. Of course she had met him in hospital, there was no need to narrate all that. He had appealed to her sympathies. But he blamed her, not the man, who only pressed his opportunity. He assumed a calm attitude until she had finished, as though he had not really heard, for he was busy putting on a mask, determined she should not see how cruelly hurt he was. Once out of the room, he could face the thing squarely, but here, she must not see.

"Of course it has all been very silly—our boy and girl romance," he said, as lightly as he could, and he found a slight pleasure in noticing he had hurt her, for she paled as she stood up.

"Silly?—you cannot think it was that, John—" she pleaded, and his heart smote him, but pride insisted on the mask. He held out his hand formally.

"Good-bye, Muriel."

Would he go like this, she thought, so blind to her terrible trial? A noise behind made him turn. A key was being fitted in the lock. She saw his face set, and its sudden tension told her more than his voice or words had betrayed. There was the sound of voices. One he knew well, would have rejoiced at on any other occasion but this,—it was Vernley's. And the other? John's eyes

met Muriel's and they felt their hearts throbbing in that
long moment. The door swung open and Vernley entered, following a young man, an officer, fresh-complexioned and of medium height and build.

"John!" cried Vernley, holding out an eager hand, but
John was looking at *him*.

"Frank," said Muriel quietly, "this—"

The man interrupted her eagerly.

"Muriel—I'm getting on fine. I've put the key in myself. Don't move, I know where you are, watch me!
There's a window on the right, the lounge on the left wall,
you're standing by it—and a chair here!" he cried, touching
it lightly with his fingers as he walked forward.

"Frank—this is my friend—Mr. Dean," she said.

The young officer halted, his hand raised for a moment.
"Oh, sorry," he cried, cheerfully. "How d'you do?"

He turned and held out his hand, but in front of John,
a little to the left, as though he might be there, and the
face turned that way, smiling at him.

A glance, and John took the misdirected hand and
looked into sightless blue eyes.

"How d'ye do, Mr. Dean?—Glad to meet any of Muriel's
friends. I'm rather sudden on the scene, eh!"

He laughed boyishly.

"And they'll wonder why she's got this blind old war
horse—won't they, Muriel?"

His laughter would have been infectious at any other
time, but now it echoed as in an empty room and was engulfed in silence. Vernley watching it all, stood by the
door. Muriel was crying now; the blind man stood
gripping the chair, sensing something unusual.

"I must hurry away now," said John. "Good-bye."

He shook the soldier's hand again, then moved towards
Muriel, and without speaking raised her hand to his lips.

For a long moment he held it so, while she looked down on his bowed head mistily. A moment later he had closed the door behind him and was in the corridor.

But he was not to go alone. Vernley hurried after him. "Scissors, my dear old Scissors!" he cried, taking John's arm as they walked towards the lift. "It's a mystery, I don't understand it, I'm sure she—she—oh damn! you know what I mean! Let's go somewhere, I'm all upside down!"

The lift took them out to the world again.

CHAPTER III

I

THEY were very patient with him at the office of the *Daily Post*. He delayed his return to the Grand Fleet again and again. Merritt, with an observant eye saw that the young man was on the verge of a nervous breakdown, but he could not disguise his surprise, when, after fourteen days' absence, during which they had no word from him, Dean entered his room and said he could not go back to Scapa Flow again, and wished to resign.

Merritt stared for a moment and poured out a flood of reasons against such preposterous folly. There was his duty to the paper, which had given him his chance and helped him to fame. Would he let Walsh down in this manner? What of the public that read his despatches so avidly? It was base ingratitude, sheer folly. The gods had poured all the good gifts into his lap.

John laughed bitterly at this.

"What's come over you, Dean? I've never seen you like this before; you've been going about with a green hue on your face for the last two weeks. Are you crossed in love?"

"That's no business of yours!" flared John.

The suddenness and intensity of the reply startled him.

Merritt veiled his surprise: he had touched a secret spring somewhere.

"Oh, I'm sorry, Dean—but you're getting a little difficult to deal with."

"I'm sick of life!" said John, dropping into a chair and beating a tattoo upon the table with his hands. Merritt let him brood awhile.

"What's the matter?" he asked, "are you tired of the Navy?"

"No—but I want to go away, right away!"

"Well—go back to France. I'll speak to Walsh."

"No—that's too near—right away, if I go anywhere."

Merritt looked at him, but said nothing. John rose.

"Come in to-morrow—Walsh may want to see you."

"Right—and I want to see him. Merritt, I've decided to throw it all up—this correspondent work—I'm going to join up."

If Merritt felt like falling, he did not show it. He was sure now that the strain had affected the boy's reason.

"Oh—well, you'll be a quitter if you do."

"How?"

"With a pen like yours, you've a duty to perform. Haven't you thought of all the people who read newspapers for a gleam of comfort? You've a sympathetic note in your work—and many a worried mother's had a little more hope to hold out with, after she's finished your column."

It was the first time Merritt had praised him.

"If you want to go—you'll go, of course, and we can't stop you—but you fall in my estimation. If it's England you want to get out of—well, we want a man in Mesopotamia."

Mesopotamia, the East! Again and again John's thoughts had travelled eastwards. In the last few weeks a deep longing for the skies of his boyhood had possessed him; he wanted to throw off all the Western civilisation now curbing and fretting him.

"If you'll send me there," he replied quietly, "I'll carry on—but I want to get right away."

Merritt had won his point. John promised to return and see Walsh in the afternoon.

The subsequent interview was short and satisfactory. He was to sail from Plymouth in a fortnight, his ultimate destination being Basra.

"It's strange, Dean, but I didn't care to propose this when I first thought of it some time ago," said Walsh, as he bade him good-bye. "I thought you'd dislike being so far from your home-base."

Downstairs again, John, with the words "home-base" echoing in his ears, laughed to himself. What home-base had he here in England, with friends dying in every trench and the world tumbling in ruin about his ears? The East —that was, after all, his true home-base. He should never have left it. To this hour it called him; its witchery was in his blood; almost he could smell the distinctive odour, hear the jingle of camel bells as the caravans wound out along the old highways.

And then a pang of regret smote him. He had friends here, good friends. Ever since that terrible night when his whole future had collapsed like a pack of cards, Vernley had been assiduous in his attention. They had passed the ensuing days together, doing nothing in particular, strolling here, eating there, talking of everything but the one thing that obsessed them both. Once only had they faced reality.

"I can't think why she did it, Scissors, I can't really. She must have been deranged with all she'd seen, and her pity overcame her—women are at the mercy of moods. I've not spoken to her yet about it—I daren't trust myself at present, but when I do, I—"

John put a detaining hand on his arm.

"Bobbie—please don't. It can make no difference now. Perhaps we are all wrong—the whole world's upside down somehow. I don't want to feel bitter—I'm not going to feel anything again, I think, and if she's happy—"

"She can't be, Scissors!" interrupted Vernley vehemently.

"Then she is suffering too—don't make it harder."

"It's her fault—no, it's his, I think—he's played upon her sympathy—he caught her with a—"

"Bobbie—don't!—We—we can't hit him—now, as he is."

Vernley whisked his stick through the air, as though beating his way through a tangle. They walked on in silence. Suddenly he stopped, and confronted his friend, his face quivering, his voice ringing with suppressed emotion.

"Scissors—you're a wonderful chap to take it like this! God! if it had been me—I'd have—I'd have—"

"Faced it, Bobbie," said John simply, "but why talk about it any more?"

But his calm belied him. To the wondering Vernley, it was marvellous self-control and astounding resignation. Even Vernley did not realise that his friend had sunk so low in the waters of despair, that a numbness was upon him; that light and air were no longer the craving of life. He was drowning, and the first fearful struggle had given place to a benumbed acquiescence in Fate. Yes, light and air had gone, that was certain.

They never mentioned the subject again, not even when they shook hands for the last time, before John travelled down to the Marshs', prior to sailing. Vernley wanted to take him to "The Croft," but that would have been too much for him, and Vernley realised the artificial naturalness they would all assume, and dropped the project.

The sun had set, and the livid upper sky tinged the sullen waters of the Thames, as in the final minutes, they paused at the bottom of Mariton Street. Vernley was walking back along the Embankment to the hospital where he was still a patient, with a shell-splintered leg now healing, two inches permanently short.

He grew philosophical in those speeding minutes, as the light died, and the lamps began to glow dimly along the curve of the embankment, running from the darkened East into the fiery West.

"What a mess it all is, Scissors—and some old blighters are making speeches about the England that is to be after the war, the era of reconstruction, of glory and peace; and here we are blasting each other off the earth, many of us dead, half of us limping, and none of us quite knowing ourselves as we were. Jove! Sedley seems like a dream— poor old Marsh and Tod, and—my God, what a mess, what a mess, I'm not sure that I care about seeing the end of it! Scissors, it has been wonderful though—we can't be robbed of that by all the damned politicians and the butchering generals. And to have had you for a friend —why it's—"

He could not finish—with a silent handshake he suddenly turned, and limped away in the gathering darkness.

When he had gained his room John sat down and thought. He sat silently there until the last gleam faded in the sky, until the room grew totally dark, and outside a large moon climbed up from the chimney stacks. Mrs. Perdie found him there when she came in to light the gas, preparatory to retiring for the night. She thought how worn he looked, and suggested a cup of cocoa, but he declined it with a faint smile of thanks. On her way to the top attic, she reflected that only youth could plumb the full misery of these tragic days.

II

In the train to Renstone, John wondered how he would find Mr. and Mrs. Marsh. He had had two letters from them since their son's death, letters written by Mrs. Marsh, full of quiet grief and patiently uncomplaining. Somehow this journey to Renstone brought Marsh's vivacious personality more vividly before him. Their days together had been without an open confession of friendship, but their attachment was deep, and Vernley's part in it equal, so that the old adage, "two's company, three's none," was proved utterly foolish.

At the station a trap met him, driven by the old gardener at the Vicarage. The sun beat down fiercely upon them on the slow drive along the country road. The regal splendour of June blazed on each side, in the woodlands and on the hills. Then the trap turned in at the familiar gates, past the central holly bush in the drive, and halted at the door. It opened as he alighted, and Mrs. Marsh stood there, hatless and smiling.

"You are just in time for tea," she said, as he moved towards her. So she had remembered his love of the tea hour and their talks! She had not altered in any way, as he had feared. Perhaps her hair was a little greyer, but of that he could not be sure; as for signs of the grief she had suffered, there was none upon that face of almost childlike grace. Far different with Mr. Marsh, however. John met him in the hall, and was shocked at the change in him. His hair was now wholly white, and the characteristic rectitude of his bearing had gone. He stooped slightly, and John felt, as he took the welcoming hand, it was a little feeble; but the irradiating kindness of his smile was there as ever, and the gentle humorous way of talking.

They had tea on the lawn, under the copper beech, with

an arrogant peacock attempting to disguise its interest in
their proceedings. The old cat came out from under the
rose bush where it had slept in the shadow; a few birds
lazily twittered in the screen of elms at the far end of the
garden, audibly tremulous in their tops as the wind passed
through them. The loudest noise was made by the wasps
crowding about the jam-dish. They talked of a dozen
things, with never a mention of Teddie's name, until after
half an hour, just before Mr. Marsh went in to his study,
he said—

"I'm afraid you'll find it very quiet here, my boy. You
see, we've not marked the tennis lawn this summer—Teddie
always did that, and there's no young people call now,
they're all away. So you'll have to amuse yourself."

He went indoors, sadly, thought John. Mrs. Marsh
watched him go.

"Poor father," she said at last. "It has hurt him
terribly."

John turned to her.

"And you?" he asked quietly.

She smiled at him.

"Perhaps I am less rebellious, John—I don't know. But
I feel, always I have felt, he has not gone, Teddie's here all
the time."

"Here?"

"Yes—in this garden. Sometimes I sit here in the
afternoon with my sewing and listen to the wind in these
trees. Sometimes there's not a murmur of sound, and yet I
feel that Teddie's here, just behind my chair, or pulling
the lawn roller down there, or lying in the sun with a
cushion under his head, 'basking' as he called it. I'm not
what you call psychic, John,— I've never given any thought
to these things, but I *know* he is not dead, that he moves
with us here, perhaps hears all we say. You know how he

loved to talk. This is foolish, perhaps,—but oh John, I am so sure I am right!"

He said nothing, but sat beside her. It was beautiful in this old vicarage garden. Generations of vicars had tended it, and June came year by year, with its profusion of roses, its climbing honeysuckle and night-scented verbena. Was it too much to believe that any one who had loved this spot, whose boyhood had passed in its peace, whose love still lingered here, should come back, unseen? This was a thought of faith, of love that would not countenance surrender; was it a thought any the less reasonable because it sprang from abiding love? He was a child in such experience, it was not for him to judge; happy for her if Faith's bright star shone in the darkness of these days.

He did not speak, he could not; any words of his would have seemed desecration. He just sat there by her side, in the flower-scented glow of the garden, while the sun dropped to the horizon and the shadow of the elms lengthened along the lawn. The birds were now twittering before sleep overtook them; the rookery over by the hall grew noisy as the sky changed from rose-red to translucent green, with an adventurous star here and there in the silver grey of the east. The dinner bell tolled at the Hall. Mrs. Marsh broke the silence.

"There, it is time we dressed. I have given you Teddie's room, I thought you would like it," she said.

Under the pergola they paused and looked back over the gardens towards the yew hedge, behind which the fading light of the horizon flamed in the heart of the sunset. Softly she repeated,

"Whose dwelling is the light of setting suns
And the round ocean and the living air.

"Oh, John, I know I am right—the living air! I can't think of Teddie as dead, he loved life too much for that; he was too joyous to end in mere nothingness."

Her eyes shone with love as she spoke, and, that moment, her faith became his.

CHAPTER IV

IN those last few days he deliberately kept his thoughts away from Muriel. Not that he was distressed by any bitterness; perhaps a little bitterness, a resentment of her injustice, would have comforted him. The inexplicable reasons of her action he ceased to ponder, and the consequences, he felt, were not his. Vernley had wanted to talk. Curiously, he now saw, Vernley revolted far more than he against the accomplished fact of her marriage. Why did she marry him? Was she in her right senses? Was she a nervous wreck? Could she possibly love this man? How could she treat her lover so callously?— all these aspects of the enigma worried Vernley in succession, and ceaselessly he battered himself, mothwise, against the undiminished, glaring fact of Muriel's marriage to a stranger. All this had not helped John, and he had tried to make Vernley see it, but the latter fretted ceaselessly against the finality of her folly.

"I don't understand women—I don't really. If ever a girl was madly in love, she was with you. She grew up with the idea of marrying you—and suddenly she turns round and bolts without reason."

And John felt also that Vernley could not understand his attitude. Vernley did not realise that henceforth he had ceased to feel anything, that he was just numb to life. Muriel had written after that dreadful interview. She made no excuses, gave no explanations, only she wanted him to know that always he had been first in her thoughts. He laughed when he read the letter, and in a vindictive moment felt he would like to ask her one question. "Who is first now?" For he knew that would distress her intensely. She could not possibly love this man, he was sure of that. She had mistaken motherliness and the protective instinct for the deeper emotions of love, and in a temporary aberration had seen in self-sacrifice something greater than a love which had encountered no real obstacles.

Had he but known, as he thought this, she was sitting in Mrs. Graham's flat seeking confirmation of her act. Mrs. Graham listened to her sympathetically, but gave her no comfort, for she affected no compromise with the hard fact that Muriel had not married the man she loved.

"Am I to blame, Mrs. Graham?—oh yes, I am, I am, but he must know I am not callous—that I still—"

Mrs. Graham smiled gently, and took the nervously clasped hands in hers.

"Muriel—in all you've said when you have said 'him', you have meant John. Need we disguise that? You can no more explain than I can. We women will never know why we throw away our lives."

At that the young wife broke down and wept in the other woman's arms.

"What can I do, what can I do?" she implored.

"Nothing," said Mrs. Graham. "My dear child you are not the first or the last sacrifice to impulse. You are not going to suffer long; your husband needs you so greatly and I think we women, if we realize it early enough, are only lastingly in love when we are happy in self-sacrifice."

She felt Muriel quiver in her arms and held her a while. Half an hour later, composed again, she went, but not before she had talked of her husband, of his cheerfulness, his eagerness to follow all she did. He had planned their whole life together, and she was not to realise she had a blind husband.

It was well she had not stayed to tea, for scarcely an hour had elapsed when the bell rang. Instinctively Mrs. Graham knew it was John. That he would come, she had never doubted. His confidence in her had touched her from that moment of boyish ardour in which he had acted as self-appointed cavalier on their first meeting at "The Croft."

When he entered she saw that he had changed. He had put on a mask, of that she was sure.

"Muriel has just gone," she said straightly, looking at him.

"Oh!" he replied, but with no surprise or embarrassment.

They sat down to tea. He talked of the Marshs, of their garden, of how Mrs. Marsh bore her loss. Mrs. Graham watched and let him talk of anything but the subject on which he really wished to talk. Then quickly, as he leaned over to take a piece of bread. "How is Muriel?" he asked, without a tremour in his voice.

"She has been here and talked to me, John. It's no use our putting masks on. You know she loves you still."

He sat silent for a few moments, then twisted his handkerchief in his hands, and looked down into his teacup.

"I never thought otherwise," he said at last. And then, dispassionately, he told her his plans. He was going away, he was going to keep away. He would never forget, of course, but she might, and that would be half the battle. If they met later and she showed that he had ceased to be first in her love, then he would not find it so hard. To go away, to stay away, only that offered hope for them both.

Mrs. Graham smiled in his face as she said—

"That is a desperate remedy," and although nothing had betrayed him in his voice, his eyes were full of dumb pain. "But John dear, perhaps you will be unable to stay away—had you thought of that?"

He laughed now, bitterly, she thought.

"Then I must make it impossible for me to return—but no woman can mean all that to a man," he added fiercely. "After all, love is the whole of a woman's life, it's only part of a man's—he has other interests."

"You don't mean that John, dear," said Mrs. Graham quietly.

"I do."

"You don't!" she reiterated, looking at him steadily. For a moment he returned her look boldly, while her hands closed over his on the table; suddenly his eyes filled with tears and he bowed his head over her hands. Neither of them spoke for what seemed a long time. She saw he could not endure this strain, and came abruptly to earth.

"More tea, John?" she asked, withdrawing her hands, and smiling at him, as though they had been foolish.

For the next hour they were very practical. He explained his plans. The prospect of his work filled him with lively anticipation.

"You know, I feel as if I were going home—as if I had a home," he said, "and if I hear Turkish spoken, although I have forgotten it all, I'm sure I shall lapse into those Amasia days again. I had a great friend there, a fellow called Ali—a Turk. I often wonder what's happened to him—whether he's been smashed up in it all. It's a silly world. Here I am, his official enemy—and we were sworn brothers. Look, I've still got his talisman here."

He opened his shirt and pulled out the moonstone with the word "Kismet" inscribed upon it.

"What a beautiful thing!" cried Mrs. Graham.

"Would you like it?" he asked, impulsively.

"No, John—you must not part with it, after all these years—and he gave it to you to keep."

"But it's only silly sentiment, Mrs. Graham."

"Sentiment is not always silly, John—'Kismet' who knows?"

He laughed out gaily, and she was glad to hear him laugh so. There was the ring of youth in it still.

"Very well then—I'll wear it because of you," he said.

"And Ali?" she added.

"And Ali," he echoed lightly. "But you shall have one gift for remembrance."

"I would like something, certainly."

"I shall not give it you except in an eventuality."

She laughed at him.

"Dear me, how formal and serious we are!"

"It's a statue—my nickname too—'Narcissus listening to Echo.' You know it? Dear old Marsh gave it to me in one of his whimsical moods. It's damaged, but it's very lovely and I have a sentimental attachment to it for his sake. I want you to keep it safely for me—and if I never come to reclaim it," he said quietly, "I want it to become yours."

She regarded him a moment, and saw that he was very serious, full of the drama of youth.

"John dear, you're talking like a novelette; 'if you never come back'—that's always what the rejected hero says in the last chapter but one. You're not made of that kind of stuff. But I'll keep it gladly—and perhaps, when you come to claim it, I shall not be willing to part with it."

He rose to go, but she saw that he had still something more to say.

"Well?" she asked him, as he stood, hat in hand, after making arrangements for her to receive the statue.

"You are wonderful, Mrs. Graham," he said, frankly. "You seem to read my thoughts."

"Oh, no, but I see you have some. Tell me, John."

He hesitated briefly, but her eyes helped him.

"There are some letters—Muriel's. I have them all—she wrote great letters from the Front. They're all numbered in a despatch box. Will you keep the box for me—and—" he hesitated again, but she waited, uttering no word, "if I don't reclaim the statue—send them to her?"

He saw that she assented, and after that he dare not trust himself longer. Almost abruptly he said good-bye and went.

BOOK VI

EAST AGAIN

CHAPTER I

I

JOHN and young Sanderson were half asleep in the orange grove that sheltered the row of tents from the merciless midday sun. All the afternoon they had dozed, just under the oranges that ripened within their reach; but about four o'clock, the noise of a Ford car coming up the boarded track to the aerodrome, from its journey to Jaffa, woke them from their siesta. A party had been down into the port on a day's excursion. It was their last probably, for early at dawn, on the morrow, the great attack was to be made and every one of the aeroplanes now receiving final touches from the mechanics would be soaring in that blue and cloudless heaven whence death would rain upon the trenches below.

"I haven't written those blessed letters after all," said Sanderson yawning. "I must do it to-night."

He stood up, a slim graceful youth in his shorts and khaki shirt. The fierce Eastern sun had browned his legs and arms, though it had not caught him so fiercely as John. He rubbed his fingers through his wavy hair and looked down at his companion.

"Do you know, Dean, I think you must be the re-incarnation of an arab sheik—I never knew a fellow who loved the desert heat like you—you're looking splendidly fit." He laughed and threw an orange at his companion as he lay in the shade. "There's something feline about the way you purr in this devilish climate."

351

John smiled, stood up and collected the letters he had written.

"Let's hear the news from Jaffa," he said to Sanderson— and strolled across the clearing towards the fringe of tents. They had been together since John's arrival two months back, and this happy-go-lucky lad of twenty reminded him at moments of poor Marsh. He had the same volatile spirits, now very elated or full of apprehension, tireless and restless, and very human and often childlike in certain moods. It was to John that he raved about Mary, the little English girl in faraway Sussex, and so deep became their intimacy that he entrusted her letters to John, for him to co-operate in his intense admiration of her wonderful epistolary style, her unbounded lovableness. John soon knew much about his mother and father, the latter a retired naval officer living in a little house on the Devon Coast; through Sanderson, he could see the gentle little lady who wrote in such a perfect hand with unbroken regularity, chronicling the small events of the domestic round. That Sanderson loved her devotedly, John knew from the light that came into his eyes when he talked of her.

"You must write those letters, Sandy," said John, as they entered the mess-tent. It was a task Sanderson hated, being always unable to find anything to write about. A letter meant much at home, and after to-night they—

"I'll do 'em after dinner," promised Sanderson.

Dinner that evening was a merry affair. The excitement of the morrow was in their blood. John looked round at his comrades, all very young, not one giving any sign of the apprehension he might feel. General Allenby was making a great push with his left flank, stretching from the sandy coast to the Jordan basin and the rising hills of Judæa. The bombing squadron was engaged in the task of cutting off the Turkish army on the line of retreat along the Ferweh-Balata road. The Turk was on the run and this might be a last great opportunity. They were to start before dawn. Early in the day, John had sought and obtained permission to accompany the squadron. Sanderson was to take him in his Bristol fighter. The spirit of victory was in the air. That evening Sanderson twanged his banjo with great spirit and sang "Glorious Devon" and his eyes watered when MacDermott gave "Highland Mary," the heavy sentiment assisted by many highland toasts. Scottish or English, it was Mary, and Sanderson almost broke down just before they retired to snatch a few hours of sleep.

"Have you written those letters?" asked John,—Sanderson stood stripped in the moonlight, shaking out his shirt.

"No."

"Then you're not coming into this tent until you have," said John firmly.

"Well, I can't write like this, can I?"

John laughed, holding Sanderson's shorts firmly.

"You promise to write at once?"

"Yes—Lord, I'm cold,"

"Here you are then, and here's my fountain pen; you can see in this moonlight."

Sanderson sat down on a box and put a writing pad on his knees. John walked across the clearing for a final survey before turning in. He climbed a ridge behind the grove, and above the tree tops a vast panorama swept into view. Away to the left in the grey void, the sea lay, the blue Mediterranean sea that glittered by day under the changeless canopy of heaven. In the night air he could hear the far-off roar of the surf, fitfully borne on a wind blowing up the ravine, laden with aromatic night-scents from the orange groves. A full moon hung in the sky, banishing many of the stars. John stood there, with a chill wind intermittently blowing upon him.

There had come to him in these days, here, in the hard adventure with kindred spirits, in the intoxication of danger and human courage, amid all that was splendid, perhaps the more splendid for its pitiful transience, a contentment with life. He was not maimed in the spirit, though he had been sorely buffeted. His greatest ally was with him, the Future. So much subservience to the omnipotent hand of Fate had this East wrought in him, he would not rebel. If Mrs. Graham could see him now, see the change that had quieted him, instead of recalling the tumult of those days when he had turned to her in his blind agony, she might wonder at the quality of his love, at a love that surrendered and was happy in the act.

"Muriel seems very happy," she wrote; "if I did not *know* I should think she loved him deeply; they are never apart and she seems unwearied in her service to him." But did she know? Who knew the heart of any woman and who could apportion duty, sympathy and love? Now he looked back, he saw that, tacitly, he and Muriel had loved, without obstacles, without trials. From the first dawn of instinct, from that wintry day by the copse, when unknown temptings of Nature and boyish impulse had made him gather her into his arms, they had followed the natural course of their early affection. For himself, even now, he had never doubted but that the fulfilment of that first impulse lay in his marriage to Muriel. Painfully, but frankly, he followed the remorseless logic of the facts. It had comforted his egotism, the eternal possessive instinct of man, to think that she had married in a mood of pity; what if she also married for love, suddenly awakened and all the stronger and more impetuous now it was really awakened?

He saw now, that throughout he had insisted upon the requital of his love, and perhaps his dominance had won until this stronger instinct awakened in her. He had banished all thought of her unfaithfulness, all reproach for the blow he had suffered. That day, for the first time, he had written to her. It had been a hard thing to do, because he realised how kindness, understanding even, would hurt her. But it was not possible to go through life with a barrier of silence separating lives that had such great memories in common, when the morning hours had been so bright for them. He had even referred to meeting again, feeling in his heart there was nothing to forbid it; and when he had written to Vernley, he had spoken of a "phase." The very word hurt him as he wrote, but it was a surgery he had to perform, and this great distance made it easier.

Rising, he retraced his steps towards the camp. He had just entered the shade of the grove, when something suddenly tensed his whole being into an attitude of listening. His heart beat, and the blood in his veins pulsed through a breathless pause. Yes, he had heard aright. Once again on the still night air it swelled and died, the old, never-to-be-forgotten, age-enduring drone of the *saz*, beaten in the Turkish trenches. Listening there, alert, his face turned to the moon-bathed valley. He was a boy again, the old impulse upon him. As a dream, his years fell from him. This was Amasia and the moon peered into the gorge, silvering the weirs of the old stream. Louder and louder, changeless and potent as ever, the night air pulsated with the immortal music of the East. He turned and went towards it, then halted with a short laugh at the strangeness of it all, a medley of thoughts dancing through his brain to those exotic strains, thoughts of deserted khans, crowded bazaars, a cowering Armenian, the tragic dumb eyes of a Turkish boy, and another boy, in a book-lined room playing a piano.

Then a voice suddenly cut sharply across the whispered suggestion of the night.

"Dean!" it rang.

"Here—coming!" answered John, shivering with a nervous chill. He blundered across the stubble, scratching his bare knees. The figure of Sanderson loomed out of the darkness.

"Good heavens, Dean, I thought you'd been kidnapped— it's twelve o'clock and we're off at four."

Sanderson had come up close now, and John's face shone clear and blanched in the moonlight. Its expression alarmed the younger man.

"I say—what's the matter?—you look hypnotised!"

"Rubbish," John laughed uneasily. "I'm cold, that's all."

They walked back to the tent in silence and turned in.

II

It seemed only a few minutes later that the batman awakened them in the dark tent. Outside there was a movement of feet and voices coming from the darkness. Hastily John and Sanderson dressed, in warm things this time, for the morning air was very cold. All the machines were out of the canvas hangars, lined up for the flight. There were muffled figures and voices. The mechanics stood by; there was an intermittent roar of an engine as it started up and died down again.

Sanderson climbs into his seat, John following. This first five minutes is trying to the nerves, his fingers are

cold and he shivers slightly. They have said good-bye
to the Wing Commander who has wished them good luck.
Some will not return again, but their thoughts do not
dwell on the fact.

Sanderson turns his head and smiles.

"All right, Dean?" he calls.

"Yes."

The propeller in front moves round slowly and the engine fires and begins with a roaring noise. Now the propeller has vanished as it gathers speed and they can see
ahead, across the clearing, to the orange groves and the
blue ridge of moonlit mountains. The mechanics are
wheeling the machine round for the run down the field,
the engine is tested with them hanging on to the wings,
Sanderson waves his hands, they let go. They are
off. Imperceptibly they lift from the ground up into the
cold air of the moonlit night. The grey-blue country
spreads around them. The stars have vanished with a
paling moon; to the east the silver of the dawn creeps over
a black ridge. The low flat roofs of Jaffa are dimly visible, here and there they catch a glimpse of moonlight
rippling on the sea. They are facing the wind, but the
roar of the engine is no longer audible, lulled by the per-
petuity of the sound. The coast line grows more distant
as their eyes become accustomed to the light. But dawn
is breaking rapidly. They are flying, for the present,
until the enemy lines are reached, in close formation; to
the left and right, like grey birds, soar the other aeroplanes. In a few minutes they will cross the enemy's lines,
over which they will have to deploy and run the gaunt-
let of anti-aircraft fire. Their crossing is well-timed, for
dawn is advancing.

"We're over—do you hear?" cried Sanderson.

Far below came on the wind a familiar sound.

Ratatatatatatatatat!

It was machine gun fire trying to find them in the darkness above. They were flying down wind now and had lost their companions. The altimeter registered 8,000 feet. And then suddenly the world was transformed. From a cloud-bank the sun emerged with a triumphant blaze of yellow light. John saw the light, like a live thing, go streaming over the hills and valleys below, flooding in a thousand hues the objects of day. Behind them now, to the left, Jaffa, with its white houses, sparkled on the edge of a blue expanse of sea, wind-furrowed. Back on the left like a dull mirror, lay the ghostly outline of the Dead Sea, with the barren hills of Judæa. The coloured contours leapt up below them, the brown face of the grainland, the grey villages, the green patches of woodland. A silver spear shot athwart a green-gold valley, where the Jordan twisted southwards to the Dead Sea. From the sand dunes of the coast to the Jordan basin a series of brown scars cut the earth's face.

"That's the last enemy line!" called Sanderson, pointing down. "They will be about, somewhere, now," and obedient to his wish, the machine lifted her nose and climbed to 12,000 feet. Already the change in temperature was noticeable. John had discarded his hat and tunic and sat in shirt sleeves, the wind blowing through his hair. They were traversing the desolate hill-region of Lower Samaria, with Nazareth, highly situated to the West, and were now nearing the wild ravines where they would find the Ferweh-Balata road. John's heart beat quicker at the approach of the desperate moment. Far off, to the north, a bright light flashed. John noticed it twice before he called Sanderson's attention to it.

"What is it?" asked Sanderson. "A helio?"

"I don't know,"

Again it flashed.

"I've got it!" cried John, putting his finger on the map. "It's the Sea of Galilee."

The next moment there floated up to them the sound of a dull report.

"That's a bomb—we've found 'em! Look out, I'm going to sweep—they're in one of these ravines. We ought to pick up the road here."

The wind sang down the planes as they banked and dropped, the country-side slowly revolved as if on a disc.

"There!" cried John, pointing to a white, ribbon-like road threading a deep gorge. "Look—it's choked with transport!"

An aeroplane ahead hovered like a hawk, then, as if inert, fell to within two hundred feet of the road, dropping its bombs.

Boom! Boom!

There were two clouds of dust high over which the swerving aeroplane swept.

Ratatatatatatatatat!—whirred its machine gun, ere the bird of death leapt skywards again.

Below on the blocked road, pandemonium broke loose. The mules reared amid a débris of destroyed wagons; some of the drivers deserted their seats and ran up the steep hillsides looking for shelter. The transport in front backed, the transport behind pressed forward, the line swayed, bulged and writhed in confusion and noise. A second aeroplane swooped and increased the panic. The road was now heaped with dead and dying men and horses, abandoned lorries, guns, carts and motor cars. There was no place of refuge in that pitiless gorge.

"Are you ready?" called Sanderson.

John's hand sought the bomb release lever.

"Yes."

The next moment they had nose-dived; at the bottom of the dive, Sanderson would pull out. John waited for the moment, his eye on the bomb-sight through which the road seemed leaping up to meet them. Suddenly, the wind caught the rigid planes as the machine pulled out of the dive. Now!

John saw the two bombs go, turn over, fall in the distance; then a pause, with the air singing in their ears and—

Boom! Boom!

They were now climbing joyously. Their companion, for some strange reason, had turned to the west and was circling wide.

"What's he doing?" asked Sanderson, but the question was answered a moment later when three enemy aircraft, their wings black-crossed, emerged suddenly from a cloud-bank.

Ratatatatatatatatatat! ratatatat! ratatatatat! went several machine guns.

Sanderson turned and climbed towards the trio swooping down upon the lonely prey. But his manoeuvre was seen. Two of the enemy planes detached themselves and turned to meet the aggressor.

"Phillips can look after himself," called Sanderson, but his optimism changed when a fourth enemy machine came out of the clouds. It was four to two now. Still Sanderson climbed. His machine was faster than theirs. John saw his intention—to make an Immelmann turn and get underneath the enemy and rake him with machine gun fire.

At the top of the climb there was a sudden *ratatata!* which sounded in their ears, ominously near. It came from above them, a fifth machine emerging from a cloud-bank, at a distance of eighty yards. John felt a sudden buffet, as though the wind had struck him. Sanderson's hand shot out to his gun, and there was an answering burst of firing, full into the belly of the machine above. It fell swiftly out of control with a wounded or dead pilot.

"Oh, good! Good!" yelled John.

Sanderson turned with a swift smile of triumph, ere tackling the machine below, but his smile changed to a look of concern.

"Dean—you're hit!"

"Hit?" echoed John, and looked down. His shirt was wet with blood. He plunged his hand into the open neck. A thin stream welled out from the left breast. Yet he had felt nothing. He was about to reassure Sanderson, when a sudden burst of firing broke on his ears. The next moment, with a fearful roar, a machine swept over them, the sparks from the exhaust trailing behind like a comet's tail. They swerved, climbed, and then fell. Down they went, leaving the enemy above; down, with an increasing roar of the wind, as they gathered momentum. Ten thousand, nine thousand, eight thousand, louder roared the wind, and John caught a glimpse of the country below as it leapt to meet them. It seemed incredible that the planes could stand this strain. Every moment he expected the machine to open up, but Sanderson knew his work; he was safe in his hands. They were falling still. Surely only three thousand feet now? Wasn't Sanderson cutting it rather fine. He could see his head in front, familiar and reassuring. Two thousand!

"Sanderson!" John called. He had no right to, of course, but something impelled him. The roar of the wind carried his voice away.

"Sanderson!"

Loud, this time, yet the head of the pilot did not move.

"Sanderson!" screamed John.

A sudden swerve, and the machine shuddered from wing

tip to tail. He was pulling out at last. No! they were falling again. John stretched forward, dizzy now with loss of blood.

"Sander—"

The cry was unfinished. Sanderson lay with his head inert on the side of the fuselage. They were out of control! Faint, John fell back; the wind screamed in his ears as they swept to earth.

CHAPTER II

AN hour before sunset, a group of Arab horsemen came over the scrubby hillocks, following the indistinct route worn by mules, which led, five miles to the north, to the main route to Damascus. Their horses were tired, for they had been hard pressed, and on the faces of the riders something of the panic of the early morning was still visible. They were alive, indeed, and fortunate in the fact, for hundreds had fallen in that dreadful massacre in the gorge. Picturesque they were, in an assorted fashion, but as soldiers they were not impressive, dressed in ragged gowns and dirty head-dresses, their beards untrimmed. More like a band of brigands, than a part of the routed 7th Turkish Army, they rode in disorder. The level sunlight flashed on the strange weapons stuck in their belts, ivory-handled knives, murderously long, revolvers of an obsolete fashion and pistols with heavy ebony handles. The young officer in command of them could ill-conceal his contempt of this rabble, and watched them with a cautious eye, knowing that they would as readily plunge their knives into him as into that of any luckless traveller. Accompanied by four juniors he rode behind, saddle-sore and depressed.

A cry at his side made him look up. His sergeant was pointing to something in the ravine below. Half a dozen Arabs had broken away from the column and were racing down the rocky steep to reach the plunder. The officer shaded his eyes from the glare of the sun. The stark outline of a shattered fuselage reared up on end from a twisted mass of machinery. A broken wing lay twenty yards apart.

It was no unfamiliar sight, this, of a crashed aeroplane. He made no effort to recall the Arabs, for his command would be ignored. The possibility of plunder shattered all discipline. Contemptuously he reined up his horse on the hillock and waited. The transport halted behind them; even in retreat they disliked hurry.

"There's nothing left, I'm sure—it's a bad crash," said the officer, surveying the twisted frame-work through his glasses. "The engine's half buried—poor devil!"

The Arabs had soon finished their inspection, and with disappointment were riding back, all but two, who suddenly turned aside and dismounted.

"Why don't they come?" asked the young Turk, turning to his sergeant. "Go—hurry them up—I will not wait."

The sergeant detached himself, his horse carefully testing its way down the steep. The officer gave the command to march, the column jogged forward in disorderly fashion, the transport drivers behind cracked their whips and swore at the jaded mules, the cloud of dust rose again on their trail along the barren hills. They had not gone a mile ahead when the sergeant overtook the commandant again.

"It was a body—they'd stripped him, but I made them give up these papers in his pocket, and this."

He handed a pocket book, some envelopes and a thin chain to the officer. On the end of the chain a pendant swung and glinted in the sunset. The officer examined it before looking at the papers. A thin strand of hair, brown hair, was tied round the link that held the frame in which an oval moonstone was set. On one side there was a minute engraving of an eye, on the other, one word, in Turkish, "Kismet."

For a long moment, the young officer spoke no word as he held the stone in his hand. The sergeant waited. As they stood, the transport column filed past them, lorries

and guns, and all the impedimenta of an army in retreat.
The men were badly shod, their uniforms ragged. They
were ill-fed and half rebellious, but the enemy were sweeping up behind and safety lay ahead; only the impulse for
safety spurred their flagging spirits.

"Where was the body?" asked the Turk, without apparent interest.

"About twenty yards from the aeroplane, sir."

"The other—there were two?"

"Yes, sir, the pilot probably—the machine fired and
there's little left."

The end of the column was in sight now. The sergeant
turned his horse as if to join the line, but his officer did
not move. The last lorry lumbered by in a cloud of dust.

"I will have a look at this machine, it may tell us something," said the officer, turning his horse. The sergeant
followed.

"No," he said, sharply. "You go on—I will overtake
you in a few minutes."

"Yes, sir." The man saluted and rode off after the
cloud of dust. The lonely horseman waited. Quiet was
settling down in the hills again. The next transport column would be an hour's march away yet; it would be dusk
ere they arrived. Spurring his horse, he went back along
the rutted road until the ravine with the crashed aeroplane
at the bottom came into sight. Dismounting, he tethered
his horse by the path and made his way slowly down
the slope, still holding in his right hand the talisman taken
from the dead Englishman. If what he feared was true
it was a strange meeting after these many years. Kismet
indeed!

He had reached the bottom of the slope now, dusty and
shaken by his swift descent. It was dusk already in the
ravine and the level rays of the sunset were gilding the

ridges of the hills above. He shivered in the cool shade, and the silence grew oppressive. The call of a jackal came from a thicket near by, a horrible, blood-chilling whine. He stumbled. The light would be gone if he did not hurry.

He could see the object he sought, a small patch on the ground ahead; breaking into a run, he approached the naked body of the dead man. Those bandits had stripped him, and he lay stretched out, his set face turned to the sky. Two birds took sudden flight at the approach of the man, and rose with a whirr of large black wings, sinister and sickening to the sight in their repulsive portent.

Flinging himself to his knees, he bent over the slim body lying so inert. For a few moments he had no courage to look into the face. Beautiful, he lay in death, like a perfect figure of marble,—the whiteness only broken on the left breast, bloody and scarred. Had the miscreants murdered him in their plundering? No, for this thin stream of blood from the wound had dried long ago.

Bending forward, the living face looked on the dead, and in that moment of recognition a sharp cry of pain broke on the desert hush. Gathering him up in his arms, he pressed the lifeless body to his breast.

"Oh, John effendi! Oh, John effendi!" he sobbed, brushing back the hair from the brow of the dead man.

"See, I have our token and thou wast faithful, John effendi! Great brother of my heart, what woe is come upon us! Dost thou not hear me? 'Tis I, Ali, thy friend of boyhood's days. O thou unfortunate one! Unhappy the servant of Allah, that these eyes thus behold thee, most beloved brother of my soul, John effendi! Oh, John effendi!"

He bent over the lifeless form, peering into the unclosed eyes of the dead man as if he would read therein some words of recognition, of greeting. He had not changed, this friend of happy days by Yeshil Irmak's singing waters. The face that had faded in distance from the fountain at Amasia was this face of death found in the desert, and the years had scarcely touched it, perhaps only to make it sterner, more handsome. Great was the will of Allah to bring them together again across the ways of the world. Thus had he beheld him on the hill on that last day of parting when the night crept over the gorge at Amasia; night crept on now, night with its stillness and its stars, and he could not go hence again. Brothers in life they were, were they not brothers in death; were not their feet wedded to the same great adventure?

With his handkerchief he wiped the sand and blood from the face of the dead man, smoothed the bruised brow. Beautiful he was, in this hour of meeting.

"O John effendi," he cried, pressing his mouth to the cold brow. "Our footsteps have gone out upon the dusty way and we are met again. Allah in his greatness willed it so!"

The darkness of night gathered about the living and the dead. Above, the brazen dome held the last flush of day. In the cool east a few stars came on the flood of darkness. From hill-top to hill-top the greyness crept and the valleys filled with shadow. The moon, low on the dark horizon, brightened; the timorous stars spangled the heavenly way with bright battalions. The hill ridges, black in the sunset, softened and sank in the encroaching tide of night.

Such silence, such peace, such coolness after the noisy, parching day! Foolish man, fretful with his bewildering schemes, his fears and frenzy, his comings and goings over the face of the indifferent earth—all, all engulfed in the enduring silence. And for the end of all—this beneficent peace.

But no, even now, the hush is broken. Out of the darkness it comes, mysterious, stirring, portentous,—the sound of a thousand years, the low insistent droning of a drum. Listening, the living hears its mournful, suggestive music, even as he heard it in the khans at Amasia. It rises, it falls, undulating. And if the dead hear, then is the call familiar,—the call of a far-off night, when, under almond blossom, a little white figure, dream-impelled, stepped towards the moonlit stream.

Nearer it comes, nearer, nearer. The night winds bear it afar down the ravine; it is the music of war, the music of a thousand conquerors marching in brief glory out to the silence of death.

Gently the living man lowers the dead from his arms. He rises to his feet, solitary and minute under the inquisition of the stars. The tethered horse on the highway stirs and whinnies. The transport column comes winding along the road of retreat. Nearer now, sound the drums; soon the riderless horse will be found.

Suddenly, shattering the night, a shot rings out, doing violence to the quiet of the valley. The echo ricochets from hill-top to hill-top and faintly dies in the distance. The deep hush flows again, the eddies of sound fade out on the pool of silence. Over the grey crest of the eastern hills the moon climbs, pouring its light into the ravine. A jackal cries and slinks away among the scrub; and again, the insistent calling of a drum.

THE END